SAVANT

Max reached into a pocket and unfolded the letter they had found in the T-55 tank. He read it aloud. '"Dear Andy, Your letter came with Red Crescent and took three weeks because of bombing. I can't say where I am but I was very happy for me to hear from you. I can now make thunder like you showed me and I can still do tricks with tennis balls. More bombing started so will finish this letter tomorrow."' Max folded the letter carefully and returned it to his pocket. '"I can now make thunder like you showed me,"' he repeated. 'We most certainly do have a manipulative savant, Leo. Maybe this Andy is not in our grasp. Not yet. But he will be.'

Leo clenched his fists in tight-lipped anger. 'And when he is, do you really think I will agree to neural-mapping him to find out what makes him tick, and possibly killing him in the process?'

Max's easy smile never wavered. 'I know you well enough by now, Leo, to know that you will.'

James Follett trained to be a marine engineer, and also spent some time hunting for underwater treasure, filming sharks, designing powerboats, and writing technical material for the Ministry of Defence before becoming a full-time writer. He is the author of numerous radio plays and television dramas, as well as fifteen novels including *The Tiptoe Boys*, *Churchill's Gold*, *Dominator*, *Swift* and *Trojan*. He lives in Surrey.

James Follett

Savant

Mandarin

A Mandarin Paperback
SAVANT

First published in Great Britain 1993
by William Heinemann Ltd
This edition published 1993
by Mandarin Paperbacks
an imprint of Reed Consumer Books Ltd
Michelin House, 81 Fulham Road, London SW3 6RB
and Auckland, Melbourne, Singapore and Toronto

Reprinted 1993 (twice)

Copyright © 1993 by James Follett
The author has asserted his moral rights

A CIP catalogue record for this title
is available from the British Library
ISBN 0 7493 1139 8

Printed and bound in Great Britain
by Cox & Wyman Ltd, Reading, Berkshire

What the true time-telling savant does is something so fundamentally different, it's almost too terrifying to contemplate. They actually *feel* and understand the flow of time and the awesomeness of space. It's as if they have their finger on the pulse of the Universe itself. Time is the one link we have with the Creation. Perhaps they are the chosen ones – the wise ones who will lead us to an understanding of the beginning of time and the Universe . . . and beyond.

Heed those with troubled minds for they have strange wisdoms.

> 6th Century BC Assyrian
> wall inscription at Nineveh,
> near Mosul, Northern Iraq

If I survive, I win.

> Saddam Hussein

SOUTHERN IRAQ
00.40 hours. Sunday, 24th February 1991

The Iraqi tank refused to die.

The first 120-millimetre HEAT (High Explosive Anti-Tank) round from the Desert Rats' Challenger battle tank should have been enough to send the T–55's turret spinning into the air like a tossed coin. But the second round produced the same effect as the first: a blinding sheet of flame that temporarily fogged driver Corporal Alan Dearborn's IR optics. His night-sights cleared to show the Iraqi medium-weight tank spurting away from the engagement at a steady twenty miles an hour, when it should have been a blazing funeral pyre for its four-man crew. From the way that it was weaving, it was obvious that the driver still had perfect control. The infra-red bloom that marked the tank's exhaust was a steady heat-cloud in the Challenger's night-sights.

Jesus Christ! A direct hit from a one-twenty HEAT and it looked undamaged!

Alan's driver's position in the Challenger was low down in the forward hull. Behind him in the cramped turret was his tank commander, Captain Jack Roper – his eyes glued to the commander's passive infra-red optics. With him was gunner Harry Williams, and loader Mike Scott. Their headsets, and the sustained roar of the Challenger's Perkins Condor 1200 horsepower turbo-charged diesel in the after hull, meant that the four-man crew was cocooned from the hellish uproar of the decisive battle for Kuwait that was raging around them.

There was no need for Jack Roper to tell Alan Dearborn to keep after the fleeing T–55. It had to be destroyed in the 1st Armoured Division's initial thrust into Iraq, otherwise it could wreak havoc with the huge fleet of fuel trucks and support vehicles trailing the armoured division. Every Iraqi armoured vehicle capable of firing as much as a machine-gun, and every gun emplacement, had to be destroyed; and they were being destroyed, with systematic, deadly precision – except for one obsolete and hopelessly out-gunned T–55 with a charmed life.

A salvo of MLRS rockets blazed light-trails across the sky like a meteor swarm as they roared towards the Iraqi positions, each missile scattering over six hundred bomblets across an area the size of a football pitch. Then another salvo was fired, and yet another. The missile tracks of heat and molten light burned across Alan's sights, costing him visual loss of his quarry. It should have been a momentary loss, no more than half a second, but when the passive IR imaging sights recovered, the tank had vanished.

Alan flipped down the Virtual Reality visor that was fitted to his headset. Suddenly he had a view of the muddy battleground as though he were perched on top of the tank. A circle of miniature multi-spectrum closed-circuit TV cameras in an armoured pod above the turret conveyed stereo images of the outside world to two tiny high-definition LCD screens in front of his eyes. If he looked ahead, he received an image of the view forward. Similarly, turning his head from left or right automatically switched in different cameras and changed the views accordingly. The experimental device worked like a dream, providing him with all-round vision – something that no tank driver had had since the first clumsy Little Willies advanced across the battlefields of the Somme in 1916.

Jack Roper's tank was the only one fitted with the device. The Ministry of Defence Procurement Executive wanted an evaluation. The understanding was that Alan didn't have to use the equipment if he didn't want to. But at that moment he was glad of it, because the moment he flipped the Virtual World visor down, the LCD screens gave him a sharp colour-corrected image of the T–55's turret, close to the desert floor and moving fast. The Iraqi tank had dropped into a depression at the exact moment that Alan had lost visual contact. Just the vague outline of the turret was enough for the visor's target recognition system to flash T–55 MBT – PROBABILITY 90% on the right-hand side of the screen.

There was a curious white marking on the turret that was lost to sight before Alan had a chance to identify it. It certainly wasn't a unit marking. It would need stupidity of a degree that was clean off the scale to paint conspicuous white markings on a tank.

Jack Roper spotted the tank at the same time. Alan heard his commands to Harry and Mike as the Challenger closed on its quarry. Then his commander was talking to him.

'Driver! That VW gizmo's got a recording facility, hasn't it?'

'Yes, sir.'

'Switch it on. If we have got a batch of faulty charges, then we're going to need some hard evidence.'

Alan blinked three times in rapid succession. Low-energy lasers detected his eye movements and switched on the Virtual World's video recorder. VT REC ON appeared at the top of the LCD display. The dapper little civilian boffin at Riyadh who had briefed Alan on the Virtual World device had explained that it represented the beginning of the new 'Looks that Kill' technology that would eventually lead to the two-man stealth tank.

'Video rolling, sir!' Alan yelled, hauling on the handlebar-like tiller-grips to send the Challenger slewing after its victim.

The T–55 was running out of the depression. Its squat hull was rising from the desert like an iron phoenix.

'Range five-five-zero!' Harry Williams's voice called out.

Alan saw the strange white markings on the rear of the Iraqi turret more clearly. A reversed swastika. What the hell could that mean?

'Load HEAT!' Jack Roper's voice crackled in the crew's headsets, but the loader had anticipated the order and had slammed another yellow-nosed shell into the tank's breech. The gyro-stabilised gun kept the doomed Iraqi tank dead-centred. The weaving wouldn't do it any good. Not with the Challenger's laser sights locked onto it, waiting to fire a shell with a muzzle velocity of two thousand metres per second.

'HEAT loaded . . . Now!'

'Fire!'

A flash of light. The Challenger shook from the recoil and the deadly armour-piercing shell screamed from the rifled barrel and into the night. The protective sabots fell away from the shell, leaving the dart-like core missile arrowing towards its target. Nothing could resist the terrifying force of a spinning HEAT shell. Even if the point charge didn't penetrate enemy armour, the pulverising impact of a direct hit was enough to punch a shock-wave through a hull or turret and shatter the armour on the inside of the tank, creating a blizzard of ricocheting shrapnel in the target's confined interior that destroyed everything inside. Behind the advancing tanks and mobile guns of the 7th Armoured Brigade were dozens of burning Iraqi tanks – their crews killed by their own armour and the deadly, unremitting firepower of the advancing Challengers.

Again the blinding flash of optic-fogging light that seemed to flare before the shell reached its target. This time the Challenger was much closer to its quarry. The force of the shattering explosion from the T–55 was enough to cause the British tank to falter in its tracks. The brilliance of the flash fogged Alan's VW visor for longer than normal. The turret's traverse gears behind his head grated harshly.

'For Christ's sake – we've got a whole fucking batch of duff rounds!' Jack Roper's infuriated voice snarled in Alan Dearborn's headset.

The sights cleared, to reveal the unharmed T–55 slewing around to present a smaller target. Its turret was contra-rotating at the same time – the two movements making the tank's outline in the infra-red optics seem to undergo a strange metamorphic change as it brought its 100-millimetre gun to bear on its tormentor. It had had plenty of time to reload its gun. All it had to do now was fire. And at that range, even the T–55's 100-millimetre pop-gun could spell a lot of grief for the Challenger.

Ever since he had arrived in the Gulf during Operation Desert Shield the previous September, from the 7th Armoured Brigade's base at Fallingbostel in Germany, Corporal Alan Dearborn had worried endlessly about this moment: the moment when he faced death. Nothing could prepare him for it, he knew; not all the live-fire exercises in the world. During the long hours of boredom, when the waiting would have been unbearable but for the frequent drills, he had imagined himself screaming in terror at this moment, or using the last few seconds of his life

4

to discover a faith that had never been a part of his twenty-five years in the deprived ghetto areas of Bristol. Now that the dreaded moment had arrived, death was the lesser fear. The real terror was that he would panic, and let his mates down.

But Alan didn't panic. At the precise moment that light flashed from the T–55's barrel, the Challenger suddenly pitched into a deep scrape, a foxhole gouged out of the desert floor by the Iraqis for a self-propelled gun that was no longer there. The heavy battle tank crashed down the steep bank, its tracks losing adhesion on the gravel and fine dust that the late winter rains had turned to slurry. There was a tremendous jolt as the massive springs absorbed most of the impact. The T–55's shell screamed over the Challenger and exploded less than five metres away, where it ploughed into the banked sand and rubble. The eruption, so close that it seemed to Alan that his tank was certain to have suffered damage, sent debris mushrooming into the air.

He didn't need Jack Roper's yelled instructions. Without thinking, he wound up the thundering Perkins diesel to maximum revs and hurled the Challenger up the steep incline, crashing through and mangling one of the wire birdcage towers that the Iraqis had erected near their positions to foil wire-guided missiles. The strange white swastika was straight ahead like a mocking beacon. That meant that the turret was pointing away from the Challenger. The traverse gears screamed their protest at having to whirl the Challenger's six-tonne turret.

'HEAT loaded . . . *now!*'

'Range two-two-zero!'

Christ! We can't miss this time!

The laser sight was degraded momentarily by a sudden squall of driving rain. And then the Challenger had target acquisition.

'Fire!'

The 120-millimetre main gun roared, spewing its deadly shell into the night. The blinding flash from the T–55 was like sheet lighting that Alan had once experienced dangerously close to on Dartmoor. A monstrous explosion whipped up a tidal wave of mush that raced outwards from the T–55. A streak of light lanced across the sky from the Iraqi tank. It was followed by an eardrum-shattering, rolling crash that sounded like thunder.

Bloody hell – it's fitted with a launcher! I never saw no launcher!

The next few minutes were a confused kaleidoscope of images that Alan would later have difficulty recalling in coherent order.

Optics clearing to show the unharmed T–55 . . .

Still slewing and weaving . . .

Now moving south at maximum speed . . .

But what momentarily grabbed Alan's attention was the glowing track of ionised gas across the sky from whatever the T–55 had fired. Then patches of white moving in the darkness on the periphery of Alan's vision.

He turned his head.

Dream-like images that didn't belong to the battle. A tide of indistinct shapes moving towards the Challenger. A dark swarm with flashes of white that seemed to rise out of the desert in front of him. He increased revs on one side so that the tank slewed to the left.

'For God's sake!' he heard his commander exclaim.

The shapes were Iraqi soldiers. So many that it was impossible even to form a rough estimate of their numbers. They were running, shambling towards the tank, some with their hands held high in the air, some stumbling, falling on their knees, clasping their hands together in prayer. The less agile floundering and coughing in the Challenger's wake as it charged past them. More men were materialising in its path. All were holding something white: towels, fragments of shirts – hurriedly ripped to shreds and shared out – maps and scraps of paper. Anything, as long as it was white or reasonably white. No matter which way Alan jockeyed the tank, they were before him: a wretched, exhausted carpet of humanity that had been deprived of sleep by a month of sustained bombing by the B52s. He slowed to avoid another scrape, turning his head frantically to left and right, using the VW visor to seek a path through the converging horde, and finding none.

'Keep going!' Jack Roper yelled as the Challenger reduced speed to a crawl. 'They'll get out of the way!'

But many of the Iraqi soldiers were too far gone to do anything other than crawl. Some, with bare, bloody and blistered feet, seemed to be paralysed with shock. Others were nursing suppu-

6

rating, untreated or clumsily dressed wounds. They were holding up fluttering squares of paper – printed in Arabic and dropped by the million from the B52s. The leaflets promised the Iraqi soldiers food, shelter and medical treatment if they surrendered. One of the soldiers actually reached out and touched the Challenger – the instrument of his final defeat. Alan saw the despair and terror in eyes that had sunk deep into an emaciated, haunted face. The image of that Iraqi soldier, about Alan's own age, gave him a sudden realisation not just of that one desperate man's humanity, but of the humanity of all the wretched creatures crowding in on the main battle tank.

Jack Roper opened his mouth to repeat his order to his driver, but closed it again. Like all good officers, he could not bring himself to give an order which he knew he would not be able to carry out himself. He opened his hatch. The horde of Iraqi soldiers was evidence that gas wasn't being used. He thrust his head and shoulders through the commander's hatch and gestured in the rough direction of Saudi Arabia.

'Food! Water! Please!' croaked a voice.

'Food. Water. That direction!' Jack Roper bellowed, waving his arm. He knew that he was taking a crazy risk by exposing himself. It only needed one soldier to lob a hand-grenade. But there was no fight in the pathetic creatures; it was impossible not to be moved by their plight.

At that moment another salvo of MLRSs streaked across the sky, and a Howitzer added its contribution to the hellish uproar. In the flashes of light across the battlefield Jack Roper caught a glimpse of a reversed swastika receding towards the darkness and the temporary safety of Kuwait.

He swore bitterly, roundly cursing the Royal Ordnance Factory that had supplied him with duff shells.

RIYADH, SAUDI ARABIA
Monday, 25th February 1991

The news blackout was getting to the press pool. A lunchtime crowd of lynx-eyed, frustrated journalists had taken to hanging about outside the Hyatt Regency Hotel, on the lookout for anyone emerging from the Saudi Arabian Ministry of Defence and Aviation building on the opposite side of the Abdul Aziz Road. The rumour flying about the pool was that Brigadier-General Richard Neal would be resuming his daily briefings at his rostrum on the hotel's fourth floor.

Max Shannon, neat and crisp in his tailored combat dress, showed his pass to the hotel security officer, pushed past the newsmen, ignored a microphone thrust at him by an Italian RAI reporter, and entered the hotel's marble-floored lobby. More journos and camera crews were thronging the interior. Someone was giving an impromptu 'I know as much as you' press conference outside the hotel's Shogun Japanese restaurant. A knot of reporters by the long reception desk spotted the dapper Englishman's approach and homed in on him like hungry locusts. For once he regretted wearing his customary combat uniform – dress that had become *de rigueur* for British Ministry of Defence civilians working in Riyadh. He possessed seven identical uniforms – a freshly laundered one for each day of the week – all cut from the same bolt of top quality cotton by his Savile Row tailor. Max had obtained the material from the stores and clothing directorate at Didcot. He used his contacts in the Ministry of Defence to secure the inconsequential with the same surgical skill that he used to win increased budget allocations.

Until now, the professionalism of the press pool had meant that Max was left alone. The journalists knew him to be an amiable but tight-mouthed civilian working at the British Forces Middle East HQ. No one had ever discovered his true role. But now his smart demeanour and purposeful step brought the information-starved mob pressing around him. As always, he was bland and smiling. No, he didn't know how the war was going. Yes, he had just come from MODA, but no, he hadn't seen General Norman Schwarzkopf or Brigadier-General Richard Neal.

There was little about Max Shannon that hinted at his importance, with the possible exception of the unobtrusive radio pager tucked in his patch-pleated breast pocket. Had he been in London he would have worn a grey business suit, with only his Brigade of Guards tie hinting at his turbulent past. But out here there was nothing for anyone to go on. His iron-grey hair, cropped very short, was just right for his slight build and confident carriage.

Max Shannon was a man held in high regard by the military of several nations – including the current enemy, Iraq. He was fifty, married, with two grown-up children, and the senior partner in a successful consultancy business which he had set up five years previously, having resigned his commission as a major. He had spent the last ten years of his military career directly involved in the designing, building and testing of clandestine weapons. Then a former defence minister had suggested that Max should set up on his own; the political thinking of the mid–1980s was that Max's work would have a greater foreign exchange earning-potential if it were in the commercial sector. So with the help of a lucrative research and development contract to get the Cybernet Consultancy started, Max had established himself in the European arms business as a man whose intuitive insights and imaginative flair – and the resulting ideas and equipment – would be decisive in determining the way future wars were fought. Now, many of his ideas were coming to fruition – although it irked him that the Gulf War had come two years too soon for some of his company's more imaginative designs to be perfected. Max had an implacable hatred of imperfection.

'Any messages for me?' he asked the desk clerk. He spoke slow but correct Arabic – another reason why his dealings with Middle East countries were successful.

The desk clerk stared blankly. He was new. Max had been staying at the Hyatt Regency since the suffocatingly hot days at

9

the beginning of Desert Shield the previous year. He had known all the staff. But with the arrival of the Scud missiles and the fear of gas warheads, many of the gas-maskless Moroccan and Pakistani guest workers had taken fright and cleared out of Riyadh. Most Saudis and all coalition personnel had gas-masks, and this was such a constant source of friction with the guest workers that many people in Riyadh carried their masks in shoulder bags instead of the proper cases, to avoid bad feeling. Max's bag was a genuine Adidas. Anything less would have been a compromise. And compromise was just another word for imperfection.

'I'm Max Shannon,' said Max patiently to the clerk. 'Room 505.'

The clerk turned to the racks of pigeonholes and unfolded a slip of paper. 'Mr Stephen Ramsay is wishing to be seeing you, Mr Shannon. He has been waiting ten minutes. I will find someone to work the paging system.' He slid Max's room key across the desk to him.

'Do you wish to check my pass first?'

The hapless clerk met the smiling grey eyes and immediately sensed the ice beneath the warmth. He muttered an apology and checked Max's pass.

'Hallo, Max.'

Max turned, and shook hands with a tall, balding man in his mid-forties. Stephen Ramsay was the same age as Max, but his unhealthy pallor and lack of hair made him look older. His grip had none of Max's power.

The senior civil servant smiled thinly at Max. 'They said you were across the road in MODA, so I thought I'd wait here. You know what it's like trying to pin down anyone in there.'

Max understood. The Ministry of Defence and Aviation complex was like a miniature version of the Pentagon. The Saudis believed in doing everything on a grand scale: Max had reckoned that it would take a hundred years before the volume of traffic in the kingdom had expanded sufficiently to justify its six-lane motorway network.

'You have something for me?' said Max indifferently.

Ramsay nodded and glanced around the crowded lobby. 'Can we talk somewhere?'

'How about a drink in my room?' Max suggested.

Max's room was on the fifth floor of the Hyatt – the Regency floor, which could be reached only by means of a special key that was used instead of pressing a button in the lifts. The tranquillity of the high-security floor, with its hospitality suite stocked with a free supply of snacks and soft drinks, was the sort of thing that made Ramsay regret turning down offers of plum jobs in industry to remain a civil servant. Even his post as the Director of Advanced Weapons Research and Development in the Procurement Executive of the Ministry of Defence didn't carry the sort of expenses that would stretch to the Regency floor at the Hyatt. His Riyadh accommodation was a clean, adequate room at a British Aerospace hostel.

'An oasis of peace in a sea of turmoil,' he remarked enviously to Max. 'Does the system keep the journalists out?'

'Some manage to get onto this floor when there's a press conference on downstairs,' Max replied. 'But that's when there's Saudi armed troops stationed all over the place. When H. Norman emerges from his black hole across the road, I have to go through umpteen security checks just to get from the lift to my room.'

Max unlocked his door and the two men entered. Ramsay looked around the room with interest. In the five years he had been associated with Max, this was the first time he had entered the scientist's private world. During his many visits to the Cybernet Consultancy's headquarters at Kimmeridge House on the Dorset coast, he had never been invited into Max's private apartment on the second floor.

Max's room in the Hyatt no longer resembled a hotel room – but then few hotel rooms in Riyadh did, these days; nearly all were being used for long-term occupancy, so it had become normal for guests to have personal effects shipped out. Here, one of the beds had been removed. In its place was a large bookcase and a draughtsman's drawing-board with a high stool. Near the window, on a desk Max had purloined from the hotel's business centre, stood a Toshiba laptop computer and a fax machine, both precisely positioned as if Max had used an engineer's square. There was not a scrap of paper in sight on the desk; if there were papers, they were probably in the rows of neatly-labelled box files. The single bed had been pushed into the far corner.

Altogether, it was an incredibly neat and efficient room for working and sleeping in. There wasn't much else to do in Saudi Arabia but work and sleep. There were no theatres or nightclubs; if you wanted night life and weren't into camel racing or football, you joined the Riyadh Astronomical Society. The only personal note in the room was a photograph of an attractive brunette about Max's age, probably his wife. Despite his outward-going good-humour, Max never talked about his family. He was a very private man. But the former Brigade of Guards officer could talk all night about the future of hi-tech warfare, as Ramsay knew to his cost.

'Something to drink, Steve? Whisky? Gin? Rum?'

Ramsay looked aghast. 'What! You've got alcohol?'

Max smiled. 'I'm lying. After five months in Saudi Arabia, I just wanted to hear the sound of the words.' He opened the mini-bar refrigerator and ruefully examined the contents. 'I've got Pepsi Cola with caffeine, without caffeine, with aspartamine, without aspartamine. And the Cokes are the same. I like to keep a well-stocked bar with plenty of variety.'

'Coke with everything,' Ramsay muttered uneasily. The Saudis were a friendly, hospitable people with a rich sense of humour – but one didn't make jokes about their neurosis concerning alcohol. Unlike Max, Ramsay, as a committed Catholic, had never come to terms with the oppressive conservatism of Saudi Arabia and its rigorous observance of the strict Hanbali Sunni Islamic code. It was a country that discouraged visitors. To obtain a visa it was necessary to be sponsored by a Saudi citizen, and even when you had one they imposed restrictions on areas you could visit and even specified the airport of entry and exit. Again everything came to a standstill five times a day for salut, the summons to prayer. Worse, salut times were different for each city . . . Also Ramsay had once witnessed the

12

religious police, the Mutawwah, at work. They had pulled up outside a shopping centre in their Nissan Patrol and attacked a girl with their switches for chewing gum. The attack had been more symbolic than physical, but it had left the poor kid badly frightened.

'So what have you got for me?' Max asked casually when the two men were settled with their drinks.

'You'll be pleased to know that Captain Roper's Challenger driver has made good use of his Virtual World visor.'

If Max was pleased, he didn't show it. 'Ah . . . Corporal Dearborn? The intelligent young man I briefed last month?'

Ramsay nodded. The glasses they were drinking from were fine Irish lead crystal tumblers. Hardly hotel issue. Max Shannon liked the good things in life.

'The visor worked well, I trust?'

Ramsay sipped his Coke. He suspected that he was getting hooked on the stuff. 'Yes, Max. It worked well. In fact, it worked bloody well. It was used with great success against several Iraqi tanks.'

Max's only show of enthusiasm was to sit slightly forward on his seat. 'He used the recording system? He had only to blink three times.'

'Yes.'

'So you've brought me the tape?' Max was now showing real interest. His customary easy smile was replaced by a hard look of anticipation.

Ramsay knew he was seeing the real Max Shannon, and the change made him uneasy. But then Max always made him uneasy, because the truth was that Max had him in his power. Five years ago Max had targeted Steve Ramsay; as shrewd a businessman as he was a scientist, he had identified the senior civil servant as the one man with the power and influence to steer profitable research and development contracts in the direction of Max's Cybernet Consultancy. Max knew that it wasn't enough for his newly-formed company to be the best in the business; one needed a little help from one's friends. He had bought Steve Ramsay's friendship with the offer of a twenty per cent holding

13

in the company and a seat on the board when he retired from the civil service.

It was all perfectly legal, of course. The British system permitted senior civil servants to prepare their retirement nest by cultivating useful contacts in industry. Naturally, the shares were in Ramsay's wife's name, and it would be difficult for a nosey journalist to put a market value on them because the Cybernet Consultancy was a private company. It was civilised, efficient, pin-stripe corruption – and it would enable Ramsay to fulfil his simple ambition of retiring early to his villa in Portugal and growing orchids.

'Yes. I've brought you a tape,' said Ramsay. 'But there's a problem. Officially, I can't let you have a copy.'

Max's grey, searching eyes opened wide. 'A security clampdown on our own development, Steve? Isn't that being just a little absurd?'

'It's not the Virtual World visor, Max. There's a bigger problem. This is strictly between you me, you understand, but Jack Roper's Challenger got lumbered with a batch of duff one-twenty mill. HEAT shells. He popped some rounds off at a T–55 and they didn't do the business. A T–55, of all things! There's a hell of a row brewing between 1st Armoured, MOD Procurement, and the ROF that made the damned things.'

'So what's this got to do with our VW hardware?'

'Everything. It recorded the failure of the shells.'

'Ah.' Max understood. Unlike aircraft, tanks were not normally fitted with video recording equipment, except when they were being used in training exercises.

Ramsay finished his drink and opened his briefcase. 'So your Virtual World visor – '

'*Our* Virtual World visor,' Max corrected. He liked to remind the civil servant of his ties to the Cybernet Consultancy at every opportunity.

Ramsay shrugged. '*Our* Virtual World visor and its associated recording equipment has provided the army with hard evidence in a top-level inquiry into what went wrong.' He produced a Sony 8-millimetre camcorder videotape cassette, and handed it to Max. 'That's it, Max. Some stock MOD Army PR footage

14

at the beginning of the tape, and a copy of your stuff in the middle. It's for your eyes only, and your colleagues' eyes if you must. No one else. Once the inquiry's over, you'll be able have it officially. All understood?'

'There's to be an inquiry?'

Ramsay nodded. 'Yes. A board of inquiry. That's how seriously it's being taken.'

'How about putting the Cybernet Consultancy on the board as advisors? We know the Virtual World equipment because we designed it. We'll be able to provide a detailed analysis of the tape.'

The senior servant considered. 'Not a bad idea, Max. But you're expensive.'

'No we're not, we're cheap because we come up with the right answers – and fast.'

Ramsay recognised the truth of that. 'That would seem sensible. I think I could swing it.'

Max beamed. 'Of course you can swing it, Steve. I have every confidence in you.'

Ramsay smiled diffidently, recognising the uselessness of trying to play down his influence. 'Okay, Max – you're on. I'll confirm it tomorrow.' He stood. 'Well, must be off. Thanks for the drink.'

'I'll buy you a real one back in London when this lot's over. By the way, how is the war going? I've not been able to find out a thing.'

The two men moved to the door. 'Bloody well,' said Ramsay with some pride. 'The real problem is one that no one expected. Iraqi POWs – thousands and thousands of them. They're surrendering in droves. Setting up "cages" is going to be one hell of a logistics problem. Well . . . Be seeing you.'

Once he was alone, Max took a shower. Although of crucial importance, the tape would have to wait. Max showered three times a day. It had become a ritual. He liked Riyadh's distilled water, from the desalination plant at Jubail on the Gulf. Purity was another name for perfection.

Once in his silk dressing-gown, a silver wedding anniversary present from his wife, he turned his attention to Ramsay's tape.

15

He fished a Sony Video Walkman from a drawer and inserted the miniature tape. Fast-forwarding through the PR footage took some time; clearly, Ramsay was aware of the risk of someone taking a casual look at the tape's contents. Max found the beginning of Corporal Alan Dearborn's tape and watched the fruitless assault on the Iraqi T–55 unfold. That the Challenger had obviously been supplied with faulty rounds was of little interest to Max. What concerned him was the way the Virtual World system behaved under battle conditions.

As far as he could see, it worked faultlessly. The pictures copied onto the tiny cassette were exactly those as seen by Corporal Dearborn when he had worn the visor. They started with the indistinct outline of a tank's turret seeming to rise out of the ground. The target recognition sub-system generated a matching wire-frame image of a T–55 tank on the right-hand side of the display, and gave a high-probability prediction as to what it was. The system's computer, concealed in a small metal box under Alan Dearborn's seat, worked in a similar manner to the human brain and a good deal faster; it took fragments of visual information, matched them with information held in its memory, and provided an instant verification of the target.

The tape Max Shannon was watching had no soundtrack. The battle was played out in eerie silence, which meant that he could concentrate on the way his system behaved. The wide-angle lenses on the cluster of miniature TV cameras in the armoured pod above the tank were, if anything, too wide. Ideally, an automatic zoom option should be available once the visor's wearer had centred his objective. Shouldn't be a problem with infra-red ranging. Max scribbled a note on a pad and returned his attention to the video walkman's screen. The white reversed swastika painted on the T–55's turret puzzled him. The picture shook from the recoil of the Challenger's main gun. Some picture-steadying circuitry was called for. Max made another note. Another round fired. At that range, Max knew that the Challenger couldn't miss.

The Video Walkman's screen suddenly dissolved to white. The light saturation cleared, and there was the T–55, unharmed and turning its gun towards the Challenger. The picture lurched and jarred. There was a few seconds' confused jumble of images, and the T-55 reappeared.

Again the Challenger fired, and again the T-55 emerged from the fogged image unscathed, fleeing for its life this time instead of fighting. Max was appalled. What was the point of the Ministry of Defence paying his company to develop advanced systems for use in the next century if they couldn't provide bloody shells that worked? To neglect something as basic as rigorous inspection procedures in the Royal Ordnance factories was inexcusable. Max could picture the justified rage of the tank commander in his cramped turret as he watched the retreating T-55.

Another shell fired by the Challenger.

This time the range was much greater, so that the resulting flash did not have such an adverse effect on the VW visor's optics. Max stared in astonishment. He wasn't certain, but it looked as if the explosion had taken place some distance from the T-55. A shell exploding before it reached its target? Surely such a thing was unheard of? Impossible.

He stopped the tape, rewound it, and replayed the scene. There was no doubt about it – the explosion was an air-burst. Maybe the Challenger had not been supplied with dud shells, but the wrong type of shells? Whatever was the cause of the strange, premature explosions, they didn't concern Max. His primary concern at that moment was that the Virtual World visor had been battle-tested and had emerged with flying colours. The security clamp-down was a damned nuisance. Max scribbled a note on his pad to ask Steve Ramsay for a debriefing session with Corporal Alan Dearborn as soon as the war was over. He picked up his telephone and dialled Leo Buller's private number in England. Buller was Max's business partner.

As he waited for the connection to be made, the Video Walkman played the last few seconds of tape, showing the distant T-55 with the curious swastika marking as it disappeared over a rise.

MUTLAH RIDGE. KUWAIT/IRAQ BORDER
Dawn. Tuesday, 26th February 1991

Lieutenant Danny Kappelhof of the 354th Tactical Fighter Wing could scarcely credit his eyes when his A10 Thunderbolt broke through the grey, forbidding cloud-base and into the strange sulphur-yellow light beneath the pall of the burning oil-well fires.

Jesus – no wonder the excited A6 pilots from the USS *Ranger* were wetting their pants! Through his rain-splattered canopy he could see that the four-lane Kuwait to Basra highway was crammed with thousands of vehicles fleeing from Kuwait. Cars, tour buses, trucks, ambulances, fire appliances, motorbikes, campers, and even tractors. Everything with wheels had been pressed into service to carry the escaping Iraqis. It was like the turn-off from Highway 1 to Myrtle Beach on a hot Saturday morning. Amid the great mass of steel heading north was a sprinkling of tanks, self-propelled guns and APCs. Because the doomed convoy included military vehicles, and because the Iraqis had not formally surrendered, the entire fleeing convoy was a legitimate target. The massive exodus had been going on all night, and a huge mass of armour had already escaped. A British armoured column was already racing across the desert in an encircling movement to cut the highway, but it had been delayed. Now the Americans were about to slam the gate shut.

In the distance wheeling A6s were already strafing the lead vehicles, plunging down like marauding birds of prey, spewing fire, scattering cluster bombs, and clawing up to gain height for the next run. Plumes of smoke were rising from the lead vehicles, and even as Danny Kappelhof levelled out, the huge convoy was grinding to a standstill. For the first time in his five-year career he had real targets beneath him, awaiting the murderous fire from his downward-angled, seven-barrelled Gatling gun mounted in the Thunderbolt's nose. The rounds in his ammunition belts were depleted uranium penetrators – almost twice the density of lead and therefore able to punch through armour as though it didn't exist. The ugly Thunderbolt (aptly nicknamed the 'Warthog') was both highly sophisticated and extremely crude. Danny Kappelhof was sitting in a protective bathtub of titanium alloy armour, and his two engines, his fuel tanks, avionics and controls were similarly protected. The plane had two wings – sticking straight out because the A10 wasn't built for speed – two engines, and two tails. In short the A10 was a flying tank, and like a tank, was designed to take heavy punishment. But the punishment it could take was nothing compared with what it could give.

The AWACs controller, sitting at a computer console in an air-conditioned aircraft circling high above the Gulf, advised Danny that he had three minutes in the designated airspace – a three-minute killing window. Mutlah was being shared out among all the pilots, especially the frustrated navy fliers who had had relatively little to do during the fighting. For many of the young men, the Mutlah turkey-shoot was their blooding. Also, Mutlah was to become the first massacre in history to be controlled by computers.

Danny reduced power, bringing the A10's ground-speed down to one hundred knots. He selected his target – an inside lane that was still moving because vehicles were using the shoulder to skirt a stopped truck. He armed the Gatling by flipping up the guard on the bright-red fire control button. The long roof of a Volvo tour bus edged into his head-up sights. As Danny levelled his wings he experienced a tightening in his groin. He thumbed the button and heard the familiar, unreal harsh whir of the multi-barrelled gun. The air-conditioning vents on the bus's roof seemed to explode as 30-millimetre slugs ripped through the thin metal, stitching a swath of holes the entire length and width of the roof.

The Volvo was replaced by a long truck. Danny's rounds shredded the driver's cab as though the pressed steel was tissue paper. A 1989 Chevvy was next, then a Buick – the same model that Danny's wife used to run the kids to school. A GM open truck followed loaded with men. They were waving frantically at the approaching A10 – probably not realising what the strange

19

whir of the Gatling signified. The impact of the wide-splayed pattern of depleted uranium slugs merged their bodies into a single bloody, writhing mass of dead and dying humanity.

The killing opened a sluice-gate of emotion in Danny that swamped logical thought. It was the same feeling he had experienced when playing arcade games as a kid – he still played them whenever he had the chance. It was a sensation that took over his whole being, anaesthetising his brain to all stimuli outside the game, yet heightening his powers of hand–eye co-ordination and his reflexes. It was this sensation that had made him such a formidable computer game player, triggering an explosive release of adrenalin that enabled him to clock up phenomenal scores that left his opponents goggling as he zapped the dancing, weaving sprites on the screen. It was a sensation too complex to call hatred yet the results were just the same.

Another tour bus, this time a sleek Mercedes. Not so sleek by the time its riddled body, with the giant windows shattered to splinters, had ploughed into a burning T–72. Women and children were running from the bus. It didn't occur to Danny that they might be Kuwaiti and Palestinian hostages taken by the fleeing Iraqis; right now they were the enemy. A pity human bodies didn't explode when hit; they just sort of fell apart. He saw a white Cadillac, pummelled by a one-second burst from the Gatling's seven barrels. It swerved off the highway, canted down a steep slope, and overturned. Again, Danny was disappointed that it didn't explode. All the targets in the games on his first Radio Shack computer, bought for him by his father, had exploded satisfactorily whenever his laser cannons struck home. After that, all the games bought for the machines of his teenage years – an Atari and an Amiga – needed to have targets that exploded properly for the game to hold his interest.

A gas tanker went up in a great whoosh of flame that forced him to bank sharply. That was better – just like the alien ships in 'Thunderfighter'. Danny gave a drunken yell of triumph and banked back towards the highway. Fire button thumbed down, the Gatling whirred death. A pick-up flew to pieces.

Danny was economical with his firing. Thumb off during those split seconds when there was no target; one eye on his ammunition counter, just as in the arcade games. No point in having the screen go blank and GAME OVER flashing up because his laser energy banks were exhausted. Funny, but the counter's digital display was exactly the same as in 'Thunderfighter'. Even the colour was the same. Green.

Green for okay.

Green for 'Go man! Go!'

Green for keep on killing.

Aim!

Fire!

Kerpow!

'Yahroo!'

A movement out of the corner of his eye.

A tank! A T–55 veering off the highway and heading for the dunes in the direction of the coast.

Jesus – a real live unscathed tank!

Praying that none of the navy pilots had seen the plum target, Danny wheeled sharply and armed a Maverick air-to-ground missile. The A10 was fitted with six of the Hughes/Raytheon infra-red homing fire-and forget missiles, each one fitted with a 57-kilo shaped-charge warhead. One would be enough to blast the medium-weight T–55 clear across the Gulf to Karq Island.

The tank dipped below a dune. By the time it reappeared the Maverick had identified it, and had target acquisition.

'Go, baby! Go!' Danny sang jubilantly as he despatched the Maverick. The missile streaked away from the A10, its control fins twitching and yawing the rocket as it homed in on the heat source of the Iraqi tank. The Maverick performed a curious pattern of little spiralling twists on the last hundred metres of its flight-path, but that was due to the constant corrections from the missile's guidance computer. Danny noticed a strange white marking on the doomed T–55's turret. It was like a swastika, only painted in reverse. Small-arms fire thudded into the A10's armour, but Danny wasn't interested. He banked left so that he would see the Maverick strike home. By rights he should have forgotten the Maverick and turned his attention to other targets, but he wanted to see the results of his first, for real tank kill.

21

And then an extraordinary thing happened: the missile exploded just before it reached the tank. It was no ordinary explosion, for it was followed by a tremendous crash of thunder that Danny heard above the howl of his engines.

'Aw – shit!'

The shock wave and fireball from the explosion blew sand and debris into the air. When it cleared, the unharmed T–55 was still weaving among the dunes, its racing tracks churning the rain-soaked sandy dust to mush.

Pull up and round! A wide circle to get the right stand-off range! Arm another Maverick! Line up! Okay – got acquisition!

Fire!

Go, baby! Go!

The second missile streaked away.

The result was the same. The Maverick blew itself to glory just before it hit the tank. Then there was the voice of the AWACs warfare controller identifying Danny, telling him his time was up.

'Another minute, for Chrissake!' Danny yelled, forgetting RT procedure in his excitement. 'Got me a Tango Double Nickel on a plate and just fired a couple of ineffective ATMs!'

The AWACs controller was unimpressed and told Danny that there were plenty more pilots waiting permission to enter the killing zone, and that someone else would deal with the T–55.

Danny switched off his vox mic and swore. But he obeyed orders and broke right, heading out to sea while piling on the power.

GAME OVER
CONGRATULATIONS, THUNDERFIGHTER PILOT.
YOUR SCORE IS THE HIGHEST TODAY. YOU HAVE
BEEN PROMOTED TO SPACE FORCE CAPTAIN, 1ST
CLASS, AND YOUR SCORE HAS BEEN ENTERED
IN THE THUNDERFIGHTER HALL OF FAME.

Suddenly, reality took over. The killing hadn't been a dream. It hadn't been a lot of computer-generated electronic head-up display wizardry projected on his screen. It had been for real.

Danny thought of the women and kids running from the coach, and wanted to be sick.

4

Behind Danny Kappelhof's departing A10 the unharmed T-55 tank, half-hidden by the dunes, spluttered to a standstill. The fuel-starved diesel engine picked up, managed a few more uneven revs, and finally died. The driver's hatch clanged open and the head and shoulders of a clean shaven, emaciated young man emerged. His eyes were sunken shadows from lack of sleep. His fair skin was stretched over his cheekbones like a fist thrust into a condom. The hands protruding from his green, tattered combat jacket were like claws. He stood on the turret and stared uncomprehendingly at the terrible dawn carnage on the Kuwait to Basra highway.

A moment later, the commander's hatch opened. The officer who emerged was in the same state as his driver. He spotted a Hammurabi Division Land Rover that had overturned nearby. The driver's lifeless hands, protruding from under the door, seemed to be clawing at the mud as though it were something priceless. The spare jerry-cans clamped to the back of the Land Rover looked intact. The officer summoned his last reserves of strength to jump down from the tank. He staggered towards the Land Rover, signalling his driver to follow him.

The young fair-haired man scanned the sky and saw another A10 coming in low, its Avenger cannon rattling rounds of 30-millimetre death at everything in its path. 'Abbi!' he cried out in Kurdish. 'Stay near me!'

But the warning came too late. One of the deadly rounds passed right through the officer's chest, hurling him backwards. But the terrible kinetic energy of the depleted uranium penetrator was far from spent. It smashed through the engine block of a ZIL truck, emerged through a wing, passed through the wheel of a truck, ploughed into the sand, and kept going for several centimetres before finally coming to rest. The A10 swept over the scene and was gone, seeking more blood from the already vanquished enemy.

The fair-haired man gave a cry and tried to scramble down from the tank, but he was grabbed from behind by the tank's loader who was climbing out of the commander's hatch.

'No, Khalid!' Nuri gasped. 'He's dead! We stay together! But we must get away from the tank!' He peered into the tank through the hatch.

'Kez!' he yelled. 'Abbi's dead! We're getting out! Come on! Move!'

The fourth member of the crew, the gunner, emerged. He was barely more than a boy and was in an even worse physical state than his comrades. Nuri and Khalid had to drag him out of the hatch and help him to the ground. His legs buckled under him, but Nuri grabbed him and yanked him upright, propping him against the tracks. With their officer dead, Nuri took command because he was the only regular soldier and because he was the oldest. Khalid, the tank's slow-witted, fair-haired driver, was a conscript, and so was their boy gunner, Kez, now hallucinating from hunger and thirst. Kez was the leanest and weakest of the three men, and therefore had the least reserves.

Nuri was shorter than Khalid, and a good deal wilder-looking due to his unkempt black beard. Although nearly dead from exhaustion and starvation, the will to live burned like a bright torch in his dark, sunken eyes. He looked quickly around and decided that their best course of action would be to hide in the dunes, well away from the road.

'We have to get clear of the tank!' he croaked to Khalid, and pointed to the dunes. 'Do you understand?'

Khalid nodded. He was about to smile but, dull-witted as he was, he realised that it would not be appropriate. The two men lifted the gunner between them and stumbled through the rain-slurried sand. When they were several metres from the T–55, Nuri turned and lobbed a smoke-grenade under its tracks. Clouds of black smoke billowed around the tank, making it appear to be on fire. Nuri's plan was for the three of them to rest up nearby; they stood little chance of dragging Kez a safe distance from the tank, so he didn't want what looked like a

24

plum target close by as an invitation for the American pilots to spray the area with their murderous fire.

Staggering under their load, Nuri and Khalid breasted a rise and half-fell, half-stumbled into the hollow on the far side. There was a ledge of sandstone protruding from the side of the dune, which provided an overhang. The two men crawled beneath it and dragged Kez's unconscious dead weight between them.

The wet sand against his face excited Khalid. He was about to shove a handful of the slurry into his mouth as though it were ambrosia, but Nuri cuffed him and yelled at him to stop. The older man pulled a handkerchief from his pocket, which he had kept in readiness as a flag of surrender, and filled it with several handfuls of the waterlogged dust. He squeezed the mass into a hard ball by twisting the material as tight as he could with his weakened fingers. Beads of moisture appeared on the outside of the material. Khalid tried to get his tongue to the ball, but Nuri pushed him roughly aside. The driver didn't mind, and this time could not help grinning. For the thousandth time Nuri wondered why he had been conscripted. But of course, he knew why; Khalid wasn't very bright but he was a brilliant driver. His uncanny judgement of speed and distance and space was such that he could hurl the T–55 at maximum speed through a gap with only a few centimetres to clear on each side. But more important than that was the smiling young Kurd's incredible good luck: shells and missiles fired at them had simply blown up before they reached their target.

Nuri cradled Kez's head on his knees and brushed the handkerchief against his parched lips. The boy's tongue came out automatically and sucked greedily on the ball of compressed sand, like a starved puppy seeking a life-giving teat.

Khalid reached for the handkerchief. 'You do the same!' Nuri snarled at him. 'Do I have to think of everything?'

Khalid's sudden grin made Nuri realise the stupidity of his question. He reached out and gave the fair-haired young man an affectionate punch. Two Intruders screamed overhead, low and menacing. One broke away, circled around and came in very slowly. The pilot was certain to see the three Iraqi soldiers

25

huddled under the outcrop. The howl of approaching turbines churned raw terror in Nuri's guts like a writhing serpent. He prayed that Khalid's good luck would hold, but the attack aircraft suddenly wheeled away. Nuri's teeth chattered as he sucked in a deep breath of relief.

'Not need luck this time,' said Khalid, still grinning.

Nuri stared into the fair-haired man's eyes and felt an icy prickling sensation in every follicle of his unkempt hair and beard. There was something behind those ever-smiling eyes. Something alien. Something that didn't equate with the Khalid he knew – good old fun-loving, trick-performing Khalid, the unit's likeable idiot who would stick his head in a bucket of water if told to do so, because he loved people to laugh at him. Being laughed at was a way of being accepted.

'That's right,' said Nuri, agreeing with Khalid. 'We don't need luck this time. We save it, eh?'

'No need to save it,' Khalid replied enigmatically. 'Always there.'

It was a simple enough answer, and Nuri wondered why it frightened him so much.

5

SINGAPORE TO LONDON
Wednesday, 27th February 1991

Mercifully, the Gulf War had frightened people off flying, so there were few passengers in the Boeing's first class section to witness the girl's increasing agitation.

'No,' she said suddenly, shaking her head with enough violence to dislodge her headset. 'At the third stroke, the time sponsored by Accurist will be ten fifteen and ten seconds. Beep . . . Beep . . . Beep.'

'Andy! Will you *please* stop that!'

Lloyd Wheeler glanced across the aisle at the disturbance. The mother was working hard to calm her daughter. How old was she? Fifteen? Sixteen? He had already guessed that the poor kid was autistic, and earlier during the flight, when he noticed her interest in his laptop computer, he had obligingly angled the screen so that she could see what he was doing. Now the kid was too distraught to take much notice of anything. Strange, how autistic children could switch in an instant from intense concentration to a near fit. Lloyd ignored the hushed, urgent tones of the mother and the moans of the girl, to concentrate on the piece he wanted to finish before the laptop's battery expired.

His sensitive, perceptive nature did not accord with his appearance; he was a big-boned, powerful man whose muscles had been developed in his youth, working on his parents' farm in Oxfordshire, and were maintained with regular squash games with his fitness-freak girlfriend. He had hair the colour of ripe corn, and enough of it to make him look ten years younger than thirty-two – and a stubborn streak as wide as the wide-body he was flying in. To get over a divorce that had snapped a ten-year partnership like a dead twig, he had thrown himself into his new job as editor of *Science UK*.

His large fingers looked clumsy and ineffective as he tapped on the small keyboard of his laptop computer. Normally he would have worked fast, not looking at the screen, but now he was pecking as slowly as a bloated wood-pigeon, trying to squeeze 4,000 words out of his abortive trip to Singapore. The annual convention of the Federation of Astrophysicists had been a shambles. The American delegation and several others had cried off at the last minute because of fears that the Iraqis were about to launch a terrorist campaign against Western airlines. As a result, several important papers scheduled to be presented to the convention had been withdrawn – and after two days Lloyd had decided to withdraw himself, and return to London.

André became restless again, twisting and turning in her seat. Laura Normanville took her daughter's hand and shushed her gently. 'It's all right, Andy – we'll be landing soon.' She caught Lloyd Wheeler's eye across the aisle and flushed with embarrassment and anger, wishing for the hundredth time that he would move to another seat, there were plenty free, and not keep glancing across the aisle each time André got excited.

Lloyd sensed her hostility. During the long hours of the flight

27

he amused himself by giving his few fellow passengers imaginary backgrounds that fitted their dress and demeanour. The elegant woman in the figure-hugging woollen dress and calf-length boots (unsuitable for flying because the feet swelled) was returning to London to rebuild her career as a model, leaving behind a broken marriage. The Hasidim who spent the entire flight with his nose buried in the Torah was obviously a Hatton Garden diamond merchant who had pulled off a spectacular deal in Singapore, and was now heading home to a floodlit, burglar-alarmed, stone-clad mansion in Mill Hill, occupied by a lonely, stoned wife.

But the mother and daughter? They defied his simplistic analysis because, although they looked remarkably alike – well-chiselled features and high, almost classical cheekbones – they were dressed very differently. The girl's pleated skirt and silk blouse had to be tailor-made to be such a perfect fit on such an awkward, coltish frame. By contrast her mother's clothes were cheap and plain, almost as if she had deliberately dressed down to appear dowdy beside her daughter. Her brown eyes cried out for make-up. Even her thick, dark hair was pulled back in an austere, old-fashioned bun, whereas her daughter's hair was a black, exotic cascade that fell between her shoulder-blades to her waist. It had a rich sheen that came from having much attention lavished on it.

'No!' said André with sudden vehemence.

'Please, Andy.'

'*No!*' André suddenly screamed. 'All wrong!' She beat a white clenched fist furiously on her arm-rest.

Laura grabbed André's hands and forced them under her daughter's seat-belt. She read the fierce strength in André's arms as the symptom of the onset of a seizure. It looked as if her desperate hope that the return flight to London would not be a repetition of the flight out was about to be dashed. 'Please, Andy,' she implored. 'Not here. Not now.' But after ten years she knew the futility of pleading with the girl when a fit was looming.

'No! No! No! All wrong!'

The few other passengers woke up and craned their heads

above their head-rests to see what was happening. Ching, the friendly Singapore Airlines flight attendant, was about to intervene when the 747 was shaken by a brief but violent shudder of clear-air turbulence that resulted in the sound of breaking glass and cursing from the upper saloon. She gave a despairing glance at the distraught girl, uncertain what to attend to first. A shout from above prompted her to race nimbly up the spiral steps.

Lloyd leaned across the aisle. 'Perhaps your daughter would like to see what I'm typing on my computer?' he offered. 'I noticed that she was interested.'

Lloyd's sudden intervention had an unexpected effect on the girl. She stopped struggling and stared at him. There was something hauntingly familiar about her stare that confused him – until he remembered where he had seen it before. The previous January, after a stormy meeting with his magazine's owner, he had cooled off by trudging around London Zoo. While he debated whether to resign or accept the challenge to double his circulation within the year, he had been captivated by the malevolent yellow stare of a magnificent black panther. For timeless moments the two had regarded each other. As Lloyd gazed into the baleful yet unfathomable yellow eyes, it had seemed to him that he was looking into a soul possessed of an awesome, all-knowing intelligence. It was difficult to accept that the sleek creature was a dumb animal. It was pretending; biding its time. He experienced the same sensation now as the unblinking green-eyed stare of this strange girl bored into him.

The spell was broken by the mother speaking:

'It's most kind of you,' she said icily. 'But I don't think André is interested in – '

'Want to see! Want to see!' André shouted, bouncing up and down in her seat. Before her mother could raise further objections, she jumped up, pushed past her mother and dived into the seat beside Lloyd.

Lloyd chuckled. 'Looks as if she's pre-empted your decision.'

'Very well. But only for a few minutes, Mr . . .'

'Lloyd Wheeler.' He felt in the handkerchief pocket of his

jacket and offered her a business card. He noticed her wedding and engagement rings as she reluctantly accepted it.

'Lloyd D. Wheeler, Editor, *Science UK*.' Beneath his name was the magazine's address, and the address of his private flat – in a converted Wapping warehouse – in the same road.

'I lead a nomadic life, thanks to my job, but you can usually track me down on one of those numbers,' he remarked cheerfully.

The woman pushed the card indifferently into a pocket in her cheap handbag. Lloyd was uncomfortably aware of her eyes fixed mistrustfully on him as he opened the machine and switched it on. A logo swam down the screen, and the letters formed themselves into the word COMPAQ. The movement seemed to intrigue André, so Lloyd pressed the reset button for a repeat performance.

'Compact,' said the girl.

'Would you like to see some of my games?'

'Games,' said André, nodding. 'Like to see games.' She watched Lloyd's fingers intently as he called up his games subdirectory. Like most laptop computer owners who use their machines for business, he had a few favourite games lurking on his hard disk. Lloyd had more games than he would ever admit to because his job often involved him in spending many hours in airport lounges or waiting for press briefings to begin. He scanned the directory, looking for a game with plenty of pattern and movement.

Scrabble? No. Chess? Hardly.

He selected MicroProse's 'StarGlider'. It was the only hunt-'em-'n-'zap-'em arcade game on his Compaq, but it was one of the best. He showed André how to use the cursor control keys to fly the spacecraft over the alien landscape and how the space-bar worked the laser cannons. The lack of response from the girl was disturbing. For all he knew, she had taken nothing in. He allowed her to pull the machine onto her lap. Her long, slender fingers danced on the keyboard with a surprising dexterity. Almost immediately there was the sound of thin, reedy explosions from the machine's tiny speaker, and the score window started clocking up points. André was zapping the fast-moving alien machines with an extraordinary skill. He turned his head and smiled across the aisle at Laura, who was still watching them anxiously.

'She's good. You must have the same game at home?'

Laura was also surprised by André's unexpected talent. 'No – we haven't got a computer at home.'

Lloyd looked at André's profile. She was staring fixedly at the screen, showing neither pleasure nor concentration. Her fingers worked the keys as though they were not a part of her. There was a spate of tinny explosions from the Compaq. He glanced at the screen and saw with some surprise that André was on level two. She must have learned how to refuel her spacecraft by flying between the Tesla towers.

'She's amazingly good,' said Lloyd, trying to keep the conversation alive. The woman intrigued him. He wanted to learn more about her and her strange daughter.

She looked quizzically at him. 'Do you think I ought to buy a computer for André?'

'Well, she certainly seems to be enjoying herself. It's a pity you didn't buy one in Singapore. You can get some real bargains there, but the prices are coming down at home. About the only thing that is.'

'How much would a machine like that cost?'

'About fifteen hundred pounds.'

Laura looked surprised. 'In that case, it's very kind of you to let her use it, Mr . . . er . . . Wheeler.'

Lloyd gave a diffident smile. 'You could get her a good desktop machine for half that.' He felt awkward talking about André in her presence, but the girl was taking no notice of them. They lapsed into silence, and the woman reclined her seat and opened her magazine, signalling an end to the brief conversation.

Although she was reluctant to admit it, Laura was grateful to the blond stranger for granting her a respite from André's tantrums. The flight out to Singapore the previous week to visit her sister had been much worse. André had become increasingly agitated at each refuelling stop, and had finally had a fit just as

31

the aircraft came to a complete stop on the runway at Changi Airport.

She felt her eyes becoming heavy. She donned her headset and turned up the volume in an attempt to remain awake, but the combination of her exhaustion and Beethoven's Pastoral Symphony had the opposite effect.

André's expression remained tense as she played. That she didn't seem to be enjoying herself was normal: few people looked as if they were enjoying themselves when absorbed in a computer game. The machine's speaker was now bleeping almost continuously as her score mounted. Perhaps her school had PCs, Lloyd thought, and the same software.

The kid continued to ignore Lloyd so he started on his news-paper crossword, glancing at her now and then out of the corner of his eye. She gave a little cry of pleasure when she reached a new level, and her hands flew up to her face in delight. Lloyd thought it strange that she wasn't wearing a watch; most teen-agers felt undressed without some sort of multi-buttoned, over-elaborate gizmo that gave the times in a dozen countries and bleeped like an electrocuted cockroach every hour.

He looked at his own watch and tried to work out what the time was in London. Singapore was eight hours ahead of London, so –

'At the third stroke, the time sponsored by Accurist will be ten thirty-one and ten seconds. Beep . . . Beep . . . Beep.'

Lloyd looked at André in surprise. She had stopped playing and was watching him carefully. Obviously she had seen him looking at his watch. Her gaze shifted across the aisle to where her mother was now asleep. He smiled at her. 'What made you say that, André? Is that the real time?'

'At the third stroke,' André recited woodenly, 'the time spon-sored by Accurist will be ten thirty-one and thirty seconds. Beep . . . Beep . . . Beep.' She lapsed into silence. Those dis-turbing green eyes were trained on him like a cat watching a mouse.

Lloyd didn't know what to make of the extraordinary out-burst. The Compaq had a real-time clock maintained by a lithium battery that he never reset when travelling. It was useful knowing what the time was in London. Like all crystal-controlled clocks, it retained an accuracy of a few hundredths of a second over a year. He decided that there was no harm in showing André what the time really was. 'Let me show you something, young lady.'

She made no objection when he took the machine from her and exited from the game. She sat back and stared at the overhead lockers. Lloyd called up the clock. He was about to show her the screen when, without looking down, she said: 'At the third stroke, the time sponsored by Accurist will be ten thirty-two and forty seconds. Beep . . . Beep . . . Beep.'

Lloyd gaped at the screen in astonishment. The digits had changed to 22:32:40 at the precise instant that André recited the third beep. There was no possibility of the girl having seen the screen. It was turned away from her, and the backlit screen was difficult if not impossible to read unless it was viewed at the right angle. His watch was out of sight, and fast, and she had kept her gaze directed upwards.

Lloyd turned the machine right away from the girl. As though guessing the rules of the game, she was now watching him. 'All right, Andy,' said Lloyd, trying to keep his voice steady. 'Tell me the time again.'

'At the third stroke, the time sponsored by Accurist will be ten thirty-four and ten seconds. Beep . . . Beep . . . Beep.'

The Compaq's clock read 22:34:10 dead on André's third beep. Lloyd could only stare at the girl and the clock, utterly dumbfounded. He thought he detected a momentary gleam of triumph in her eyes at his expression, but the look was gone in an instant.

A fluke, he told himself. But he knew that he was deluding himself. This amazing kid, supposedly retarded, or at least suffering from a severe form of autism, had an astonishing ability to tell the time to the second. He recalled a television programme about Stephen Wiltshire, an autistic boy who could draw buildings with amazing detail from memory, having seen them for only a few minutes. His undisguised amazement seemed to encourage the girl.

33

'At the third stroke, the time sponsored by Accurist will be ten thirty-five and thirty seconds. Beep . . . Beep . . . Beep.'

Lloyd gaped at the screen. It was unbelievable.

'At the third stroke, the time sponsored by Accurist will be ten thirty-five and fifty seconds. Beep . . . Beep . . . Beep.'

'*How dare you!*'

Lloyd and André looked up, startled. Laura was standing over them, her face livid.

'How dare you make André do that!'

'I'm sorry, but I didn't make – '

'I thought I could trust you! Instead I find you taking advantage of that trust!'

'Now look,' said Lloyd calmly. 'I can't see that – '

But he never got a chance to finish the sentence. Laura seized André's arm and jerked her to her feet. 'I might've known!' Laura spat, pushing André across the aisle into her window seat. 'I might've guessed that you couldn't be trusted!'

Lloyd shrugged and returned to his newspaper. He toyed with the idea of giving the woman an hour to cool off and then apologising to her. No – he rejected the idea. Why the hell should he say sorry? He had done nothing wrong, and as far as he could tell the kid had enjoyed demonstrating her talent. Maybe it could be the subject for an article? One of those little fillers that he liked to keep on hand to pad out column settings. He worked out the opening paragraph in his head. He was good at starting articles in his head. Getting them down on paper was more difficult . . .

He dozed off while composing the second paragraph, and had an airline-food bad dream in which a pair of haunting, mocking green eyes were floating before him against a backdrop of the galaxies and vast dark clouds of universal matter. Whichever way he turned, the amazing spectacle lay before him – myriads of galaxies, stars and star clusters shining so brightly that it was impossible to look at them directly. What was odd was that the billions of points of light were not moving away from each other – the universe was not expanding in his dream, but contracting. And superimposed on the extraordinary collapse of the universe were those haunting green eyes, and an expressionless, echoing voice that kept calling out the time every ten seconds.

'. . . forty-two and fifty seconds . . . Beep! Beep! Beep! And forty seconds . . . Beep! Beep! Beep! And thirty seconds . . . Beep! Beep! Beep!'

The collapse of the universe was accelerating, and time was running backwards. The girl's voice rose in pitch like an accelerating tape-recording until it became a continuous, high-pitched shriek.

A sharp pain in his temple woke him. His pillow had slipped to the floor and his head was jammed against the arm-rest. He sat up, feeling badly shaken. He rubbed his temple and saw André watching him. She had been watching him dream, and that made him feel uncomfortable. He gave her a little wave but she refused to acknowledge it.

He rose and climbed the spiral stairs to the bar, where excellent coffee was available throughout the flight. The Hasidim engaged him in conversation. The Orthodox Jew was not a diamond merchant but a good-humoured dentist with a fund of funny stories about dentistry. Drinking and talking killed a couple of hours. When Lloyd returned to his seat he saw that André was becoming agitated again. After thirty minutes she was snapping the window-blind up and down and rolling her head from side to side. Laura did her best to comfort her daughter. She caught Lloyd's glance and stared right back at him, her brown eyes cold and angry – daring him to say or do anything.

The distant whine of the engines changed, and the aircraft canted down very slightly. The PA chimed. The captain announced that the 747 was at the top of its descent to Heathrow. 'We will be landing shortly, ladies and gentlemen. Will you please ensure that your trays are stowed and that your seats are back in the upright position. Please observe the No Smoking signs when they are switched on. Thank you.'

'Wrong,' André muttered, rolling her head as though trying to shake off a hallucination. 'All wrong.'

Ching and another stewardess appeared and passed through the section, making sure all seat-belts were secure.

'Ladies and gentlemen, we will be dimming the cabin lights for landing in accordance with normal procedure.'

A popping in Lloyd's ears warned him that the captain had equalised cabin pressure with the outside world. There was the rumble of the main gear being lowered. The necklace of lights of the M4 appeared in Lloyd's window as the Boeing banked and lined up for its final approach. He glanced across at André. She was now badly disturbed – twisting in her seat and banging her knees against the seat in front of her.

'All wrong!' she cried. 'All wrong!'

Laura took a firm grip of André's hands and talked incessantly in a low voice, not pausing for a reply because none was expected. In the ten years since the accident Laura had learned to keep up a steady patter without stopping to think what she was saying. The sound of her voice, always warm and reassuring, usually had a more powerful calming effect on André than any drugs.

Lloyd couldn't hear what she was saying, but he saw the real love the woman had for her daughter and was moved. Two years before he had researched the treatment of autistic children for an article, and had been impressed by the care and devotion many parents showed their disadvantaged children.

On the flight deck the co-pilot banked slightly. He took a professional pride in always dropping his nose main-gear smack down the centre of the runway. It was a clear night. The runway's VASI lights had been visible from the top of his descent, and he had a good line-up.

Two hundred metres to touchdown.

A twenty-knot cross-wind. Another minute correction.

One hundred metres . . . Fifty metres . . .

He eased back on the control column to flare the aircraft, and the Boeing's main-gear smacked down on the runway. He applied reverse thrust, causing the hurtling aircraft to decelerate rapidly.

André's eyes rolled frighteningly and she gave little whimpers of misery and pain. Laura tightened her grip on the girl's hands. 'Imogen said that she was so pleased to see us that she'll come and stay with us in the summer. That'll be nice, won't it? You got on so well with her.'

'*No!*'

The Boeing had shed more than half its landing speed and was down to sixty-five knots. It was going to be a perfect landing.

'Isn't it exciting to be back, Andy? Though I expect the garden's a bit of a mess. I do wish we'd had more time to do a really good clear up before we left.'

'*NO!*' André tore a hand free and beat furiously on the seat in front of her. Luckily it was unoccupied. Laura grabbed the flailing hand and struggled to hold it still.

The explosive report was heard plainly on the flight deck. The immediate reaction of the three-man crew was that they had a nose-wheel blow-out.

At least two tyres to have made that noise, thought the captain. There were two decks and the hold between the Boeing's flight-deck on top of the bubble and the 747's nose gear. He radioed his suspicions to the control tower. The co-pilot did everything by the book. He left the brakes alone and continued to rely on reverse thrust to slow the jet.

'I have nose-wheel steering,' he reported when the engines had brought the jolting aircraft down to fifty knots. He gave his skipper a puzzled glance. 'She feels fine.'

Although everyone had heard the bang, none of the passengers were aware that anything was amiss. Laura was doing her best to pacify André. 'The first thing we must do when the shops open is get your snaps developed. Wasn't it kind of Imogen to buy you that camera? I'm sure those pictures you took of the orchids in the botanical gardens will look marvellous.' She struggled to keep her voice calm.

The 747 was down to forty knots and had used up two-thirds of the runway. In the control tower they had binoculars trained on the aircraft and were reporting to the captain that all the main-gear tyres looked fine. Nevertheless, the co-pilot was taking no chances. He was careful with the brakes. Something *had* to be wrong to have caused a report like that. He steered off the runway onto the taxiway. The engines died to a subdued whine, dropping the aircraft's speed to twenty knots.

Ching was unaware of the problems on the flight-deck, although her more experienced colleagues in first class guessed there had been a tyre blow-out and were not unduly concerned. Such an event was more common than airlines liked to admit. She picked up her handset. 'On behalf of Singapore Airlines, we welcome you to London Airport, Heathrow, ladies and gentlemen. We hope you have had a pleasant flight and look forward to seeing you again. Would you please remain in your seats with your seat-belts fastened until the aircraft has come to a complete stop.'

As always, the announcement was ignored. Passengers, relieved to be able to stretch their legs after the long flight, were standing and reaching up to the overhead lockers. Laura hoped that the sudden bustle of movement would distract André, but the girl was enveloped in a world of misery. At the precise moment that the Boeing rolled to a stop, she let out a shrill, agonised scream and arched her back off the seat.

There was a sudden crack of thunder that sounded like lightning striking the aircraft. There was a flash outside the flight-deck windows, as if someone had popped a giant flashbulb. At the same time, the entire airframe gave a convulsive shudder as if it had ridden over a cattle grid. For a few hairy moments the 747's captain was convinced his nose gear was about to collapse. The watchers in the control tower had also seen something, although they weren't sure what. Two observers suspected a lightning-strike. But if it was lightning, it hadn't so much struck the aircraft as seemed to leap away from it.

The tremendous crash of thunder and the violent shuddering of the aircraft caused consternation in all the passenger sections – which was partly quelled by a quick-witted chief cabin services officer explaining over the PA that there had been a very near lightning-strike, and that there was nothing to worry about because the aircraft was designed to cope with them.

The 747 captain was also thinking fast. He could order an emergency evacuation. But he could see the headlights of four self-propelled embarkation steps speeding towards him, the ground crews already having been alerted that there was a problem. Several fire appliances were also converging on the aircraft.

With only eighty passengers on board, the chances were that he could get them all off and into buses more quickly by normal means than by breaking out the chutes. The chief cabin services officer reported over the interphone that the passengers were edgy and anxious to disembark but there was no panic. The skipper thanked him and decided on a normal deplaning, but on the taxiway.

André thrashed her skinny legs and slipped to the floor with her seatbelt caught around her neck. '*No! No! No!*' she screamed. '*All wrong! Everything wrong! At the third stroke . . . !*' The rest of the sentence was choked in her throat by the seat-belt.

Ching heard the commotion, but the anxious passengers piling into the aisle and crowding towards the exits prevented her from intervening. Laura struggled to release André's seat-belt but the girl's fists were pummelling the air. Lloyd dived across the aisle, pushed a gaping passenger out of the way and managed to grab André's wrist with one hand and release her seat-belt with the other. He knelt beside the girl and helped Laura ease her back onto the seat. The child's spine seemed to have gone rigid with shock but her arms and legs continued to thrash.

Then the chief cabin services officer spoke over the PA: 'We're very sorry, ladies and gentlemen, but all the jetties are busy, so we shall be disembarking here and taking you to the terminal by bus.'

'*All wrong! All wrong!*' André screamed.

'You must let me help you off the plane with her,' Lloyd offered.

'I can manage,' was Laura's defiant reply. 'She can't stand anyone but me touching her.'

At that point André fainted. Lloyd ignored Laura's protests and scooped André up in his arms. A youthful nipple erupted beneath his fingertips; she was heavier than he expected. Her eyes were closed but there were rapid side-to-side eye movements behind her eyelids. 'You bring my briefcase and computer,' he instructed Laura, 'and I'll look after André.'

He headed towards the exit without waiting for a reply, twisting his body sideways to prevent André's feet catching on the rows of seats. The girl's eyes continued their alarming oscillations. The doors were already open and passengers were filing quickly down the steps; Lloyd muttered a goodbye to the stewardesses and refused their offers of help with André. He set her down by the waiting bus and was pleased to see that she had recovered sufficiently to stand. Laura gave Lloyd his briefcase and computer, and threw her arms around her daughter. 'Thank you,' she said curtly, taking André firmly by the hand.

'If there's anything – '

'I can manage now, Mr Wheeler. Thank you for your help.'

André was no more trouble, but she appeared to be in a trance as they boarded the bus.

6

SOUTHERN ENGLAND
Thursday, 28 February 1991

Once all the passengers had been bussed to the terminal, the captain, co-pilot and engineer carried out a 'visual' – the walk-round inspection that was normally carried out before a flight. They could see nothing wrong with the big jet. Main-gear, control surfaces, tyres, oleos, everything – all sound. Not so much as a smear of leaking hydraulic fluid to be seen.

Two ground engineers joined them and quickly came to the same conclusion. The senior engineer was confident the aircraft could be moved, so he returned to his van and radioed for a tug.

There had been so few passengers on the flight that it was difficult for Lloyd to get near Laura and André in the baggage hall without them noticing him. His plan was to edge close to them by the carousel, in the hope of reading a name and address on their luggage tags. André spotted him first; those green eyes missed nothing. She spoke to her mother, who turned and scowled at him, and turned her luggage trolley away. He caught a glimpse of the name 'Laura' but that was all. He saw his valise from the corner of his eyes. It was passing out of reach, so he made a badly timed grab and caused a pile-up that brought the conveyor to a brief stop. By the time the log-jam was sorted out, André and her mother had vanished.

Damn! It would have been a good article – enough to redeem the Singapore debacle. He hurried after them, but a diligent customs officer in the green channel, curious as to why Lloyd seemed to be in a rush, decided to turn his valise out. When Lloyd finally emerged, all the passengers had disappeared.

He didn't have the heart to call Sarah and drag her out of bed at this hour, so he took a taxi back to his flat at the Jute Wharf in the heart of London's restructured Dockland.

The eighteenth-century Wapping warehouse in which Lloyd had his flat was home to a motley collection of small businesses that included photographers, scenery builders, sail-makers, piano-makers, two brothers who ran a car restorer's which had supplied Lloyd with his Lotus Super Seven the previous year after his promotion to editor of *Science UK*, and even a wig-maker. His apartment on the sixth floor was a fifty-foot-square expanse of polished pitch-pine boards. Dotted around the area, in no apparent order, were islands of furniture and fittings devoted to bathroom functions, kitchen functions, sleeping, eating and relaxing. The bathroom and toilet were guarded by office-type movable partitions which, like the plumbed-in hot-drink vending machines and everything else, had been bought at auctions. The overall effect was of a miniature exhibition hall rather than a flat. The 'bedroom' was in the precise centre of the floor, where three king-size mattresses were piled up on the shining boards and covered with four giant duvets – all deemed necessary because the flat was unheated. In summer it was a simple matter to move the 'bedroom' into the shuttered loading bay overlooking the Thames, where the cast-iron derricks – still attached to the side of the building – had once unloaded giant bales of jute from the waiting barges moored below.

Lloyd undressed quickly without turning on the lights, and scrambled into the multi-layered bed. Finding Sarah in the huge bed depended on getting in between the same layers. But this time her pink, warm body was nowhere to be found in any of the layers, and the first thing he noticed when he turned on the

lights was that the chromium dress-shop rail that served as her
wardrobe was missing her favourite clothes. He wrapped himself
in a duvet and padded around the flat like a bored Tiberius in
his villa on Capri until he found a note in Sarah's spiky EEG
handwriting. Another interior design commission, this time in
Nassau, and she had no idea when she would be back. All her
beachwear and squash gear had been left behind, though – Sarah
didn't believe in mixing business with pleasure, which meant
that she was rarely gone for long. He always missed her when
she disappeared. She played mean, ego- and body-bruising
squash, and had a sexy way of kissing them both better. He
drank a cup of warm chocolate from the vending machine – the
thermostat was on the blink again – and sank into the soft womb
of his empty, wobbly bed.

Sleep was impossible. Every time he closed his eyes he saw
André standing before him, staring down at him with those
hypnotic green eyes. And when he did eventually drift off, she
stayed with him, her lips moving gently as she counted off the
remaining years, hours and minutes of his life.

7

Only when she was clear of London and well into the back lanes
of Surrey did Laura relax and ease her foot off the Metro's
accelerator. Ten years ago it had all been so different; with
David she had shared a love of the city, the bright lights, the
traffic and the uproar; the receptions, the smart parties given
by David's wide circle of friends. In the city they had felt they
were alive. The country was a place where those who could stay
on a horse chased foxes; those who couldn't used it for wild
weekend parties in ivy-covered mansions, where pot was acceptable and cameras weren't . . .

Ten years ago, being married to David was the most wonderful thing imaginable. He came from an old family with old
money, and plenty of it. They hadn't approved of Laura at first,
but made the best of the match by accepting Laura as new blood
– like a filly bought by a decaying stud farm to spike up the

lineage. Not the best blood, but new. David's mother was convinced that Laura had married her son for his money. It wasn't true – Laura loved David passionately. Even Laura's mother, always loyal to her wayward daughter, had secretly thought the same, and with good reason.

As a teenager, Laura's cavalier attitude to money and responsibilities had been a constant worry. When she had money, she blew the lot on clothes. And not practical clothes, but designer gear: Laura had expensive tastes. Later, when she was at teacher training college, she usually managed to get through a quarter's allowance in the first month. Between the ages of seventeen and nineteen she had crammed in more heavy relationships – all ending in tears and tantrums – than her older sister, Imogen, had managed with her six-year head start. After Laura's marriage to David, when she was twenty, and three months pregnant with André, there had been the unspoken feeling in both families that Laura would make a lousy mother and David an equally bad father. In a way, they had been right. As soon as André was born, she became a carrycot baby, lugged from one weekend house party to the next.

The accident happened after such a party on a dank, miserable Sunday night in 1980 when André was five years old. She was sound asleep when David carried her from the house where they had been staying and laid her across the back seat of their Porsche. It was decided that David had drunk too much, so Laura drove. She loved driving the sports car and she loved driving fast.

Of the accident, Laura could remember nothing but a vague patchwork of static images, like strobe-frozen dancers in a disco.

The A27 – the main coastal trunk route. A fast road, but a mass of intersections where it was crossed by other roads radiating out from London.

Traffic grease on the inside and outside of the windscreen, breaking up approaching headlights into the smudged, disembodied flares of homing missiles – each blinding flare fading out of the corners of Laura's vision, to be replaced by a new one.

Chevrons marking a bend that she didn't see until it was too late. David's warning cry.

The Porsche was a superb piece of engineering. As safe as any machine could be at 100 m.p.h. But with one proviso: that all four wheels remained on the road. With all four wheels off the road – without the adhesion of those four tiny areas of rubber biting on asphalt – the machine's tonne plus of ABS anti-lock braking systems, high sheer alloy torsion bars, drag-links, roll-bars and low-profile tyres, all became useless lumps of ballast that merely added to the vehicle's deadly kinetic energy.

Laura's memories stopped at the moment the car left the road. They started again with her sitting with her mother in a cheerless waiting-room at St Richard's Hospital near Chichester. Laura couldn't recall how long they had clung to each other. The police doctor had taken a blood sample from Laura because the breathalyser test had been positive. Each time someone entered the waiting-room, they looked up, hoping for news from the casualty theatre where surgeons were operating to remove the section of door pillar that had speared David's heart. And then the kindly sister had approached them, and they both knew from her expression that David was dead.

Laura's injuries had been a bruised forehead and a broken finger.

At first light there had been the journey in her mother's car to the Atkinson Morley Hospital where André had been taken by a Royal Navy helicopter. They had to pass the place on the A27 where Laura had lost control of the Porsche. The remains of the car were still among the trees, surrounded by fluttering police bunting, as though the scene were the site of a macabre celebration.

At the Atkinson Morley they were allowed to see André through a window in the recovery ward door. Her head, which had smashed through the Porsche's windscreen, was swathed in bandages. She looked so vulnerable, but she was alive, her heartbeat and breathing regular.

'She's amazing,' said the surprisingly forthcoming nurse. 'As tough as they come. Mr Houseman says he's sorry to have missed you but he was called from his house when André was admitted, so he's catching up on his sleep.'

Laura had sat in silence, letting her mother do all the talking.

44

The nurse steered the older woman into the corridor and spoke in low tones. 'Mr Houseman said I could tell you what happened. It was a real freak accident. The windscreen wiper passed right between the cerebral halves of the brain . . .' She touched her head in the centre, just above the hairline. '. . . Here. It caused little damage to the frontal lobes but it lodged in the hippocampus.'

The name meant nothing to Laura's mother. 'It's the innermost core of the brain itself,' explained the nurse, sensing the woman's bewilderment. 'It's rarely damaged by itself because the frontal lobes are invariably damaged first. But that hasn't happened in this case. It's very unusual. But her face is okay. The windscreen must have shattered a split second before she hit it. There'll be a scar, but it'll be hidden by her hair.'

'So what will happen to André? Will she be all right? What shall I tell my daughter?'

The nurse hesitated. 'We can't answer any of those questions just yet. But Mr Houseman doesn't think André will lose any motor control or speech abilities.'

'*Doesn't know? Doesn't think?* Well, what exactly *does* Mr Houseman know?'

The nurse nodded understandingly, not seeming to mind the outburst. 'No neuro-surgeon can predict how a brain operation will turn out. Only time will tell. We shall know a lot more in the next few days but it's much too early to make predictions. I'm very sorry.'

'So what do I tell my daughter?' Laura's mother demanded despondently. 'Why couldn't this Mr Houseman have waited?'

'He is very concerned, please believe me. He said that first thing in the morning he's going to look through all the case histories of brain damage that's restricted to the hippocampus. The truth is that our experience of such cases is limited.'

'You really mean non-existent, don't you?'

The nurse hesitated and nodded. 'André's injuries are the result of an amazing freak accident,' she admitted. 'We don't know what we're up against but we do know that we're going to do everything we can for her . . . You will tell your daughter that, won't you?'

The accident had profoundly changed Laura. The social worker assigned to her, sensing this, had persuaded the police not to prosecute her and recommended that she should be allowed to keep her daughter.

Laura had shouldered all the guilt for what had happened, and although still only twenty-five she had put André's interests above all else. She turned her back on David's family and smart friends, gave her wardrobe of chic clothes to Oxfam, and completed her interrupted teacher training. She resolved to use David's considerable inheritance for André and André alone. Perhaps one day a cure would be found. In the meantime she would earn a living and support André as best she could, using the interest on David's capital only where André was the main beneficiary. Mr Houseman thought André should live in the country rather than be exposed to the stresses of city life, so Laura took out a mortgage on a small house in the village of Durston in Surrey, nearly on the West Sussex border, and worked as a supply teacher in the surrounding villages. In short, she settled for the sort of humdrum, country village way of life she had always ridiculed. It was best for André, and that was all that mattered.

And now she loved the countryside: the winding lanes with their sombre hedgerows picked out in the car's headlights, the sudden glow of a fox's eyes, the frantic scurry of a rabbit across her path. Singapore had been a mistake, as she had known it would be. The long flight, the uproar and bustle of the place was too much for André. Well, it was a mistake that Laura would not make again.

'Isn't it lovely to be home, André?'

André made no reply but sat staring straight ahead at the patch of illuminated road disappearing under the Metro's bonnet.

'It was lovely seeing Imogen again, wasn't it? But I really don't know how my sister can stand the place. So hot and humid, and the sun setting and rising at the same time each day throughout the year. Twelve hours of darkness, twelve hours of daylight. No seasons. God – it must be boring. Just think – we've got the spring to look forward to now. Do you think the

46

same house martins will come back this year? Jeff Harcourt reckons that five summers is their limit.'

After ten years Laura had developed a technique for maintaining a near continuous stream of prattle when she and André were alone. 'Communication is important, Mrs Normanville,' Mr Houseman had stressed a year after the accident. 'Even though André doesn't respond, you must talk to her as much as possible. She does understand, and it's most important that she doesn't feel isolated.'

As Laura talked, she kept an eye on the mirror, especially on the straight stretches. That journalist had definitely been trying to read the tags on her luggage. She was certain that he had been unlucky, but there was always the chance that he was following her from Heathrow. God, how she detested him, making André tell the time like that. The monumental arrogance of the man! But why had André done it so willingly? Hadn't six years of drumming it into her that it was wrong had any effect? After all, André hadn't made thunder since . . . Laura blocked out the ugly episode of the only time she had ever struck her daughter. Six years was long enough to develop a technique of side-stepping painful memories.

No one was following the Metro.

The signposts became familiar. Witley, Godalming, Plaistow, Northchapel. The very names were a comfort. This was a part of England that time and progress ignored. There were no motorways nearby, and the summertime grockles, speeding on their way to the coast in their Cavaliers and Escorts, had not the time or inclination to discover the magic that was only a turn of the steering-wheel away from the main road. The Metro passed the darkened windows of Jacko's Café, set back from the road in front of a clinker-and-ash clearing rolled flat by lorries, cars and motorbikes. Another mile and they passed the wooden bus shelter, visited more often by courting couples than by buses.

Laura slowed. Even after living here for ten years she still had to look carefully for the entrance to Durston Wood, hidden among the tall, alien conifers and spruces that the Forestry Commission had wished on the old Wealden Forest. The turning was all too easily overshot at night. She turned into the estate and slowed down to negotiate the sleeping policemen. The asphalt humps across the road could smash the springs on a tank if they were taken too fast.

Durston Wood, on the outskirts of Durston village, was a very un-English estate. Instead of selling to a developer who would build a mass of look-alike, ready-made houses and sell them off, the landowner had sold individual quarter-hectare plots. The result was that Durston Wood was a strange mixture of styles, from five-bedroom mansions in buff Bargate stone to sturdy Scandinavian-style lodges with wide verandas and shallow-pitched roofs. Most of the older timber bungalows had generous overhangs, roofed with shingles split from the great elms of the forest before the disease took them. All the houses were set well back from the road, and every one was different; yet there was an overall look of rightness about the place, as if this small estate belonged to the remnants of the ancient forest that surrounded it.

Laura's house was a modest three-bedroom timber-framed bungalow on a spur road, and therefore well-hidden among the brooding pines and spruces. The Metro's headlights picked out a dozen little reassurances as she turned into the long drive. Oscar, for example, André's rabbit, looking well-fed and sitting on his hind legs in his hutch. Everything was in place. There was nothing new or complicated to make André uneasy or afraid. Laura stopped the car in front of the cedarwood garage and applied the handbrake.

'Home,' she said, more to herself than André. Then she smiled at her daughter and squeezed her hand. 'Oscar looks fine. I bet young Janice has been giving him twice as much food as he needs. We're home, darling. Everything's going to be all right now.'

8
MUTLAH RIDGE. KUWAIT/IRAQ BORDER

It was the distinctive whine from the Apache's sand filters rather than the thrash of the helicopter's rotors that woke Nuri. Until he encountered the A10 Warthogs, the gunships were the one thing he had feared above all else. They owned the night, flying low, following rills and valleys so that the uneven ground cloaked the sound of their muffled engines. They could sneak up on a tank squadron and blow it to pieces with their terrible fire-power. That was the difference between this war and the long and bitter campaign against Iran that Nuri's unit had been involved in. During the Iranian war both sides stopped ground fighting at night. But not these new enemies. The Americans and the British owned the night. Moving their armoured columns like ghosts across the desert, not showing a light. Circling around, unseen and unheard, and then attacking from an unexpected direction. What chance did you have when you were under the command of a despotic, murdering megalomaniac who decided to take on NATO forces that had been equipped and trained to fight the mighty Soviet war-machine, not just during the hours of daylight but around the clock?

Nuri had been a regular soldier for fifteen years and was one of the longest-serving Kurds in the army. He had survived eight years of the bitter Iran/Iraq war, having been wounded twice. With three years to go before retiring with a generous gratuity, the air force had gassed his two sisters in a raid on his home town of Halabji in 1988. Until then his ambition had been to open a garage in Halabji, perhaps even get married. But the savage attack had changed all that. He had decided to complete his service, grab his gratuity, and use his skills and money to form his own pershmarga guerilla unit made up of other Kurds in his company. But now, after this latest debacle, they were all dead, and he would never see his long-promised gratuity. From now on, for many years, there would be an army of occupation in Iraq who would be unlikely to honour the contracts of defeated soldiers.

He tried to press the backlight button on his cheap digital watch, but his numbed fingers made the simple task virtually impossible. He could wake Khalid, of course. Reciting the right time was one of the young man's tricks. But he eventually managed to press the button and focus his eyes on the digits.

Twenty minutes after midnight. There was no moon, no stars. Nothing could get through the layer of oil-smoke that lay over the scene like a shroud. During the day the temperature had hardly crept above the norm for night. A change in the wind had shifted the unseen smoke towards Mutlah and was causing Nuri's eyes to smart. Kuwaiti crude is rich in salt and sulphur, so that the burning oil was combining with atmospheric oxygen to produce chloride and sulphur dioxide. The levels of the toxic gases were high, but not dangerously so; the real danger over the years to come would be the long-term cancerous effects of inhaling particles of heavy metals.

Nuri looked anxiously at the shapeless huddles of his two sleeping comrades. Despite their wretched condition – their raging thirst, gut-gnawing hunger and rain-soaked clothes – they had managed to sleep, albeit fitfully, for over fifteen hours. Sleep was the only thing their frozen bodies had craved above all else. For over a month they had been subjected to almost continuous bombing and shelling. It was paradoxical that they had, at last, found some respite from the war near the scene of its greatest carnage. By midday the killing at Mutlah was over and the American ground attack aircraft had left the scene.

The helicopter faded into the distance. Nuri listened intently before he dared move. There was an occasional rumble of gunfire from the north. Had Basra fallen already? And if so, how long before Baghdad also fell to the Americans and the British? Who would have thought that the British would return to Mesopotamia after so many years? At school he had learned about the vicious campaigns the British had fought against the Kurds in the aftermath of the Great World War. Nuri guessed that the battle for Baghdad would be particularly bloody. He had never shied from fighting, but he was glad not to be caught up this time. If he could escape from this mess at least there was the possibility of being able to live out the rest of his life in his homeland, free of the dark shadow of Saddam Hussein and the Ba'athists. Perhaps this time the British would ignore the sensitivities of the Turks and their hatred of the Kurds, and agree to the setting up of an independent Kurdistan.

He moved around Khalid to Kez and shook him gently. The young conscript was from the same part of Halabji as Nuri. He knew the boy's parents and had promised them that he would keep a special watch over their son. The boy had never been strong and should never have been conscripted.

'Kez!' he whispered, and shook him again.

The boy stirred and mumbled. Nuri felt a wave of relief. For a terrible moment he thought the lad had finally succumbed to their misery and deprivation.

'Kez! I'm going to look for supplies! Do you understand?'

Kez's lips moved but there was no sound. Khalid sat up and looked inquiringly at the older man.

'Look after Kez,' said Nuri curtly. 'I won't be long.'

'You must stay with me!' Khalid pleaded.

'Don't be such a coward!' Nuri snarled at the younger man – and immediately regretted his venom. Cowardice was one thing Khalid could not be accused of. During the heat of battle he had retained amazing control over their tank and had actually seemed to relish danger.

'Not a coward, Nuri,' Khalid pleaded, clutching at Nuri's anorak. 'Stay near me and you will have good luck.'

Nuri ignored the outburst. He pushed Khalid away, crawled to the top of the rise and cautiously raised his head above the rocky ledge. The night was heavily overcast, promising little respite from the infernal marrow-chilling wind and drizzle. An eerie light from burning vehicles suffused the scene, turning the great mass of twisted ironmongery into a clashing mosaic of colours, like the ghastly images of hell in a surrealist painting. The helicopter he had heard was about a mile away, playing powerful searchlights on the scene, probably to discourage beduin looters.

Nuri knew all about the beduin and the other nomadic Shiite

Arabs that lived in the vast expanse of the Majnoon Marshes at the confluence of the Tigris and Euphrates. At night they could steal up unheard on even the most alert soldier, slit his throat, rob him of his weapons, and slip back into the night without having made a sound. Nuri knew this region well. He had been an infantryman in the decisive 1988 Fao Peninsula offensive that had eventually driven the Iranians out of Iraq's narrow corridor to the sea, which they had occupied since 1986. Nuri didn't know it, but it was that Iranian advance that had panicked the West. Once the Iranians were in Iraq there had been nothing to stop them sweeping through Kuwait and into Saudi Arabia. The West had seen Saddam Hussein as a bulwark against the spread of Shiite fundamentalism, and had supplied him with virtually anything he wanted in the way of arms and equipment.

Deliberately choosing an area well away from the give-away light of a burning truck, Nuri scrambled down the slope and threw himself flat behind a hummock. He listened, not knowing what devilish devices the Americans had for monitoring the darkness. He decided that it was as safe as it was ever likely to be, and darted into the shadowy tangle of shot-up cars and trucks. The burst of effort was a huge drain on his meagre reserves of strength, but desperation and determination drove him on.

He found a Cherokee pick-up. Nuri felt no pity for the Iraqi colonel slumped over the wheel with most of his head blown away. These were the bastards who had shot men in his unit in the back when they suspected them of trying to desert. They had picked on the Kurds unmercifully, reserving particular venom for Christian Kurds. Nuri grabbed the AK–47 assault rifle off the passenger seat and stuffed the spare magazines into his anorak pockets. He decided that he might as well have the weapon, even though it wasn't primarily what he was after. The same applied to the Bank of Kuwait polythene bag containing a thick wad of new $100 bills that he found in the glove compartment. There was no time to relish the sensation of having more money than he had ever seen in his life. If he could hang onto it, at least he had his gratuity.

A Chieftain camper was his next target. Once inside, the

stench of gasoline was so overpowering that he dared not use his lighter, but there was just enough light flickering through the shattered windows from a burning SA–9 Gaskin missile-launcher for him to see. The camper's roof had been riddled down the centre, leaving the bulkhead fittings on each side remarkably unscathed. The prize find was a full ten-litre water container. He was so weak he had to push the container on its side to drain off half the water before he had the strength to lift it to his lips. He drank greedily, slopping water down his anorak, but the useless material was soaked through anyway. The long draught of sweet heaven gushing down his parched throat cleared his senses. A galley closet was full of booty. He grabbed a carton of Mars Bars, broke it open and crammed most of the chocolate bars into his pockets. He stoppered the water-container and half-fell out of the camper. He staggered doggedly back up the rise, laden with his trophies, and slithered down the far side to the overhang.

For once Khalid wasn't smiling when Nuri returned. He gestured anxiously to Kez and started to chatter, but Nuri silenced him with an angry cuff. The two men lifted their unconscious comrade into a sitting position. Nuri filled a plastic cup with water and raised it to Kez's lips. The boy's head lolled forward and the water ran down his chin. Nuri hooked his arm around Kez's neck with the intention of tilting his head back. It was then that he realised there was no pulse in his comrade's neck. He frantically tore open Kez's anorak and tunic, and listened fearfully with his ear pressed against his pale chest while Khalid looked on. After a few moments Nuri straightened up, but his head remained slumped forward in private despair and grief. He stared down at the son of his lifelong friends, then bent to kiss him on the cheek. There was nothing he could do for the boy now except anoint his body with tears.

RIYADH

Failing to shut his car door properly that morning was a seemingly insignificant incident that was destined to change Max Shannon's life. Because the door hadn't been shut, the interior light had remained on all day and had drained the battery. The Toyota's starter motor cranked the engine a couple of times, and died. Cursing his uncharacteristic carelessness, Max returned to the hotel lobby. It was 10 p.m. The war had ended that day, and the lobby was thronged with journalists awaiting taxis to take them to the airport. Most news editors, conscious of the enormous expenses their scribes had been running up despite the lack of alcohol, were recalling their charges to the fold as quickly as possible.

The pressmen were laughing and joking, most of them looking forward to getting stewed out of their minds once their aircraft was airborne. Bellhops were standing guard over trucks piled high with ENG video equipment. Taxi drivers were doing brisk business with fast runs back and forth to King Khalid Airport.

Max used a lobby phone to notify the hire company of the misfortune that had befallen their car. They promised to deal with it immediately. He had planned going to the Intercontinental Hotel that evening to sample their special 150-Riyals-a-head Victory Carvery Celebration. Steve Ramsay and his colleagues in MOD Procurement would be there.

He considered calling a taxi, and then decided that he couldn't face a large meal or Steve Ramsay and his fellow civil servants. The entire city was on a euphoric high following the crushing defeat of the Iraqis. There were parties going on all over Riyadh. Max had tried to do some work at the British Forces Middle East Headquarters that morning, and had given up. He had returned to his hotel room to write a detailed report which he had faxed to Leo Buller. By rights he should now be hungry, but he wasn't. It was a cool evening, so a stroll to the Shoula Shopping Centre for a hamburger and a coffee, followed by an early night, seemed a sensible alternative.

A laden tanker roared low overhead as he set off. These days Max hardly took any notice of the giant Lockheeds as they struggled to gain height, and they no longer disturbed his sleep even though the hotel lay under their flight path. They had been flying out of Riyadh AFB around the clock for almost a month, fuelling the enormous coalition war effort. Now they were ferrying fuel north for the return of the armoured and mechanised divisions. The war had been over hardly twenty-four hours and already General H. Norman Schwarzkopf's mighty war-machine was in fast reverse.

He turned into the Shoula Shopping Centre, crowded with parties of black-veiled women laden with bulging plastic bags. Some were with their husbands. Only a few years before there had been different shopping times for men and women. Things were changing in Saudi Arabia, and the quiet revolution was powered by the women. Shortly after Max first arrived in the country, he had witnessed the extraordinary spectacle of several Saudi women driving Cadillacs in convoy along Malek Fahed Road. Male drivers had hooted their indignation. It turned out that some fifty Saudi wives had organised a protest demonstration against the law that forbade them to drive. Journalists staying at the Hyatt Regency had been in a quandary, knowing that to report anything critical of the Saudi way of life could lead to their visas being revoked. Eventually the press pool had decided that the story was too good to sit on, and all of them had filed it at the same time, daring the Saudis to boot the entire press corps out of the country. As it happened, the Saudis decided to take no action, and even the women who had ousted their chauffeurs got off lightly.

Max walked up the ramp that spiralled around a fountain and led to the upper level. He was disappointed to see that the tables outside the café that served the best coffee in Riyadh were crowded with a noisy mob of British and American servicemen. They were about as boisterous as it was possible to get on 7-Up and Cokes.

'In less than two hours,' a Welsh soldier declared in a booming voice, 'it will be St David's Day. Long enough for you Yankee heathens to learn to sing "Men of Harlech"! God forbid, but we'll even let the English join in if they know the words.' He started to sing in a rich baritone that Max would willingly have listened to, but the Welshman had to give up in the face of a sustained barrage of good-natured catcalls from the USAF airman.

Max decided that there was no room at the café. Also he felt a bit of a fraud in his immaculate combat dress, in the presence of men who had been in the thick of the fighting. He was about to move off when a friendly hand owned by a 1st Cavalry sergeant grabbed him and pulled him down on a seat. 'Hey – no need to be shy, feller. Plenty of room even for pseudo soldiers.'

For the next few minutes Max made cheerful small-talk with the servicemen and found himself enjoying their reminiscences. Like all soldiers, they were already exaggerating the decisive role they had each individually played in bringing about Saddam Hussein's defeat. One airman of the 354th Tactical Fighter Wing was boasting about his part in the Mutlah Ridge turkey-shoot.

'You're talking crap, Danny,' said a marine captain. 'An hour ago you were telling us you couldn't even blow away a crummy T–55.'

'For Chrissake,' Danny Kappelhof protested. 'All I said was that that goddamn T–55 had a charmed life. Like those Iraqis were eating Lucky Luck's pussy right there in their tank.'

Max was immediately interested, although he didn't show it. 'A lucky T–55?' he inquired.

Danny nodded and took a swig from a Coke can. He was about to speak but one of his comrades got in first.

'Yeah – they were lucky to have you around with your lousy shooting, Danny.'

Danny Kappelhof began to get angry. 'How many times do I have to tell you gooks,' he protested. 'I fired two fucking useless Mavericks at it. *Two!*'

'A hundred thousand bucks-worth of guided missile and our Danny has to miss.'

56

'Hey, Danny – reckon if the Iraqis had battleships you would've missed them as well?'

'What happened, Danny?' Max asked quietly.

Danny looked suspiciously at the Englishman. It was one thing to gripe about weapon failures to fellow countrymen, quite another to talk about it to a Brit. But then the Brits had been right in there, and their Tornadoes had taken one helluva hammering with their low-level attacks. 'I got caught up in Tuesday's turkey-shoot at Mutlah.'

Max nodded. 'I heard about it. You boys did a good job.'

'Yeah,' said Danny laconically, remembering the women and kids he had cut to pieces and wishing he could get blind, stinking drunk. 'Fucking good job.'

'Tell me about the tank.'

Danny shrugged as if he was trying to shake off a bad dream. 'Fired off a couple of AGM–65 Deltas at a Tango Double Five when it headed for the desert, and it got lucky. Real lucky. Both stores blew up before they hit the target. I've never known warheads blow like that. They made a sound like thunder. Didn't get another chance because my time was up.'

'Someone would've nailed it,' said another pilot. 'Nothing got out of Mutlah. Everything got wasted.'

'Were there unusual markings on the turret?' Max inquired, keeping his voice very matter-of-fact.

'Red crescent on a circle?' Danny queried.

'No – not that.'

'What, then?'

'Well . . . Like a white swastika, only painted backwards?'

Danny was about to take another pull at his Coke can. Instead he set the drink down and met the Englishman's gaze. 'Now how in hell do you know that?'

10

SOUTHERN ENGLAND

No matter how deeply Lloyd burrowed into the duvet layers of his bed in a determined attempt to de-jetlag himself after the flight from Singapore, nothing could shut out the day-time sounds of the Jute Wharf. It started when the scenery-makers on the ground floor received a consignment of sawn timber delivered by a Thames lighter. The ancient derricks creaked and clattered all morning, and when they had finished, the industrial sewing-machines of the sail-makers on the floor below started up. Around midday the sound-recording studio at the far end of the venerable building declared war on the three-feet-thick walls with a Kango hammer. Lloyd gave up. He showered and shaved, and nuked himself a frozen lasagne in the micro-wave. The meal's icy, crunchy centre, which he discovered when he sat down to eat, did nothing for his mood. Maybe his mother was right, maybe it was time to start living sensibly.

He listened to Fleetwood Mac on headphones, but the Kango hammer drove him out of the flat in the middle of the afternoon.

Miss Millicent Dyson, the wig-maker and theatrical cos-tumier, was outside her tiny workshop busily flattening card-board boxes and cramming them into the industrial waste-bins that were lined up against the wall in the narrow, cobbled street. She was a prim, grey lady – sour as real yogurt, with a Ghurka-knife tongue, and totally deaf.

'Dreadful row,' she complained as Lloyd helped her crush the last of her boxes. 'It's that fat beatnik friend of yours with his recording studio.'

Lloyd thought that some sort of preservation order should be slapped on Millicent Dyson; no one said beatnik any more. 'I'm surprised you can hear anything at all, Miss Dyson,' he replied. The woman was such a skilled lip-reader that it wasn't necessary for him to frame his words carefully, but he did so out of courtesy.

'I can feel vibrations,' Miss Dyson snapped. 'I'm not com-pletely without senses, you know.'

'Rik said something about having a desk taken out,' said Lloyd, edging away.

'I'd like to have something take him out,' Miss Dyson retorted. 'Preferably a Scud missile. Some people have no con-sideration. You're the chairman of the Tenants' Association

– you're to speak to him, otherwise I shall complain to the landlords.'

'I'll have a word with him now,' Lloyd promised. He left her and walked to the entrance at the far end of the building, where he found Rikki Steadman, obese and sweating, struggling with two men to persuade a Neve recording desk to go through a widened doorway and onto a waiting truck.

'I thought the old cow was deaf,' Rikki complained when Lloyd conveyed Miss Dyson's complaint.

'She says she can feel vibrations.'

'Tell her if she wasn't so ugly I'd give her some very special vibrations,' Rikki growled. 'We'll be through in ten minutes.'

Lloyd passed an edited version of Rikki's reply to Millicent Dyson, and walked the hundred yards to the offices of *Science UK*. The magazine was housed on the ground floor of a small modern office building in the crimson-brick-and-phoney-slate-roof style of the late '80s. On paper, the block blended with the old warehouses, but in reality it looked like something out of Legoland.

Della Smith, the magazine's receptionist, looked up from her VDU as Lloyd pushed his way through the glass doors. She was thirty, and had the self-confidence and poise that comes from surviving two broken marriages and several broken relationships.

'Hallo, Lloyd. Got your fax saying you'd be back early. Singapore not too good?'

She liked blonds, but she particularly liked Lloyd. People mistook his innate sense of fairness for a tendency to be easy-going, but underneath he was uncompromisingly tough. It didn't do to cross him.

'Singapore was a waste of time,' Lloyd grunted, looking through the mail that Della was dealing with. He used to have his own secretary, but that was before the swingeing staff cuts he had been forced to make the year before. Now Della doubled as secretary, receptionist and postal clerk, and she even looked after the advertising accounts. Times were tough, even for a small monthly journal whose subscription list and acrimonious correspondence columns suggested that it was the unofficial

59

house magazine of the Royal Society and the Massachusetts Institute of Technology. *Science UK* had the good fortune to be owned by a wealthy trust, which made it possible for it to defy economic gravity, even with its minuscule circulation of 15,000. But that hadn't stopped the chairman of the trustees forcing through a massive cost-cutting exercise, with Lloyd as his unwilling tool.

'I'll be working in my office for a while, Della. I'm not officially back yet. It was a lousy flight and I've not slept properly; and I feel as if I'm walking on eggs. You'd better warn anyone who wants to see me that my human condition is marginal. Furthermore, I've lost my squash partner. Sarah has sodded off on a commission.'

'Understood, Lloyd. How about some coffee? Some of my real coffee?'

Lloyd knew that she provided the coffee out of her own pocket. He managed a wan smile despite his black mood. '*That* could cause me to forget my rules about sexual harassment and do something out of character.'

'In that case,' Della replied, rising, 'I'll make it right away. Harassment I can handle. Improper invitations to become your squash partner are more difficult.'

They both laughed at that. Their bantering exchanges always made Lloyd feel better. He entered his tiny office behind the reception area and read through the mail that Della had marked for his attention. There was nothing that couldn't wait. He had other, more pressing matters on his mind.

He remembered that his magazine had published an article on gifted children when he was assistant editor – perhaps as long as five years ago, but he wasn't certain. He could check the back numbers box-files, but the computer was quicker. He switched on his LAN terminal. After a quick check to see how the page make-ups for the next edition were proceeding, he carried out a word-search of the phrase 'gifted children'. Several entries scrolled down on the screen, each one flagging when the phrase had been used against the issue number and page number. He worked methodically, calling up each entry in chronological order, sifting through fillers, readers' letters and articles. There was nothing of substance, although one useful concordance was the word 'savant'.

Della came in quietly with a coffee, but he was too engrossed to notice her. She was used to Lloyd and his off-days. Sometimes they were off-weeks.

He called Gary Pepper on the intercom.

'Gary. Do we have any experts on savants in this country?'

'Gifted kiddiwinks?'

'Yeah. I've been wading through back numbers, but all the experts seem to be Americans.'

'There is one. Can't remember his name off-hand. Give me ten.'

Gary called back after five minutes.

'Edward Prentice. A child shrink. Private, with a contract to look after the MRs, SLDs and autistic kids at Horton Manor Children's Centre near Epsom. Do you want his number?'

'Please.'

Gary gave Lloyd the information and warned: 'Mike says our lamented sister mag. ran a story about him and his work about five years ago, which Prentice resented so much that he wanted to sue them. He can be prickly, but he's the best.'

'I'll treat him with kid gloves,' Lloyd promised.

'Better if you used mesh-reinforced industrial gloves,' Gary observed drily. 'I gather you had a lousy trip and are in quarantine?'

'Thanks for the info, Gary.'

Lloyd cut the conversation short by punching for an outside line and calling Edward Prentice's number. He got through to a private secretary.

'Mister Prentice is an extremely busy man,' said the woman tetchily. 'He's attending a convention at the moment. An appointment is most difficult to arrange until he gets back.' She sounded as though arranging for anyone to meet her boss would result in the automatic loss of her job. Lloyd persuaded her that the matter was important. 'Very well, Mr Wheeler. The earliest is next Tuesday – fourteen hundred hours, Tuesday the fifth of March. But I shall have to confirm it on Monday.'

Lloyd thanked her, and hung up.

Damn! He hated waiting.

11

Friday, 1st March 1991

Suddenly the porpoise gave a convulsive shudder. The movement dislodged several of the neural mapping probes that were inserted into the creature's brain. Although it was unconscious, its powerful tail thrashed wildly, striking a tray of surgical instruments and scattering them on the floor. It was prompt action by Leo Buller's assistant that saved the 486 Viglen computer from being smashed. Helen Frost shoved the computer trolley clear of the operating-table, yanking more probes from the porpoise's brain in the process. She looked up in wide-eyed concern at her boss.

'I'm sorry, Leo.'

'Dammit, Helen,' Leo muttered, moving quickly to reinsert the probes. 'Computers are easier to come by than porpoises.'

The glowing trace of the porpoise's heartbeat on the cardiac monitor became erratic. Helen tapped a dislodged layer of moisturising foam latex back into place around the porpoise. 'It was an instinctive reaction.'

Leo checked an impulse to swear. He was a tall, spare, and somewhat thoughtful man, rarely given to displays of temper. His control over his emotions was as tight as his control over his experiments – even when experiments as important as this one went wrong. 'We'll give him a couple of minutes to stabilise. What you did is not your fault but the failing of the human brain.' He pressed a function key on the adrenaline regulator while watching the porpoise intently. 'We still have to put up with instinct overriding logic in emergencies, Helen. A hardware bug that four million years of evolution has failed to eradicate. Your God was always weak on R and D.'

Helen didn't bite. She was a Catholic, and had learned that Leo's frequent needling of her beliefs was not out of perverse pleasure but because he was genuinely puzzled as to how any rational, intelligent being could persist with a belief in God.

Leo removed his rimless spectacles and polished them absent-mindedly while screwing up his eyes to watch the cardiac monitor. He was forty-nine, and had reached that infuriating stage when his optician could not keep up with the rapid shortening of his sight.

A minute passed. The mammal's breathing and heartbeat returned to normal, so Leo resumed neural-mapping the creature's hippocampus – the most primitive part of the inner brain. He was using controlled bursts of light, and measuring the brain's reaction. Helen sensed the scientist's tension and remained silent. The monitor showed a sampling capillary being eased into place and capturing a tiny measure of the hormone safely into the tube. Leo looked up from the eye-pieces and gave a half-smile of triumph.

'We've done it, Helen.'

'It's a hormone?'

Leo nodded. 'It's probably a form of melatonin or something very close to it. Whoever would have thought that it could be produced in the hippocampus and with such little light stimuli? Amazing.' He withdrew the sampling capillary from its insertion sleeve, and sealed the ends before sliding it into a protective glass tube. He relaxed, and chuckled. 'You ought to write up today in your diary, Helen. You'll be able to tell your grandchildren that you were in on the discovery of a new pesticide that eradicated disease-carrying mosquitoes from the planet.'

'How will it work?'

'If we screw up their circadian rhythms with a new hormone, we can also screw up their breeding cycles.'

Helen smiled. 'Well, if it doesn't work, Leo, the chances are that you've stumbled on an aphrodisiac that really *does* work.'

'What?'

Helen pointed to the comatose porpoise. It was sporting a wickedly-proportioned erection that had forced its way through the layers of moisture-conserving foam rubber.

12

An hour after Helen had gone home, Leo sat in the first-floor office he shared with Max and wrote out his notes in longhand. He was exhausted, it was nearly midnight, but this task had to be done. When he came to the report's conclusions, the enormous significance of what he might have achieved began to get through to him. He crossed to the window and stared out at the lights of the inshore fishing boats in the bay while he sorted out his thoughts.

Normally he relished the quiet and isolation of the chunky granite mansion on the Dorset headland. There were those days when the army firing range was busy, but they were getting rarer. Kimmeridge House had been built a century before for a shipping magnate, and later became a hotel which failed through bad management. During the war years the extensive grounds leading to the cliff edge had been used as a huge ammunition dump, and last year there had been a scare when a gardener unearthed an ancient unexploded shell. Now the mansion's thirty or so rooms were offices, laboratories, a machine shop and a library for the Cybernet Consultancy's ten employees. The largest suite had been converted into an apartment for Max and wife, and there was a smaller flat for Leo.

He returned to his desk and struggled to compose succinct sentences. Damn this place. It was like living in a Daphne du Maurier novel. He wanted to phone up some of his old and trusted former colleagues in America and tell them the fabulous news. He needed to talk. He needed someone to bounce ideas off. He even considered telephoning Max with the good news, but he was too tired to work out what the time was in Riyadh. Anyway, Max was only interested in neural mapping that could be used to produce artificial networks with military applications, such as optical target-recognition systems.

The infra-red laser neural-mapping technique that Leo had developed had worked perfectly with any area of the brain except the hippocampus – the most primitive and yet least understood region of the inner brain. No matter how careful he was, his attempts to map the hippocampus had always ended in disaster. It was as if an outside force were saying: 'This far and no further'. But Leo didn't believe in God. The brain was a machine – albeit an incredibly complex machine – and depended on the interactions between nerves and chemicals. And like all machines, tiny parts of it could be duplicated as artificial networks – as the Cybernet Consultancy had already demonstrated with great success.

The company was owned jointly by Max Shannon and Leo Buller, and it was making money. Real money. The flow of design ideas from the combination of Leo's neurological work and Max's electronic genius had resulted in the successful registration of over a hundred patents. They had started their business five years before with simple speech-recognition microprocessors that had a host of applications: the synthesised warning voices in most modern aircraft that informed the flight-deck crew of impending problems and hazards were based on preliminary research work carried on by the two men. Max Shannon had developed the micro-processors, and their embedded software was based on Leo Buller's work on how the brain perceived and responded to stimuli from the outside world. That their start had been so successful was largely due to Max's willingness to spend money on good patents agents, and his unwillingness to get bogged down in manufacturing.

'We're scientists, innovators and businessmen in that order,' Max had insisted when they forged their partnership. 'We're not going to be production engineers. Production engineers are two a penny. Half the population of Japan are production engineers. We'll have a few small workshops for building prototypes to test design concepts, but that's as far as we go in making anything. There's no point in wasting time mass-producing our ideas when we should be getting on with the next project. Our products will be our patents. We'll license others to make better mouse-traps – not make them ourselves.'

Leo was glad of it; he had recognised from the outset that Max shared his own ambition for riches and fame. Leo's ambitions went a stage further, however: earlier in his career he had craved a Nobel Prize. And with the success of his work at Stanford University, California, into the memory storage functions of the brain's 'messengers' – monoamines and peptides – a Nobel Prize had looked a distinct possibility. Much of Leo's genius stemmed from the way in which his brain could picture in three dimensions the complex interactions of compounds and molecules. In his remarkable mind, lustreless slices of brain tissue as seen under the electron microscope were transformed into living networks of nerves and electrical charges.

His career in America had come to an abrupt halt on a TV discussion programme in which he condemned God as an incompetent bungler for inventing the time-wasting and hopelessly inefficient evolutionary approach to design.

'It's "suck-it-and-see" technology at its worst,' he had declared. 'It doesn't permit intellectual leaps. If we designed aircraft like God designed creatures, the space shuttle would have a rudimentary second set of wings because we'd be reluctant to give up the biplane approach.'

A prominent evangelist on the panel took grave exception to his remarks, whereupon Leo had ripped his shirt open and pointed to his nipples, saying: 'You tell me what use they are and I might consider worshipping your God.'

Two decades earlier John Lennon had made a similar error of judgement, and as a result, free-speech-loving Americans built bonfires of Beatles' records. Leo's later admission that his real error of judgement had been the two whiskies he'd had to steady his nerves before going on air didn't stop an outraged army of the self-righteous from burning his articles and books, or his American wife from divorcing him and denying him access to his daughter. Following that, he had had no option but to return to England and accept Max's offer of a partnership.

Leo was caught in a trap. In his twenties he had marched with the nuclear arms race protesters, and he had seen his work in an idealistic light as serving mankind. Now his principle work with Max was on the interactions between men and machines; more particularly, men and fighting machines.

'No one ever went broke from thinking up ways of making bigger and better bangs to end the life of one's fellow man, whereas getting involved in pharmaceutical R and D is a sure-fire way of going bust,' was one of Max's favourite responses whenever Leo suggested increasing their efforts in socially useful fields. As always, Max had been right: military work guaranteed a cash flow.

The Mamba two-man stealth tank was a case in point. There was a model of the thing in one of the labs; a low-slung, mean-looking mass of hardware crewed only by a driver and a gunner. It was still a design exercise – a machine for the next century – yet the concepts embodied in the Mamba had already interested Vickers and the Ministry of Defence.

But the most important current military project centred around the flight simulator they had had in Kimmeridge House's main gallery. It was the main tool in the programme the two men were now concentrating their resources on with the aid of a Ministry of Defence R and D contract. The idea was to build a flight control system that could work like the human brain, but at several times the speed. To build an artificial intelligence that worked like the brain, of course, it was first necessary to understand fully how the brain worked. And the trouble was that Max was much keener on exploiting the preliminary results of Leo's neural mapping than on encouraging him to continue with his research.

Leo yawned, and glanced at his watch. A few minutes to midnight. Twenty years ago he could work around the clock and think nothing of it. The phone rang, and he groaned inwardly. It would be Helen to say that her car had broken down yet again on the way home, or Max's wife calling from her flat, asking him to turn the central heating up.

But it was neither – it was Max.

'Max! You must be telepathic. I was just thinking of calling you. We've had a breakthrough with the – '

'Sorry, Leo,' Max cut in. 'It'll have to wait. Something urgent's come up. You're needed out here. And fast.'

Leo's mind raced. 'In Riyadh? But the war's over. Anyway, I don't have a visa for Saudi Arabia.'

'You will have. Listen carefully. Take your passport along to the visa section of the Royal Embassy of Saudi Arabia tomorrow, with your birth certificate and two passport photographs, and they'll issue you with a military-sponsored visa right away.'

'Yes, but Max, we've had a major breakthrough – '

'I'm not interested,' said Max, using a mild tone that Leo recognised as dangerous. 'This is much more important, Leo. Extremely important. Everything's been arranged this end. That's Belgrave Square tomorrow, with your passport, birth certificate and two photos. You need only be out here for a couple of days. Call me with your flight details and I'll meet you at the airport. Okay?'

'What's this all about, Max?'

'You'll find out when I see you. I can't discuss it on the phone.'

Leo gave in. He always gave in to Max. 'Okay. I'll call you tomorrow from London when I'm fixed up.'

'Fine,' said Max, sounding pleased. 'One more thing, Leo. Bring a sunhat – it's beginning to warm up here.'

13

SOUTHERN IRAQ

The two filthy, unkempt men following the goat-track through the dun-coloured, barren foothills looked like ghostly wandering dervishes – which was exactly what Nuri wanted them to look like. They had discarded their uniforms in favour of jubbahs. The fine gowns had been new when they found them at Mutlah, but they had aged them by rolling them in mud so that they were now caked and stained. Nuri kept the AK–47 hidden under his jubbah. Their tough vinyl back-packs, doubtless looted by the fleeing Iraqis from a safari store in Kuwait, had received similar treatment. Nuri's footware was a pair of magnificent Texan leather boots. He knew it was crazy wearing new boots when they had a long walk ahead of them, but he was proud of them. Unlike Khalid, Nuri came from a poor family who could not afford such luxuries; until he joined the army he had never seen an indoor cold-water tap. The fit of the boots was not helped by the $5,000 in $100 bills that he had packed inside,

68

around each foot. Originally the feel of the money had been a source of comfort, but now it was giving him blisters. Khalid was wearing givas – the comfortable but hard-wearing woven camelhair shoes that were favoured by the traditionalist riverine Arabs who scorned the universal fashion for trainers.

The night was freezing, but mercifully it wasn't raining. Khalid rewound his red-spotted keffiyeh around his face and settled the double loop of the black camelhair aagal more comfortably on his head. As a Kurd, he was not accustomed to wearing the traditional Arab headdress, but he appreciated its usefulness in keeping his head warm at night and protecting it from the sun during the day – not that the two men had seen much sun. In dry, desert conditions the simple but effective garment made an excellent dust and sand filter, and in marsh-lands it protected the face from mosquitoes.

They walked slowly up the steep slope, looking neither right nor left but carefully down at the broken, uneven ground. Nuri had insisted that they take particular care. A twisted or broken ankle now would be fatal. If the Iraqis found them, they would be shot as deserters; if the Americans found them, they would be shot as spies; if a band of beduin found them, they'd be shot as impostors, because that was the way of the Shiite marsh Arabs, who had an almost pathological hatred of the Iraqi Sunni. They were unlikely to accept that two travellers were Christian Kurds.

The two soldiers had been walking for two nights, sleeping soundly during the day in goatherds' shelters, and living on chocolate bars, dates and raisins. After his initial enthusiasm for Mars bars, Nuri had been more selective in subsequent raiding forays at Mutlah, and as a result both men were in much better physical condition than when they had set out. Also they were in good spirits. Despite Nuri's depression over the death of Kez, he found it was impossible to be down-hearted for long in Khalid's company. As always, the fair-haired young man's good-humour was irrepressible, and he was always ready to make light of any misfortune. Nuri was developing a protective, fatherly fondness for the retarded youngster. He was learning that Khalid was a soul completely devoid of malice; although

69

Khalid had shown great enthusiasm for returning to his home-land, Nuri suspected it was out of a desire to be reunited with his family rather than from a driving ambition to fight Saddam Hussein and the Ba'athists.

Khalid had been a late arrival at the Kuwaiti front. He had been attached to their tank crew as a driver when their original driver crushed his hand during an engine change. At first the other three members of the tank crew had been suspicious of Khalid; a simpleton was a liability. But his remarkable skills as a driver and his easy-going, smiling manner soon won them over. Everyone liked Khalid. Also, he was an accomplished conjurer and had kept them entertained with tricks during the long hours of boredom while they waited for the war to begin. And when it did begin, so did the amazing streak of luck that Khalid had promised his three comrades. Despite the massive bombing of their positions by B–52s, and shelling from the sea, no bombs or shells had landed near the scrape where their tank had been hunkered down.

When other units in their armoured brigade saw the incredible good luck that the despised Kurdish tank crew were enjoying, they were ordered out of their position – whereupon that posi-tion, with its new occupants, suffered a direct hit. During the last air raid before the beginning of the land war, their T–55 had been forced to occupy an exposed position; yet it had escaped. It was the same story during the land battle – not one enemy shell had struck home, although a number had exploded uncomfortably close. Even the Americans' deadly air-launched anti-tank missiles had blown up prematurely at Mutlah. But not even Khalid's extraordinary good fortune could prevent the elderly T–55 from running out of diesel fuel.

The travellers reached the crest of the hill and stopped for a rest in a hollow that was out of the wind. Far to the south they could see the hellish glow of the oil fires at Al Ahmadi. Nuri loosened the buckles on his Texan boots, while Khalid made a shelter of stones for the camping Gaz cooker and kettle. Nuri wondered if reception might be better on this hilltop, so he dug the tiny radio out of his pack. It was an FM-only set, and so far had been useless, especially now that its two batteries were dying. Several times he had considered discarding it, but there was always the possibility that it would be useful when they were further north. He switched the set on and tuned around. Basra was still off the air, which was hardly surprising because the port at the head of the Shatt-al-Arab waterway was a major target for bombers. Baghdad was there, but too faint to make out, even when he held the radio above his head. A slightly stronger station came through that Nuri hadn't heard before. He spoke very little English but he could recognise an American accent.

'Khalid! What are they saying?'

Khalid stopped making tea and listened. 'War over,' he said simply. He grinned. 'Cease-fire agreed in a tent between Iraqi generals and Americans.'

Nuri was dumbfounded. Was it possible that the whole of Iraq had been overrun so quickly? Did it mean their beloved homeland had been liberated?

Khalid did his best to hear what he could of the fading signal by pressing the speaker to his ear, but the batteries finally expired before he could make more sense of the report.

'Too much Saddam Hussein shouting has made radio deaf,' Khalid joked.

But Nuri wasn't amused. In fury, he hurled the useless set into the night.

They settled down to sip the tea that Khalid had made, but Nuri was preoccupied. He was totally at a loss to know the best thing to do. Then there was the unmistakeable rumble of gunfire from the east, from the direction of Basra. He jumped to his feet and stared across the darkened hillocks. If there was a cease-fire, why the fighting? What was going on?

They finished their tea, repacked the rucksacks and continued their long northward trek. Two hours later they paused at a fork in the track while Nuri checked their bearings with a pocket compass. The large-scale road map of the area he had found at Mutlah was virtually useless, but it was all they had.

'Left path is away from Basra Road,' said Khalid.

'You're sure?'

It was a stupid question; Khalid's sense of direction was like his luck – uncanny.

Khalid smiled, nodded vigorously and stuffed some dates in his mouth. 'Left is away from the road.'

They took the gently descending left fork. Nuri had good reasons for wanting to avoid the highway. Even if the Americans didn't shoot them as spies, the last thing he wanted was to spend months, perhaps years, in a POW camp. He had work to do in his homeland.

Logic told him that the Americans could not have driven the Iraqi forces from Kurdistan in such a short time. Hadn't President Bush repeatedly said that America didn't want another Vietnam on its hands? And yet the Americans had given the impression that they wouldn't rest until they had destroyed Saddam Hussein's war-machine. Nuri's sole ambition now was to get home. If Saddam Hussein's forces still held sway there, then he would stick to his original plan and organise an uprising to drive them and the despised Iraqis out of Kurdistan. Until now, such ambitions had been doomed from the outset; previous uprisings had been dealt with by Saddam Hussein with the utmost ferocity, even to the extent of gassing villages suspected of planning insurrection. Hadn't the despicable tyrant murdered his sisters? But the terror of Mutlah Ridge was a testament to the terrible fire-power of the Americans and the certainty that Saddam Hussein's forces had been annihilated. Nuri prayed that it was so, but there was always that niggling doubt. Saddam Hussein seemed to be as indestructible as the legends that had risen up around him.

'Men,' said Khalid quietly, as Nuri was pushing the compass back into a pocket in his rucksack.

Something in the younger man's tone alerted Nuri. He wheeled around, and his heart sank. Resistance would be useless. At first he thought there were about five of them, but the dark shadows separated and he saw that there were at least double that number of the black-shrouded beduin. Their eyes and rifle-barrels gleamed menacingly in the darkness. They had materialised like ghosts out of the night, and had them surrounded.

'Too close for good luck to work,' Khalid observed expressionlessly, reading Nuri's thoughts.

A torch snapped on and the beam played on Nuri and Khalid in turn. The leader of the beduin spoke rapidly in a dialect that Nuri didn't understand.

'We are Kurds,' said Nuri firmly, certain that the word would be understood. '*Christian* Kurds,' he emphasised.

The beam flicked back to his face, blinding him.

'Kurds?' The answer was spat out from behind the dazzling light.

'Kurds,' Nuri confirmed. He started to explain but was silenced by a warning growl. His rucksack was yanked roughly from his shoulders. Searching hands quickly found the AK–47. It was unclipped and thrown on the ground. He could hear Khalid receiving similar treatment. He was about to protest, but realised that it would be useless.

The gang conferred in low tones. Suddenly a different voice spoke from behind the light.

'What are your names?'

Nuri could scarcely believe his ears. The question had been asked in Kurdish! From the Mosul region, judging by the man's accent. He started to gabble who he was and where they were from, but the new speaker cut him short.

'Very well. And your friend is also Kurdish?' The torch went back to Khalid, who promptly bowed and blew kisses to an invisible audience as though the beam were a stage spotlight. The sudden mime produced some guffaws. The interrogator was not amused and repeated his question.

'I am a Kurd,' Khalid agreed. He gave his name and where he was from.

'You will come with us,' said the Kurdish-speaker.

Nuri and Khalid were allowed to gather up their rucksacks, and the group threaded their way single-file down the steep left-hand track. There were nine men in the gang; tall, erect, taut as piano wires, and moving with a graceful, almost feminine bearing. Nuri wasn't sure which of the men was his fellow-countryman; they all kept their faces carefully covered with their black keffiyehs, and refused to answer his questions.

Khalid tried to joke with one of the Arabs, and received a curt warning to remain silent. He subsided into silence, but did produce laughs when they had to negotiate a part of the path that was broken away. Instead of flattening himself against the rock face and edging along sideways, in a remarkable display of agility he leapt from rock to rock, holding extended forefingers against his ears in impersonation of a mountain goat.

'Your friend is a little crazy,' the Kurdish-speaker remarked to Nuri, and Nuri had to agree.

They walked for another hour without speaking, often well strung out as a precaution against land-mines. If there was communication between the Arabs, it was by sign-language. It made Nuri realise just how formidable these Majnoon marsh Arabs were as guerillas.

The ground levelled out and became soft underfoot. From the map, Nuri knew that they were on the edge of the vast tracts of featureless marshland at the confluence of the Euphrates and the Tigris, which covered most of Southern Iraq.

After another thirty minutes the going became decidedly heavy, with his fine boots squelching deep into the soft, clinging sedge. Soon the water was sucking greedily at each footstep, and the disturbed mosquitoes rose in swarms. Khalid pulled his keffiyeh even tighter around his face, hiding his eyes behind a narrow slit. Then they were walking through an expanse of rushes, whose deep, water-seeking roots helped keep the low-lying land drained and firm until the floods came. The growth of the rushes was new and green. By the autumn they would be taller than a man. Nevertheless, quicksands abounded, and at one point they passed the humped outline of a truck roof protruding a few centimetres above the mire. There was no obvious trail through the featureless terrain, but Nuri knew they must be following one. Only the marsh Arabs could move with impunity through the vast, treacherous swampland.

In 1987 Nuri had been forced to work round the clock when the Iraq army tried to lay a brushwood road from the west, so that they could bring heavy guns to bear on the Iranians dug in on the Fao Peninsula. The enterprise had failed abysmally.

On one occasion four trucks loaded with fresh troops and supplies had been swallowed by the swamp.

They came to an expanse of water, gleaming dully in the weak moonlight. In another month or two, with the melting of the snows on the Anatolian Mountains in Nuri's and Khalid's homeland far to the north, the swollen rivers of the Tigris and the Euphrates would turn this great delta into a vast estuary covering hundreds of square kilometres.

Two of the men used long poles to push aside a floating island of reeds, to reveal a narrow-beamed bellum. Khalid's eyes lit up at the prospect of a boat ride. These ancient, canoe-like craft had been built by the marsh Arabs to ferry supplies to Basra before the building of the Shatt-al-Arab waterway, and were still in use. This one was large, at least ten metres long. Nuri and Khalid were motioned to sit on what looked like an engine box, but turned out to be a mass of truck and car batteries linked together to make one large, high-capacity power supply. As soon as the craft was cast off, a powerful DC electric motor hummed into life and the bellum accelerated smoothly to about twelve knots. They moved rapidly, in almost total silence, across the brackish water.

Thirty minutes later, the helmsman reduced speed and picked his way through a maze of channels, eventually steering the craft towards a ghostly blue glow. They passed under a camouflage net supported on high poles, and came alongside a jetty. The net covered an area about thirty metres in diameter. Beneath it was a huddle of large, army-issue cotton duck tents arranged in a circle around a communal eating area consisting of aluminium picnic tables laid flat and surrounded with ornate cushions. The eerie blue glow was from several ultra-violet mosquito-traps, strung up on the poles, whose elements were constantly crackling as they electrocuted victims from the swirling swarm. Several women were sitting gossiping around the remains of a meal that had been cooked in pots on a modern, trolley-mounted gas barbecue. They broke off and stared curiously at Nuri and Khalid as the party disembarked from the bellum.

'Welcome to our camp. My name is Nidel.'

75

The two men turned. The Kurd had pulled his keffiyeh away from his face. He was about Nuri's age, clean-shaven and with startlingly blue eyes. He shook hands with each of them in turn using the warm double hand-clasp of the Kurds. Nidel introduced them to other members of the party, but there were too many strange names and faces for the two men to remember. The helmsman turned out to be the leader, a tall, striking, alert-eyed man with curiously European looks that hinted at Ottoman blood. He bowed, and exchanged greetings by copying Nidel's handshake before turning to the staring women and giving them orders in rapid Arabic.

14

Saturday, 2nd March 1991

The rich lamb stew with carrots and sweet potatoes was the first real meal that Nuri and Khalid had eaten in over two months. They gratefully wolfed down second and third helpings while the others sat cross-legged in a circle, drinking coffee that the women served. The two travellers had washed and shaved, and been given clean gowns. The conversation during their meal, with Nidel acting as interpreter, was slow and uneven, but Nuri and Khalid had as much listening to do as talking. Nidel had been an army conscript who had deserted in March 1988 when news reached him that his home town, Halabji, had been the victim of a savage mustard-gas attack.

'*You* are from Halabji?' Nuri interrupted in surprise.

'Near the old carpet bazaar on the Arbut road,' Nidel answered. 'And you?'

'Qara.'

A bond born out of mutual suffering was formed between the two men. They recounted their vicissitudes. Nuri's parents were already dead, and he had never married; he had lost his two much-loved sisters in the terrible air raid. Nidel's home had been nearer the centre of the town, with the result that three generations of his family had perished, including his wife and their two children. As soon as news of the atrocity reached him,

76

he deserted and joined up with the Shiite marsh Arabs, who made good use of his knowledge of the army and its ways. Nidel had been instrumental in the planning of a number of successful raids against the Iraqis. He had even been responsible for the electrification of the larger bellums, turning them into effective war-canoes.

'A brilliant idea,' Nuri enthused. 'You can go anywhere with them. We used to use amphibious landing-craft in the marsh-lands that were always getting their engine intakes clogged with reeds. We had no reliable way of getting around. Also, being below the rushes means that your boats cannot be detected by radar.'

The leader nodded as Nidel translated. Then the tall Arab looked at Nuri and Khalid in turn, and spoke to them directly. The other members of the camp nodded in agreement.

'Ali is inviting you to join us and fight,' Nidel translated.

Nuri frowned. 'Who is there to fight here now?'

'Saddam Hussein and the Ba'athists, of course.'

'But surely they have been smashed!'

There was a brief flurry of translations for the leader's benefit before Nidel answered. 'Haven't you heard the news? The United Nations forces have stopped their advance. There is an uprising in Basra – perhaps in the north – but the allies are doing nothing to help us. The French were close to taking Baghdad but they were called back.'

Even Khalid, who had been having some trouble following the conversation, was stunned by the news and stopped smiling, but Nuri had risen to his feet in fury. 'But that's impossible! You are telling me that the Americans put together a force big enough to destroy Saddam Hussein, and they stopped!'

Nidel nodded.

'But it is unbelievable!'

'Unbelievable but true,' said Nidel sadly. 'As for Saddam Hussein being destroyed, he lost two-thirds of his tanks – that still leaves him with over a thousand. He lost only a few aircraft and hardly any helicopters. And now the Americans and all the rest are going home as quickly as possible.'

Nuri subsided into the cushions. The enjoyable meal he had

77

just eaten had become a cold, indigestible ball of despair in his stomach. Khalid did not understand many things, but he understood his friend's distress. He touched Nuri's arm.

'Perhaps,' Nidel ventured, 'the army is now very weak in the north. There is the chance of an uprising succeeding there this time.'

'Saddam is dangerous when he is desperate,' Nuri countered bitterly. 'That's when he uses gas. It's cheap and efficient.'

'So what do you want to do, Nuri?'

'What is there to do but to go home and fight? Thank Ali for his invitation, but we wish to return home. Like you, I am trained. I will join the PKK and fight.'

'Fight,' Khalid echoed, grinning broadly.

Nidel looked worriedly at the young man. 'You will take him with you?' he ventured cautiously.

Guessing what Nidel was thinking, Nuri put an arm protectively around Khalid's shoulders. 'Yes. He has brought me good luck.'

'A precious commodity,' Nidel observed, not convinced but touched by the obvious affection that Nuri had for the younger man.

The leader raised his fingers to his lips. All fell silent. The women cleaning up after the meal were shushed. In the stillness of the night only the croaking of frogs could be heard, and the soft purr of a distant petrol generator. There was the low boom and rumble of distant gunfire that Nuri and Khalid had heard before.

'Basra,' said Nidel simply. 'The fighting there is bitter. Even at night. We have contacts there. Yesterday the Shiites thought they were winning. No supplies were getting through to the Republican Guard – we were making sure of that. And then the British release two thousand prisoners of war and suddenly Saddam Hussein has two thousand reinforcements. And then the helicopters start flying in supplies and the Americans do not interfere.' He paused and listened again. 'It will be over soon.'

Nuri shook his head, trying to make sense of the madness. 'What is happening at home?' he asked.

Nidel shrugged and looked downcast. 'We are getting reports

of sporadic fighting at Mosul and Arbil, but the pershmargas are badly organised. What chance do they have?'

'We want to join them,' said Nuri grimly.

Nidel nodded sympathetically. He understood his countryman's feelings too well to attempt to dissuade him. He glanced at the others, then spoke rapidly in Arabic.

Like most Kurds, Nuri could speak Arabic (the teaching of Kurdish was illegal), but he could make little sense of the local riverine dialect. Whatever it was that Nidel was saying, however, made Ali so irate at one point that he jumped to his feet and started firing questions at him; he did not seem to be too pleased with the answers. Eventually the leader calmed down and signalled to one of the women, who brought him an Icom two-way radio. After a few exchanges into the set with a guttural, protesting voice, he resumed his place in the circle and spoke again with Nidel. The Kurd listened attentively, and turned to the two guests.

'It has been decided to help you return home,' he said in Kurdish. 'For you to go by road would be too dangerous. Mukharabat agents and informers are everywhere. Also, every large bridge has been bombed. It is safer and easier by river. A merchant at Umm Qasr has a cargo of dried fish for Baghdad; it has to go by motorised mahaila because there are too many wrecked bridges across the Tigris for the lighters and barges to navigate with safety. You will help crew the boat until you are near Baghdad. But for you to enter Baghdad would be very dangerous.'

Ali suddenly broke in with a spate of questions. 'Do you have any identification papers?' Nidel asked when the leader had finished.

Nuri shook his head. 'We left everything in our tank.'

'Do you have money?'

'A little,' Nuri admitted cagily. 'Some American dollars we found at Mutlah. A dead officer had no further use for them.'

Nidel gave a half-smile. 'We can arrange your IDs but they will cost five hundred dollars each. Can you afford that?'

'I think so,' Nuri answered cautiously.

'From south of Baghdad it would be best if you travelled as

Kurdish businessmen. They are common enough there, and it would cover your reason for wishing to travel north. Will you have enough money left over for Western clothes? They are the best passport of all. For you to wear Kurdish or Shiite dress would be suicide.'

'There will be enough money,' Nuri replied. Anxious to change the subject, he asked: 'How far is it by river to Baghdad?' He knew that it was over five hundred kilometres by road and that the road ran virtually parallel with the Tigris for the entire distance; but the river had many more twists and turns.

'Six hundred kilometres.'

The news shocked Nuri, although he was careful not to show it. Six hundred kilometres upriver in a mahaila river boat, with spring floods starting, was not to his liking. The upstream journey would take at least two weeks.

'The Tigris is not in flood yet,' Nidel pointed out, seeming to read Nuri's thoughts. 'The boat doesn't leave for two days, so you have plenty of time to rest. Also we will need to take some Polaroid photographs of you for your papers.'

Nuri bowed his head in acknowledgement and thanked his hosts. There was little else he could do, but he had no intention of sacrificing two weeks. If there was to be a war, he wanted to get home as soon as possible.

15

RIYADH

Max looked up from the satellite photographs that were laid out on his desk. 'So where are the pictures of Mutlah Ridge, Steve?'

'Mutlah?'

'A large number of military vehicles were shot up there.'

'You don't suppose the tank made it that far?'

Max smiled at Ramsay. He had no intention of passing on what Danny Kappelhof had told him about the T–55 that had refused to die at Mutlah Ridge. 'I never suppose anything, Steve. You should know that. I abhor guesswork. So where are the Mutlah photographs?'

Ramsay looked uncomfortable and glanced down at the aerial prints of Kuwait. Such was their pin-sharp resolution that they looked like aerial photographs taken from an aircraft at four thousand feet rather than from satellites in space. The pictures were the work of KH-11 Keyhole military surveillance satellites following highly elliptical orbits which, at their lowest point, their perigee, passed within two hundred kilometres of the surface. Their cameras could resolve detail down to ten centimetres – fine enough to identify a T-55 tank.

'The Americans are being cagey about Mutlah Ridge,' Ramsay admitted. 'From what I've been able to find out, they don't want anyone to see them. At least, not yet. Anyway, the chances that the T-55 made it as far as Mutlah are pretty remote.'

'The chances of it having the luck to encounter several dud rounds of 120-mill. HEAT were also pretty remote,' Max observed drily. 'Okay, Steve. I appreciate that your resources are stretched, so I'll give Mutlah a personal once-over.'

Ramsay looked aghast. 'You go to Kuwait? You can't.'

'Why not?'

'Because you can't!'

Max gathered up the photographs and returned them to their folder. 'You underestimate your abilities, Steve. Anyone who can get hold of pictures like these should have no trouble in fixing me up with transport to Kuwait ASAP.'

'It's a sensitive area.'

'Not as sensitive as Royal Ordnance being accused of supplying dodgy ammo to our brave lads. If I'm to take part in an inquiry, it would be nice to be able to report that I received one hundred per cent co-operation from everyone involved.'

The civil servant knew when he was beaten. 'You know what I'd like to call you, Max, were it not for my good manners and breeding?'

Max chuckled. 'A bastard?'

'Precisely.'

16

The inflatable plastic doll that Henry Wilt was struggling with on the cover of the Tom Sharpe paperback had bright crimson, bloated nipples that upset the sensibilities of the smiling Saudi customs official as he turned out Leo Buller's luggage.

'Very sorry, sir,' he said, tearing the cover off the paperback. 'But such things are not permitted in Saudi Arabia.'

Leo bit back a curt rejoinder. To get this far across the arrivals hall at King Khalid Airport had already taken two hours. Long enough for his resentment at being summoned away from his work by Max to become a smouldering anger. An hour was the normal time needed to pass through immigration, but the procedure for clearing the passengers from the British Airways 767 was slowed down by the Saudis deciding to man each computer terminal with four officers, each one with a different idea on how the dual Arabic/English keyboard should be operated.

'You have a permit to use this camera, sir?'

'I didn't know I needed one,' said Leo stiffly. 'But I expect the British army will have arranged it.'

'One needs a permit to breathe in Saudi Arabia, sir,' the customs officer commented with an unexpected flash of humour. He gave Leo a warm smile and permitted the tall, stooping figure to pass through his examination station on his way to tread the holy sands of the Prophet.

Max was waiting for Leo outside the terminal building, where taxi drivers were gathered beneath the floodlights like predatory white moths.

'I'm not happy at being dragged out here, Max,' said Leo, ignoring Max's offered hand. 'I had just established a link between the optic nerve and the hippocampus when you called.'

Max took Leo's case. 'You should know me well enough to know that I would not want you here unless it was important.'

'That's what makes it even more annoying. Two hours to get through their crazy bureaucracy! Two hours!'

'I did warn you.'

'*And* they took exception to a paperback I bought at Heathrow.'

Max chuckled. 'They've even banned *Private Eye* since it started saying unkind things about the Saudi royal family.'

Leo grunted and looked disapprovingly at Max's neat combat dress. 'Why are you wearing that crazy get-up? I thought the stupid war was over?'

'The car's this way.'

Leo fell in step alongside Max. As they crossed the road, he glanced up at the dark sky and was disappointed. He had read about the low humidity of Riyadh, the world's hottest capital city, and had expected to see the illuminated splendour of the Milky Way. But the sky was heavy and overcast.

'The weather's been atrocious,' Max commented in answer to his colleague's query. 'The locals are blaming it on the oil fires.'

'I saw them as we came in. Looks like something Dante dreamed up.'

'You've seen more than I have,' said Max curtly, releasing the central locking on his Toyota and tossing Leo's case on the back seat.

'So why am I here?' Leo demanded, once he was settled in the car. His anger was evaporating now that the long flight was over.

Max drove out of the car park. 'Firstly, Leo, please believe me when I say that I'm really very sorry for having to drag you out here. But the truth is that I've come up against something I can't handle myself.'

Leo glanced at his companion in surprise. Such an admission from Max was wholly out of character.

'It's all about an Iraqi tank with a charmed life,' said Max, not taking his eyes off the airport feeder road. 'Let's talk about it at the hotel.'

The two men made idle chat on the broad highway to Riyadh. The smooth, quiet tarmac encouraged fast driving. The road was well-lit and there was only a sprinkling of late-night traffic. Fifteen minutes after leaving the airport, Max picked up the huge ring road that completely encircled the city. They passed the regular, monolithic dark hump of a Patriot anti-missile battery.

'Was there a blackout when the Scuds started arriving?' Leo asked, looking with interest at the giant floodlit mushroom-shaped water-tower that dominated the skyline.

Max glanced at his passenger, who was taking in the strange, money-no-object architecture of the city. 'Didn't you watch the news on TV?'

'Some. I've been too busy,' Leo commented. 'On the odd occasion when I did switch on, it was always some prat telling us what he thought might happen instead of what actually had happened. I reckon I'm the only person in the world who hasn't spent the last month glued to a box.'

'This break might be good for you, Leo. You've been overdoing it. What is the point of a blackout against ballistic missiles?'

'Not a lot,' Leo admitted. 'But I seem to remember some design work we did for SAAD 16 about four years ago for a device that provided bright light terminal guidance for their Al Hussein missiles. As long as Teheran doesn't have a blackout, the device would steer the warhead smack into the middle of the city centre. Your exact words, as I recall.'

'You're to keep your mouth shut about our SAAD work,' said Max softly. These days it was best to play down his many contacts in Iraq.

Leo chuckled. He enjoyed winding up Max – no one else could do it. Their verbal exchanges were an essential part of their success as a team, because they acted as devil's advocates for each other's ideas. Before they assigned research funds and resources to a scheme, it had to survive an obstacle course of logic-fuelled scorn. It was rare for their verbal duels to spill over into outright animosity – which Leo attributed to his partner's lack of a sense of humour. Anyway, Max always got his own way in the end – and he was right to be sensitive about the consultancy work they had carried out for SAAD 16; it was the Iraqi guided weapons research and development establishment at Mosul in Northern Iraq. The Iraqis had been good customers; prompt payers most of the time. But then they had been provided with massive financial aid by grateful Saudis who saw

Saddam Hussein's protracted war against Iran as stemming the dangerous spread of Shiite fundamentalism in the Gulf.

The Toyota pulled up outside the Hyatt Regency Hotel. 'Home,' said Max. 'I've booked you into the room next to mine. The place is emptying fast now.'

17

The Hyatt bathrobe fitted Leo's spare frame like a woolly parachute. He perched on the edge of the bed in Max's room, watching the television intently. The Video Walkman was running the tape of the battle between Captain Jack Roper's Challenger tank and the Iraqi T–55.

'So what do you think?' Max asked when the tape ended. He had been watching his partner carefully.

'Let's see it again.'

Max rewound the tape and replayed the brief scene.

'So what am I supposed to think?' Leo inquired when the tape had finished. He sipped a Coke.

'Isn't it obvious?'

'The flashes are very obvious. Your conclusions aren't.'

'For God's sake, Leo. What more do you want? Three direct hits and the tank gets away unscathed.'

'Logic dictates that the Challenger was supplied with dodgy shells.'

Max gestured impatiently. 'That's nonsense. We're not talking about shells being mass-produced under wartime pressures. Those 120-millimetre nasties are made in small batches. They're rigorously inspected, and tested several times during every stage of production. The Royal Ordnance Factory is adamant that it would be impossible for faulty rounds to be issued.'

Leo was unimpressed. 'Seems to me that the only way to really test the buggers is to fire them. That's exactly what the army did.'

'What about the A10 pilot? Two Mavericks failed against a T–55. *Two!*'

Leo stretched out on Max's bed, crumpling the neatly turned-down sheets. 'So what?' How many millions of missiles and shells and bombs and mines and God-knows-what-else have been dropped, fired and generally gone bang over the last five weeks? So you've found a few that have failed to go off. Big deal.'

'We're talking about missiles and shells that have failed against the same tank.'

'You don't know that, Max. That cross could mean anything. Probably a unit marking. Probably hundreds of tanks with the same cross.'

'It's not a unit marking,' said Max with some irritation.

'You've checked?'

'Of course.'

Leo grunted and shot a thoughtful glance at his colleague. 'And knowing you, you've probably done your usual efficient scratching and found out exactly what it does mean.'

Max nodded. He was a good enough actor not to show his discomfort, but Leo spotted it. 'So what does the reversed swastika mean, Max?'

'Actually it's Hitler's swastika that's reversed. It's an old Indo-Mesopotamian symbol of good luck. The word "swastika" is Sanskrit for "good luck".'

The information did not please Leo. He sat up and glowered at Max. 'That proves my point, you idiot. Christ – you've dragged me away from some vital work to look at a bloody cross that's as common as camel shit around here. Probably been painted on hundreds of Iraqi tanks if you look.'

'As I said, it hasn't been painted on hundreds of tanks, or any Iraqi vehicles, because I've been making inquiries,' said Max icily, maintaining his customary calm. He was used to his partner's occasional abrasiveness. 'I'm convinced someone in SAAD 16 has developed a means of destroying incoming shells and missiles.'

Leo snorted. 'Those clowns couldn't develop a roll of Box Brownie film without outside help.'

'There were some competent engineers among them,' Max observed. 'Kerhan, Hailid, and several others.'

86

'Egyptians. And Saddam Hussein made their life hell and chased them all out. Why else did the Gyppos fight on our side?'

Max nodded. 'I agree with you that it's unlikely that the Iraqis have developed any form of anti-missile or anti-shell system, but an A10 Thunderbolt *and* a Challenger failing to knock out the same tank is too much of a coincidence. The Iraqis have *got* something, Leo. Something that we ought to know about.'

Leo thought for a moment. 'Okay. Let's assume that the Iraqis have come up with something. With fifty billion dollars-worth of aid to chuck at a problem, maybe anything is possible. But *if* they have got some sort of tank defence system, do you think they'd fit it to a crappy old T-55 that rolled off the assembly line when we were kids? Like hell they would – the Republican Guard would've grabbed it for their T-72s.'

'It could have been a prototype.'

'Which they'd risk falling into enemy hands?'

Max was silent. Leo had made a number of valid points, all of which had been troubling him already. He shook his head. 'Maybe you're right, Leo. I don't know what to think. But that A10 pilot was certain that there was nothing wrong with his Mavericks, and there's no arguing with the evidence of that tape.'

'Anyway, surely we're too late? The intelligence munchkins would've latched onto it by now.'

'No,' said Max sharply. 'I'm the only one who's collated the intelligence from the Challenger *and* the A10 pilot. There's no chance of it being collated now, not with the way the Americans are falling over themselves to go home. You and I have *carte blanche* to come up with the reason why some shells didn't work. No one else must find out what we suspect.'

'Because there might be money in it?'

'Exactly.'

Leo shrugged. 'So what can we do?'

'We're taking a Charlie One-Thirty RAF transport up to Kuwait tomorrow, and we're going to look for that tank.'

18

KUWAIT
Sunday, 3rd March 1991

Leo cupped his hand against the RAF Hercules' window and stared down in astonishment at the Saudi Arabian desert. The countless thousands of track-marks on the desert floor were thrown into sharp relief by the long shadows of the rising sun. Between the broad gash of the Wadi-al-Batin in the east and the soft sands of the Samiyah Desert far to the west was a ten-mile-wide swathe of tracks. They stretched almost as far as the eye could see on both sides of the low-flying transport, ranging from the deep, patterned ruts of tanks and self-propelled guns to the parallel gouges of countless hundreds of assorted military vehicles. The desert was scoured, so that the entire expanse of dun-coloured dust resembled an unimaginably vast marshalling yard for the gods.

'Holy shit!' Leo shouted at Max, trying to make himself heard in the uninsulated cabin above the roar of the transport's four engines. He climbed out of his aft-facing seat and squeezed his bulk alongside laden cargo pallets lashed to the floor, where he could goggle in disbelief at the stupendous tide of tracks vanishing towards the horizon ahead of the aircraft.

Max joined him and shouted something in his ear. Leo began to wish he paid more attention to the news. He knew that the steel land-armada that had advanced on Iraq and Kuwait was big, but he had no idea that it was on this monumental scale. It was unbelievable, unnerving. As he stared ahead, he picked out the discoloured thread of a distant convoy of trucks heading east towards the coast. A minute later he saw that it was no ordinary convoy but a continuous line of trucks that stretched northward to the elongated layer of black smoke that marked the well fires of Kuwait's oil-fields. There was something odd about the trucks. It took a few seconds for him to realise what it was: the windscreens had been removed from every vehicle so that there was nothing to catch the light of the rising sun. Leo's guess was that at night the vehicles would have been a ghost convoy.

They passed over the border town of Khafji where, for thirty-six hours at the beginning of February, an Iraqi incursion force had fought with a savagery and tenacity that had given the coalition forces a bad fright and had led to a major rethink of their whole Gulf War strategy.

A few minutes later, both men caught their first glimpse of Kuwait City as the Hercules banked over the Persian Gulf and lined up for its approach into the airport south of the city. At first there appeared to be little evidence of the much reported plundering of the city by the occupying Iraqis. In the distance the now familiar water-towers, and the onion domes of the Emir's elegant Dasman Palace, looked unharmed. South of the city, bright dots of light marked the burning oil-wells at Al Ahmadi, and there were more of the hellish glows lighting up the underside of their black palls to the north at Sabriyah.

The friendly flight-sergeant who had seen them settled into their seats at Riyadh reappeared. 'Landing in ten minutes, gentlemen!' he shouted, gesturing to their seats. He stayed to ensure that his civilian passengers were secured, then returned to the flight-deck.

Leo coiled his awkward frame into his seat and fastened his four-point harness. Aft-facing seats and proper seat-belts – the RAF could teach civil airlines a thing or two about air safety.

The Hercules lowered its main gear and unpacked its flaps. It came in steep, the runway racing up at alarming speed. It flared with seconds to spare, and dumped its 150,000 pounds on the concrete runway with an unnerving, shuddering crash. The note of the four Allison turboprop engines rose to a howl as they went into reverse pitch at full power and brought the big Lockheed to a standstill in a surprisingly short time. There was no taxiing off the runway. The engines were cut immediately, and an airport tug hauled the big transport onto the taxiway, the driver looking anxiously over his shoulder as he steered the aircraft over sheets of heavy-gauge steel plate laid over bomblet holes.

The hairy landing made Leo decide that maybe the civil airlines were easier on their aircraft than the military. He glanced at his companion and was amused to see that Max's face was haggard.

The flight-sergeant reappeared. 'Sorry about that, gentlemen,' he cheerfully apologised. 'Landing space is still at a premium until we get all the potholes properly filled. A real pitched battle was fought here last week.'

The passenger door opened. Once down the steps, the two men were able to see the extent of the damage the airport had sustained. All the windows of the control tower were smashed, and the sides pockmarked with small-arms fire. Halfway down the building was a hole caused by a heavy artillery shell – possibly a 100-millimetre. The other buildings had fared no better; the passenger terminal was shot up, and a small building virtually demolished. Around the perimeter were the blackened wrecks of several T-72s – the most formidable tank of all from the Soviet armaments factories. Two had had their turrets blown off and were still smoking. But most spectacular of all, at the far end of the apron was the gutted wreckage of a British Airways 747.

This was Flight BA149, lying on the concrete like the picked leavings of a whale barbecue. The unfortunate aircraft had arrived at Kuwait Airport the previous August on the night – almost on the hour – that the country was invaded. During the first invasion of Kuwait by Iraq in 1961, the British Foreign Office gave airlines advance warning of the impending storm; nearly thirty years later, in August 1990, no such warning had been given because there was a faint hope that the aircraft might be used to evacuate embassy staff. But all the passengers and crew of BA149 had been seized and held as hostages by the Iraqis. And now, eight months later, several British soldiers were having their photographs taken standing in one of the yawning engine intakes, which looked curiously undamaged.

Leo and Max moved out of the way of a team of soldiers who scrambled into the Hercules' hold and set to work unshackling the cargo pallets. Both men were carrying their day's rations – hotel packed lunches – which they had been told to bring. Everything was in desperately short supply in Kuwait – even drinking-water. Max sniffed in distaste at the faint but pungent smell of burning oil.

A Nissan Prairie bearing Saudi plates and several large BFME pennants drew up. It was driven by a petite, dark-haired WRAC sergeant in a tight-fitting combat uniform. Max eyed her appreciatively as she slid the Prairie's driver's door open.

'Mr Shannon and Mr Buller?' She spoke with a Midlands accent.

Max and Leo shook hands with the girl and showed her their blue MOD passes, which she studied carefully. They climbed into the people carrier's rear seats and drove off. The WRAC driver introduced herself as Sergeant Caroline Morgan – their MOD minder. 'We'll be driving briskly through the city,' she explained. 'I take a northern detour into the city, but at the moment it's all a bit Wild West lawless until the police manage to confiscate all the fire-arms the locals have got hold of. Don't worry if you hear bursts of fire – it's their way of saluting us. But in case of trouble, I speak Arabic, which is why I'm your minder. But I don't think we'll have any bother. We're rather popular at the moment.'

19

Sergeant Morgan's idea of brisk driving involved hammering the Prairie along the broad, litter-strewn avenues of Kuwait with her foot hard on the floor. None of the traffic-lights were working and in many cases were missing altogether, but that didn't worry her; she merely flashed her lights, leaned on the horn and kept going. Smiling, waving pedestrians obligingly jumped out of her way. Most of the men seemed to be armed with AK–47s which they held by the curved magazine and waved in triumph at the speeding Nissan. One boy, who looked about twelve, was sporting a modern AKS–74 assault rifle. A sinister-looking woman, veiled in black, was wearing a webbing belt from which a cluster of RGD–5 hand-grenades dangled. Sergeant Morgan returned her wave and swerved sharply to avoid a group of children playing with a burning tyre. Bursts of automatic fire into the air marked the speeding Prairie's progress through the devastated city, past derelict buildings and gutted, looted shops, their steel grilles ripped out and strewn on the sidewalks.

The two passengers were silent, grateful for the girl's non-stop commentary which saved them from having to comment on scenes they had difficulty in accepting as real.

'The Iraqis went berserk before they pulled out,' said Sergeant Morgan. 'They took everything they could lay their hands on. Maybe they wanted souvenirs of their mother of all retreats, I don't know, but they even took shop signs.'

The Prairie picked up the main Highway 8 heading north. The road widened to a four-lane motorway, with the inside lane and shoulder littered with the wreckage of burnt-out trucks and APCs. An Iraqi T-72 had crashed into one of the huge electricity pylons that lined the road. The delicate-looking lattice structure was now being held up by its own power cables. Both men looked carefully at every T-55 they chanced upon. At one point Max asked the driver to stop so that he could investigate a T-55 turret that was jammed by its gun-barrel into a lawn like a giant lollipop. After a cursory examination he returned to the Prairie and they resumed their journey on what the press would later dub the Highway to Hell.

The sentinel-like row of graceful street lights along the central reservation added an incongruous touch of normality to the scene, as did the overhead gantry signs pointing to the appropriate lanes for Baghdad, Basra and Umm Qasr. More than anything else the signs were monuments to the peace, albeit uneasy, that had once existed between Kuwait and Iraq.

The shops and malls thinned out and gave way to smart apartment blocks set in well-tended gardens. Strangely, the apartments looked undamaged.

'Some parts the Iraqis left alone,' Caroline said in answer to Leo's question. 'Weird, isn't it? Don't ask me to explain Iraqi thinking. Don't ask anyone to explain.' She pointed to the entrance to a Wild West theme park. 'That place got stripped. They took these electric bucking bronco things that the kids used to try and stay on for a minute. Just ripped them out and left the control systems. They even took the miniature golf course. Madness.'

The road followed the bay eastwards out of the city before swinging north. A watery sun broke through the sullen clouds, lending an inappropriate sparkle to the sea. Parties of French mine-clearing legionnaires were working on the beach, cautiously digging out the millions of Italian-made anti-personnel mines planted by the Iraqis. The bombs, in their yellow plastic cases, were in neat piles awaiting disposal. They looked like children's toys.

'I thought the whole area would be awash with oil,' Leo commented. He caught Sergeant Morgan's bitter look in the mirror.

'The oil spill wasn't nearly as bad as the press made out,' she said. 'Most of it evaporated, and the rest amounted to not much more oil than gets spilt in the Gulf in the course of a year anyway. There was a two-mile stretch of beach in Saudi Arabia that got hit pretty bad, and that's where all the news teams went to set up their cameras. The joke was that the slick wasn't from the Iraqi sabotage at this end of the Gulf, but from a tanker. Cleaning up the seabirds keeps the Saudi wives happy – it's about the only work they're allowed to do.'

'The first casualty,' Max commented drily.

'What is?' Leo demanded.

'In war, the first casualty is truth,' Max enlarged. 'You sound very bitter, young lady. I hope your superior officers don't hear you talking like this.'

The girl's sudden vehemence took both men by surprise. 'A lot of us have got bitter since we've been in Kuwait,' she said, tightening her grip on the steering-wheel in her anger. 'The only people who really fought the Iraqis last August were the Palestinian residents. They put up a hell of a fight, while the Kuwaitis scooted off to Saudi Arabia as fast as their air-conditioned limos could carry them. And now the Kuwaitis are giving Palestinians and Bedoons hell just because Yasser Arafat supported Saddam Hussein. Most of the Palestinians in Kuwait consider themselves Kuwaitis first and foremost, because it's their home. They've no time for Arafat, never have had. It's the Palestinians who've run Kuwait. They've always formed the bulk of the professional and civil service class; they're the traders. Your average Kuwaiti couldn't run a nose with a cold. The only thing they're any good at is taking out leases on homes anywhere but in Kuwait. They'll do anything for their country except live in it. Did you know that the ungrateful bastards charge three hundred dollars a night for British servicemen to stay at the Sheraton? No water, no electricity, no lifts. Three hundred dollars a night!'

She lapsed into an angry silence and concentrated on her driving, sensing that she had said too much. Not that she cared. Another three months and she would be married and out of the army.

By now the Prairie was on higher ground so that the outline of Kuwait City, looking strangely normal across the bay, began to shimmer slightly in the haze generated by the strengthening sun. But the warmth did not last for long once they reached the great smear of smoke from the oil fires near Sabriyah. The sunlight took on a curious khaki hue as the road continued to rise, and there was an increase in the number of wrecked vehicles that had been bulldozed off the highway. Then they came upon parked British army vehicles in dun-coloured camouflage paint. At one point Sergeant Morgan had to slow to a crawl to negotiate double-parked low-loaders belonging to the Royal Engineers. An armed corporal signalled them to stop.

'This was Objective Cobalt,' the girl commented, checking her map. She held out the blue passes to the corporal, but he ignored them.

'Sorry. We're closed,' he announced.

'These gentlemen are MOD civilian scientists,' the WRAC driver explained. 'They're here on a weapons assessment recce.'

'Sorry, sergeant. I've strict orders. No one passes this point.'

'This is absurd,' said Max mildly, poking his head out of the window. 'We've come all the way from England. Our passes have been issued by the British Forces Middle East HQ in Riyadh. Take a look at the stamps, please.'

The corporal looked respectfully at the neat Englishman and studied the passes. He was undecided. A Range Rover drew up behind the Prairie. A door opened and slammed. The corporal looked relieved and returned the fresh-faced major's salute.

'Anything wrong, corporal?' the major asked.

'These civ . . . These gentlemen have passes from BFME HQ, sir.'

It was the major's turn to examine the passes.

'It's imperative that we're allowed to examine the site,' Max said, smiling affably. 'We have to carry out a detailed operational research survey. It's all been arranged – '

'Yes, I'm sure it has,' said the major smoothly. 'The trouble is that things are moving so quickly that one hand doesn't know what the other is doing.'

'So why all this palaver?' Leo demanded. 'What's the big secret?'

The major looked uncomfortable. 'No secret, sir. It's just that the area is being prepared for visits by the press. We have to make sure everything is safe. There's ammunition and heaven knows what else lying about.'

'We're weapons experts,' said Max. 'We can look after ourselves.'

'Have you brought cameras?'

'Well, of course.'

The major thought for a moment and came to a decision. 'Very well. Leave all your camera equipment with Corporal Roberts and you can go through. He'll look after everything for you.'

Max's easy smile nearly deserted him. 'I'm sorry, but we must have our camcorders. That's the only reason we're here.'

The major moved towards his Land Rover. 'I'm sorry, gentlemen. You either leave your equipment or you don't go through.'

Max and Leo had no choice but to accept the compromise. Corporal Roberts's search was thorough. All he allowed Max and Leo to keep were their water canteens, sandwiches and notebooks. He even relieved Max of his Psion Organiser, but grudgingly permitted him to keep his binoculars before waving Sergeant Morgan on.

The Prairie breasted the rise and stopped. 'My God!' the

driver breathed, her voice a shocked whisper. 'I had no idea it was like this. No idea . . .'

Max remained silent, while all Leo could muster was one word: an awed, 'Fuck.'

It was a scene that confounded and stunned the senses, and at the same time commanded them, challenging the observers to close their eyes or look away. Less than a week had passed since Danny Kappelhof had flown over Highway 8 in his A10. Then the dreadful carnage was only just beginning; now it was complete, but the image of tangled, still-smoking wreckage stretching into the distance was too stark, too recent, for Mutlah yet to add its name to Wounded Knee and My Lai. Legends demanded misty memories and faded photographs; not the Technicolor starkness of a shot-up Spar supermarket truck or a Hertz Buick, or a riddled John Deere tractor, or an APC whose burnt-out hulk was still radiating heat. The props were wrong. They didn't fit. Reality was a gruesome inconvenience which the Royal Engineers, busy with their JCB excavators, were doing their best to bury in huge, hastily dug pits at the side of the road.

Max pulled the Prairie's sliding door open and stepped onto the black tarmac, which was warming in the sun. Leo followed him.

'I don't know how long we'll need,' said Max to Sergeant Morgan. 'I thought a couple of hours would be enough, but . . . looking at this . . . we might be much longer.'

The WRAC driver nodded. Her face was white, as were her knuckles gripping the steering-wheel tightly as though the resilient plastic were a source of comfort. 'I'll wait for you back at the checkpoint. I could do with a cup of tea.' Her customary driving skills deserted her for the moment, for as she turned she managed to crunch the gearbox and stall the engine. She restarted the Prairie and drove back.

'So . . . So where do we start?' asked Leo. His voice was curiously strained.

Max made no reply. He pulled his binoculars from their case and focused them along the breaker's-yard highway. As in a breaker's yard, a lane had been cleared through the centre of the devastation. Every shot-up, burnt-out bus, truck and car clamoured for attention, but he was interested only in the military vehicles. An amphibious PT–76 with a gaping hole blasted right through it; of no interest. The binoculars moved on. A T–72 hull minus its turret; no interest. A Zil truck sitting on its wheel-hubs, the black globs of its tyres clinging to their rims and still smouldering, adding the stink of burning rubber to the stench of death and the grey pall hanging over the stillness like a shroud; no interest. A T–55. Max's binoculars paused in their careful sweep.

'Found one,' he murmured. 'And another.'

'We'd best make a sketch-map from here, where we've got some height,' Leo suggested.

Max nodded. 'Good idea.'

The two men spent the next twenty minutes pinpointing every T–55 it was possible to identify from where they were standing. Leo drew a rough map, marking the position of each tank with a cross.

'That's enough to be going on with,' said Max when they had identified twenty likely tanks. 'Come on. Let's get stuck in.'

Leo began to sweat as they skirted the vehicles. He wondered how Max always managed to look so cool and trim. In some cases the heat radiating from gutted tank hulls and engine blocks was so intense that they were forced to circle them by scrambling up the gravelled slopes. There was a faint, all-pervading buzzing noise that Leo was unable to identify.

That was when they drew near the first of the Royal Engineers' 'Graves Commission' details. The soldiers had used a JCB to dig a deep pit and were lining the bottom with cloth-wrapped corpses. The men were masked and anonymous, carefully positioning the bodies; more from a need to make efficient use of the space than out of respect for the dead. There was no way of telling how many layers of bodies there were in the deep trench, but the corpses, already beginning to bloat, emitted loud groans and farts as the soldiers walked on them. An NCO used a hand-held GPS receiver to note the precise position of the grave on the clipboard. Somehow it seemed appropriate that the first victims of a computer-controlled massacre should occupy the first mass graves to be marked not by headstones or memorials or tears, but by a satellite navigation system. The dry sands of the deep pit would desiccate and mummify the pitiful remains, so that thousands of years hence, perhaps, Mutlah would be the only story of the region left for archaeologists to piece together.

The Royal Engineers worked silently, ignoring the strangers. Most of the bundles looked too small to contain men, and some were particularly small. A tiny blackened hand protruded briefly and accusingly from one, and was quickly kicked out of sight.

'Jesus Christ,' Leo breathed. 'They're burying women and children.'

It was a rule that the Americans had insisted on: women and children first. It didn't matter if the press saw the corpses of Iraqi soldiers. But it was important to preserve the myth of Mutlah Ridge until it was a safe, time-sanitised legend for airmen to relate to wide-eyed, adoring grandchildren.

'The Iraqis took Kuwaiti women and children hostages,' said Max indifferently, consulting Leo's sketch and walking along the road. He pointed to a turretless T–55. 'Let's see if we can find its turret. It can't be far.' The hideously grinning skulls of the tank's incinerated crew didn't seem to bother him. But they bothered Leo. They bothered him a lot.

It was then that Leo realised what the curious buzzing sound was: it was flies. Swarms of them, rising up in a black cloud at their approach and quickly settling again as they passed by.

They found the shattered mass of cast steel that had been a turret some twenty metres away, lying on its back like a stranded turtle. Max peered under it and shook his head. 'Nothing,' he said. 'But a hundred-mill. layer of our Chobham armour would've saved it.'

The next four tanks were the same. Leo scrambled down from the side of an overturned truck and mopped his forehead. His drawn features were even more gaunt than usual. In contrast Max looked cool, neat and unruffled. He pointed.

'There's another one on the right – near that artic.'

The articulated truck had jack-knifed around the T–55; it was like the passionate embrace of a strange mechanical lover.

Leo didn't see the truck-driver's blackened hand hanging out of the cab window until it brushed against his shoulder. He gave an involuntary cry.

Max turned and looked at the hand and his ashen-faced colleague. 'What's the matter, Leo?'

Leo grimaced and ducked under the mocking hand. 'Christ, man. Isn't it obvious? Look – we're not going to find anything, Max. For God's sake, let's get out of here.'

Max regarded his colleague dispassionately. 'We won't find anything unless we look, Leo.'

'This is a terrible place.'

Max glanced around the fearful carnage. 'Terrible. But this is reality, Leo. If you can't stomach a battleground then you shouldn't be in the weapons design business.'

'This isn't a battleground, for Chrissake! This is a bloody massacre!'

'What's the difference, Leo?'

Leo had always known about Max's streak of ruthlessness. In business it had always been an advantage, and it was why he was happy for Max to look after their financial affairs. But this was very different. 'There's women and children back there!'

'So?'

'For Chrissake, Max, isn't that enough?'

Max sat on an ammunition box that was spilling 9-millimetre rounds into the sand, and removed the water canteen from his pack. Rather than swig from the canteen's neck, he poured a measure into a beaker and sipped it appreciatively as though it were a fine wine. 'So you believe in categories of human life, do you, Leo?'

'What the devil are you on about?'

Max pointed to a fruit-machine that had, literally, fallen off the back of a lorry. 'Sit down, Leo. Have a drink. It's getting hot.'

Leo sat on the one-armed bandit and took a long pull from his canteen. Max pointed to a Pontiac's rear bumper. It bore a sticker that said: BABY ON BOARD. KEEP YOUR DIS-TANCE. A reconnaissance vehicle had ploughed into the back of the big saloon. The impact had wrenched the bumper from its mountings so that it stuck up in the air at an odd angle.

'What does that bumper sticker tell you about the people who stuck it on their car?'

'I'm a neurologist – not a shrink,' Leo muttered. 'What the devil should it tell me?'

'That the people who bought that sticker may consider themselves to be Allah-fearing or God-fearing souls. They would be horrified to know that they're the sort of people who could've become guards at Auschwitz or Belsen. That sticker says that they regard a baby's life as more important than an adult's life. You may think your horror at the discovery that women and children died here last week is commendable, but is it? You're putting human life into categories – dangerous categories. That's what the Nazis did with Jews and gypsies.'

'We're talking about defenceless women and children!' Leo snapped. He never did like Max's logic-rooted views.

Max nodded. 'Ah. So the value of human life varies to the degree that it's able to defend itself? Once you accept that all human life is of equal value, Leo, it will be as if a veil has been lifted from your eyes. You will see the false morality of jailed murderers who beat up child-molesters. And you certainly would have seen through the morality of Richard Neal's statements when he said that every effort was being made to avoid civilian casualties, and that he was "comfortable" with what civilian casualties there were.' Max gestured at the hellish scene around him. 'This is real warfare, Leo. The sort of warfare we're going to be involved with in the next century. The old medieval idea of just killing soldiers is obsolete. The enemy's civilian populace is the sword; the soldiers are merely the cutting edge.'

Max suddenly stood and swung his pack onto his shoulder. He was quietly angry, but Leo wasn't certain if the anger was directed at him. 'Come on. Let's find that tank.' He paused, and pointed to a Mercedes tour bus that looked remarkably intact. Not a window broken. 'See if you can get onto the roof of that coach, Leo, and take a look around. They sometimes have a ladder at the back.'

There was no ladder, but the passenger boarding door was open. Puzzled, Leo mounted the steps. Strange patterns of sunlight dappled the coach's interior, breaking up outlines and confusing the eye. At first Leo thought he was looking at brightly-coloured bundles of laundry that had been strewn everywhere. Then, with mounting horror that churned the bile in his stomach, he realised what it was he was seeing. It was impossible to tell if the mangled remains mixed up with the mass of blood-stained rags were men or women. A mass of limbs; a tangle of humanity like a still picture of a macabre orgy. One of the curious, swimming blobs of sunlight illuminated a man's face. He was staring at Leo through half-closed eyes, and smiling in secret ecstasy. Leo raised his eyes and saw the reason for the strange patterning effect of the sunlight. The entire width and length of the coach's roof was riddled with bullet holes. Not the small, neat holes he was accustomed to seeing punched through cars in television footage of the aftermath of a Northern Ireland killing, but jagged, fist-sized holes; and there were hundreds of them.

A movement near his feet. Something touched his ankle. He looked down and stared at the fingers that were slowly clasping and unclasping, trying to get a feeble grip on his shoe. The fingers were slim and white. A woman's hand. There was a muffled moan. That someone was alive after a week was horror enough; that the survivor was trying to involve him in this hideous scenario was even worse. For Leo to do something – to go running to the army post for help – would spell an emotional link with Mutlah. Leo didn't want that. He didn't want to do or say anything that might interfere with the process of memories fading with time. To be involved would mean a sharing of the guilt of this dreadful place.

He stumbled blindly out of the coach and ran towards the dunes, in the direction of the distant sea. It was the sea that beckoned. It was clean and pure. He heard Max yell after him, but he ran on, his inadequate shoes dragging in the soft sand. He reached the crest of a dune and nearly lost his footing as he slithered down the far side. Mutlah was lost to sight now, but even here there was an abandoned army vehicle. He stopped running, braced himself against it with one hand, not noticing the touch of cold steel, and threw up his breakfast. He groped for his canteen and nearly dropped it as he unscrewed the stopper, so badly were his hands shaking. A long draught cleared the foul taste from his mouth, but the images of the coach's interior and the slim, white hand reaching for him still danced before his eyes.

Dear God. Make me forget. Please make me forget!

'Well done, Leo! Well done!' It was Max's voice. Leo opened his eyes. Max was walking towards him, grinning broadly. It was unusual for Max to look so pleased. 'I wondered what made you take off like that.'

Leo realised that the vehicle he was leaning against was a tank.

A T-55.

Marked on its turret in bold, broad strokes of white paint was a reversed swastika.

20

Max compared the swastika on the T-55's turret with a still picture he had taken from the videotape made by Corporal Alan Dearborn. The match was perfect. He walked slowly around the tank and noted that the only damage appeared to be to the shattered left-hand track and mangled idler-wheels, which looked as if they had stopped several rounds of depleted uranium. The T-55 hadn't driven off the track, as often happens, which suggested that it had been stationary when it was hit.

'Hardly any damage,' Max remarked to Leo when he had completed his inspection. 'Even the machine-gun's still armed. Okay – let's take a look inside.' With that, he scrambled nimbly onto the tank and helped Leo up after him. Max peered into the commander's hatch. No one had died in there, for which he was thankful – he didn't want to get blood on his combat uniform, which still looked crisp and smart.

'If there is some unusual equipment in there, it might be

102

booby-trapped,' Leo warned as Max lowered himself through the hatch.

Max nodded in agreement. 'Risky old business we're in, Leo,' he remarked, and disappeared.

Being small, Max had little difficulty in taking stock of his surroundings. He felt a pang of disappointment. There was nothing here of any significance. No sophisticated weaponry; no unusual aiming-devices. The T-55 wasn't even equipped with the advanced Swiss optics that had been discovered in the Iraqi tanks captured at Khafji. It was a very ordinary and very obsolete T-55 – not so different from the World War II T-34 in the British Army's tank museum at Bovington. Most of the ready-use ammunition racks were filled with 100-millimetre shells. It hadn't seen much fighting.

'Anything?' asked Leo, peering down from above.

'Nothing,' Max replied curtly. He checked the driver's position low down on the right-hand side of the hull. Again, there was nothing of interest.

A Henri Winterman wooden cigar box caught Leo's eye. It was wedged behind a power cable. Hanging from the box by a chain was a silver St Christopher. He reached down and removed the box. It felt heavy.

'I've found your secret weapon, Max.'

Max looked up quickly. He was not pleased to see the St Christopher swinging by its chain from Leo's fingers. 'If you think that's funny, I'm afraid I don't share your sense of humour.'

'I don't think it's funny – I think it's odd.'

Max levered himself out of the hatch and sat opposite Leo on top of the tank. 'What's so odd about a St Christopher?'

'The Iraqis are Moslems, aren't they?'

'Not all of them. There are many Christian and Jewish communities in Iraq, and have been for centuries. Didn't you hear about all the fuss there was when a synagogue got bombed? For all his many murdering faults, Saddam Hussein doesn't go in for religious persecution. And he's only as much of a Moslem as it takes to satisfy other Moslems. He's only made one haji to Mecca.'

While he was talking, Leo opened the cigar box. It contained family photographs and a number of neatly folded letters written in Arabic.

'I just don't understand it,' Max was saying. 'This is the right tank. There's no doubt about it.'

Leo wasn't listening. The paper quality was surprisingly good. From the state of the letters it was obvious that they had been read many times, and been carefully looked after. Some were in envelopes with stamps bearing pictures of an Arab who wasn't Saddam Hussein. They were of Sa'd bin Abi Waqqass, the tyrannical Mesopotamian ruler with whom Saddam Hussein liked to identify himself.

He turned to the photographs. They showed a smiling mother and father in expensive Western clothes, holding the hands of a serious-looking boy aged about ten. What surprised Leo was that the boy, like his mother, had remarkably fair hair for an Arab. In contrast, the father, dressed in a well-cut business suit, was quite dark. His eyes were alight with good humour. They were comfortably off, enjoying the good life. The next photograph was an even bigger surprise. It had obviously been taken at the same time and in the same place as the first one, but the camera angle was different, revealing the precise nature of the location.

Both photographs had been taken on Westminster Bridge, with the Houses of Parliament in the background.

There were several more pictures: one taken outside a bank with the family grouped around an XJS Jaguar. The sign on the bank proclaimed it to be the London branch of the Kurdish National Investment Bank. Some of the remaining pictures were taken in a garden that looked remarkably English. There was a picture of the father standing proudly beside the Jaguar on the forecourt of a small block of smart apartments. The car was obscuring the first syllable of a sign by the block's lobby that said: -INGHAM COURT. In the last photograph the mother was alone. She was smiling at the camera, looking slim and elegant in a print dress, her fair hair tied back with a ribbon.

'Take a look at these,' said Leo, breaking into Max's flow of thoughts.

Max examined the photographs without enthusiasm.

'So what do they tell you, Max?'

'What should they tell me? That one of our Iraqi crewmen was a well-off man who could afford holidays in England. Interesting.'

Leo shook his head. 'I don't think the man in those photographs was in this tank. It was the boy. Take a close look at the car numbers in the car park, and the number of the Jag. All about ten-year-old registrations. That boy would be twenty-ish now. Old enough to be a conscript or a reservist, wouldn't you say?'

Max nodded. 'Possibly. You'd better put everything back. Let the army deal with it. They'll see that the Red Crescent return everything to the boy's family.'

Leo didn't hear him. He was staring at a letter that was still attached to a writing-pad. 'Good heavens,' he muttered. 'This is in English.'

Max took the letter from him and read:

DEAR ANDY
YOUR LETTER CAME WITH RED CRESCENT AND
TOOK THREE WEEKS BECAUSE OF BOMBING. I
CANT SAY WHERE I AM BUT I WAS VERY HAPPY
FOR ME TO HEAR FROM YOU. I CAN NOW MAKE
THUNDER LIKE YOU SHOWED ME AND I CAN
STILL DO TRICK WITH TENNIS BALLS. MORE
BOMBING STARTED SO WILL FINISH THIS
LETTER TOMORROW . . .

The few lines had been started at the top of the sheet, and it was obvious that the writer had meant to write more. The entire letter consisted of carefully printed capitals, as if he were not accustomed to penning Roman characters. Max flipped through the rest of the writing-pad, but it was blank. He read the strange letter through again and looked up at Leo. His normally genial expression had vanished.

' " . . . I can now make thunder like you showed me . . .",' he muttered. 'By God, Leo! That's what the A10 pilot said about his Mavericks. Thunder! And the Challenger crew said the same thing about this T-55 when they attacked it! That there was a noise like thunder!'

21

SOUTHERN IRAQ

It was hard to believe that the flat, dreary, night-shrouded Sumerian landscape passing on both sides of the big, high-prowed mahaila was the scene of five thousand years of recorded history that pre-dated even the First Dynasty of the Pharaohs; yet this fifteen-metre craft on which Nuri and Khalid were travelling was virtually identical to the boats that had plied this stretch of the Tigris since the beginning of civilisation. Even the lateen sail, now furled because an elderly Kelvin TVO engine was thumping the boat up-river, was the same as those depicted on the wall carvings in the ruins at Kut, Nineveh and Opis. All the riches of Babylon had passed along this river and its sister, the Euphrates: silks, gold, jewels, spices from the East and hardwoods from North Africa.

It was the great ruler Hammurabi, forty centuries earlier, who had brought stability to the region and made this rich trade possible. It was he who had codified the already ancient laws of Babylonia, leaving behind him cuneiform scripts that dealt with every aspect of life in his enlightened land: trade and employment, marriage and inheritance; libraries, universities and schools; civil rights, including the equality of women. Later, invaders and new influences had changed the land; there had been long periods of darkness when the country fell to despotic rulers. But there had never been a darkness to equal that which this latest tyrant had brought to Babylon. No previous ruler had treated his own people so barbarically, nor, by his arrogance, greed, cruelty and ambition, brought such powerful and vengeful enemies to his door.

The villages and hamlets along the river were blacked out, with only the occasional flicker of a single oil lamp, or an isolated cluster of lights powered by a generator. The power-stations serving the region had been systematically bombed. Pumping stations were not working, which meant that the flood outfall pipes that served every town and village were discharging raw sewage into the river. On the left bank was the Basra to Baghdad highway which followed the Tigris all the way to the capital and continued north to Kurdistan. Much to Nuri's surprise, the highway was surprisingly busy. During the day most of the traffic was military: pristine new trucks taken from storage, armoured personnel-carriers, mobile guns, and low-loaders carrying sleek new T-72s in 10th Armoured Brigade unit markings, all heading south to smash the Shiite uprising. There was, it seemed, plenty of fuel for Saddam Hussein's still mighty military machine. But there was also a fair sprinkling of civilian traffic, cars, coaches, and even Baghdad taxis with their distinctive coloured wings.

A drop in engine revs and a shout from the mahaila's skipper in the midships wheelhouse intruded on Nuri's thoughts. The Arab was gesturing ahead to the tangled remains of yet another box-section bridge whose slab-sided spans had been neatly jack-knifed in their centres and dropped into the Tigris by precision bombing. A small floodlight, consisting of a car headlight hanging from a cable, illuminated a narrow passage where a fallen section formed a triangular arch against its stone buttress. Nuri grabbed a long boathook and prodded Khalid's sleeping-bag with a Texan boot.

Manoeuvring the mahaila under the bridge delayed them for an hour, because other small rivercraft were already awaiting their turn to negotiate the arch. No doubt the hold-ups would get worse as they travelled further north. Beyond the wrecked bridge was a pontoon bridge consisting of several steel road-sections bolted across the gunwales of river barges. The centre span could be raised and lowered by a power winch to permit the passage of river traffic. All the major bridges across the Tigris and the Euphrates that had been destroyed by the Allies had been replaced soon after their destruction by these simple but ingenious bridges. When an air-raid threatened, the barges had been quickly unhitched and dispersed, thus making their destruction virtually impossible.

Once under way again, Nuri conferred in low tones with

Khalid. They decided to leave the boat when they reached Amarah. 'If need be,' said Nuri in answer to Khalid's query, 'we've got enough money to take a taxi to Mosul. The world's gone mad anyway, so we might as well join in.'

22

SOUTHERN ENGLAND
Tuesday, 5th March 1991

At thirty-two Lloyd Wheeler still had that boundless energy that in ten years' time would cause him to look back at the amount of work he used to get through and wonder how he did it. By midday he had held a preliminary planning meeting for the magazine's June issue, approved the layouts of the next issue, had a meeting with the bank manager, typed on his trusty Compaq some belt-tightening proposals to get rid of three leased cars, and had even managed to revise his filler on his abortive trip to Singapore. As always when he was busy, lunch was desk-bound: a chicken sandwich provided by Della, and a plastic cup of tasteless coffee while he approved some commissions. It was now rare for him to join his colleagues at the pub down the road for lunch.

It was his capacity for dogged hard work that had earned Lloyd promotion at *Science UK* when his predecessor died in harness. Another year, and he would move on. He dutifully visited his mother and father once a month on their highly profitable smallholding-cum-farm-shop near Oxford, and even enjoyed helping out behind the counter. His mother disapproved of his avant-garde warehouse flat – she was convinced that it was overrun with rats – and of the girlfriends who passed through his life on their way to better things. She was a forceful lady, and of the opinion that it was time for her son to 'settle down' – two words that filled Lloyd with dread.

At twelve thirty he left a note for Della saying that he could be contacted on his portable phone, and headed his bright yellow Lotus Super Seven towards Epsom. The car was something else his mother disapproved of; she said it was old, noisy, cramped, and ruinous on insurance. She was right on every count, of course, and no doubt she would have been horrified to know what it was worth. Lloyd had made up his mind to own one when, as a kid, he had watched Patrick McGoohan in the TV series 'The Prisoner' hammering one of the crazy little kit-cars through central London every Sunday evening to slam down his resignation on George Markstein's desk.

23

Ted – he loathed 'Edward', which he considered pretentious – Prentice was a small, outspoken man with an acid sense of humour and a wild crop of white hair that made him look older than his sixty years. His skills as a psychiatrist were matched by his remarkable capacity for making enemies – talents which he strove to improve each day. His fondness for referring to the new breed of budget managers in the National Health Service as 'Tuppence-off Tesco bookkeepers' ensured that the latter ability was forging ahead. Lloyd took an immediate liking to him, even though he was not too happy about having to conduct the interview in the sprawling grounds of Horton Manor Children's Centre. He had been looking forward to thawing out in a warm office after the drive from London.

'Has to be outside,' Ted Prentice barked, sitting on a bench near the touchline of a miniature tarmac football pitch. 'The moral terrorists who run this place have actually written a termination clause into my contract about my pipe. I got away with it at first, by promising to smoke only herbal tobacco. Took the little wankers six months to discover that all tobacco is herbal. Anyway, the sole purpose of my agreeing to see you is so that I can exact a grovelling apology from you over that article you wrote about me.'

'That you won't get,' said Lloyd, standing over the doctor. 'Firstly, I didn't write it. Secondly, it appeared in a sister magazine that is now defunct.'

'No apology?'

'No.'

'Fair enough. You can bugger off, then.' The older man proceeded to stuff Condor ready-rubbed into a briar.

'I didn't come here to grovel. I came here to talk to you about savants. If you want your ego massaged, the general misguided opinion is that you're a leading authority on them.'

'*The* leading authority,' Prentice corrected, lighting his pipe with a pocket flame-thrower. 'You'd better sit down.'

Lloyd sat. He would have preferred to keep walking. His windsurfer jacket and slacks were hardly the right clothes for March; he was convinced that a severe case of hypothermia was only minutes away. On the other hand, Prentice, old enough to be Lloyd's father, was one of those depressingly robust outdoor types who never felt the cold and probably took a cold shower every morning.

'So what do you want to know about idiot savants?'

'That's not a word I would use,' Lloyd countered, feeling that the interview was off to a bad start.

Prentice laughed. 'Of course you wouldn't. You've been brainwashed by the legions of moral terrorists who've debased our language. "Idiot" used to be an accepted medical term until the language loonies started wetting themselves every time they heard it. You can go to the electric chair in America for using the words "cripple" or "blind" these days. "Physically challenged" or "vision-impaired" are the Orwellian Newspeak crap terms the harpies of hate insist you use now. Idiot savants was a term coined by Langdon Down in the last century.' He turned his intimidating bushy eyebrows on Lloyd. 'You've heard of him, of course?'

'The man who first described Down's Syndrome?'

The doctor grunted his approval. He was about to say something but was interrupted by a large group of noisy youngsters in wheelchairs filing onto the football pitch. He returned their friendly waves. 'Our Tuesday football match. You might find this interesting.'

The children started playing a noisy, aggressive form of five-a-side football that involved them having to manipulate a huge, tough, balloon-like ball with their wheelchairs. They were aged from ten to thirteen. Despite their handicaps – some couldn't even support their heads properly – they were all having tremendous fun. The two teams were equally divided as regards physical ability. There was the frequent clash of aluminium on aluminium, and play often had to stop while wheelchairs were disentangled. Every delay produced whistles and catcalls from the little knot of onlookers.

'I'm the only one left using the term idiot savant,' Prentice remarked when the game had settled down. 'The others wouldn't dare. We are now in the age of the politically correct – with the thought-police scouring minutes of meetings for evidence of undesirable thinking, and local-health-authority-sponsored Ministries of Truth restructuring our language. Words are bullets. In Down's day, "idiots" was the medically accepted term for those with IQs of around thirty and below. Use the term today and hordes of loonies will descend on you and cart you off to the local Nelson Mandela House of Reform and Re-education. So now we use the expression "Savant Syndrome". It keeps the apparatchiks off our backs.' He chuckled, apparently unconcerned that his words were being captured on the tape-recorder that Lloyd had placed between them. ' "Savant" is a French word. It means "wise one". So what do you want to know about them, Mr Wheeler?'

'As much as possible. I saw the BBC Equinox documentary on Stephen Wiltshire. That's about the sum total of my knowledge, although I once wrote an article on the treatment of autistic children.'

A goal was scored, and the onlookers, some of them also in wheelchairs, cheered lustily.

Doctor Prentice sucked on his pipe. 'Stephen Wiltshire is a remarkable boy. But he's not the only one. There's Richard Wawro. If you ever see his pictures, they'll blow your mind. An IQ of around thirty, virtually blind, and yet he produces brilliant crayon sketches of anything he's seen on TV or in a photograph. He's produced thousands of drawings, and can remember every one. Margaret Thatcher's got a collection of Wawro originals. Then there's the most famous savant of all. Leslie Lemke. An American. Blind. Hopelessly retarded. Yet Leslie can play *any* piece of music on the piano having heard it once. And not only play it perfectly, but add his own improvisations and harmonies. Musically, he's a genius. Mentally, he's a child. His repertoire seems to be unlimited, and once he's heard a piece of music, he never forgets it.

'Then there's Nick Mollart who works for a private detective agency in London. An IQ of forty. He can't feed himself but he knows over ten million names and addresses and phone numbers off by heart, from skimming through all the UK telephone directories. Give him a name and address and he'll come straight back with the phone number. Give him the number and he'll give you the name and address. Ask him to list all the numbers that don't appear and he'll give you those as well. Useful, if you're matching ex-directory numbers. Where the new directories have got post codes, he can rattle those off as well. He can even list all telephone subscribers by their post code. He doesn't stop there – he can do much the same with electoral rolls. Then there are the calendar calculators and lightning calculators. Would you like to meet one?'

The question took Lloyd by surprise. Before he could answer, Prentice suddenly bellowed: 'Paul! Come here a minute!'

A golden-haired boy aged about nine detached himself from the group of spectators and steered his electric wheelchair towards the bench where Prentice and Lloyd were sitting.

'There are talented savants, and what we call prodigious savants,' said Prentice. 'Paul is a prodigious savant.'

Lloyd shook hands with the lad and smiled to put him at ease. He noticed that the boy had André's blank, indifferent gaze.

'Paul is a calendar calculator,' Prentice explained. 'Give him any date and he'll tell you what day of the week it fell on. And not only that, but he can juggle with the calendar any way you wish. Ask him to list the dates of all the Fridays in 1066 and he'll reel 'em off. And he can work out Easters over the next million years. I've got a computer in my office if you won't take my word for it.'

Lloyd remembered his laptop Compaq in his shoulder-bag and fished it out.

'Got a calendar program in it?' Prentice asked.

' "Sidekick",' Lloyd replied, opening the machine and switching it on. 'Sidekick' was a useful background program that kept tabs on his appointments. Among its features for the busy executive was a useful calendar facility that enabled one to make appointments up to two hundred years in the past or two hundred years in the future.

Paul waited patiently while Lloyd called up the calendar on his screen.

'Okay, Paul. What day of the week was the 19th of March 1856?'

'That would be a Wednesday,' Paul replied promptly.

'Well done, Paul.'

The boy's blank stare was replaced by a shy smile.

Lloyd tried his date of birth. 'How about the 20th June 1960?'

'That would be a Monday,' Paul answered without hesitation.

'That's excellent, Paul.'

Paul's smile widened to a broad grin.

Lloyd scrolled his computer into the past and selected the first day of the twentieth century. '1st January 1901?'

'That would be a Tuesday.'

Lloyd's cold was forgotten. He traded grins with the boy. It was obvious that the lad loved showing off his talent. 'That's good. How about the first day of the next century? 1st January 2001?'

'That would be a Monday.'

Lloyd tried ten more dates. In each case Paul trotted out the right answer the instant Lloyd gave the year. It was a remarkable demonstration.

Prentice asked a question. 'How many seconds in a hundred years, Paul?'

This time there was a pause before the boy answered. He closed his eyes tightly and said, 'That would be 3,155,760,000 seconds, allowing for 365.25 days per year.' He recited the number as a string of digits and, to his obvious delight, received a warm hug from Prentice. The doctor thanked the boy and allowed him to return to his game.

'Amazing,' said Lloyd, shaking his head in disbelief as the boy steered his wheelchair back to his friends.

113

'Yet if I had asked him to add two and two, he would have been stuck, and would've got upset.'

'He can perform amazing feats of mental calculation and yet he can't add? Why not?'

'I didn't say he couldn't add. Like many savants, Paul can't handle abstracts. If I were to ask you to add two and two, you'd answer "four" without having to ask, two and two what? But days, months, years are not abstracts, so Paul can handle them.'

'So how does he do it?' Lloyd asked, watching Paul talking to his friends. 'Does he work out every date, or has he memorised the entire calendar?'

'If he used memory, he would be a talented savant and limited to a hundred-year span or so either way. No – he works it out. You saw the hesitation before he gave the answer to the number of seconds in a century.'

'Was he right?'

'Oh yes. He even qualified his answer, as you heard. Give him a specific century and he would have calculated all the leap years exactly.'

'How can you be sure he doesn't use memory? You've obviously asked him that question before, otherwise you wouldn't know the answer yourself.'

Prentice shook his head. 'Paul's retentivity is almost non-existent. Show him four items on a tray and he will not be able to remember them when you take the tray away. And yet his calculating speed is fast – phenomenally fast, even by the standards of most prodigious savants. But, as you saw, it's possible to slow him down with silly questions about the number of seconds in a century. He can be slowed down even more than that?'

'How?'

'Questions about Easters. The date of Easter each year is fixed by a weird and very complicated formula the Catholic Church dreamed up around 325 AD at the Council of Nicaea; it's so weird and complicated, in fact, that Easter can vary by a month from year to year. So Paul finds calculations involving Easter a pain in the arse. Ask him when Easter will fall in one million AD and it'll probably take him a long time to work it out.'

'How long?'

'About ten seconds. No more than fifteen.'

Lloyd chuckled. His liking for Prentice deepened. 'Actually, Paul is now the second savant I've met.'

'Who was the first? I'm sure I know of all the UK ones.'

Lloyd told him about his meeting with André on the flight from Singapore and her ability to tell the time.

Prentice was immediately interested. 'What was her name?'

'André.'

'Her full name?'

'I didn't get a chance to find out.'

'And you call yourself a journalist?' Prentice broke off and relit his pipe. 'André rings a bell.' His face creased in a frown. 'No – it escapes me. Getting old, that's my trouble. A female time-telling savant? Now that is unusual on both counts.'

'Why's that?'

Prentice explained that among savants, calendar calculating ability and exceptional musical or artistic talent was usual, whereas time-tellers were almost unheard of. Only one was believed to be alive. Also, female savants were extremely rare. 'I've only met one time-teller, but not a female savant, so I'd be very interested to meet this André. I suggest you find her.'

'I intend to. Since meeting her, and now you, the subject has aroused my interest.'

'And you've no idea where she lives?'

'No.' Seeing Prentice's contemptuous expression, he added in his defence: 'The mother didn't like her daughter showing off her ability. She really got mad at me and dragged the girl away before I had a chance to find out much.'

'Stupid woman. All savants love showing off their talent, as you've just seen. It gives them a feeling of much needed confidence; superiority, even – but it doesn't do any harm. It brings them out of their shell and enables them to acquire a few social skills. Watch a Stephen Wiltshire draw or a Leslie Lemke play – that's when they're at their happiest. To suppress and deny their talent is a monstrous cruelty. All the famous savants have blossomed because they had a loved-one who encouraged them and provided motivation.'

115

Lloyd told him about André's disturbed state that reached its climax on arrival at Heathrow. 'The moment the aircraft came to a standstill, she had a really bad fit that ended with her fainting. I had to carry her off the aircraft. There was a lightning-strike that came within an ace of hitting the aircraft when it stopped, but she was getting in a state before that.'

The doctor grunted. 'Probably the disruption of her routine that upset her. Singapore is a hell of a distance. Stability and routine are very important for autistic kids.' He waved his hand at the football match. 'We play that game at the same time, twice a week, all through the year. If the weather's bad, we play in the gym. We never cancel it.'

The two men watched the game in silence for a few seconds. 'So how *do* they do it?' Lloyd asked him at length. 'Why is it that they can do things that seem impossible to us?'

Prentice sighed. 'Have you got a couple of years to spare? Firstly, it's important to understand that savants are not child prodigies. They're autistic children whose brain failed to develop normally in their mother's womb and therefore works in a totally different way from ours. Then there is the complex effect of sex hormones on the brain in the womb, which usually ensures that savants are male. Then there is acquired savantism – usually as the result of an accident. But that's so rare that it's not worth considering. It's outside mainstream Savant Syndrome.'

The doctor paused. 'But you want to know how they do it. As I talk to you now, it's the left-hand hemisphere of your brain that is processing my speech. I make a string of noises, your brain understands them. Speech, rules of grammar, mental calculation – all are controlled by the left hemisphere. The left stands for logic and order and discipline. Serial input. Serial output. If two people talk to you at the same time, you get confused because you're having to process parallel data with a serial facility. On the other hand, our little-used right hemisphere is concerned with vision and artistic ability. It has formidable powers that we're only just beginning to understand. Remember, we know a hell of a lot about brain structure, but bugger all about brain function. You could watch a wall of a

116

hundred televisions all running different programmes, and your right-hand hemisphere would be able to spot immediately if one of the televisions had a faulty picture. But if you were played a hundred different tunes and one was being played out of tune, your left-hand hemisphere would give up the ghost.'

The tape-recorder switched off with a click. Lloyd turned the tape over.

'Of course,' Prentice continued, 'what I've just said is shot full of over-simplifications. Occasionally the left side decides that it can't cope and there's a sudden migration of functions to the right side. This happens when we're learning to ride a bike or drive a car, or swim, or master a new piece of software. We struggle for hours, overloading our left-hand hemisphere with functions it can't handle, and then, Bingo! It suddenly becomes automatic, so that we wonder why it was so difficult in the first place. The right side has taken over. The process of learning is the process of forcing the right-hand side of the brain to take over functions connected with vision and perception of the world about us. The left side is day-to-day order and reason; the right side is artistic ability and anarchy, enabling us to do complex things automatically. Normally, we have no choice in which side of the brain we use. The left side, with all its shortcomings, is dominant.'

'And savants use their right-hand hemisphere automatically?' Lloyd ventured.

Doctor Prentice nodded. 'Pretty well – yes. But it's possible to use your right side at will in a small way. Try a little experiment before you go to sleep tonight. Tell yourself repeatedly to wake up at a specific time, and choose a time you don't normally wake up at. The left-hand side has to do a lot of work at night when we're asleep – disposing of the day's accumulation of unwanted memories and transferring essential data to long-term storage. If we had a better-organised brain, by the way, we probably wouldn't need to sleep; some savants don't. Now, the presence of a wake-up program will get in the way of your left hemisphere performing its night-time functions, so the program will be transferred to the right-hand side. The result? You'll wake up at pretty near the time you requested because you've brought into play a hormone in your brain's hypothalamus that controls your circadian rhythms – your body clock. There's a savant in all of us, Mr Wheeler.'

The interview ended in Prentice's office. He gave Lloyd a batch of photocopied papers which he thought would be of interest. 'And you'd better have this, but I want it back.' He handed Lloyd a VHS videotape. 'It's a Channel 4 documentary I made with the grant that you were so critical about. "Out of Their Tiny Minds." It was broadcast about six years ago. We advertised all over the country for savants and auditioned about thirty for the programme, although only a few were used in the final cut. We rented London Weekend Television's rehearsal room on Waterloo Station for the auditions to cut down on all the travelling expenses we had to shell out.'

'Were there any female savants among them?'

Prentice frowned and banged out his pipe. 'It was all some time ago . . . Yes – one was in the group we auditioned. Damned if I can remember her name. But her mother said she could make thunder.'

'What?'

Prentice managed a bleak smile. 'We were sceptical as well, but we had her along to the rehearsal room.'

'And could she?'

The doctor snorted. 'Have you ever been in LWT's rehearsal room in the old news theatre? Waterloo Station is not the quietest place in the world, believe me. We did a test, but no one could hear anything except bloody music and announcements. The mother swore that her daughter could only make very distant rolls of thunder. Very quiet. We refunded her fares and sent her home. A time-waster – there were several. But look, if you really want a story, you ought to track down a young Iraqi boy we used in the programme. Khalid al Karni. I've tried to find him, but I've given up.'

'What was special about him?' Lloyd asked.

'He was a time-teller like your André – the last savant in the programme – but he had another amazing ability that we couldn't use in the documentary for various reasons. It astonished us, and it even astonished his mother.'

118

'And what was that?'

Prentice rummaged in a desk drawer and handed his visitor a curious-looking ball covered with an uneven layer of matt latex. 'What do you suppose that is?'

Lloyd turned the ball in his hands. Around the centre of the ball was a series of circles and dots moulded into the rubber. A small hole had been cut in the side, just large enough to accept his forefinger. The inside of the strange ball felt furry. 'I've no idea. Some sort of rounders or baseball ball? A practice cricket ball? And why the hole?'

Prentice grunted. 'Close. Actually, it's a tennis ball that was turned inside out by the Iraqi savant. A Dunlop production engineer cut that hole. He confirmed that it was definitely one of their balls. Those circles and dots are the batch control codes they set up on the moulds.'

There was silence for a few moments. 'You're kidding,' said Lloyd softly.

'No.'

Lloyd turned the hole to the light and peered into the ball's interior. He could see the furry melton nap that was normally on the outside. 'I don't believe it. You're telling me that a boy took an ordinary tennis ball and did this to it?'

'Yes.'

'What did he do? Say abracadabra?'

'Actually, I don't blame you. We were all shaken in the rehearsal room. It started when some of the kids found a box full of tennis balls and began chucking them about. It was bloody chaos in there, so a bit more didn't matter. I was actually talking to Khalid's mother at the time, when her son came over to us with one of the balls. "I can turn inside out," he said.' Prentice nodded to himself at the recollection. 'We pulled his leg about it. He got cross, threw one of the balls at the wall. One of the kids caught it and gave it to me. That's the ball you're holding.'

'Good grief,' Lloyd muttered.

'He did it again a few minutes later when we got a camera on him. But another attempt about an hour later failed. He couldn't do it again, and that made him mad.'

119

'Was his time-telling ability affected?'

'Not at all. You'll see him perform on the tape.'

Lloyd stared at the ball in his hands, his mind performing mental exercises in topography to work out if it were possible to cut a small hole in a tennis ball and then turn the ball inside out through the hole. He gave up. Common sense alone dictated that such a feat was impossible. 'And you say that you didn't use this in the programme?' he asked incredulously.

Prentice refilled his pipe. 'The idea I sold to Channel 4 was for a programme about savants – gifted autistic kids whose abilities could be demonstrated at will in front of the camera. Talents which are extraordinary, but fact. There's no argument about them. You can watch them draw, or listen to them play, or test their mental calculation feats with a pocket calculator. But turning tennis balls inside out? Manipulative savants? Uri Geller bending spoons in sealed glass tubes; Dale Rothman transferring jewels from a safe to his pocket on television? That's wandering into fringe stuff like ESP and telekinesis.' He took the tennis ball from Lloyd and stared at it. 'Mental savantism is explainable; manipulative savantism isn't.'

'And this Khalid did the trick in front of the camera?'

'Just the once. It's among all the audition takes and out-takes at the end of the tape. Don't forget that I want it back. I'm running short of copies.'

Lloyd thanked the doctor and promised to return the tape. The two men strolled out to the car park.

'Do you intend to track down your time-telling savant?' Prentice asked as Lloyd climbed behind the wheel of his Lotus.

The young man nodded. 'Definitely.'

'Well, when you do, I'd like to meet her.'

'I'll do my best. But first I've got to find her. And when I do find her, there's going to be the problem of her mother.'

'You've *got* to find her,' said Prentice with a sudden intensity that took Lloyd by surprise. 'That young Iraqi time-teller is probably dead by now, poor sod. Your time-telling savant might be the only one alive in the world. They're very special. They don't perform calculations or play around with calendars or have prodigious memories. What the true time-telling savant does is something so fundamentally different, it's almost too terrifying to contemplate. They actually *feel* and understand the flow of time and the awesomeness of space. It's as if they have their finger on the pulse of the Universe itself. Time is the one link we have with the Creation. Perhaps they are the chosen ones – the wise ones who will lead us to an understanding of the beginning of time and the Universe . . . and beyond.'

24

Lloyd drove back to his flat, going over the interview in his mind. Even the frozen state his feet were in was forgotten. A sudden chorus of car horns behind him shook him out of his reverie. To his surprise, he found himself in Wapping, having stopped automatically at a familiar set of traffic-lights because the junction was usually busy. But on this occasion the road was clear, the lights were at green . . .

Very embarrassed, he drove on, wondering what other mistakes he had made on the journey from Epsom. Had he jumped lights? Had he exceeded the speed limit on the A3? He knew all about the so-called 'automatic pilot' in most drivers, but just because it had a name that didn't explain how the mass of eye-brain-hand co-ordination was handled. How was it that he had driven for an hour through dense evening traffic from Epsom to London and couldn't recollect anything of the journey except his thoughts?

In a way, it was rather frightening.

25

It was nearly 11 p.m. when Lloyd finished work and returned to his flat. The place was dark, and as welcoming as an abandoned abattoir. There was an emptiness, with Sarah gone. She would have waited up, and had a chilli simmering on the cooker. They would have discussed their respective days over the meal,

121

watched a tape, argued about their last squash game, and tumbled into bed for an hour's love-making before drifting off to sleep in each other's arms. He missed her. He missed her quite badly.

Supper was a cheese sandwich. He had forgotten to take a loaf out of the freezer that morning, so he had to prise the rigid slices apart with a knife. He stuck them in the microwave for a moment, then sat in the living-room area, watching television while trying to suck sustenance from the corners of his icy meal. By midnight he had had his fill of studio pundits pondering the fate of Saddam Hussein and re-fighting the war. There was the tape that Doctor Prentice had lent him, but he wanted to tackle that with a fresh mind. It had been a busy day, he was tired; an early night seemed a good idea.

Before drifting off to sleep in his multi-layer, Sarahless bed, he remembered Ted Prentice's suggested experiment and told himself repeatedly that he had to wake up at 4.30 a.m. – a suitably ungodly hour when he reckoned he was usually in deep sleep.

He dreamed of André's strange green eyes. They were floating before him, unblinking, unnerving. Moving away at first, and then drawing nearer and nearer. Her strange green irises swelled and vanished beyond the periphery of his vision as her pupils expanded and dwarfed his consciousness. The blackness of her gaze devoured him until he found himself floundering in space, surrounded by all the stars of the Milky Way and all the countless glowing galaxies of the Universe. He looked frantically in every direction and realised that he could actually see the expansion of the Universe, the parallactic difference between the motion of stars close to and those further away. Time was running towards and accelerating away from the strange orange glow at the very centre of the universe which – in his dream-wisdom – he knew to be the epicentre of the Big Bang: the site of the Creation.

And then he was awake, wide awake and sweating. Blood pounding in his ears. He closed his eyes, but the darkness was too frightening to face again. He opened them, and discovered that the orange glow was the soft flare of the sodium street lights on the warehouse's varnished pine ceiling-joists.

Hell – that was a lousy dream. What had he eaten last night to deserve that? His throat was dry, so he threw back the duvet, padded into the kitchen area and drank some milk straight from the bottle. He saw his watch as he closed the fridge door.

4.34 a.m.

His experiment! 4.34! That meant that he must've woken up on the stroke of 4.30!

There's a savant in all of us, Mr Wheeler.

Lloyd sat at the breakfast bar and tried to organise his thoughts. The coldness of the milk-bottle in his hand was reassuring. This was crazy. Setting an internal alarm-clock to wake oneself up at an unusual time was something everyone did at some time or another.

Yeah. But it's not a very reliable system and yet you woke up dead on 4.30.

Then Lloyd remembered Dr Prentice's parting words:

'It's as if they have their finger on the pulse of the Universe itself. Time is the one link we have with the Creation. Perhaps they are the chosen ones – the wise ones who will lead us to an understanding of the beginning of time and the Universe . . . and beyond.'

He took another swig from the bottle without thinking what he was doing, and there was the sudden sting of cold milk dribbling down his chest. He looked at his hand and saw that it was shaking.

It was stupid to feel the way he did; irrational yet understandable. He was alone, after all, and shaken by a bad dream; and it was an unholy hour of the morning when the spirit was at its lowest ebb, and logic and reason refused to assert themselves . . .

What he was experiencing was fear.

26

SOUTHERN IRAQ
Wednesday, 6th March 1991

Corporal Willie Mellish of the Queen's Own Scottish Borderers
had had a lousy war, and now the peace was providing to be as
bad.

The biggest enemy was the sand. Not the real sand that he
knew from his holidays with his parents in Greece, but a fine,
wind-driven dust that got everywhere. Next was the rain,
because it turned the dust to a gooey yellow mud, and that
got everywhere too. Then there was the unending, desiccating,
blustery wind that sucked up moisture and quickly turned the
desert back into dust. After that there was the boredom – you
couldn't read all the time. Then the pressmen. Bloody pain in
the arse they could be. Last of all were the twelve hundred Iraqi
POWs in his care. They were so little trouble that they hardly
counted as an enemy any more, but they were the only reason
why Willie was here and not on a celebratory boozing binge
with some of his mates who had scrounged a trip to Bahrain.

Willie pulled his cape around his shoulders, glanced up at the
sullen sky and contemplated the advantages of shooting himself
if it started raining again. He moodily surveyed his Iraqis, and
lit a cigarette. Some of the prisoners nearest him looked long-
ingly at the cigarette, but Willie had learned to stop handing
his fags out. A party of sappers had fenced off the 'cage' with
a barbed-wire entanglement, the coils stretched out to the point
of uselessness because the stuff was so scarce. The previous
week the temporary 'cage' had been nothing more than a giant
square marked out on the desert floor with white ribbon, which
the POWs were told not to step over.

Willie's compound in the middle of the desert was about two
hundred metres square. His charges had been given hundreds
of polythene sheets to use as shelters. When it rained, they
crawled under them to keep dry, and when it stopped raining
they sat on them to keep out of the mud. They were a pathetic
sight; hollow-eyed from lack of sleep as a result of a month of

naval and aerial bombardment, and emaciated from lack of decent food. The majority of them had inadequate clothes: bottle-green anoraks that stayed wet after heavy rain – not even the right colour for the desert – and cheap, ill-fitting boots that fell apart when they got wet. A couple of hard-pressed MOs were still sorting out those who had had toes shot off by their officers to prevent them deserting.

It was incomprehensible to Willie that soldiers should have been treated so badly. The poor bastards didn't even have a system of identity tags, thus obliging the British to invent one using hospital patients' plastic ID bracelets. The abject misery of the POWs was reflected in their eyes, but at least they were looking better now than when Willie had first been put in charge of them. They were getting daily food packs – rather like airline cold meals, but with the contents and instructions printed in Arabic – and there was a plentiful supply of fresh water from the huge mattress-like bag that lay in the compound looking like part of an inflatable fairground fun castle.

At first the POWs had been uneasy about being captives of the British. The majority of them were conscripts from poor backgrounds who believed that the infidels ate Moslems; they had wanted to be the prisoners of the Saudis – their brother Arabs. But now they accepted their lot and sat around in disconsolate groups on their polythene sheets, talking in low tones and anxiously watching the sky for rain. Some were sleeping – making up for the previous month. A few of them could speak English. They usually tried to engage Willie in conversation. Right now, they sensed his mood and left him alone.

Willie toyed with the idea of going to his tent and making himself a mug of tea. It would pass an hour. First one had to get the Gaz burner working, which meant cleaning the sand out of the jets; the bloody stuff even crept under the threads of his water-bottle cap. He had tried filtering the water with the Cona coffee filters he had pleaded with his mum to send him, but the sodding dust was so fine that it passed straight through the paper. Then cleaning out his mug was always a big problem because his J-cloths got impregnated with sand – as did his teabags. No matter what precautions he took, he always ended up drinking gritty tea. Christ knew what it was doing to his teeth.

Willie was having a lousy peace.

Another hour, and his relief would take over. Even then there was nothing to do except read. Willie had never read much in his life; now he was devouring the donated paperbacks that were arriving by the sackful. The boundless generosity of people back home astounded and touched him. The other consolation was that he could read in comfort because he had managed to scrounge a US camp-bed. The Americans had decent aluminium-framed camp-beds that were high enough to sit on. Not like the six-inches-off-the-ground British army 'Safari' camp-bed that sank into the mud and soaked your arse if you didn't use a groundsheet. There had been a comment in the *Sandy Times* that some 19,000 US-issue camp-beds had been subject to inter-force ownership transfer (stolen), and that the Americans were not pleased about it.

The drone of a vehicle approaching from the south. A Nissan Prairie with a loud-hailer mounted on its roof-rack.

Another bloody TV news team coming to feast their cameras on the POWs. A news team had already dropped Willie in the shit. The previous week, a famous sandy-haired newscaster had turned up with a cameraman and sound-recordist; this was before the 'cage' was properly organised, when Iraqi soldiers were still converging on the camp with their hands up to surrender and throwing away their helmets. Willie had kept the cameraman well back so that there would be no close-ups, because that was the rule: the British did not want to be accused of violating the Geneva Convention requirement that POWs should not be exposed to humiliation. But Willie had underestimated the power of modern zoom lenses. That evening, close-ups had gone out on television showing grateful Iraqi POWs kissing the hands of the famous sandy-haired newscaster. It turned out that the newscaster had not been operating within the pool agreement and wasn't even properly accredited. Willie had been standing nearest the fan, and copped more than his fair share of the flying brown stuff as a result. Since then he was wary of all journalists.

126

Willie waved the vehicle to a parking area well away from the 'cage', and it stopped beside the huge cache of arms – a pile of rifles and ammunition that had been rounded up from the area or removed from the prisoners. The Nissan was driven by a WRAC sergeant, but her two passengers were civvies – one a pseudo-civvy in combat dress. He had close-cropped hair and a warm, engaging smile that was wasted on Willie.

'We're MOD scientists from Riyadh,' Max explained, showing Willie their passes. 'We're scouring all the "cages", looking for the crew of a particular Iraqi tank. We need to question them about some special equipment they were issued with. They don't have to answer, of course; there'll be no pressure. We'll address them *en masse* with the PA, so we'd like to take this vehicle into the compound.'

Their passes were in order, they had no cameras on board, so Willie had no objections. He signalled to the private manning the makeshift gate, and the Nissan drove through and stopped near the wire. All the POWs watched the new arrivals with interest. Those in the latrines sensed that something was up and emerged from behind the canvas screens. Even those who had been asleep, woke and sat up. The appearance of the Nissan was a welcome break from the dreary monotony of their daily routine. They gathered around the vehicle, waiting for something to happen.

After two days touring the 'cages' with Max Shannon and Leo Buller on their mysterious search, Sergeant Caroline Morgan had a standard patter worked out. Under the watchful eyes of Willie and the privates under his command, she sat on the Prairie's roof with the PA microphone in her hand and addressed the POWs in fluent Arabic, explaining how some letters addressed to Khalid al Karni had been found in a T-55 on the Kuwait to Basra highway. Also, some property belonging to Khalid had been found in the tank, which the British were anxious to return to him. No bodies had been found in or near the tank, so the chances were that he and the rest of his crew had surrendered. Was he among the prisoners? And if not, did anyone know what had happened to him?

As she spoke she cued Max and Leo, who each held up a

127

poster-sized enlargement of a photograph of the T-55 with the reversed swastika clearly shown.

'I give you our solemn word that no harm will befall Khalid or his comrades,' Sergeant Morgan concluded. 'But these gentlemen would like to talk to him. We'll talk right here, where you can all see what is going on.'

The circle of dark, sullen faces stared blankly back at Sergeant Morgan. It had been the same at all the other 'cages'; either the POWs didn't trust them, or they didn't understand why their captors should wish to single out one of their comrades. Not that she could blame them. Doubtless many of the POWs had been involved in the unspeakable atrocities that had been perpetrated in Kuwait and were only just coming to light. They would want to keep their heads down and await their inevitable repatriation, which couldn't be that far off.

A figure some twenty metres from the Prairie held up his hand. 'I know of Khalid,' he said, speaking in slow but good English.

Max and Leo exchanged glances and signalled the Iraqi to come forward. He was about twenty; taller than his comrades, and lacking the obligatory moustache. Like most of his fellow countrymen he was wearing shapeless trousers and a bulky, ill-fitting anorak with bulging pockets crammed full of sweets. He smiled uncertainly at the new arrivals. At first he was reluctant to enter the Prairie, but he relented when Leo reversed the two front seats so that they faced aft. He sat in the back seat, facing the two Englishmen. Sergeant Morgan stood by the open driver's door in case her Arabic was needed. POWs crowded silently around the Prairie, staring in at the windows.

Leo took out a notebook and switched on a cassette tape-recorder. He glanced at the Iraqi's plastic ID bracelet and noted down the number before giving the POW his full attention. Leo would be watching for those subtle but difficult-to-hide variations in posture, gesture and expression that would signal whether or not the POW was lying. He was skilled in such analysis and was confident that cultural difference would not affect his ability.

'What is your name?' asked Leo, smiling genially to put the

POW at his ease. The Iraqi's worried expression suggested to Leo that he was now wishing he had remained silent. In fact he was glad that the tall, thin man had addressed him; he looked more friendly than the man with the close-cropped hair, who had 'officer' stamped all over him.

'Adnan Barhadin.'

Leo wrote it down phonetically.

'You are a conscript, Adnan?' asked Leo.

Adnan nodded. Leo guessed that he came from a middle-class family, and asked a few questions about his background, simple questions to put the young man at ease. When he had finished he nodded to Max, who went ahead with the more serious questions.

'You knew Khalid al Karni?'

'First you must tell me if he is in trouble.'

'He's not in any trouble,' said Max. 'I give you my word on that.'

The Iraqi studied Max's fixed smile and decided that perhaps he could be trusted.

'So you knew Khalid?' Max pressed.

'A little. He was in my armoured unit. He came late.'

Max opened the cigar box that Leo had found in the T-55. He showed the family photographs to the prisoner. 'Is Khalid one of these people?'

The Iraqi looked at the photographs. 'Ah – I have seen these pictures before.' He pointed to the boy. 'That is Khalid. Much younger there.'

'Is his hair still blond – fair?'

The POW mustered a faint smile. He was beginning to relax.

'Yes. We used to . . . joke him . . .'

'Tease him?'

'Yes – tease him about it. He was a Christian Kurd but his mother and father live in Baghdad. He tell me they have a summer home in north. There are some Kurds like him – very pale. And with money.'

'What did his father do?'

'A manager. In a bank. Important men – man, I think.'

'Well, he could afford holidays in England,' Leo observed,

holding up the family group photograph with the Palace of Westminster in the background.

Adnan looked at the tall man and shook his head. 'No, I have seen that picture before . . . Khalid have two homes . . . No, three homes. He live in Baghdad, and London, and family home in Kurdistan.'

'When did he last live in London?'

The Iraqi tried to think and shook his head. 'Very recent. In January, I think he say, but I do not remember.'

'January this year?'

'I think – yes.'

Leo made a note.

Max changed tack. 'Why did he paint a cross on his tank?'

This time Adnan's smile was unselfconscious. 'Not Khalid. *We* paint the swastika.' His pronunciation was Arabic – *svastika*.

The faint smile at the corners of Max's mouth lost a trace of its permanence. 'Why?'

'Because he was lucky.'

'Why was he lucky?'

Leo could see that the question confused Adnan. The Iraqi glanced at Sergeant Morgan and spoke quickly in Arabic, faster than Max could follow.

'Because he was lucky,' she translated. 'How can I say why? He used to say that the enemy would never get him. And we believed him. He was blessed by Allah. He was . . .' She broke off and asked Adnan a question. He replied by tapping his head.

'Stupid?' Max suggested. 'Retarded?'

'Retarded,' said the Iraqi. 'Yes – that is a good word. But he was good tank driver. Very quick. Accurate. He could miss eggs each side of his tracks. The men in his crew love him. His tank commander love him. We all love him. Because he was lucky, we think we all share luck.'

Max's gaze hardened, challenging the young Iraqi to look away. 'Was he looked on with favour by his officers? Did his tank receive special equipment or special treatment?'

The question seemed to amuse the Arab at first. Then the

130

sad shake of his head spoke more words than any answer. 'Our officer was a Tikriti. You understand?'

'Tikrit is Saddam Hussein's home town,' Sergeant Morgan explained. 'The Tikritis worship him and get all the best jobs.' She would have been surprised to know that Max had stayed in the town's best hotel as a guest of the Iraqi government.

Max was silent for a moment. He was getting somewhere, and yet nowhere. The tape-recorder hummed softly. He unfolded the letter that Khalid had started to write and showed it to Adnan.

'Can you read English?'

'No.'

'Who is Andy?'

'I am sorry?'

'In this letter he has started to write to someone called Andy, but there is no address. Who is Andy?'

'I don't know.'

'Someone in England, perhaps?'

'I don't know.'

Max caught Leo's nod. The POW was telling the truth. Max leaned forward slightly and waited until he had the Arab's full attention. 'Could Khalid do tricks?' He repeated the question in his slow but good Arabic to ensure the POW understood.

Both Max and Leo noted the sudden discomfort that the question caused the Iraqi. He was an open young man who could not conceal his feelings easily. Adnan glanced around at the faces of his comrades peering in at the windows. 'Tricks? I don't understand.'

Sergeant Morgan started to translate, but Max interrupted her, not taking his eyes off Adnan for an instant. 'I can follow him. I think you do understand, Adnan . . . Don't you?'

The young Iraqi saw the hardness beyond the smiling grey eyes. He sensed that it would not be wise to try to keep anything from this man. He began to understand why the British were such good soldiers. They didn't scream at their men or brutalise them. They didn't have to. No one would disobey this man with the compelling grey eyes.

'Could Khalid do tricks?' Max repeated.

131

The POW looked uncertain. 'Tricks?'

Sergeant Morgan spoke to him briefly in Arabic, not wishing to see the prisoner unduly pressurised.

'Yes,' he admitted at length. 'But you will laugh.'

'We won't laugh.' The eyes were relentless. 'What sort of tricks?'

'He could tell the time. Without a . . .' He tapped his watch. 'You ask him the time and he would give it. Always perfect.'

'What else?'

'Nothing else.'

Leo cleared his throat.

'What else?' Max repeated. He didn't acknowledge Leo's signal but his voice was harder.

'He . . . He could make thunder.' The answer was blurted out.

Leo stopped making notes. He stared thoughtfully at the POW.

'What sort of thunder?' asked Max, moderating his tone.

'Well . . . Thunder.'

'Loud thunder? Quiet thunder? Far? Near?' Leo knew Max well enough to recognise the quiet tension in his voice.

'Thunder in distance. Loud or long way. But not many times. He listen and tell us to stop making noise. And we hear thunder. He say he make thunder any time. We laugh. One day I say to him to make thunder. And then he make big thunder. Very loud. We think American ships shelling again.'

'What else could he do?'

For a few seconds Adnan was undecided. Again he met the hard, grey eyes and again he realised that nothing could be hidden from this strange Englishman with the close-cropped hair. He unzipped a pocket in his bulging anorak, felt in its depths and produced a ball with a smooth, matt, rubberised surface.

'Tennis ball,' he said. 'My tennis ball. Khalid throw it at wall. Then he gets it from air – what is the word?'

'Catches?'

'Yes – then he catches ball and give back my ball. But it is like that.'

132

Max took the ball, examined it, squeezed it, and gave it to
Leo. It was the right weight and size for a tennis ball, and had
the right degree of resilience.

It was a tennis ball in all respects except one.

It was inside out.

27

SOUTHERN ENGLAND

It had been a happy day.

André wasn't expected back at the Candice Webb Special
School after the Singapore trip, and the education office didn't
have any supply-teaching vacancies available for the moment.
Normally Laura worried when she was out of work, but this
time she decided to put the free time to good use.

Mother and daughter spent the day repairing the ravages of
winter. They cut back the fruit trees which were getting over-
grown; went on the attack with billhooks and reclaimed another
few metres of wilderness from the pine forest encroaching on
the end of the long garden; creosoted fences, repaired panes of
glass in the greenhouse, and cleaned out the rabbit and chickens.
At dusk Laura lit a bonfire, much to André's delight. The girl
loved throwing debris on the blaze and watching sparks burst
into the sky. Several times Laura had to warn her that she was
standing too close.

'A shower,' said Laura when they finished work. It was dark,
they had used the light from the bonfire for the final clearing-
up. She raked the embers into a more compact heap. 'We both
stink of bonfires. And afterwards, toast made in front of the
fire. What do you say?'

'A shower,' André agreed. 'And "Neighbours" in twenty
minutes and thirty seconds from . . . Now.'

Laura frowned. She didn't like André using her time-telling
talent, even in an oblique manner. 'They never start on time
and you always get annoyed,' she pointed out.

'Not toast,' said André quietly.

'Why not, Andy?'

'Wednesday.'

Of course. Wednesday. Laura was disappointed. She had hoped that André would forget the date, what with all the upheaval of travelling halfway around the world. No . . . Silly to think that she might forget. Where time was concerned, Andy never forgot. Wednesdays had become very special for her.

'You've had a busy day, Andy. You've been a tremendous help. Wouldn't you rather stay in this evening with me?'

As Laura expected, André was not going to be deprived of her Wednesday evening. The girl shook her head and regarded her mother steadily. 'Like going out.'

Laura smiled to hide her disappointment, and put her arm around her daughter's shoulder. 'Sure you do,' she said as they returned to the bungalow. 'Sure you do. Tell you what, the water's going to take a while to heat up, so what say I do something in the microwave for a quickie snack, and then we take a shower together?'

Taking a shower together was something they hadn't done for at least six months. Since her long-overdue first period the previous year, André had become self-conscious about her mother seeing her. Not overly so, but enough for Laura, always attuned to her daughter's feelings, to sense that she now needed more privacy. But this time André didn't mind because Laura was the first to strip off and step into the cubicle.

Laura's feelings were mixed as she soaped her daughter's body. Just how much André had developed in that time was a shock; she knew her breasts were filling out, but she hadn't realised by just how much, and the girl's fine down of pubic hair was now a dense, dark growth. Laura guiltily suppressed her resentment at the way nature was turning her daughter into a young woman. André was no longer a child, and Laura knew that the love and care she lavished on her 'little girl' would have to be modified for the growing woman.

'We must make a trip to Guildford on Saturday, to buy you a few bras,' said Laura cheerfully, adjusting the shower-head so that André received the full blast.

'Will they hurt?'

134

'No.'

'Yours make dreadful marks,' said André, running her finger along a weal on her mother's midriff.

Dreadful – that was a new word in André's vocabulary. God, how she was changing, and not just physically. Laura laughed, and worked shampoo into her daughter's long, dark hair. She looked forward to drying it and brushing it, admiring the lovely sheen that always appeared as if by magic. 'I only buy cheap ones. Yours will be the best – the very best.'

'Why don't you buy the best, mother?'

The question was innocuous enough, yet caused Laura to give an inward shudder of fear. It was the first time André had called her 'mother' instead of 'mummy'. And it was the first time she had queried Laura's insistence on always buying the best for her daughter. The child psychologist who visited André's special school every month to carry out assessment tests was right: André was changing.

'She's shown an increase of ten points over the past three months on the Vineland Social Maturity Scale, Mrs Normanville. She now has a vocabulary of three hundred words – perhaps more. And her general IQ is going up as well. It really is a most extraordinary improvement.'

At the time Laura had rejected the psychologist's opinion out of hand, saying that André never showed any emotion except when her routine was disrupted or when something wasn't in the right place.

'The day I'll believe that she's changing will be the day that she smiles,' Laura had stated flatly. 'She never smiles. She never laughs. She sometimes cries, but . . . she's never ever put her arms around me and returned a hug.'

The lack of bitterness in Laura's voice had caused the psychologist to look searchingly at the young mother and wonder why she was so keen to reject his findings. In his experience, parents of autistic children latched eagerly onto any suggestion of even the slightest improvement in their offspring. Without exception, they always nursed that tiny glimmer of hope that their child's affliction was only temporary.

'Don't you want her to improve, Mrs Normanville?'

135

'Well, of course I do!'

The vehemence of Laura's reply had led the psychologist to suspect that there was denial at work. Perhaps the mother needed her daughter's retarded state as a well into which she could pour her love and devotion; love and devotion that stemmed from guilt. Once the psychologist had had a case of a mother who was still breast-feeding her son when he was three years old. The woman had a compulsive need to give milk and didn't want her son to grow up. Perhaps Laura was afraid that once André no longer needed her love, the love would dry up – like mother's milk. Perhaps the giving of love was now the only purpose Laura's life had. Such things were, sadly, not uncommon, and always frightening when exposed.

Laura sat André at the expensive Elizabeth Anne dresser and vanitory unit in her daughter's bedroom and brushed the wondrous sheen into her hair. As a child, Laura had dreamed of having such hair, and now, in a way, she did. As she brushed, Laura kept up the endless chatter she always fell into when the two of them were alone together; after a decade of caring for André, it came almost automatically.

'It's wonderful what we've got through today. I was thinking that we'd have to pay Jeff Harcourt to tackle that jungle at the bottom, and you know what he charges us. It would be a good idea if we got him to fix the cultivator so that we could grow potatoes down there for a couple of seasons. Keep still, darling.'

André had reached forward and was running her finger around the silver-framed photograph of Khalid that she kept on her dresser. The simple gesture set off a whole train of worries in Laura's mind. Khalid and André used to go for long bicycle rides whenever the young Kurd stayed at Durston Wood, and until now she had seen them simply as two retarded children who got on well together. But Khalid wasn't a child any more; to the despair of his parents, he had been old enough to be conscripted. And, as she had just seen, André was blossoming into a young woman. Supposing she and Khalid had . . . ? No! It was unthinkable! She pushed the unwelcome thought from her mind.

'Those pines have probably made the soil quite acid down

there,' Laura prattled on, 'so potatoes are probably the only vegetables that'll grow, unless we use a lot of lime. Tomorrow we could tackle digging out a bean trench in the vegetable garden. Gosh. How time flies. If we don't get some sowing done soon, we'll be too late. Sorry, darling, was that a snag?'

Laura left André to tease out the snag with her mother-of-pearl comb, and slid the wardrobe doors open. All André's clothes were top-quality. Mothers of younger children at Durston Wood were always in eager competition for the hand-me-downs from André's wardrobe. She selected her daughter's favourite Lacoste track suit and her white Reebok trainers.

'No,' André said when Laura set the clothes down on the quilt bedspread.

Laura looked surprised. 'What's the matter, darling?'

'Skirt,' said André.

Laura was taken aback. André adored her track suits. 'You want to wear a skirt, darling? Well – of course.' She returned to the wardrobe and selected a long plaid skirt.

'No.' André went to the wardrobe and unhooked a short skirt in white.

'André, darling. You can't wear that any more. It was fine last year, but you've grown out of it the way you've shot up. It's much too short and you'll catch your death on your bike.'

But André ignored her mother's pleas. She stepped into the skirt and wriggled it over her hips. In that instant Laura was taken back nearly twenty years.

Laura! I absolutely forbid you to wear that skirt! Frank! Will you do something about your daughter! She's going to that party looking like a tart!

To compound her mother's shock, André selected a white cashmere sweater that Laura had planned to give to Sally Freeman during the coming spring clear-out. She pulled it on without bothering with an underslip, and regarded herself in the mirror as she pulled strands of hair from under the sweater's high neck.

You'll wear a bra if I say so, my girl! Do you want boys staring at you? Is that what you want?

The difference now was that André didn't stand with her

137

hands on her hips and glare defiantly at her mother. Defiance was an emotion. André rarely showed emotions, except when she was upset.

Dear God, thought Laura. How am I going to handle this? She caught André's eye in the mirror and managed a warm smile despite her inner turmoil. Experience, and a resolve made many years ago that she would never shout at André as her mother had shouted at her, came to Laura's aid. 'You look lovely, André. Really lovely. Turn around.'

André turned round.

Good grief, if she rode her bike in that the skirt would ride right up over her thighs, and those panties were virtually transparent. Laura put her arms around her daughter. 'You look sensational, Andy. You'll knock 'em all out at Jacko's. But will you do me a favour, darling? A really big favour?'

André made no reply.

'It's a terribly cold night. You'll freeze to death in an anorak. So will you wear your long, zip-up leather coat for Mummy, and keep it on?'

'Which one?'

'The fur-lined one with the hood. You've only worn it once. It's a lovely coat.' Laura felt André trying to push her away, and tightened her grip. '*Please*, Andy. I'll only be worried sick about you. You don't want that, do you?'

André shook her head.

'And you promise to keep it on all the time?'

'Hot in Jacko's.'

'I know, but will you *please* promise me to keep it on.'

This time André relented and nodded. Laura sensed a little victory. 'Say promise.'

'Promise,' said André flatly.

Laura relaxed and smiled. Once André was programmed, she would keep her promise.

28

The night was blustery when André wheeled her Dawes ten-speed sports bicycle out of the garage. Laura glanced anxiously up at the thrashing pines and the sky as she closed the garage doors. Rain wasn't forecast, but this flat pocket of land at the western end of the Sussex Weald, sandwiched between the North and South Downs, could produce its own weather.

André stood patiently holding her bicycle while Laura made doubly certain that her fur coat was securely zipped from hem to chin, and that her reflective safety-belt was properly fastened.

'Got everything, darling?'

'Money,' said André. She went into the living-room and took a red purse from Laura's handbag. It was used solely for her needs. She found a £10 note inside the thick wad of £50s and thrust it into her coat pocket. It was her weekly pocket money. Laura gave her a hug when she returned. 'Have a good time, darling. You will be back at nine thirty, won't you, and you will promise me you'll 'phone if it rains?'

'Promise,' said André flatly, nothing in her tone suggesting that she was anxious to be off. She said goodbye to Laura, switched on her lights and pedalled down the long drive.

Laura watched her anxiously, as she had done every Wednesday evening that year. Her rear light was amazingly steady – no wobble as one would normally expect from a push-bike, but a steadily receding red blob. But then André's prowess on the machine had astonished everyone on the estate when Laura bought it for her the previous Christmas, while Khalid was staying with them. On Christmas day Sam Crittenden had nearly choked on his turkey when he saw André cycling along the top of his garden wall. She was showing off to the young Kurd. It was a single-brick wall – one brick wide and topped with vee-shaped concrete cappings. Until he had seen André pedalling along the top of the wall he would have staked his pension from the Forestry Commission that such a feat was impossible.

'Kid may be retarded,' he had remarked to his wife. 'But the way she can ride, I reckon Laura should put her in a circus.'

Laura closed the bungalow's front door and returned to the

living-room. The open log fire cast a golden reflection in the polished pitch-pine floorboards. It was a simply furnished room; the three-piece suite had been old when Laura bought it from the Women's Institute jumble sale nine years previously. The loose covers and curtains were made from the same material, and were her first attempt at needlework on a second-hand Singer. They were faded, but they belonged, as did the pine dining-room table and chairs that Laura had laboriously stripped and treated with Solignum. The elderly Hitachi's cathode-ray tube had long gone 'soft', so that the colour control had to be kept fully wound up. André's television in her room was a stylish Bang and Olufsen in ivory-white.

Laura left the door open so that she could hear the telephone. She threw another log on the fire and tried to watch television, but was unable to concentrate. She idly prodded the control box, channel-hopping. She hated Wednesdays. It was the one day of the week when the outside world invaded this secure retreat she had built, and claimed André away from her.

She should never have given in and bought André the bike, but Laura had never been able to refuse her daughter anything. Not that André ever made demands. But if she saw something she liked in a shop window, she would stop and stare at it. She had stopped and stared at the Dawes bicycle in Halford's window when the two of them were on a Christmas shopping expedition in Guildford. A week later, Laura had opened the red purse to purchase the machine.

One week into the new year and André had expressed a desire to visit Jacko's Café by herself. The steamy truck-drivers' pull-up was about two miles from Durston village. With its ancient, much pounded pinball-machine, formica-topped tables and blaring juke-box, it was a popular evening venue for local kids; they preferred it to the Durston Youth Club with its wholesome badminton-and-table-tennis ideas on what kids wanted.

'Let her go,' Sally Fielding had said when Laura confided in her neighbour. 'Little bit of independence won't hurt her. My Janice used to go there, and Jacko and Freda don't put up with no nonsense.'

'But she wants to go in the evening, Sal. By herself and on her bike.'

'So? There's a footpath all the way there. And the way Andy can ride her bike – well, I don't know what you're worried about. Look – I know it's difficult living out in the sticks. Took me ages, getting used to Janice and Simon going off, but you've got to give kids a bit of independence. Otherwise you'll lose 'em for good when they're old enough.'

'She usually hates any change in her routine,' Laura had complained. 'And now she wants to do this.'

'She's growing up, Laura. Kids change. Even a kid like Andy has to grow up. Let her go. Nothing can happen to her at Jacko's – they're all the local kids there, and you know how protective they are to Andy.'

Laura had reluctantly agreed with Sally, and André's first evening trip had gone without a hitch. After that the girl had absorbed her Wednesday evening excursions to the café into her routine.

Laura threw another log on the fire. Silver birch. It burnt up in no time. She had complained to Jeff about it, but he said they had to start on the birch now – all the fallen chestnut and oak from the great hurricane had nearly gone. She smiled to herself. Ten years ago, all trees had fallen into two categories: those that looked like Christmas trees, and those that didn't. Now she knew enough about them to know how they burned.

When the Nine o'Clock News started on BBC1, she went out and looked at the sky. The wind had dropped. She felt a few spots of rain on her face and wondered whether or not to get the car out and collect André. Jacko and Freda wouldn't mind looking after André's bike overnight. She told herself that she was being silly and went back to watch the news, trying to ignore the uncomfortably prickling sensation at the nape of her neck telling her that something was wrong.

29

André leaned her bicycle against the Pepsi Cola sign outside Jacko's Café and padlocked it. She pushed the door open and entered Jacko's and Freda's steamy, evening world, where the day's fried leftovers filled doorstep sandwiches that had to be held with two hands to stop the greasy contents slithering onto laps. During the daytime the café served high-cholesterol meals to truck-drivers working between Guildford and Chichester. Jacko's was a dump, but it was a popular dump, especially with kids who were too young or too well-known to drink in the local pubs.

There were about a dozen youngsters present this evening, including two tough-looking older youths, Dabber Young and Greaser Evans, wearing motorcyclists' black leathers and taking it in turns to play/assault a battered pinball-machine. As André came in there was a chorus of hallos and smiles from the girls she knew. The spotty boys sitting at the tables with the girls ignored her; André was considered too weird to notice. To speak to her amounted to a huge loss of street cred.

Freda's round face was lit with a warm smile by the time André reached the counter – which was dominated by a hissing, steam-wreathed, chromium-plated, gas-fired monstrosity that could brew two gallons of tea to neat tannic acid in one minute flat.

'Hallo, Andy luv. Wednesday already, is it? Don't time fly? Usual, is it?'

André nodded, but Freda had already snapped the cap off a bottle of warm Coke and inserted a straw. She scooped up the £10 note and counted out the change into André's hand. Anyone else offering a £10 note for one drink would have received a stern verballing from Freda, but not André. 'There you go, luv. Cold old night, innit?'

André nodded. She put her drink down on a vacant table near the two bikers and crossed to the juke-box. The £1 coin she dropped in the slot entitled her to six plays. She punched buttons 13 to 18, not bothering to read the labels. The previous week she had pressed buttons 7 to 12. Next week she would select 19 to 24. That was André's system. Dire Straits were exploring their Telegraph Road as she returned to her table and sat down to watch Dabber's and Greaser's efforts to wreck the pinball-machine. The two yobs pointedly ignored her. André Normanville – Yuck!

Freda jabbed Jacko in the ribs. He was built like his wife – overweight – with the addition of a permanent two-day stubble and a temper that made public health inspectors reluctant to visit his grease-encrusted, fly-blown premises. He was trying to repair a Dualit catering toaster. Having pulled the elements out, he wasn't sure how they went back. 'Wot's up?'

'Andy's here. Take a look at that coat.'

Jacko peered around the tea-maker's gleaming superstructure. The girl was sitting with her back to him. Her long leather coat nearly touched the grease-stained lino. 'What about it?'

Dabber and Greaser thought Jacko was looking at them, so they eased up on their torture of the pinball-machine.

'What do you mean, what about it? She always wears nice clothes but that coat's real leather, it is. Must've cost her mother several 'undred.'

Jacko grunted, and went back to the toaster.

'How does she do it on a teacher's money, that's what I'd like to know,' Freda demanded.

'How does this bleedin' toaster go together, that's what I'd like to know,' Jacko growled into his stubble.

A squabble broke out at a table, over ownership of a pop-magazine poster of Jason Donovan. A warning bellow from Jacko was enough to end hostilities. No one argued with Jacko.

At 8.30 p.m. André finished her Coke and bought another. She returned to her table and continued watching the flashing score-panel on the clattering pinball-machine.

'Reckon she fancies you, Dab,' murmured Greaser.

'Fuck off,' growled Dabber, not taking his eye off the steel ball while frantically working the flippers to keep it in play.

It was hot in the café, and André felt uncomfortable in the long, fur-lined coat. She had promised her mother to keep it on, but that didn't mean she couldn't unzip it. She released her

143

reflective safety-belt and tugged the coat's fastener down to the hem.

Greaser rested his leather-clad elbow on the pinball-machine's glass top and spoke to Dabber behind his hand. 'Don't look now but I think the Normanville bird is trying to tell us something.'

Dabber lost his last ball and glanced at André while pretending to check the wall clock. He took a swig from his Coke bottle to hide his surprise. 'Fuck,' he muttered, turning his gaze back to the score-panel. 'She's actually got legs. Not bad, neither.'

'And tits, and a pussy.'

Dabber took another casual glance in André's direction. The shortness of the girl's skirt, which had ridden up around her thighs, and the tightness of her sweater, bore evidence to the accuracy of Greaser's observation. 'For fuck's sake, Grease. She's a retard.'

'So? She's sixteen. Don't take brains to screw.'

Dabber couldn't think of a suitable reply. He looked at the girl out of the corner of his eye. She was not looking at them but staring at the score-panel. Even so, the way she was sitting, legs apart, skirt nearly round her neck . . . Well, it added up to one big come-on, didn't it?

'Reckon she's a virgin?' Greaser asked.

'Sure to be.'

'Fuck.'

'Yeah.'

Greaser and Dabber did things together. Both lived in the nearby Surrey village of Witley; both worked in the same warehouse in Guildford; both rode Kawasaki Z1000s; both had lost their virginity at the 1989 Reading Pop Festival to the same girl, in the same hour, in the same tent. Greaser was the more dominant, and marginally more intelligent.

'When she leaves, we leave,' he decided. 'Only we don't make it obvious. Highest score on next round goes first.'

There was a loud buzz of massed two-stroke engines arriving in the car park.

'Christ – here come the moppets,' Greaser growled.

A motley collection of local sixth-formers pushed their way into the café and crowded noisily round the counter.

André zipped up her coat, finished her drink and left.

Freda got embroiled in an argument over change. By the time she had sorted out the dispute and taken all the orders, she noticed that André had gone, and Greaser and Dabber had also vanished. That was the trouble with those big bikes; quiet as ghosts when they wanted to be – not like the noisy little fart-boxes that this load of delinquent moppets rode.

30

There was no sign of André's rear light on the long, dark stretch of main road through the forest. At first Greaser thought the girl had taken one of the numerous asphalted Forestry Commission tracks as a short cut, but then Dabber spotted the red light about two hundred yards ahead: she was riding on the track that ran alongside the road. They mounted the grass and skil-fully steered their powerful machines across the verge and onto the track. Their headlights caused the girl's reflective safety-belt to glow as they closed the gap. She must have heard and seen them, yet she maintained a steady pedalling in a straight line, looking neither left nor right. Both youths dropped into low gear and came up alongside André, flanking her; Greaser on the inside, Dabber on the outside.

'Hi!' Greaser called out, pushing up his helmet visor.

André glanced at him and carried on pedalling.

'Thought we might get to know each other a bit better,' said Greaser. 'You're André, aren't you?'

The path narrowed, causing the fairing of Dabber's bike to nudge André off course. She wobbled, tried to steady herself, and bumped against Greaser's machine. Her handlebars caught on his mirror.

'Hey!' Greaser yelled. 'Don't you scratch my bike, bitch!'

Dabber hooked in front of André, causing her front tyre to squeal on his fairing. She braked hard, and dismounted before she lost her balance. The youths stopped, and lifted the bikes onto their stands. They left their engines ticking over and their lights on. The finely balanced engines with their tuned, resonant mufflers burbled softly.

'Thought you might like to have a ride on a real bike,' said Greaser. He reached out and stroked André's hair before gathering a hank in his hand. 'And after that . . .' He broke off and smiled. 'You can give me and Dabber a ride.' She was staring at him, but without fear. Maybe that was what she wanted. Maybe she liked a bit of rough. 'What do you reckon, Dab? Sounds fair, don't it? A ride for a ride?'

Dabber grinned. Already he was getting an erection at the thought of the sport that lay ahead. 'Sounds real fair, Grease.'

Greaser let go of André's hair and pulled her coat zip-fastener down. It was a chunky zip, and slid easily. He dropped his hand to her thigh and pushed his fingers between her legs. She continued to stare at him, with cold, dispassionate eyes of a green so intense that it made him feel uncomfortable. Christ, he thought, suddenly angry with himself. A retard. What the fuck were they doing, messing about with a retard?

He jerked his hand away. At that moment André suddenly brought her knee up and connected with his balls. At the same time she thrust her bike at Dabber. Greaser let out a loud 'ooof!' and doubled-up in pain.

'Bitch! Fucking bitch!'

Dabber was too taken by surprise to make a grab at André. Greaser lunged at her, but tripped over the girl's bicycle and went sprawling. 'Get her!' he yelled, but André was already running along the track. By the time the youths had mounted their machines and swung their headlights in her direction, she had vanished.

It was Dabber who saw the entrance to the Forestry Commission tractor path as they flashed past. 'Grease!' he yelled, and slewed his Kawasaki around on the narrow strip.

Greaser saw his mate apparently disappear into the forest, and roared after him. At full throttle the Kawasaki engines had a distinct, harsh crackle. The metalled track through the dark, silent pines was less than three metres wide, designed for tractors and trailers. It was André's reflective safety-belt that betrayed her. It was a glowing come-and-get-me beacon about a hundred yards ahead of the bikers.

Greaser dropped into low gear, opened the throttle and surged ahead of Dabber. Their exhausts boomed off the trees. Then their headlights picked out the running girl, and the huge pile of cut pine-logs across the track that blocked her escape. Forestry Commission contractors had been working long hours to clear the ravages of the October 1987 hurricane and the less severe gale of the previous year.

She suddenly dashed off the track and plunged into the pines, just as Greaser was about to grab a handful of her hair. He swore, and slewed his machine after her. Dabber came up alongside him. They had to drop their speed as they swerved to avoid the densely-planted trees that loomed up in their headlights. But they were skilled riders, and this obstacle course wasn't so different from the traffic cones they had weaved effortlessly around on their driving-test. A branch Greaser didn't see until it was nearly too late chewed a chunk out of his machine's fibreglass fairing. He swore, and corrected the skid, his tyres spinning on dry pine-needles.

André slipped and fell. She scrambled to her feet and staggered on again. She was exhausted; her heart was pounding. The engines right behind her were a terrifying crackle that filled the dark forest. Every time she jumped across a drainage gully she was able to gain a couple of metres, but it was only a matter of seconds before she collapsed from exhaustion and her pursuers were upon her. Then the madly swinging headlights, stabbing clinical white light into the undergrowth ahead of her, picked out a stout chain-link fence on the far side of a deep drainage ditch. The wire-netting stood three metres high; she knew she wouldn't have the strength or time to climb it.

With her feet slipping on the muddy edge of the ditch, she turned to face her tormentors, her coat wide open, legs splattered with mud, her slim body bathed in the powerful, hellish, halogen glare from the two machines bearing down on her.

'NO!' she screamed in anguish as she lost her balance and fell backwards. 'ALL WRONG! ALL WRONG!'

147

31

The explosion shook Jacko's Café and shattered several windows. Jacko could move fast when he had to. He shot his bulk from behind his counter and was first through the door and into the car park. The explosion gave way to a continuous, echoing roll of thunder that lasted longer than any thunder Jacko had ever heard. It gradually died away to a resonant distant rumble like a receding Concorde.

But the strange glow in the sky was to the south – in the opposite direction from where the eerie rolls of thunder had sounded. Freda was right behind her husband, followed by a noisy clamour of young customers.

'Bloody hell!' Jacko breathed. 'Looks like it's over at Tanner's Plantation.'

'Gas-bottle?' a moppet suggested, hopping onto his two-stroke and stamping on the kick-start. All the kids were anxious to track down the cause of the explosion.

'That was no bottle,' said Jacko, not taking his eyes off the glow. 'That was a plane from Dunsfold or something.'

'Look, Jacko,' Freda pointed. 'What do you make of that? See it? Looks like a beam of light.'

Jacko stared upwards; a fading path of luminous gases marked a straight line across the sky, from the flickering light in the distant trees to the place where the strange thunder had died away.

'Plane's bought it,' Jacko decided grimly. 'Poor buggers.'

32

Forestry Warden Rob Jones was thinking exactly the same thing as he scrambled up the fire-watcher's tower: an aircraft, either landing at or taking off from British Aerospace's airfield at Dunsfold, had come down in Tanner's Plantation. Odd – he had an idea that Dunsfold never operated at night. And why had the noise like thunder that followed the explosion gone on for so long? Weird.

Rob had never climbed the tower in the dark before. Thankfully, he didn't need to go right up to the observation platform; once clear of the crowns of the fifteen-year conifers, he could see the impact zone. Flames were flickering among the trees about half a mile to the south, in the direction of the main road. Once they got a hold on the resinous top-growth there would be no stopping them until the entire strip of a couple of million quids-worth of spruce and pine between the wide fire-break lanes was burnt out.

But there was something about the beginnings of the fire that wasn't right. He blinked to clear his vision, but it was still there: a streak of dull light, almost like a dim searchlight beam, shining across the sky from the direction of the fire. Even as he stared, it was fading fast. He held onto a rung of the ladder with one hand, pulled his Telecom Ebony portable cellphone from his pocket, wedged it against the ladder with his chest, and called the police house at Durston village. While he was holding the handset awkwardly against his ear, listening to the ringing tone, he noticed that the strange streak of white light had vanished.

33

The shattering explosion, and the reverberating rolls of thunder that followed, flushed all the residents of Durston Wood out from in front of their televisions and into the road.

'Someone's gas-bottle, do you suppose?' Laura asked Sally Fielding. She had often worried about the large gas-bottles in her outhouse. The estate did not have a mains gas supply.

'Don't think so,' said Sally doubtfully, looking up at the sky in the direction she thought the sound had come from. The surrounding trees made it impossible to see anything. 'I remember a bottle going up on a caravan site when I was a kid. It was loud – a big bang. There weren't no thunder – nothing like that.'

Someone produced a portable radio and tuned it to 'County Sound', but there was only music.

'André will be cycling home about now,' said Laura anxiously, looking at her watch. 'I ought to go out–'

'She'll be all right,' said Sally firmly. 'What time should she be in by?'

'Nine thirty.'

'Well, that's not for a few more minutes,' said Sally practically. 'Give her thirty minutes. If she's not back by then, you go out and I'll stay by your 'phone.'

Laura's reply was interrupted by the howl of sirens hurtling along the main road. During the next ten minutes several more sirens were heard in the distance. Eventually the small crowd got bored with not knowing what was going on, and started drifting back indoors.

'Go inside and stop fretting,' Sally told Laura firmly. 'She's not due back for another five minutes, and she's probably watching the fire or whatever it is, anyway.'

Laura thanked her and went indoors in time to pick up a report on the kitchen radio of a mysterious explosion in the Durston village area on the Surrey/West Sussex border. She was about to make a cup of tea when she heard a sound outside. She opened the side-door. André was propping her bicycle against the side of the garage. Her beautiful leather coat was stained and torn, and she was splattered with mud. Her luminous green eyes blinked in the sudden light.

'Andy! My darling! What's happened?'

André disentangled herself from her mother's embrace and entered the kitchen. She went straight to the sink and poured herself a glass of water. In the fluorescent light Laura could see, to her immense relief, that her daughter was uninjured. She wanted to make a fuss, but she knew it would be futile; calmness was the best way to tackle this. She helped André out of the torn coat.

'So what happened, Andy?'

'Can't hear.'

A little gremlin of panic nudged Laura; she remembered an earlier time when she had worried about André's hearing following a loud bang. 'What do you mean, you can't hear? What happened?' Laura raised her voice. '*What happened!*'

'Came off bike.'

'Are you hurt?'

No reply.

Laura raised her voice again to repeat the question. André shook her head and sipped her glass of water, watching her mother out of the corner of her eye. She shrank against the sink unit when Laura looked closely at her – a reaction that alarmed Laura, although she was careful not to show it. Not since André was ten years old had the girl been given any reason to fear her mother; since the accident, André had been the recipient of Laura's unselfish, unswerving love. But there had been an exception. Just one occasion, when André was ten. And even that brief display of fury by Laura had been deliberately calculated so that she would never have to show it again.

The fear that André's green eyes had shown then was now back. Laura shook her head. No . . . It wasn't possible. She wrapped her arms around André and held her close. 'You heard that loud bang and thundery noise about twenty minutes ago? You must've heard it.'

André nodded.

'And all the sirens?'

André nodded again.

Laura gave a little shudder of relief. Of course. The explosion, or whatever it was, and the wailing of the fire-engine and police-car sirens had frightened her. What else could cause André to fall off her bike? She never fell off her bike. That must have shaken her up, too.

'Oh darling. You've had a bad fright and Mummy's frightened you even more by shouting at you. I'm so sorry. Please forgive me.' She held her daughter tightly until she could feel the tension in the frail young body ebbing away. Laura kissed André's forehead – and saw the singed hair-ends. In places André's fine, dark hair was shrivelled and scorched light brown. She held André away from her and noticed that her eyebrows were also partly crisped.

'Andy . . . Your hair and eyebrows are singed!'

'Singed?'

'Burnt!'

'Bonfire in garden.'

Of course. Laura remembered André causing showers of sparks that afternoon. She had stood too close to the bonfire when stoking it up. But something puzzled her. 'I never noticed that your hair and eyebrows were burnt when I brushed your hair after the shower.'

'Bonfire,' André repeated. 'Too close.'

Laura sighed. She didn't know what to think. André was always truthful. She liked to think that was because her daughter was basically an honest girl; it was easier to believe that than face the truth that André didn't have the intelligence to lie. Anyway, what did it matter? The important thing was that she was home and safe. Laura smiled, and smoothed her daughter's hair.

'Anyway – you're not going to win any beauty contests in this state. I'll run you a bath. You look as if you need a nice long soak. Come on, young lady. Let's get you out of those clothes.'

Thirty minutes later André was in bed, watching her television. The moment Laura had left the bedroom, she turned the sound right up.

I'll have a word with her in a minute about that, Laura thought as she opened the washing-machine. She added André's soiled skirt, sweater and underwear to the week's load and picked up the fur-lined leather coat. The damage didn't look so bad on close examination. The mud would clean off, and the tear was along a seam so the chances were that it could be repaired.

And then Laura noticed something that closed a cold, clammy hand around her heart. Her legs suddenly lost their strength, forcing her to sit suddenly on a kitchen chair. Her hands shook so much that she nearly dropped the coat.

Please, God, no. Tell me it's not true. I couldn't bear to have to start all over again. There's a recession on – I'd never sell this place. I love it here. We both love it. We're happy here. Please don't spoil it. Please.

But the bitter years since the accident had taught Laura the uselessness of prayers. There was no outside force she could turn to. As always, André's security depended on her and her alone, and on her readiness to do whatever had to be done, no matter how unpleasant. This was the dominant thought that gave her the strength and resolve to stand and walk along the hall to André's room, clutching the incriminating coat in her hands. She opened the door. The sound of the television rolled out to meet her.

André looked up at her mother framed in the doorway. Her eyes dropped to the coat and she knew. She pressed the mute button on the television control box. The silence was as sudden as it was shocking. Laura held the coat out without going any closer to the bed. There were tears in her eyes when she spoke.

'The fur trim is singed, Andy. You see? Burnt. Yet you didn't wear this coat in the garden this afternoon, did you?'

André's eyes went round with fear.

Laura advanced into the room and stood over the bed. This time the fury surfaced like an underwater eruption.

'*DID YOU!*'

'*Had to do it!*' André screamed. She threw back the duvet and bounced up and down on her knees, beating her pillow with her fists. '*Had to! Had to! Had to! Had to! Had to!*'

'*WHY!*'

Laura grabbed André and threw her on her back.

'*WHY!*'

'*They were going to hurt me!*' André screamed back.

'Who?'

'Two boys. From the café. Followed me.'

Laura thought she was going to faint. She turned to André's luxury vanitory dresser and picked up the mother-of-pearl hair-brush. As she did so, she knocked the framed photograph of Khalid to the floor, shattering its glass.

André gave a wail of despair. She buried her face in the pillow and sobbed piteously. Laura was stunned. It was one shock on top of another. She dropped the hairbrush and touched her daughter tenderly.

André was crying. For the first time since the accident, when she was barely more than a baby, she was actually crying.

34

AMARAH, SOUTHERN IRAQ

Amarah was a brash and cosmopolitan town, a place where the dialects of the riverine Arabs to the south were hardly spoken, and where Nuri and Khalid felt more at ease – despite the raw sewage overflowing into the gutters.

The first trader the two travellers encountered in the crowded, dirty back streets was a money-changer who exchanged $200 of Nuri's money at a rip-off rate of three dinars to the dollar. When Nuri protested, the wrinkled old Beni-Lam Arab merely shrugged and remarked that silence had a price: he had spotted the rest of the money in Nuri's wad. After that salutary lesson Nuri was more circumspect, visiting several money-changers and trading only one $100 bill at a time until he had exchanged $1000 and the money pocket in his jubbah was bulging with dinar banknotes and weighed down with fils. At least they could now go shopping without arousing suspicion.

To turn themselves from stevedores into businessmen required careful planning. Their first purchase was two medium-sized suitcases into which they transferred their belongings, including Nuri's Texan boots, which he was determined to keep. The haversacks which had served them so well were dumped in a skip – and promptly rescued by two delighted barefoot boys who scurried off down an alley with them, whooping with pleasure. A barber trimmed Nuri's unkempt hair and beard.

They found a covered courtyard where the traders made and sold a wide range of footwear, ranging from cheap sandals to traditional, beautifully-crafted, upturned shoes inlaid with jewels. Nuri haggled over sober black-leather shoes and thin cotton socks for the two of them, and paid what he considered was a reasonable price. After that, a Turkoman draper matched up a pair of lightweight business suits for his two strange customers. White shirts, each with a fashionable tie, completed their ensemble. Nuri was careful to ensure that their new clothes were not too expensive. The rest – the purchase of underclothes, toothbrushes and other toiletry items to fill out their luggage convincingly – was easy.

The two well-dressed men who eventually stepped out onto the streets of Amarah's old town hardly warranted a second glance. One was short and thickset, the other tall, with fair hair and a seemingly permanent smile. Nuri examined his reflection in the mirror outside the store with some pride. He had never owned such a suit, in fact, with the exception of army combat dress, it was the first time he had worn Western-style clothes.

They hailed a taxi which took them to the smart four-star Iris Hotel, set in pleasant gardens to the north of the city and overlooking the broad sweep of the Tigris. The taxi driver recommended it because it had its own generator and water-purification plant, but driving out to it cost them a two-dinar fuel surcharge.

The hotel receptionist was more interested in the football match on his portable television than the registration cards that Nuri filled in. The room had to be paid for in advance, but he was not surprised by the $100 bill that Nuri offered. Since Amarah was a riverside city, its people were used to handling virtually every negotiable currency in the East, and US dollars were still in wide circulation. Few Arabs permitted their hatred of America to extend to American dollars. He pushed a key across the counter without looking up from the miniature screen, and rang for a bellhop.

In cloak-and-dagger movies, new guests registering at hotels often attract the attention of sinister figures in the lobby who are invariably reading a newspaper. The man in the charcoal-grey suit sitting in one of the hotel lobby's comfortable arm-chairs did not look particularly sinister, and he was reading *Paris Match*. Nor did he normally hang about in hotel lobbies, on the look-out for strangers. Rather, he had been waiting for a colleague to show up. Nevertheless, it was bad luck for Nuri and Khalid that he happened to be in the lobby when they registered. He waited until the new guests had left for their room, and then strolled across to the desk. This time the clerk took notice, and turned off the television. It paid to treat the Mukharabat secret police with respect.

The clerk showed the man the cards for the two guests who had just registered, and promptly obeyed a request to provide photocopies. The man also examined Nuri's $100 bill with great interest. He thanked the clerk politely, returned the banknote, and strolled casually into the sunshine.

There could be nothing in it, of course, but one couldn't be too careful. On 18th August 1989 there had been a massive explosion at the missile solid-fuel manufacturing facility at Al Hillah, fifty kilometres south of Baghdad, and since then some highly sensitive research had been switched to a remote centre at Rifa. The nearest town to Rifa was Amarah. The *Observer* journalist, Farzad Bazoft, had asked questions about Rifa and Al Hillah, and had even visited the site of the explosion with a British nurse. Other foreign journalists had been to Al Hillah, too, but none of them had shown any interest in Rifa; which was why they were still alive, but Bazoft had paid for his curiosity with his life.

Since then there had been a covert tightening of security in the Amarah area. Normally, checking up on the two new guests at the Iris Hotel would be a simple matter of a routine call to Baghdad, to the Mukharabat's IBM mainframe computer; but an unlucky bomb had destroyed the computer, and now there were problems transferring the back-up tapes to the new Bull computer that had been shipped from France through Turkey. So finding out just who the two strangers were might take a bit of time.

35

SOUTHERN ENGLAND
Thursday, 7th March 1991

There was a buzz of activity at the main office of *Science UK* when Lloyd arrived for work. The previous night a large meteorite was believed to have impacted in a Forestry Commission plantation near the village of Durston on the Surrey/West Sussex border. There was a huddle of Lloyd's colleagues around a television in the main office, watching Sky News aerial shots of the devastated pines in Tanner's Plantation. It reminded Lloyd of the time when an Airbus had carved a swathe of destruction through a pine forest at a French airshow.

Gary Pepper was keen to cover the story, but Lloyd vetoed the idea. 'We'll let the tabloids have their field-day,' he decided. 'Then we'll run a proper feature when the furore has died down.'

'But there's no trace of any wreckage, Lloyd,' Gary pointed out. 'Something very odd's happened down there.'

'Nothing like as odd as the expenses you guys can run up on a half-day coverage,' said Lloyd curtly. 'We'll take the story off wire for the In Brief column. If it's still a live issue in a month, then maybe we'll run something. You're in the wrong part of Wapping if you want to be in tabloid journalism.' He turned and entered his office. He didn't slam the door – that wasn't his style – but he closed it with sufficient force to let it be known who was boss.

There was a double-deck VCR in his office. He set the machine to make a copy of the videotape Ted Prentice had lent him, and decided that he might as well watch the tape while it was being duplicated, before the normal working day got into its stride.

'Out of Their Tiny Minds' was a reasonably competent twenty-five-minute studio-bound documentary made for Channel 4 by Mindway Films – an independent production company. According to the label on the tape box, it had first been broadcast six years earlier in 1985. Ted Prentice was named as the executive producer. The talents of several remarkable savants were examined: Tommy Jefferson, a ten-year-old with a musical gift similar to the American savant, Leslie Lemke; two lightning calculators, a calendar calculator with a plus-or-minus-a-hundred-years span; and lastly a fifteen-year-old fair-haired Iraqi boy, Khalid al Karni, who could tell the time. He had to be the Iraqi time-telling savant Ted Prentice had talked about.

Lloyd replayed that segment of tape. The Iraqi boy's talent was the exact match of André's ability: he could maintain perfect synchronisation with the Speaking Clock. A younger-looking Ted Prentice confirmed that he had carried out a series of tests on Khalid over several days, during which the boy had been denied access to any form of clock. Whenever he had been asked the time, his answer was always correct to the second. For the purpose of the documentary, his parents had agreed to his being kept in a windowless room for twenty-four hours, watching endless Tom and Jerry cartoons, which he loved, on a closed-circuit television. Every two hours Khalid had been asked the time, and each time his answer had been correct.

The programme's closing credits rolled. The picture on the office television flickered and changed to one of a nervous-looking boy sitting in a chair. A clapperboard identifying the child and his special skill was snapped shut in front of the camera.

Lloyd wanted to keep watching, to see the out-takes Ted Prentice had mentioned, but thirty minutes was as big a bite out of Lloyd's day as *Science UK* could spare. Towards the end of the programme, letters were dropping out of the fax machine, Della was darting in and out with papers that demanded his attention, and staff were tapping cautiously on his door and creeping away again when they saw that their boss was occupied. Lloyd cursed the pressures on him. It was frustrating, not being able to concentrate on the subject that was now dominating his mind. He switched the television off, leaving the double-deck VCR to hum softly to itself as it continued its task of duplicating Dr Prentice's tape.

36

AMARAH, SOUTHERN IRAQ

Once Khalid had shown Nuri how everything in the hotel room worked, the older man decided that America probably wasn't the great world pestilence that the newspapers and television would have him believe. Any country that could invent the pulsating shower-head and the single-lever hot-cold mixer tap couldn't possibly be all that bad.

Nuri rose at 6 a.m., had a shower, and went back to bed. He bounced out of bed three hours later, while Khalid was still sound asleep, had another shower, and dived back between the sheets. They were satin; he had never known such luxury and he revelled in it. Going to bed made him look forward to having a shower, and having a shower made him look forward to going to bed. A keying error with the television remote-control brought in the CNN Middle East news feed at full volume, and woke Khalid.

'Sorry,' said Nuri cheerfully as a mop of fair hair emerged sleepily from under a sheet. 'Just playing with the room. You may be used to this sort of living, but I'm not. But with practice, I think I could get used to it.' With that, he slid out of bed and had another shower. He emerged fifteen minutes later, having covered himself in every lotion and shampoo he could find.

'You smell like my mother,' Khalid remarked, smiling.

'Whether that's an insult or a compliment depends on your mother, I suppose,' Nuri remarked, critically examining his newly neat beard in the mirror.

'She's a very lovely lady.'

Nuri looked sharply at his companion in the mirror and saw a fleeting look of pain. It was unusual for the young man to show any emotion other than his usual good-humour, and he rarely mentioned his family. 'Maybe your good luck runs in your family, Khalid.'

'I don't think so. Nuri . . .' he hesitated, and then blurted out: 'Nuri – will we be going near Baghdad?'

'We'll be going around Baghdad,' Nuri corrected. 'Nidel said that Baghdad would be too dangerous for us.'

'My parents live in Baghdad. I would like to visit them.'

The older man was surprised. 'But I thought they lived in Kurdistan?'

'In the summer – yes. We have a lovely lodge on the lake near Duhok. But now they are in Baghdad. They have a house at Mansour.'

Nuri remained silent. Although he had never been to Baghdad, he had heard of Mansour. It was the pleasant garden suburb near the racecourse, where the wealthy of Baghdad lived; where the Mercedes and the swimming-pools vied with each other for numerical supremacy, and where Saddam Hussein's loyal Tikritis bought plots of land at favourable prices. But making a detour to Mansour was out of the question. His plans for getting to Kurdistan were deliberately vague because advance planning was impossible, one had to deal with circumstances as they arose; but it would be suicidal for two Kurdish conscript deserters to venture into Baghdad, no matter how good their disguise and false papers.

He was about to veto the idea out of hand; but then he thought about the lengths he would go to if he had a family, and he changed his mind. He put his arm around Khalid's shoulders and gave the young man an affectionate hug. 'Are the bedrooms at home like this?'

'Much better.'

'Then we'll go to Baghdad.'

The happiness in Khalid's eyes made the appalling risk they would be taking almost worthwhile.

They had a late breakfast in the hotel's dining-room. Khalid showed Nuri how to negotiate the obstacle course of the buffet: how to use the automatic toaster and how to obtain coffee from the dispenser. Afterwards Nuri questioned one of the waiting taxi drivers in the hotel's forecourt and rewarded him with ten dinar for his information. He returned to the lobby, where Khalid was waiting.

'The best thing is for us to buy a second-hand car,' Nuri announced. 'They're going cheap now, because most people are trading them for pick-ups so that they can drive out to the farms to buy food direct. There's no gasoline rationing now, though there are shortages which amount to much the same thing. But apparently most dealers will sell a car with a full tank and throw in a couple of cans of gas.'

Khalid's eyes lit up. 'You will let me drive, Nuri?' he asked eagerly.

Nuri laughed and clapped his comrade on the shoulder. 'I wouldn't try to stop you.'

They checked out of the hotel. The helpful taxi driver dropped them at a used car lot, where Nuri parted with $750 for a ten-year-old Escort that looked clean and well-maintained, and

had sound tyres. Fifteen minutes after completing the trans-
action they were driving in bright sunshine along the fast highway that skirted the east bank of the Tigris. The only sign of
the recent war they saw was a narrow bridge for light traffic,
dropped into the river by a single bomb that had probably cost
more than the bridge. Barges were not available to form a
pontoon bridge for such an unimportant crossing-point, so a
number of enterprising boat owners had pooled their resources
and built a crude boat-bridge with lashed planks, and were
charging car drivers a five-dinar toll.

Khalid drove at a steady 100 k.p.h. through the flat,
uninteresting but fertile countryside, and would have driven
faster if Nuri had not warned him to conserve fuel. Not that
petrol was likely to be a problem, because they passed several
filling-stations doing brisk business, but the car dealer had
warned them that the main highway got priority deliveries and
that the patchy supply situation was worse further north. Khalid
made up for the gaping hole in the dashboard where the radio
had been by singing out of tune in English at the top of his
voice. Nuri decided that whereas he might get used to Khalid's
singing, he would never get used to his overtaking. Several
times he found himself working phantom pedals while Khalid
hurled the car through gaps that turned out to be only just wide
enough to squeeze through. It had been the same with the
T–55: the young man had an unnerving ability to judge time,
movement and distance with total accuracy.

'*Please*, Khalid,' Nuri begged after a hair-raising duel with a
twenty-wheeler that Khalid won, earning himself first prize of
a sustained, angry blast on the truck driver's horn. 'The last
thing we want is a ticket for dangerous driving.'

'Trying to get rid of Peugeot,' said Khalid simply, grinning
inanely.

'We're not in a race.'

'Following us since we left the hotel. Driver was in the lobby
yesterday and this morning.'

'What!' Nuri craned around and saw a blue saloon about half
a kilometre behind them. It had just overtaken the truck but
was maintaining its distance. 'The blue 408?'

'Same man,' said Khalid, still grinning. 'He was in lobby twice. He followed us to the car dealer's lot and he is still following us.'

For the first time the young man's mental disability aroused anger in Nuri. 'You crazy idiot! Why didn't you say!'

'No need. He doesn't have my good luck.'

Before Nuri had a chance to answer, he had to brace himself as Khalid suddenly forked off the highway onto a narrow unmade farm track that cut due east across a field bright-green with early maize.

'It didn't work,' Nuri growled when he saw the Peugeot following them. He was now very worried. If Khalid was right about the driver having been in the hotel lobby, there was little doubt that he was a Mukharabat agent.

The road rose gently on a ridge and dipped down on the far side into a depression, so that the deserted field was out of sight from the highway. Khalid accelerated hard and executed a neat handbrake turn on the far slope, so that he could see back along the track through his side-window – which he quickly wound down when the Peugeot appeared over the ridge. It stopped some three hundred metres from the Escort. For seconds nothing happened. Then the driver stepped out of his car and stood regarding them. The AK-74 assault rifle he was holding did not go well with his charcoal-grey business suit, but Nuri considered it unlikely that fashion aesthetics preyed on the man's mind.

The Peugeot driver beckoned to the Escort. When that didn't produce the desired result, he started walking slowly towards the car. From the way he was holding the rifle it was obvious that he knew how to use it. Also, it was the very latest 5.45 mm. model with the improved muzzle brake that damped all recoil muzzle-climb, enabling even a mediocre marksman to deliver bursts of automatic fire with deadly accuracy. If he got much closer he would be able to riddle the Escort and its occupants with ease.

'Okay! Now go!' Nuri snapped, thinking that Khalid had stopped as a clever ruse to gain time. If they took off now it would cost the man several seconds to race back to his car. But

Khalid continued to stare at the man. 'Get going!' Nuri yelled, his voice now a scream of fear. 'Don't let him get any closer!'

The man suddenly ran forward, dropped to one knee and raised the automatic weapon. Despite the bright light and the distance, Nuri saw a muzzle-flash. Roundly cursing Khalid for his monumental stupidity, he threw himself out of the Escort and rolled away, at the same time twisting his body at ninety degrees to the car to reduce the target area he presented to the gunman.

37

SOUTHERN ENGLAND

Instead of joining the lunchtime exodus to the pub, Lloyd remained in his office to watch the copy of Prentice's videotape that he had made. As always, the double-deck Panasonic VCR produced a copy that was indistinguishable from the original. He found the beginning of the auditions and used the remote-control to picture-search through them until he spotted the fair-haired Iraqi boy. The scene showed the teenager in a group of over-excited children milling noisily around a large room. Lloyd paused the action and checked the hastily scribbled notes he had made after his meeting with Prentice. The venue used for the programme was the London Weekend Television rehearsal room on Waterloo Station.

He punched the remote control. The tape resumed. A wide-angle shot showed parents seated around the edge of the room, chatting in small groups and sipping from plastic cups while their children indulged in some good-natured brawling and running around. Several of the kids appeared to be blind. A clapper-board marked the next shot, which was of the fair-haired Iraqi boy sitting uneasily in the interview chair.

A studio manager yelled for silence. Once he had achieved it, there was a delay while distant PA speakers announced a platform change for the departure of a Portsmouth train.

Ted Prentice was out of shot but his voice was recognisable. 'Mummy says you can tell the time, Khalid. Is that right?'

The teenage boy stared straight into the camera lens and nodded. 'You say now, and I say what the time was when you say now.'

'Okay, Khalid. Are you ready?'

The boy nodded nervously.

'What is the time . . . *now?*'

'One-one-five-six and ten seconds.'

'Eleven fifty-six and ten seconds – that's excellent, Khalid. Spot on. Okay – go back to your mother and the studio manager will be talking to you.'

Lloyd fast-forwarded the tape. He was looking for the incident where Khalid turned the tennis ball inside out. Prentice had assured him that it was definitely on the tape. He found it near the end.

The fair-haired youth was holding a tennis ball and looking uncertainly off-camera. Children were shouting and shrieking in the background, pushing and shoving to get into shot and ignoring a harassed-looking studio manager.

'The camera's recording now, Khalid,' said Prentice, making little effort to conceal the note of excitement in his voice. 'I want you to do what you did just now, but first hold the ball out to the camera.'

The youth clumsily thrust a tennis ball at the lens. When the focus sharpened, there was no doubt that it was an ordinary tennis ball.

'When I count to three I want you to throw the ball at the wall. Do you understand?'

Khalid nodded anxiously. An unseen woman spoke to him in Kurdish and he relaxed. The shot loosened to wide-angle.

'One . . . Two . . . Three . . . !'

The Iraqi boy threw the ball hard at the wall. It rebounded at an angle off a radiator. A girl with long dark hair leapt to catch it.

Her sudden appearance caused Lloyd to snatch up the remote control and freeze the picture. The four-head VCR did its job well. Despite the speed of the action across the frame, the image on the television screen was sharp and clear, with no picture 'bounce'. He had frozen the tape at the moment when the girl's

164

fingers were about to close around the ball. He pressed the advance button and allowed the action to continue frame by frame, as a procession of still pictures. She was six years younger – a gawky ten-year-old – but there was no mistaking that lovely black hair swirling around her shoulders. Or those vivid green eyes.

He had found André.

38

SOUTHERN IRAQ

Nuri tried to burrow his entire body into the soft ground to avoid the inevitable burst of fire from the Mukharabat agent's AK-74, but it never came.

He heard a second shot zing over his head, which was followed by a tremendous crack and a deafening roll of thunder that took several seconds to die away. He raised his head and peered under the Escort in the direction of the agent's Peugeot, but the rise of the ground obscured his view. The Escort's passenger door was open from the moment when he had thrown himself out of the car.

Convinced that Khalid was dead, Nuri crawled towards the front wheel and peered cautiously around the bumper in the direction of the Peugeot. There was no sign of the gunman. He quickly scanned the hectares of maize, but the crop was too short to provide effective cover for Khalid unless he had found a hollow. Perhaps at this moment the unseen gunman had Nuri in his sights, and was about to open fire. He cried out 'Don't shoot!' and stood with his hands high above his head.

Nothing happened. He wheeled fearfully around, his eyes darting everywhere, expecting to see the Mukharabat agent rise out of the field, covering him with the AK-74. But all he saw was Khalid grinning at him through the windscreen. The young Kurd climbed out of the driver's seat and pointed to the Peugeot.

'What happened?' Nuri spluttered in bewilderment, still frantically scanning the field. The wind and clouds created dappled,

165

eye-deceiving patterns on the billowing corn. Each sudden change of colour and texture had Nuri jumping.

'Gone,' said Khalid with a casual shrug.

'What?'

'He ran into my good luck.'

Nuri stared at Khalid. 'Good luck? What are you talking about? It sounded like a bomb!'

'And thunder.'

Nuri gave up trying to make sense of what his companion was saying and walked towards the Peugeot. There was no sign of the agent, but he did find a fragment of his AK–74's magazine. The remains of the plastic case were partially melted, as if it had been chopped in half with a blunt, red-hot axe.

'A booby-trapped rifle!' he exclaimed, showing the piece of heat-distorted plastic to Khalid. 'I've heard of them. The magazine is a dummy packed with explosives.' He looked sharply at Khalid. 'I should never have thought it possible, but your crazy luck seems to be holding. If he is Mukharabat, it looks as if they've been infiltrated.' Nuri broke off and glanced around, frowning. 'But where is he?'

'Big bang,' said Khalid. He suddenly became serious. 'Nuri – you must listen to me.'

The uncharacteristic tone caused Nuri to look at his companion in surprise. For once Khalid wasn't smiling.

'Okay. I'm listening.'

The young man stared at the spot where the gunman had disappeared. He had a struggle finding the right words. 'I always have good good luck.'

'I'll go along with that.'

'But it is more than that. In future you must stay close to me when there is danger.'

'I would never abandon you, Khalid. You know that.'

'That is not what I mean . . . You jumped out of the car.'

The comment angered the older man. 'Of course I jumped out! I didn't want to be shot at like a sitting duck!'

The stress of trying to communicate clearly made Khalid ball his fists against his temples. 'I am not saying it right. If Abbi hadn't left our tank he would still be alive.'

Nuri remembered the moment when their officer was cut to shreds by the American aircraft. 'You mean, when he tried to get some fuel?'

'Yes. I tried to make him stay but he took no notice. Nuri – my good luck is more than good luck.'

Nuri wanted to get away from the area as soon as possible, before a curious farm worker came along. He turned away, but Khalid suddenly gripped his arm with astonishing strength. Nuri had never seen his normally unemotional comrade looking so upset.

'Please, Nuri. If there is danger again, you must stay near me.'

The usual blank stare of what Nuri had always assumed was the window on a crippled mind, was gone. Behind the imploring eyes the older man sensed that there was another Khalid, desperately seeking a way of compensating for his inadequate communication skills.

'You must always stay near me.'

Nuri shrugged. 'Very well, Khalid.'

'Promise!'

It was turning into a children's game. The best thing would be to humour him. 'Okay. I promise.'

Khalid released his grip on Nuri's arm. The blank smile returned, and he nodded happily.

Nuri resumed searching the area. He expected to find bits of the agent scattered everywhere, but there was nothing. Not so much as a button. He knew that modern explosives such as Semtex B had incredible detonation velocities, but he would never have believed that any explosive in the quantity that could be packed into a rifle magazine could atomise a grown man. But the evidence, or rather, the lack of it, was proof that it could and did.

He checked the Peugeot, and was relieved to discover that it was not equipped with a two-way radio. The chances were that no one knew where the agent was. Nor was there anything in the vehicle to identify the driver; no personal possessions or papers. That alone indicated that he had probably been a Mukharabat agent. The Peugeot's keys were in the ignition so Nuri locked the doors and threw the keys in an irrigation gully. That ought to delay matters when the car was found. The agent's colleagues would think that he had locked up and left the car for a reason.

'Come on,' he snapped. 'Let's get out of here.'

This time Nuri didn't complain about Khalid's fast driving. Only when they had put a hundred kilometres between themselves and the scene of the agent's mysterious disappearance did the older man begin to relax.

39

SOUTHERN ENGLAND

The trouble was, thought Detective-Sergeant Grahame 'Yorkie' Barr, that everyone was bomb-happy these days. He hauled on his left foot. The mud glugged obscenely on his green wellie, and the effort caused his right foot to sink even deeper into the disgusting mire. A blast in the Surrey woods (why couldn't it have been a few hundred metres to the south, in West Sussex?) had everyone leaping about yelling, 'Bomb cache!' The army training course he had been on told Yorkie that this hadn't been a bomb or even a cache of explosives. Bombs blew holes in the ground; bombs scattered debris over a huge area; bombs stripped branches from trees, leaving bare trunks. Bombs did all sorts of nasty things. What they did not do was flatten trees so that they fell *towards* the centre of the explosion. Nor did they create long swathes of destruction like a crashing bomber.

Another thing: bombs didn't start fires, at least, not out in the open. The blackened, fallen pines all around him were evidence of fire, as was the mud that he was now sinking into. The Forestry Commission had panicked, and summoned every fire appliance in two counties to saturate the area with umpteen million litres of water so that the entire bloody site was now a quagmire. Fat chance of finding any clues in this mess if it had been a bomb.

He struggled to the beginning of the avenue of damage (or was it the end?), near a steep drop with a high chain-link fence at the foot of the slope, and looked back towards the track where his car was parked behind the ancient Land Rover belonging to the Forestry Commission warden. He lifted his camcorder to his eye and rolled some more videotape. The gash through the pines was about fifty metres wide and at least two hundred metres long. His PMR radio squawked his call-sign. It was Surrey Constabulary HQ at Mount Browne, wanting to know if he was committed.

'Answer, no,' said Yorkie wearily.

'You'll be pleased to know that the Home Office and the army have confirmed your finding. Over.'

The army bomb disposal team and the Home Office experts had combed Tanner's Plantation last night, and later surveyed the scene at daybreak from a helicopter. Since then there had been helicopters buzzing around all morning like wasps investigating a jam trap.

'I'm overwhelmed,' Yorkie replied.

'We're ordering a stand-down. Can you RV with a Professor Gordon Walters from London University? He's heading now. Should be with you in two-zero. Over.'

Yorkie agreed to await the arrival of the professor. He trudged through the mud to his car. Rob Jones, the Forestry Commission warden, climbed out of his Land Rover to meet him. 'You've just missed an attention drawn on your main-scheme.'

'I daresay it'll catch up with me,' Yorkie commented sourly, dumping the camcorder on the passenger seat of his Escort and yanking off his boots. 'One day, Rob, someone less understanding and less loveable than me will nick you for listening to police transmissions.'

'Something about a couple of bikers from Witley missing. They didn't return home last night. Last seen in Jacko's dump. Probably dead with food-poisoning in a ditch somewhere.'

'I don't suppose I'd bother to go home if I lived in Witley,' Yorkie remarked. 'There's a bod from London University on his way. Maybe he'll tell us what caused all this.'

40

CENTRAL IRAQ

Nuri swore softly under his breath when he saw the army checkpoint ahead. All vehicles heading north were being waved onto a coned-off shoulder on a section of dual carriageway. The proceedings were watched over by the Republican Guards' favourite toy for intimidating the civilian populace: a 12.7 mm. heavy machine-gun mounted on a Toyota pick-up truck. Luckily, cars were dealt with briskly by the soldiers in their search for arms. A quick check on the underside with mirrors, a search in the boot, the spaces under the seats and the engine compartment, and Nuri's and Khalid's Escort was on its way.

The reason for the soldiers' vigilance became apparent a few kilometres further on, where the road skirted the smoking ruins of a Shiite village that appeared to be surrounded by Republican Guard artillery. Blood-soaked bundles were being dumped unceremoniously into ambulances. There was even a woman's leg lying ignored by a children's crossing sign. For once Khalid was not smiling. The two men drove on in silence.

It was mid-afternoon when they reached Kut at the confluence of the Tigris and the Shatt-al-Hai. The journey had passed without further incident. According to the proud sign beneath the inevitable photograph of Saddam Hussein in the Elf garage shop where Nuri had to pay nearly double the official rate for a tankful of petrol, the filling-station was built on the site of the massive defeat the British Army suffered at the hands of the Turks in 1916 with a loss of twenty-one thousand men.

The two fugitives cleaned up their suits as best they could in the filling-station's modern toilets. Luckily the ground in the maize field had been reasonably dry, so the suits still looked smart. Nuri purchased a simple road map from the attendant – all proper maps had been withdrawn at the beginning of the Iran–Iraq war – and they decided that rather than enter the ancient city of Kut, they would take the ring road and stop at a Wimpy bar for a meal and a chance to study the map. They were within one hundred and twenty kilometres of Baghdad.

The highway continued to follow the Tigris, but from here on across the fertile flood-plain it took a more direct route and no longer hugged the east bank of the meandering river.

'We've got to enter the city about six, when the evening rush is on,' Nuri reasoned with his mouth full of king-size hamburger. 'That's when there's less chance of roadblocks. Do you know the way to your parents' place once we get there?'

'I'll find it,' Khalid promised, mopping up his maple syrup pancake and smiling happily. Soon he would be reunited with his beloved mother and father. There was a radio blaring behind the counter, and a government official was denouncing Kurds as the enemy within and declaring that new restrictions on their activities would be announced soon.

Nuri finished his hamburger and regarded his companion thoughtfully. 'You love your parents, don't you, Khalid?'

The young man nodded. 'Very much.'

The spokesman on the radio was now almost ranting. Nuri glanced around the restaurant. The customers were well-dressed and affluent; the chances were that there would be a sprinkling of Tikritis among them. There was even a family party at the centre table, celebrating a child's birthday with doughnuts and milkshakes. Across the road on some waste ground, several peasant women shrouded in black abayahs had set up simple stalls and were selling their household possessions to raise money for food. Nuri leaned across the table and lowered his voice.

'Will you want to stay with them?'

'Of course.' The young man was surprised at the question.

'You realise that we're deserters?'

Khalid's grin broadened. 'Lucky deserters.'

'So far – yes. But do you know what could happen to your family if they're caught sheltering a deserter? Even if he is their son?'

'My father is a rich man. He has many friends.'

'Your father is a *Kurd*! Right now he has no friends. Use your ears and listen!'

'Listen to what?'

'The radio!'

171

Khalid listened for a few moments, but the diatribe did little to undermine his fixed smile or his simple confidence.

Nuri resisted an urge to shake some sense into him. He stood abruptly, angry with his companion, angry with the other customers, the peasant women across the road, the glitzy Americanism of the restaurant – everything. 'Come on,' he said curtly. 'We'd better get moving.'

They drove on through the late afternoon. The traffic became heavier as the main highway picked up more and more vehicles from the increasing number of feeder-roads. The army checkpoints were becoming more selective about the vehicles they searched. Several times the Escort was waved on without having to stop, which led Nuri to suppose that their car number had been radioed ahead by the first roadblock they had stopped at. They passed the devastated Salman Pak industrial zone that straddled the highway – the worst results of allied bombing that they had seen so far. The highway widened to two lanes and then three.

There was an hour's daylight left when they joined the Dora Expressway and drove past the two huge hoardings of Saddam Hussein that marked the city limits to the south. But it wasn't the giant pictures of the tyrant that aroused a mixture of bitter hatred and icy fear in Nuri's Kurdish heart: it was the name of the city itself, emblazoned on a giant illuminated sign in Arabic script and Roman lettering.

This was the city that, with British help, had for generations orchestrated a policy of brutal repression against Nuri's people. From this city orders were given for light trainer aircraft to drop canisters of mustard gas on his home town of Halabja in 1988, killing five thousand souls, including his beloved sisters. This was the fabled capital of Mesopotamia which in the seventh century AD had possessed over two thousand public libraries, and whose scientists had mapped the heavens and invented algebra. This was the city where Scheherazade had spun the erotic fantasies of *One Thousand and One Nights*. This was the city whose golden spires, minarets, domes and magnificent gardens were among the wonders of the world. Once its name had been synonymous with enlightenment and learning. Now it was a name that conjured hatred and fear.

Baghdad.

41

SAUDI ARABIA

The HEAT round fired by the Challenger smashed into the T-55. The report of the explosion reached the observers just as the spinning turret reached the top of its arc, and fell amid a cloud of dust some twenty metres from the tank, which had burst into flames at the moment of impact.

Captain Jack Roper, sitting half out of the Challenger's commander's hatch, folded his arms and watched the burning tank with some satisfaction. 'I think, gentlemen,' he commented to the three civilian observers who were watching the T-55 through binoculars, 'that we can now say that honour is satisfied.'

The test had taken place a few kilometres outside Dahrain, where the 7th Armoured Brigade's tanks and equipment would soon be loaded into freighters for shipping back to Germany. An army tank-transporter had been used to bring the intact Iraqi tank from Kuwait before the US 1st Armoured grabbed it for their museum.

Corporal Alan Dearborn, sitting in the Challenger's driver's seat, had mixed feelings as he watched the plume of black smoke rising from the T-55. A fire appliance had moved in and was smothering the flames with foam. That they had hit the tank now, didn't explain why they had been unable to destroy it during the hundred-hours ground war. Nothing made sense.

Leo Buller lowered Max's binoculars. His gaunt, angular frame seemed to have acquired even more of a dejected stoop. The flames, the rising column of smoke, were the last things he had wanted to see. They meant that the strange chain of events surrounding the T-55's apparent earlier invulnerability could have only one explanation – an explanation he could not bring himself to believe in.

Jonah van Elkmann had been crazy, hadn't he? He had

believed that the human brain had telekinetic powers – which explained the spoon-bending talents of people like Uri Geller. But van Elkmann's ideas made a mockery of modern logical theories on the functions of the human brain – theories that Leo himself had contributed to. How could he come to terms with the possibility that he had been wrong all his life? It was like the Pope being confronted with irrefutable evidence that Christ had never existed. In Leo's case, the irrefutable evidence was an inside-out tennis ball in the hotel's safe back in Riyadh. His last hope was that the tennis ball was a fake – but something told him it was genuine.

'Thank you for your co-operation, captain,' said Max.

The tank commander looked down at the always smiling dapper little scientist, and wondered how he managed to look so smart compared with his two companions. He nodded. 'My pleasure, Mr Shannon. Er . . . Mr Ramsay – a word, please.'

The civil servant looked questioningly at the army officer, who jerked his thumb at the armoured pod on the Challenger's mast, which contained the Virtual World miniature television cameras.

'If and when you and your procurement colleagues at MOD do decide to order the Challenger II from Vickers, I'm going to recommend very strongly that Mr Shannon's and Mr Buller's Virtual World visor is fitted as standard equipment. Along with the GPS navigation system, it's a war-winner.'

'Your comments will be taken seriously, captain,' said Stephen Ramsay frostily.

The officer grunted, and spoke into his headset microphone. 'Driver.'

'Sir?'

'Have we got enough fuel to drive home to Germany?'

'Don't think so, sir.'

'Okay – it'll have to be Dahrain.' He raised his hand to Ramsay, Max and Leo. 'Good day to you, gentlemen.'

The Challenger's diesel roared. The main battle tank wheeled noisily on its tracks and headed back towards the road, towing a cloud of dust.

The three civilians climbed into the Nissan and were driven

across the scrubland to the T-55. Once the foam had been hosed off, they spent some minutes examining the wreck. Max left Ramsay peering into the gutted interior and wandered across to Leo, who was staring forlornly down at the turret. It was lying the right way up. The tall man didn't look round as Max's slight shadow fell across the turret.

'Penny for them, Leo.'

Leo didn't answer immediately. He touched the reversed swastika, as though hoping the magic powers the ancients credited it with would somehow surge through his fingertips, providing instant enlightenment. He straightened, and shook his head. 'I don't know, Max. I've gone over everything a hundred times in my mind, and nothing makes sense. But there is something . . .'

Max propped his briefcase against the turret. He knew Leo well enough to know when not to press him, and sensed that he was wrestling with something he was having difficulty accepting.

'Have you ever heard of the term telearrestáre?' Leo asked at length.

'No.'

'No – of course not. It's crazy. I don't even know why the thought crossed my mind.'

'So tell me what telearrestáre means.'

'A telearrestáre is a manipulative savant.'

'A what?'

'Twenty years ago a neural researcher published a crazy paper on an autistic boy who the researcher believed could stop matter.'

'You mean, move matter? Like poltergeists? Telekinesis?'

'Something a lot more profound than that, Max.'

Max sat on the turret and indicated that Leo should do the same. The two men sat in the hot sun, watching Ramsay taking photographs of the smoking T-55.

'What was this guy's name?' Max asked.

'Jonah van Elkmann. He died about five years ago, and his loony theories died with him. Elkmann said that the present universe was in an unnatural state. He accepted that the universe was expanding from a singularity; it was self-evident, he said,

175

that all the matter in the universe was formed from such a singularity or body before the Big Bang.'

'Good for him,' Max remarked drily.

'But he said that the escape velocity of such a primeval mass would be far higher than the speed of light, which meant that the Big Bang which started the expansion of the universe was an unnatural event. In other words, our entire existence is supernatural – abnormal, and "normal" is for all particles of matter to exist as a super-massive body, at rest, at the centre of the universe.'

'He had a point,' Max admitted. 'The escape velocity of black holes is greater than the speed of light, which is why we can never see them, because they can't reflect light. Which is also why nothing can ever leave them.'

'And all the black holes, and all the billions of galaxies, and all the billions and billions of stars in those galaxies, all started from one super mega-mass. And *that* is the natural state of the universe. The Big Bang could not have happened.'

'And yet it did happen. Otherwise you and I wouldn't be sitting here on this damned turret. Right?'

'Right,' Leo agreed unhappily. 'Van Elkmann stood all thinking about manipulative savants on its head. He said that they restored normality – that what they were doing was restoring matter back to the beginning of time, and therefore back to the moment of the Creation.'

Max broke the silence that followed. 'I take it your feelings about this van Elkmann are similar to the feelings that Egon Ronay probably has about McDonald's and Burger King?'

The tall man gave a reluctant smile and nodded.

'And yet the world is full of McDonald'ses and Burger Kings and their eager customers.' Max made a pattern in the sand with his foot while he marshalled his thoughts. 'Van Elkmann was right in some respects. Mathematically speaking, the natural state of the universe is a super-massive black hole in the form of a perfect sphere due to massive gravitational collapse. The Big Bang should have been a perfectly even explosion that gave rise to a perfectly uniform universe, with billions of equally spaced galaxies containing billions of stars all the same size and all at the same stage of development. The universe *ought* to look the same, no matter which direction we look. But it doesn't. There was a tiny unevenness at the moment of the Big Bang that has been amplified ever since the beginning of time to create the chaos in the universe that we have today. We've explained it with the uncertainty principle. The uncertainty principle tells us why everything is different; we've built it into the laws of physics.' He smiled. 'And the end result is two totally baffled blokes who look different from each other, and who think differently from each other, sitting on a tank turret in the middle of a desert.'

'And wondering what to do next,' Leo added.

'Wrong. I know what we must do next.'

Leo met his partner's cold grey eyes. 'And what must we do, Max?'

'I should have thought the answer to that was obvious. You've already proved with your neural-mapping techniques that it's possible to build artificial neural networks which duplicate the cognitive functions of the brain, and those of sight, movement, colour, co-ordination, recognition. Now we have a function to work on that will be worth billions if we succeed . . . And we will succeed, Leo.'

'You're crazy.'

Max smiled. An easy smile. 'Your exact words when I proposed integrating your profile-recognition network into a single microprocessor. Our target-recognition patents are now our most profitable.'

'For heaven's sake, Max. We use porpoises to neural-map those brain functions that they have in common with humans. I've never carried out the technique on a human being because it's dangerous. And besides, to SPECT neural-map a manipulative savant we'd have to find one.'

Max opened his briefcase and took out the inside-out tennis ball. He had bought it from the Iraqi POW for six hundred cigarettes. The two men stared at it in silence for some moments.

'There's Khalid al Karni who did this,' Max observed.

Leo snorted. 'Chances are he's dead now.'

'True,' Max agreed. 'But there is also the mysterious Andy.

177

But according to our talkative POW, Khalid's parents had a home in England until January. I've already tried London directory inquiries, and there's an al Karni who's an ex-directory subscriber. That alone tells me that they were living in the London area, so it shouldn't be too difficult to trace where. And from that we can find their contacts, circle of friends and so on.'

'Maybe,' said Leo. 'But there's one thing we've got to get straight here and now, Max. There's no way I'm going to use my SPECT neural-mapping technique on humans in its present state. It's too dangerous.'

Max smiled blandly and stood up. Leo could be manipulated when the time came – but not now. 'Our work's finished here,' he said. 'So we might as well go home. Can't say I'll be sorry.'

'I'll second that,' Leo remarked.

Max frowned. 'What puzzles me, Leo, is the sound of thunder that the Challenger crew heard when their shells failed. The Warthog pilot also heard thunder when his missiles failed. And that Iraqi POW said Khalid could make thunder. It's a common thread, but what, I wonder, does thunder have to do with the control of matter?'

Max sensed Leo's sudden tension. The tall man was staring across the scrubland.

'Something the matter, Leo?'

'Nothing.'

'I think you ought to tell me.'

Leo looked up at Max and saw beyond the easy smile to the ice beneath. 'It's not important.'

'I think it is.'

Leo knew the uselessness of trying to conceal anything from Max. He would keep returning to the subject again and again with that infuriating smile of his, until he extracted what he wanted to know. 'It's something I've just remembered. A woman kept writing to me some years ago from England, about her daughter. Acquired savantism as the result of a head injury. She claimed that her daughter could make thunder.'

'Interesting,' Max observed casually after a pause.

'This was when I was in America. She had read an article

about me or something, and thought I would be able to help her daughter. Her claims were so stupid that I ignored them.'

'But you kept the letters, of course?'

'You've seen some of the letters I get from crackpots. I usually bin them.'

Max smiled again – that infuriating, supercilious smile that meant he was keeping his anger on a tight leash. When he spoke, his tone was mild, almost dismissive. As though the matter was of no consequence. 'Well, let us hope that you did not do so in this case, Leo.'

42

SOUTHERN ENGLAND

'A meteorite!' declared Professor Gordon Walters, standing in the middle of the devastation in Tanner's Plantation, oblivious of the mud splattered on his jeans. He raised his Canon to his eye and took more pictures of the snapped and scattered pines. 'The telly pundits are right for once.' Enthusiasm radiated from him like radioactivity from a reactor meltdown.

Yorkie grunted. By his lights, university professors were ancient, stooped old men who wore shabby cardigans and had a beautiful daughter in tow. They did not wear jeans and Garfield T-shirts and talk like Prince Charles. 'In that case,' he said, 'shouldn't there be a crater?'

'Ah. Good point.'

Yorkie considered his point was more than good; it was bloody excellent. But then he wasn't the one wearing the Garfield T-shirt.

'But none of the seismic labs in the South of England have reported any abnormal shocks,' the professor added, frowning.

The two men squelched through the mud to the steep ridge where the damage ended.

'What it looks like is a total atmospheric burn-out immediately before impact,' said the professor, stooping and squeezing a handful of mud through his fingers. 'Most meteorites are pebble-sized. Thousands of them hit the earth's atmosphere at around fifty kilometres per second every day and are burnt up long before they reach the ground. I would put this one in the category of a small asteroid. Maybe as big as twenty metres across when it hit the atmosphere.'

'Like the one that clobbered Siberia around the turn of the century?' Yorkie asked. He was a fan of BBC2's 'Horizon' programmes.

The young man dug a stick into the ooze. 'The Tunguska impact was probably a comet nucleus. It exploded at a height of several kilometres, flattening trees over an area of a thousand square kilometres, but left no fragments or a crater. Ah . . .' He plunged his left hand into the gunk and fished out what Yorkie thought was a piece of slate until the professor wiped it clean with his handkerchief. It gleamed dully.

'What is it?' Yorkie asked, sensing the scientist's suppressed excitement.

'A tektite. In this case, a piece of vitrified clay – caused by intense heat. It's fascinating. No wonder there've been no seismic reports. I guessed right. The meteorite must have been completely annihilated an instant before it impacted, and the resulting heat was enough to do this.'

'Then why,' asked Yorkie, pointing to the smashed pines, 'are the bloody trees pointing *towards* us?'

The professor looked at a loss. 'That's what's puzzling me,' he admitted. 'What I think must've happened is that the meteorite ionised the atmosphere in its wake – created a vacuum – and what you see here is the result of an atmospheric implosion when air rushed in with tremendous force to fill the vacuum.'

'Doesn't sound very plausible.'

'Why not? It's a common enough phenomenon. Thunder is the sound of air imploding into the vacuum created by a lightning flash.'

43

BAGHDAD, CENTRAL IRAQ

In the fading light Nuri and Khalid saw the results of over a month of sustained Allied bombing. Until now, what little evidence they had seen of the Gulf War outside the battlegrounds of Kuwait and Southern Iraq had been bombed bridges and blacked-out towns and villages. Now, in the industrial zone, where entire factory complexes had been systematically obliterated, there was evidence all around them. It was over two weeks since the last raid on Baghdad, yet smoke was still curling into the air from some of the ruins. But the biggest surprise was the number of anti-aircraft batteries with their stockpiles of ammunition in steel ready-use cases bearing Jordan Army markings. The muzzles of triple-A gun-emplacements pointing at the darkening sky were everywhere – proof that Saddam Hussein had not been lying when he boasted that Baghdad was the most heavily defended city in the world.

The altered landmarks and the numerous diversion signs confused Khalid, and caused him to take a wrong turning off the ring road. They blundered into Saddam City, one of the poorest quarters of Baghdad, where the potholed streets between the squalid high-rise blocks were running with sewage; where the expressionless white faces of the women looking out from their black abayahs were the faces of those who had lost all hope. The two men in their smart business suits attracted envious stares and the attentions of young girls and boys offering sexual services. One persistent girl clung to Nuri's door and pulled her dress open to display her still-developing breasts. She claimed that she was eleven – which was probably true – and that she was a virgin – which probably wasn't. At times the traffic slowed to a crawl as drivers took extra care with their nearly bald tyres on the rough road, knowing that a burst tyre would render their cars immobile for good.

They passed a long queue of wretched humanity at a government food-distribution truck, where men were tossing packages of rice, sugar and army rations to eager, outstretched hands.

There was no order. The strong forced their way through the crowd to the truck and got double their share, while the weak, and small children, had their food snatched from them or were trampled into the filth. When the food suddenly ran out and the men yanked up the tailboard, there were no remonstrations, no shouting as the truck driver started his engine. The women who had been unlucky accepted their misfortune and melted back into the dark, unlit streets. Further down the street a group of young children were playing in the mire-filled gutter, their legs already starting to bow outwards – the first sign of rickets. It was an area where an outbreak of cholera was waiting to happen.

Closer to the city centre, Nuri saw that pack-animals had returned to the narrow alleyways around the Kadamiya mosque, some so overloaded with firewood that their burdens scraped along the walls and ancient, clench-nailed doors. Along the embankments of the Tigris, built by the British to contain the annual spring floods, the rows of graceful palm trees had been hacked down for fuel, leaving raw stumps like rotting teeth. Blind beggars wearing nightshirt-like galabiyas lined the parapet, holding out imploring hands.

And yet less than three hundred metres away was a great splash of light blazing in the city centre, reflected from the pall of smoke hanging over Baghdad from the thousands of wood fires burning in the dark suburbs. This island of luxury, Khalid told Nuri, was Abu Nawas Street, on the east bank of the Tigris near the destroyed 14th July Bridge, with its smart restaurants and nightclubs. Beyond that were glittering shopping precincts, and bazaars with stores stuffed to their fluorescent light-fittings with sanction-flouting stocks of cameras, jewellery, and hi-tech electronic trinkets from the East. For five millennia Baghdad had been at the hub of the great trade routes between East and West, and the tradition of commerce was so deep-rooted that even now, less than two weeks since the end of the Gulf War, fleets of the smaller motorised mahailas were arriving at the wharfs of Baghdad – loaded with goods from, of all places, Kuwait . . . In the Middle East, politics and trade were disciplines to be kept firmly separated. Even during the long and bitter Iran/Iraq war, the centuries-old lines of commerce between the two countries had been kept open – so open that the arms dealers of Teheran and Baghdad had actually continued to do business with each other.

As they passed the Al Rasheed Hotel, unmarked by war like most of the city's commercial centre, the Toyotas, BMWs and Mercedes were already arriving, bringing wealthy Tikritis and their families and hangers-on to dine in the hotel's Ishatar restaurant, or to while the night away at the Thousand and One Nights disco.

'We've got to get out of this,' said Nuri uneasily when they came to yet another hooting snarl-up.

Khalid tried to peer beyond one of the double-decker Routemaster buses that had once plied the streets of London. 'All the bridges must be destroyed, Nuri. But we have to get across the river somehow. Our house is on the west bank. The bus station is on the other side, so there must be a bridge.'

'Then follow the bus!' Nuri snapped irritably.

The mass of traffic surged north along the broad boulevard of Rashid Street which ran parallel to the Tigris. There were no left turns – Khalid was right, all the bridges were down: the Jumhuriya, the Sinak, the Ahrar, the Rushata. But eventually they crossed the Tigris by a pontoon bridge, and once they had crossed the Mosul railway line, Khalid was able to get his bearings. Within thirty minutes they were driving through the broad, well-kept avenues of the Mansour commercial district where the street lighting still worked and the embassies were still lit: the neighbourhood's electricity was provided by an army mobile generator which stood in a local park so that its continuous roar should cause the least disturbance to inhabitants of the large, detached houses near the racecourse. One particularly large villa had a floodlit hibiscus garden with a fountain shooting a column of sparking water into the air.

'Why did the Americans bomb all the power-stations?' Nuri complained. 'What was the thinking behind that? Surely they know that all military installations and communications centres have their own generators? They *must* know: all our generators are American-made. All they've done is wage war on the poor.'

183

He fell into a brooding, angry silence, thinking of the streets of Saddam City running with sewage, and the many thousands of children who would surely die the following winter. The Allies had said they were intent on destroying Saddam Hussein's weapons of mass destruction, yet they had handed the tyrant the oldest and most deadly weapons of all: hunger and disease.

'This is my road,' said Khalid excitedly, turning the Escort into a narrow road lined with recently planted palm trees. He pointed to a pair of high, wrought-iron gates hung on stone pillars. 'And that's our house! Why aren't the floodlights working? My father was so proud of his garden.'

'Drive past it,' Nuri snapped when he saw that the house was in darkness. Khalid started to protest but Nuri cut him short. 'We don't want the neighbours seeing that you're back.'

'But they are our friends!'

'Do as I say!'

Khalid drove a hundred metres past his house, and parked in the shadows between two street lights as Nuri directed. They locked the car and walked back to the house in silence.

The gates were ajar. They pushed them open and walked up a gently sloping drive towards a large, whitewashed house with a Western-style pitched roof and small verandas on the upstairs rooms. In the suffused glow of the street light it was possible to see that many things were wrong: the electric up-and-over door to the double garage had been forced so that it hung buckled and forlorn from its guides; downstairs windows were either smashed or wrenched from their frames. Most ominous of all, the oak front door was hanging open by one hinge.

'Stay here,' said Nuri curtly. There was no need to repeat the order; Khalid had stopped and was staring at the house. His jaw moved but no words came out.

Nuri squeezed past the broken door and paused in the hall to allow his eyes to become accustomed to the gloom, but his nose picked up the smell immediately. It was the stench of the latrines in Kuwait and the streets of Saddam City. The house had been more than ransacked, it had been vandalised. His feet echoed on the bare cedarwood boards, and his even breathing had a resonant quality as he moved to what he assumed had been the main living-room. There was no door, and the barbed hooks of carpet-grippers snagged on his shoes as he crossed the threshold.

It was a large, elegantly proportioned room. At the end nearest the kitchen was a dining-area, once screened off by a delicate alabaster wall that had been smashed down. Everything of value had been taken, even the air-conditioning grilles had been ripped out. The only fitting left was a dummy fireplace in white marble, and even that was half-pulled from the wall.

As Nuri stared dumbly round at the ravaged room he remembered the times when, as a boy in Halabji, he had played hide-and-seek in the burial chambers of forgotten Persian princes and princesses that lay long abandoned by tomb robbers and archaeologists. Many times he had wondered what the chambers were like when they were filled with treasures. He felt the same now. His own home had been little more than a hovel; he had never been in such a house as this, and he wondered what life must have been like here. He had a feeling that it had been a happy home, as his had been, because Khalid had always spoken of his parents with simple pride and love. The destroyed splendour of this house, the mindless vandalism inspired by hate and jealousy and greed, seemed to symbolise the terrible disaster that had overtaken Babylon – once the most civilised country in the world.

In the gutted kitchen the source of the dreadful stench became apparent. Smeared on the tiled walls in brown Arabic script was the legend:

LONG LIVE SADDAM HUSSEIN

The unknown scribe could not have selected a more appropriate material to write such a message.

Nuri left the house. Khalid had not moved. He was still staring up at the whitewashed façade and didn't seem to hear his companion's approach. Nuri felt sorry for the young man's feelings. After losing loved ones, the greatest devastation anyone can suffer is to see their home destroyed.

'Not there, are they, Nuri?'

'No.'

'Where are they?'

'I'm sorry, Khalid, but there's no message. There's nothing.' Khalid took a step forward but Nuri grabbed his arm. 'There's nothing there,' he repeated harshly. '*Nothing*. The place has been stripped of everything. Do you understand?'

The fierceness of his friend's tone forced understanding on Khalid. He nodded dumbly. 'But I would still like to go in, Nuri. It is my home.'

Nuri nodded understandingly. He dug in his jacket pocket and handed the young man a cigarette-lighter. 'You might need this.'

Khalid entered the hall. In the gloom he could see the terrible misfortune that had befallen his home. He cried out for his mother, expecting her to come bustling out of the kitchen, but all that answered was his own voice, echoing off the bare walls and floors – frightening him with its booming resonance. His mother and father, and his home, had always been at the tranquil eye of his cerebral hurricane. Now everything was gone. He mounted the stairs, drawn to his bedroom where everything would surely be the same. He would get into bed, pull the covers over him, and be secure until his mother came home.

He pushed his bedroom door open and a little cry of distress rose in his throat. There was nothing left but a few of his clothes scattered on the floor. Whoever had raided his built-in wardrobe had ripped out everything, including the brass rails.

He stared about him in despair, tears pricking his eyes. On the floor was a photograph that had once been mounted in a silver frame. He picked it up and looked at the colour picture of the girl. She had long black hair, arching eyebrows, and green, compelling eyes that were gazing straight at the camera without a hint of self-consciousness.

'André,' said Khalid softly to the photograph. He pressed it to his lips and tears flowed from the strange reservoir of his emotions. His thoughts went back to the happy times in England, the long bicycle rides through the Surrey lanes. The last such ride with André had been only a few weeks before, at the beginning of the year, but already it seemed like a lifetime ago. He had lost her letters, but now he had her photograph. He slipped it into his breast pocket and made his way downstairs to the front door, where Nuri was waiting for him.

The older man was about to chide Khalid for the length of time he had been gone when he realised that his companion was gazing fixedly over his shoulder. Nuri wheeled around. A shadowy figure in uniform was watching them from the gates. Outside in the road was a police car; he hadn't heard it, it must have freewheeled to a standstill. Khalid gave a cry and ran towards the man – who immediately unfastened his holster and levelled his pistol.

44

SOUTHERN IRAQ

Even though Corporal Willie Mellish knew he would be on his way home within seventy-two hours, his peace of mind was evaporating by the minute. He and Private Ian Hunter stood in their capes in the relentless drizzle like khaki Draculas, watching the line of headlights that was materialising out of the desert from the north. On the other side of the rectangle of barbed wire that marked their 'cage', the twelve hundred Iraqi POWs had also seen the lights. Sleeping comrades were shaken awake, and they all rose to their feet and stared at the convoy of trucks. The line of low-wattage floodlights shone on their faces, which showed neither hope nor fear, mostly resignation. Some peered at their cheap plastic-strapped watches. They all knew that in ten minutes' time they would no longer be prisoners.

The lead truck stopped a hundred metres from the 'cage', bringing the other vehicles to a standstill. They waited, their diesels idling, headlights picking out the spears of falling rain.

Seven minutes to go.

'Just doesn't make sense,' Private Hunter breathed. 'Handing 'em over, just like that. Twelve hundred men – rested and fed.'

'And their kit,' said Willie, nodding to the piles of helmets and small-arms – at least twenty tonnes in full ammunition boxes alone. There had been plans to move the stuff, but the promised transport had never materialised.

The POWs were now crowding towards the wire where the two NCOs were standing.

Five minutes.

'Just doesn't make sense,' Private Hunter repeated to himself.

But it made sense to Willie. During the long hours of guarding the Iraqis he had taken to reading Franz Kafka. The madness that was about to unfold had a crazy logic about it that the Czech writer would have understood. The Geneva Convention required POWs to be repatriated as soon as practical after the war; but Willie's 'cage' was on Iraqi soil, so all the British Army had to do was walk away and leave the prisoners behind. Technically, the POWs were already home; technically, they were still serving soldiers in the Iraqi Army. And at midnight they would once again be under Iraqi command.

That afternoon Willie had overheard two officers discussing the lunacy of the hand-over.

'The trouble is,' the captain had said, 'the Foreign Office look upon Iraq as their particular baby. It's a country they welded together in the twenties, after the break-up of the Ottoman Empire, and they don't want it to fall apart as a result of this uprising.'

'So we help Saddam Hussein out by giving him twelve hundred men,' Willie's commanding officer had replied.

'Our political masters don't think he'll survive,' the captain replied. 'But they want Iraq to survive. They want it both ways.'

The sudden roar of the lead truck broke in on Willie's thoughts. It was pitching and bumping along the rough track towards him. Gears were engaged in the following vehicles and the whole convoy of thirty canvas-covered trucks moved forward. The lead truck was a new Soviet-built Zil. It stopped near the two British NCOs and a small swarthy man in combat dress jumped down from the driver's cab. He was a colonel in the Popular Army. Unable to see the rank of the two British soldiers under their capes, he saluted them.

'I have come to collect our men, sir,' he announced in correct English.

At that moment the distant thunder of heavy mortars far to the north rolled across the desert. The Iraqi cocked his head

188

and smiled uneasily at Willie. He looked at his watch, and what he saw seemed to give him confidence. 'It is now midnight, sir.'

Without a word, Willie and Private Hunter dragged a section of barbed wire aside. It was the signal. Cab doors opened and slammed. Someone started addressing the former POWs in Arabic over a portable PA unit. The men shuffled forward, but without any show of enthusiasm. Some turned despairing faces towards the British soldiers, whom they had learned to trust. Their expressions spoke of betrayal. Willie avoided meeting their accusing gaze. Some infantrymen were examining the piles of small-arms. They threw aside the mud-splattered rifles in disdain and organised a human chain to pass the wooden ammunition boxes to the trucks in the rear of the convoy.

Willie and Private Hunter watched the men boarding the trucks for some minutes, then realised there was no point in staying. They shut down the portable generator and hitched it to their Land Rover. Willie drove, heading towards liberated Kuwait.

The swarthy Iraqi officer watched their lights receding into the drizzle and spat contemptuously into the muddied sand.

45

BAGHDAD

'Hazma!' Khalid cried joyously. 'It's me! Khalid!' He would have thrown his arms around the policeman, but the man pushed Khalid forcibly away.

'Put your hands on your head!' The order was barked out.

'But, Hazma!'

'Do as I say!'

Crestfallen, the young man did as he was told.

The policeman swung his pistol towards Nuri, who was on the point of racing for cover among the hibiscus bushes. But when the policeman played a powerful torch beam on his face the situation was obviously hopeless, so Nuri remained still and put his hands on his head before he was told to do so.

'Now come here!'

Nuri went forward and stopped beside Khalid.

'Hazma,' Khalid whimpered. 'It's me.'

The policeman switched the flashlamp off, clipped it to his belt and jerked his pistol towards his car. 'Get in.'

Nuri and Khalid sat in the rear seat and the policeman sat in the front passenger seat. He switched on the interior light and studied his captives for a moment with dark, suspicious eyes. He was about Nuri's age, badly shaven, with cuts on his face as though he had to cope with blunt disposable razors, although his moustache was neatly trimmed. Nuri was in no doubt that the pistol was aimed straight at him through the back of the front seat. The police officer's hard expression suddenly relaxed a little, but he remained alert. Eventually he pushed his pistol back into its holster. 'What are you doing here, Khalid? I thought you were dead.'

Khalid suddenly started talking, piling one question on top of another without giving the policeman a chance to reply, and only falling silent when the policeman ordered him to be quiet.

'Now,' said the policeman, 'why are you here and why aren't you in uniform?'

'I wanted to be with my parents. Where are they, Hazma? Please – you must tell me.'

The policeman redirected his question at Nuri.

'We're on our way back to our headquarters at Mosul.'

'In civilian clothes?'

'We used what clothes we could find. We lost everything.'

'You're deserters.' It was an accusation rather than a question.

'There was nothing left to desert from,' said Nuri simply. 'Our entire brigade was cut to pieces. Wiped out.'

The policeman was silent for a moment. His dark eyes turned to Khalid. 'Your parents thought you were dead. Your name was not on the Red Crescent lists from the Americans and the British.'

'We thought we were dead too,' Nuri remarked drily.

The policeman ignored the comment.

'*Please*, Hazma – where are my parents?'

'We received orders that all Kurds were to be rounded up,' said the policeman harshly.

'But my parents have always been loyal!' Khalid cried. 'And they have always been good to you.'

Nuri looked at his companion in surprise. Khalid normally had trouble selecting the right words, but now, in his distress, he was showing a remarkable degree of eloquence.

'Five days ago we received orders that they were to be rounded up,' said Hazma flatly. 'We came out the next day, and they had gone. Food, blankets, jewellery, money and car – all gone.' A thin smile showed beneath his moustache. 'Someone must have tipped them off.'

'Who stripped the house?' Nuri asked.

Hazma shrugged. 'It could be anyone. Kurdish property is not safe. The Hablas' house has also been stripped. And they too have fled.'

'Tikritis,' said Nuri savagely.

'I did not say that,' the policeman replied evenly. He looked sharply at Khalid. 'Do you know where your parents have gone?'

Khalid nodded. 'Yes, of course. They will have gone to – '

'Don't tell me!' the policeman suddenly snapped angrily, holding up his hand.

The young Kurd fell silent and stared at the policeman with hurt eyes.

Hazma held out his hand. 'Give me your papers.'

Nuri hesitated. This man knew Khalid's real identity, so their forged documents could get them into even more trouble. But what was more trouble? He reluctantly pulled the sheaf of papers from his breast pocket and handed them over. The policeman studied them carefully for a few moments. He opened the car's glove compartment, rummaged through some papers and report pads, and produced a self-inking rubber stamp. Using the drop-down glove compartment door as a makeshift desk top, he went through the documents, writing notes on them and stamping what he had written. He folded the sheaf of papers and returned them to Nuri.

'They now show that you've reported to the police and have permission to travel north,' said Hazma. He brushed aside Nuri's thanks in some irritation, and ordered them out of the

191

car. He slid into the driver's seat and started the engine. Before moving off, he wound down his window. 'It would be best if you left Baghdad as quickly as possible.' His hard face unfroze into a half-smile. 'Good luck.' As if angry with himself for his last-minute display of compassion, he revved the engine hard and let in the clutch sharply.

'Hazma would have tipped my parents off,' said Khalid, watching the police car's receding tail-lights.

'I guessed,' said Nuri. 'We'd better do as he says.'

He took hold of Khalid's arm and the two men walked slowly back to their car.

46

SOUTHERN ENGLAND
Friday, 8th March 1991

Lloyd was appalled. He pressed the telephone harder to his ear. 'No notes?' he echoed. 'What, none at all?'

'Mindway Films were a small company that went bust about three years ago,' Ted Prentice explained. 'All their records went in a skip. Are you sure it's the same girl you saw on the plane? Kids change a lot in six years.'

Lloyd stared at the office television. He had paused the video-tape on a clapperboard shot that showed André sitting on a chair, facing the camera. 'I'm on the shot now. It says on the clapperboard: "André Normanville – makes thunder". There are also some shots showing her mother. She's hardly changed.'

'I remember her now,' said Prentice after a pause. 'Yes – Laura Normanville. She saw our ad and phoned up. Said her daughter could make thunder. So I invited her along to the rehearsal room. We stuck the kid in front of the camera, rolled sound and asked the kid to make thunder. Zilch. Another time-waster, so we booted her out. Why didn't she say at the time that her daughter was a time-teller? Doesn't make sense.'

Lloyd had watched the audition sequence of the abortive attempt to get André to make thunder and had asked himself the same question. 'When I find her, I'll ask her,' he promised.

'I hope you do find her,' said Prentice gruffly. 'As I said to you before – time-telling savants are special. I'm damn annoyed that I let one slip through my fingers.'

Lloyd promised to keep the psychiatrist informed, and hung up. As he replaced the telephone, the video recorder objected to being held on picture-pause for so long, and the time-out circuitry switched the machine off – causing the television to default to Sky News, which was showing for the twentieth time aerial shots of the devastated pines in a Forestry Commission plantation in Surrey. Another shot showed residents of Durston village repairing broken windows.

Lloyd stared at the screen, deep in thought. He rummaged among some proofs awaiting correction and found a list he had made of the video counter numbers of interesting shots. He spun the videocassette to the shot that showed André sitting in the corner of the rehearsal room with her mother. Next was a medium shot of André and the Iraqi boy, Khalid al Karni, talking by themselves. No sound, but André seemed animated – alive, and totally out of character for an autistic ten-year-old. As she turned her head briefly towards the camera, it seemed that her green eyes were alight.

If only there was sound!

But there was sound-track accompanying André's actual audition takes. The clapperboard was snapped and whipped away to show her sitting on a stool, looking ill at ease. There was a hubbub of conversation in the background, and the sound of distant music – probably the Waterloo PA system that Prentice had complained about.

'Are you okay, André?' asked Prentice's voice off-camera. He sounded gentle and persuasive.

André nodded.

'Mummy says you can make thunder. Would you like to make thunder for me?'

André nodded again.

'Shall I count to three?'

Another nod.

The studio manager's voice calling for quiet had only a marginal effect on the general level of background noise.

193

'One . . . Two . . . Three . . .'

André closed her eyes and screwed up her face in concentration. A voice in the background announced the imminent non-departure of a Portsmouth train, but there was no sound of thunder.

'Shall we try again, André?' asked Prentice, still out of shot.

The scene was repeated three times, with the same negative result each time.

The last shot was the one that showed André catching the tennis ball Khalid had thrown at the wall. It ended with the studio manager holding the inside-out tennis ball close to the camera lens for a huge close-up.

Lloyd sat deep in thought. He had an idea, and called Rikki Steadman's studio. There was a faint possibility that the sound engineer would be able to help.

47

CENTRAL IRAQ

By now Nuri and Khalid had a smooth routine for dealing with roadblocks and vehicle checks. Both men would get out of the car before they were asked to do so, Nuri would produce their papers before they were requested, and Khalid would open the boot. Their movements suggested that they had passed without trouble through many such checks and were accustomed to them. Nuri believed that it gave the inspecting police or soldiers confidence.

But this roadblock, fifty kilometres north of Baghdad on the road to Kirkuk, was different because all traffic was being turned back. The sullen soldiers weren't interested in papers, or searching the few vehicles, or people's reasons for travelling. And the only assistance they offered was to the driver of a large, open truck as he struggled to turn it in the narrow road.

'Kirkuk sealed off,' said a corporal in answer to Nuri's friendly inquiry, accepting the offered cigarette.

'Any idea why?'

The soldier shrugged. 'Kurds planning trouble in Kirkuk and Arbil, we've heard.'

Nuri thought fast. Kirkuk was at the sensitive centre of an oil-rich region on the edge of Kurdistan, in the north-east. Arbil, further north, was a large Kurdish town with an anti-government population of 200,000 that had always been a source of trouble. There was a huge army barracks at Kirkuk, set up specifically to guard the oil pipeline to Jordan. Officially, the pipeline was no longer in use, but the barracks were fully manned and even had helicopter gunships; the rumour was that the pipeline was now pumping to Jordan in exchange for arms. It was a region best avoided at any time, but Nuri's plan had been to skirt Tikrit and then try to head north-west towards Mosul, where the PKK Kurdish resistance organisation had a base. If Kirkuk was dangerous, Tikrit was infinitely more so. It was Saddam Hussein's birthplace and the home town of his most fanatical followers, the Tikriti families who held all the important posts in Iraq.

'If you want to go north, you'll have to double back and head for Tikrit,' said the soldier helpfully. 'Maybe the road's open from there, but I wouldn't count on it.'

Nuri thanked him, climbed back into the Escort and told Khalid to turn back.

Tikrit!

Well, they had been through danger before. Maybe it wouldn't be any worse than what they had experienced so far.

Khalid was about to turn the car round when he had to wait to allow a convoy of six flat-top transporters to pass: the soldiers waved them through without making them stop. On the back of each vehicle was a bright-yellow JCB – the digging-buckets and hydraulic back-acters of the excavators were lowered to give them stability as the transporters ground by. None of the JCBs bore registrations, and all looked new.

'What are they wanted for?' Nuri called out to the soldier.

The soldier shrugged. 'Road repairs, I suppose. A lot of bomb-damage in the north.'

As they retraced their route, they met several more JCBs and giant International bulldozers being moved north. The ubiquitous JCB diggers, with their bulbous herring-bone-tread tyres unmarked by use, made Nuri uneasy. Why were so many of the excavators being pressed into service, and why did the transporters have military registrations?

48

SOUTHERN ENGLAND

In more prosperous days Rikki Steadman's well-equipped sound studios were much in demand by aspiring pop artists wishing to make professional demo tapes, established groups, and advertising agencies. Now the recession was biting hard, which meant that he considered himself lucky to get three bookings a week – and the resulting trickle of fees was barely covering the interest charges on his banks of harmonisers, synthesisers, mixers, MIDI systems, and multi-track recorders. Despite his problems, Rikki, an obese one-time hippy of the 1960s, was always willing to do favours for his friends, provided it involved keeping his audio skills honed and working. Now as he listened to and watched the videocassette that Lloyd had brought round, the pained expression on his florid face suggested that he was regretting his generosity.

'Bloody hell, Lloyd. A bloody analogue copy of a copy of a copy of a recording made in a crap studio with no audio isolation from what sounds like St Pancras Station PA announcements.'

'Close, Rik. It's Waterloo Station, actually.'

Rikki rewound the segment of tape that showed André's abortive audition and played it again.

'Pretty kid,' he remarked.

'Even more so now,' Lloyd replied.

'And you think there might be a roll of thunder lurking under all that crud? It has to be thunder, doesn't it? Low-frequency sounds are a pig's ear to isolate.'

'I'm sure you can do it, Rik,' said Lloyd, knowing that flattery always worked with the ex-hippy.

Rikki grunted. 'Well – maybe I could find something. But

anything below a couple of hundred Hertz pulled out of that . . . You're not asking much, old son.'

'Give it a try, Rik. Please.'

Rikki set to work. He converted the analogue recording to digital so that it could be processed through a computer, and systematically eliminated all unwanted sounds with a mouse as they appeared on the screen. He worked with pictures of the sounds, occasionally using his headphones to check his progress.

'Tell you what, Lloyd – there's something odd lurking under there.' He pointed to a densely packed spiked pattern. 'Probably a tube train.' He rewound the computer-enhanced digital tape and pressed the play key.

Prentice's voice filled the small room. It was sharp and clear, with the background noise of the rehearsal room and Waterloo station reduced to an unobtrusive buzz.

'Are you okay, André?'

A brief silence.

'Mummy says you can make thunder. Would you like to make thunder for me?'

Pause.

'Shall I count to three?'

Another pause.

'One . . . Two . . . Three . . .'

The reverberating roll of thunder that crashed from the studio speakers was at such a level that Lloyd could actually feel the shock waves on his face caused by the displaced speaker cones. The incredible roar was sustained for some seconds and then began dying away – not as though the roll was losing its strength, but as though it were receding at tremendous speed through the atmosphere.

The recording ended. 'A lot of enhancement to fill in the gaps, but that's pretty well it,' the sound engineer commented flippantly. 'Tell you what, Lloyd, old son. If you ever run into that kid, you might ask her from me how she did it.'

49

'Mrs Normanville?'

Laura's glance took in Detective-Sergeant Barr's warrant card and the uniformed woman police constable who was with him. Yorkie saw the sudden flash of alarm in the woman's eyes, but realised that it could simply be due to seeing a police uniform on her doorstep. Nevertheless, it was noted. Also, he knew this woman.

'Yes?'

'I'm Detective-Sergeant Barr, and this is WPC Williams. We're making some routine house-to-house inquiries about a couple of local lads, bikers, who disappeared on Wednesday night. May we come in?'

'I'm sorry but I don't know anything about – '

'They were last seen playing the pinball-machine on Wednesday night at Jacko's Café. We know your daughter was there that evening, so maybe she spoke to them or overheard their plans? Could we talk to her, please?'

During ten years of protecting André from the outside world, Laura had developed a certain cunning. She knew that to protest would only arouse police suspicions. Instead she opened the door wide and treated the two officers to a welcoming smile. 'Yes – of course. Please come in.' She showed the police officers into the living-room.

'I believe we've met before, Mrs Normanville,' said Yorkie, smiling.

'Really? I don't remember . . .'

'Oh – it must've been about five years ago, when I was in uniform doing a door-to-door. An old drunk, Crabbie Howard, disappeared one night after he'd been boozing.'

Laura gave a quick smile. 'Oh, yes. Was it as long ago as that?' She opened the French windows and called out, 'Andy! A lady and gentleman to see you!'

What Yorkie and his colleague didn't see as André entered the room from the garden was the warning look Laura gave her daughter.

'There is something you ought to know, Sergeant Barr,' said Laura when they were all seated. 'André is . . .'

'Yes – we know,' the policewoman interjected. 'Don't worry, Mrs Normanville. We under – '

'How do you know?' Laura demanded, immediately regretting any sharpness in her voice.

'Your neighbours told us.'

Laura nodded and took André's hand. 'Andy – this man and woman want to ask you a few questions. Will you answer them for Mummy?'

'Hallo, André,' said Yorkie, smiling at the girl. 'Would you like to help me?'

André redirected her stare from the policewoman's uniform to the questioner. Yorkie found her unblinking gaze disturbing.

'You know Jacko's Café, don't you, André?'

André looked at her mother for reassurance, and nodded.

'Jacko and Freda said that you were there on Wednesday evening. Yes?'

'She goes every Wednesday,' said Laura, seeing her daughter's blank look. 'I'm sorry, sergeant, but André doesn't have much grasp of time.'

Yorkie produced recent photographs of Dabber and Greaser sitting on their Kawasakis. 'Did you see these two men in the café, André?' He held them out, but the girl made no attempt to take them or even look at them properly, though she did nod.

'You watched them playing on a pinball-machine?' Yorkie made a gesture of pulling back and releasing a firing plunger.

'Yes,' said André, speaking for the first time.

'Did you speak to them?'

'No.'

Yorkie pocketed the photographs and glanced at his notebook. Jacko and Freda had been certain that the girl hadn't talked to the missing youths.

'Did you see them leave the café on their motorbikes?'

'No.'

'Did you leave before them?'

Again it was a question that seemed to puzzle André. 'Surely Jacko or Freda would know that, wouldn't they?' Laura asked.

'They were busy at the time, Mrs Normanville.' Yorkie tried the question again and got the same result. He closed his notebook. 'Thank you, André . . . Mrs Normanville. I don't think we need bother you again with any more questions.'

'What will happen now?' Laura asked.

Yorkie shrugged. 'Not a lot. They're both over-age. They've both got money; and they've both got a reputation for taking off when the whim grabs them.'

The two police officers returned to their car. 'Anything?' Yorkie asked the policewoman as he fastened his seat-belt.

The WPC shook her head. 'The mother didn't signal the daughter by look or deed. She only stepped in when the girl was uncertain or confused.'

'Nothing else?'

'No. Should there be anything else?'

Yorkie started the car's engine. 'Just that the mother wasn't interested in the bikers' names. She didn't even try to look at the photographs. Everyone else we've seen has wanted chapter and verse. I reckon that's odd. And it's odd that she didn't ask me about old Crabbie Howard's disappearance.'

'Can you really remember a face after a door-to-door five years back?'

'Oh yes,' said Yorkie, letting in the clutch. 'I never forget a face . . .'

In the bungalow, Laura was close to tears as she hugged André and kissed her on the cheek. 'Well done, darling! Mummy's so proud of you. We won't have to move after all. Isn't that wonderful, darling?'

The roots of Laura's concern went back ten years, to 1981, a few months after the accident . . .

Laura sat on a blanket on the hillside overlooking the Solent, watching her daughter throwing a stick for Senator. It was hard to believe that the accident had been earlier that year. The speed of André's physical recovery had astonished everyone, including Mr Houseman, the consultant neurosurgeon at the Atkinson Morley Hospital.

Senator, her mother's good-natured Labrador, bounded down

the slope to seize the stick before it landed, and raced back to André. It was a warm afternoon in autumn; a perfect sky, the song of a late lark, high and invisible, reaching from the blue. Under such conditions it was almost possible to believe that nothing had ever happened – that the terrible events of that year had been a bad dream.

But there was no David beside her, with his arm around her waist and his thumb always trying to toy with her breast, even in company. The last time she had sat on the grass like this had been at Sandown Park, when David's horse romped home at 5 to 1 – and that was an excuse for everyone to get slightly drunk on champagne. Their friends had parked their cars in a tight circle; boots open, picnic hampers everywhere. Laughter and idle chatter between races. The McArdles did things in style; they had brought along their butler who acted as everyone's runner, placing bets and serving cold chicken and caviar while they waited for the next race. Laura remembered tripping across the picnic blanket and joining in everyone's laughter as egg mayonnaise ran down her face. Everyone loved André. Such a sweet, happy little girl. Always laughing. A little smidgeon of sunshine, Lindsay McArdle called her. They all told Laura and David how lucky they were . . .

Laura returned André's wave and gazed at the glittering sweep of water. The Solent was dotted with sails – owners grabbing the last fine days of the season before laying up their craft for the approaching winter. The Blakes' yacht *Takapuna* was down there somewhere. But hadn't they said they would be taking it to Bermuda for the winter of '81/'82?

Why was she thinking about them? She didn't care what they did with their yacht; or who would be invited next year to the Nadinaris' August-long house party at their villa in the South of France; or whether the Hon. Cordelia Smythson-Watt's marriage to her diamond merchant would last another year. Not one of them had sent as much as a card after the accident. That life was finished. It had ended with the ending of David's life; it was part of another existence. And somehow her denial of that brief but flamboyant period in her past made her guilt over what had happened – what she had made happen through her own selfishness and stupidity – a little easier to bear. Learning to come to terms with that guilt was proving much harder than putting a new life together; she wasn't rebuilding from the shattered remains of the old life but had discarded them completely.

'Mummy!'

André was much nearer now, throwing her stick high into the air. A five-year-old playing with her dog on a grassy hillside: only a close observer would notice that the little girl never laughed or smiled.

Laura waved. She treasured the weekends, when she could devote all her time to André. Her weekdays were taken up at the teacher training college in Portsmouth, where she would qualify the following year. Home was her mother's house at Petersfield. Her father had died the year before, and her sister, Imogen, was living in London with her latest boyfriend and making plans to marry him and live in Singapore, so there was plenty of room at the family home – and her mother loved looking after André.

'Mummy!' André was only a few yards away, swinging a small branch that Senator had found; he didn't like mere sticks. The dog was barking and racing in circles, trying to keep up with the end of the whirling branch.

Laura waved again. Mapping out the future made it that much easier to face. As soon as she finished at college she planned to buy a small house, using the money her father had left her and a small amount of David's money. She ought to be able to meet the repayments on a fifty per cent mortgage. Nothing pretentious, but a place in the country where the locals would be understanding and protective towards André. Somewhere not too far from her mother, and within practical driving distance of Ivor Houseman's private consulting rooms.

At first Laura had taken André to the neurologist every fortnight, now it was once a month. On every visit her question had been the same: 'Have there been any developments? Will André ever be cured?' And on every visit his answer had been cautiously optimistic:

'I'm sure that by the end of the century the neural mapping

202

of the human brain will have been completed, and nerve regeneration will be commonplace, Mrs Normanville. Once those goals have been achieved, then I'm sure there will be a hospital somewhere in the world that will be able to repair the damage to André's brain. But it's love that André needs above all else; love and understanding and stability.'

André let go of the branch and fell over.

'Andy!' Laura scolded. 'That stick's much too big. Can't you find something smaller?'

The little girl ignored her mother and started whirling the branch again.

Ivor Houseman's optimistic view of future developments provided Laura with a slender ray of hope that reinforced her determination to use none of David's money for herself. It was all for André – every penny. And with interest and compound interest, the capital should more than double by the end of the century, even though she was using some of it to give André the best of anything she needed.

André's anguished scream broke in on her thoughts.

'Mummy!'

Laura looked up. The small branch André had been whirling around a few yards away was boomeranging straight at her.

'Mummy!'

The implosive force that followed the terrifying crack of thunder lifted Laura momentarily off the ground even though she was sitting, and tossed her onto her side. The thunder rolled away, but there was no silence for Laura – her tortured eardrums continued to maintain a screaming protest. Winded and deafened, her first thought was that an aircraft had crashed. She pushed herself up and opened her eyes.

Senator was miming frantic barking, rushing back and forth between her and André; André was sitting on the grass holding her hands over her ears. Laura staggered to her feet and immediately lost her balance because of the screaming noise that was tormenting her inner ears, but after a few moments she found she could crawl to André. She tried to say something, but not being able to hear her own voice made articulation impossible. Half-expecting something to come crashing down from the sky,

203

she threw her body protectively across her daughter. Seconds or minutes passed. The noise in her ears diminished to shrill ringing, and she began to hear Senator's frantic barking. She sat up, and the labrador was upon her, joyously licking her face. She helped André up. Instead of looking frightened, the child's face was alive, her vivid green eyes blazing a strange fire.

Laura made certain that André was unhurt, then looked around. Everything was strangely normal. The sky was blue, the Solent sparkled, and the invisible lark was still singing. The only thing that was wrong was a blackened patch of ground nearby, about a metre in diameter. Laura stood and examined the burnt area. The soil had been turned to a dull, glassy substance that caught the sunlight so that it looked like a pool of water. She touched it. It felt warm, but that could be from the sun. André's hand stole into hers.

'I think,' said Laura unsteadily, 'that we've just come within an ace of being struck by lightning.'

'Andy make bang,' said André simply.

Laura smiled, and shook her head in the hope that it might clear the ringing. At least it was diminishing, although her immediate concern was that André's hearing might have been damaged. But the child was tugging playfully and unconcernedly on Senator's collar.

'I think it's time to go home and see what granny has for tea, young lady. Where's that stick?' Laura looked around for the small branch that she had last seen flying towards her. It was nowhere to be seen. 'Where's that big stick, Andy?'

'Make go with big bang,' said André simply . . .

Two further demonstrations of André's remarkable thunder-making talents that year convinced Laura that whatever was wrong with her daughter's brain, it must be something so fundamental, so obvious, that it would be easy to put right. Her frantic telephone calls and visits to Ivor Houseman produced no reassurances, largely because he refused to believe her, and because André had difficulty in producing the phenomenon at will. Only when subjected to sudden distress could she reproduce the deafening thunderclaps. Undeterred by Ivor Houseman's attitude, Laura started subscribing to every journal that covered neurology. She learned about savants and their extra-ordinary abilities, and saw that manipulative savants were rare, and were almost invariably exposed as hoaxes.

An article in the *British Medical Journal* about Leo Buller's impending return to England to continue his neural-mapping research prompted her to write to him, care of the journal. She told him that she thought her daughter was a manipulative savant like Russell Freeman, the American telekinetic. There was no reply. She wrote several more times, and only gave up when Buller eventually sent a scribbled reply politely telling her to stop wasting his time. A savant specialist in Ohio expressed an interest, but he died after an early exchange of letters.

Early in 1985 she spotted an advertisement in the *Surrey Advertiser* asking parents of savants to call a London telephone number. It was several days before Laura marshalled the courage to ring, and when it was explained that André might be invited to appear on a television film, she almost put the phone down straightaway. But when the representative of Mindway Films heard that André was a girl, not a boy, and that she had acquired savantism as a result of head injuries, he was so interested and so encouraging that Laura agreed to attend the audition.

The disastrous outcome of the audition caused Laura to wish that she had followed her original instincts. She emerged onto the concourse of Waterloo Station with the ten-year-old André clutching her hand.

'But I *did* make bangs, Mummy,' André said, sensing her mother's annoyance.

Laura could never be angry with André for long. She knelt down and straightened her dress. 'Of course you did, darling,' she said giving André a reassuring hug. 'Mummy's not cross. Gosh, you are shooting up now. There's lots of shops here. This is a big town – much bigger than Guildford. Shall we buy you a new winter coat? And afterwards we could go and see the new Star Wars film and have a Big Mac. Would you like that?'

A few hours later, after a happy evening in London, they caught the last semi-fast Portsmouth train from Waterloo and got off at Witley, where Laura had left the car. The remote country station was the nearest to Durston Wood. As they drove back through the dark, winding lanes, Laura maintained her customary chatter.

'Do you remember that nice Iraqi boy? What was his name? Oh dear – one of those funny names – '

'Khalid al Karni,' said André quietly.

Laura was surprised. It was most unusual for André to break into her flow of talk. It could be that the specialist was right to insist that André should be talked to as much as possible. 'That's right, darling – Khalid. Anyway, I got chatting to his mother – Sajii I think her name was. Wasn't she pretty? They have to return to Baghdad every few weeks, and she was wondering if you and Khalid would like to write to each other as you seemed to get on so well together. Pen pals.'

'Pen pals?' André didn't understand.

They came to a straight stretch of road. Laura put her foot down. 'You write to each other every month and tell each other what you've been doing. Like the diary you have to write at school. You could copy it out and send it to Khalid. I've got their address in Baghdad. And they've got a lakeside home in the north of their country. And a flat in Swiss Cottage. They sound very well off. Of course, pen pals hardly ever meet, but Khalid returns to England with Sajii and his father several times a year, so – '

'*MUMMY!*'

There was a vague shadow in the road. Laura's feet slammed to the floor. The Metro's brakes screamed and locked. She fought to steer the car into the skid.

Not again! Please, God! Not again!

This time she was going to keep the car on the road. She took her foot off the brake to regain steering control. As she did so, the sickness that rose up in her stomach like a malignant serpent told her that she had no chance of avoiding the drunk reeling across her path.

There was a terrible thunderclap. A flash of blinding light. And the drunk seemed to vanish. The car shuddered to a sideways standstill in the middle of the road. The smell of burning rubber filled the Metro's interior. Laura ignored the ringing in

206

her ears and jumped from the car. She was convinced that the
man had gone right over the roof and that he couldn't possibly
be alive.

*I must have been travelling at about fifty. That's not fast for this
road.*

As she ran back along the road, she could hear herself pleading in court. What would happen to her if she went to prison?
What would happen to André?

The road was empty. He must have gone into the ditch. Oh
no – it's too dark to see anything.

She ran back to the car and reversed until the headlights were
shining back along the road. The black, accusing streaks of her
skid marks showed up plainly on the gravelled top-dressing. A
farmyard dog barked in the distance, but there was no other
sound or sign of life.

*He must have been drunk to have been staggering like that. If I
find him, the police will test his blood. It'll be all right. It's got to
be all right.*

She thought she saw something against a hedge but it turned
out to be a plastic feed-sack. Had the impact been hard enough
to send him right over the hedge and into the field? No – that
was impossible.

'Gone. Bang make man go.'

Laura looked up from where she was on one knee, trying to
peer into the ditch. André was silhouetted against the Metro's
blazing headlights.

'Bang make man go,' she repeated.

Laura scrambled to her feet and gripped André's shoulders.
'Andy – what are you trying to tell me?' It was hard to keep
the hysteria out of her voice.

'Man gone.'

'Gone? Gone where? *Tell me where he's gone!*'

'To beginning.'

'What!'

'Beginning.'

Realising the danger they were in if another car came by,
Laura pulled the Metro off the road by a farm gate. 'Andy,' she
said quietly. 'Did you just make thunder?'

207

André nodded.

'Because the man was there?'

Another nod.

Laura didn't want to ask the next question because she dreaded what the answer would be. But it had to be asked. 'And where is the man now?'

The green eyes stared at her in the glow of the interior light. 'Gone.'

'You mean, he's dead?' It was impossible to hide the panic in her voice.

'Not dead. Gone.'

'Gone where?'

'Beginning.'

Laura gritted her teeth. It took all her self-control not to shout. 'Beginning of what, Andy?'

'Time.'

'Time?'

'Time. At the third stroke it will be eleven fifty-one and ten seconds. Beep . . . Beep . . . Beep . . . At the third stroke it will be eleven fifty-one and twenty seconds. Beep . . . Beep . . . Beep . . . At the – '

'Stop it!' Laura seized hold of André's shoulders and shook her hard. 'You mean, he's dead? Gone?'

'Not dead. Gone,' André corrected.

'Oh my God. This is terrible, Andy. What have you done?'

'Made thunder,' said André simply.

Somehow Laura managed to get the Metro back to Durston Wood. She packed André off to bed and returned to the garage to inspect the Metro more closely. There was no sign of any impact damage, only the minor knocks and dents the car had already acquired. There was some slight distortion of the front bumper, as if it had been exposed to intense heat, but it hardly showed. What did show was a patch of discoloured cellulose on the nearside wing. She looked closely and saw that this also looked as if it had been caused by heat. She hunted through the shelves in the garage and found a tin of T-Cut she had bought to restore the enamel on a second-hand refrigerator. She went to work on the wing. Five minutes' vigorous rubbing brought the paintwork up like new. Only by looking carefully at an angle was it possible to see anything wrong.

The task gave her a chance to sort out her confused whirl of thoughts. Looming uppermost in her mind was the ugly realisation that André's talent could result in her daughter being taken away from her. It was lucky the audition had been a failure: the thought of André's ability being aired on television after what had happened tonight was too awful to contemplate. Laura thought about the first time André had made thunder. The tremendous crash, the burnt grass, Senator barking madly, and the ringing in her ears that hadn't stopped for several hours. Why hadn't it occurred to her then that this was dangerous? André would have to be persuaded that she must never make thunder again. But how? How did one persuade a kid with an IQ of 40 never to do something again? If the conditioning had started five years ago, it might have been possible – like conditioning a toddler not to wet the bed. But André was now ten.

A shock? Would that work?

It would have to be something so terrible that André would never, ever think of making thunder again.

By the time Laura had locked up the garage and returned to the bungalow, she had decided what would have to be done. The thought made her sick inside, but it was nothing compared with the sickness she would feel if André were taken from her.

André's bedroom television was blaring through a late-night movie. Laura pushed her daughter's door open and entered, and the girl looked up from where she was sitting on the bed. In that instant, vital communication passed between mother and daughter. Laura turned the television off and picked up the mother-of-pearl hairbrush.

'Andy,' said Laura quietly. 'You must never, ever make thunder again. Not as long as you live. Do you understand?'

The girl clasped her hands around her shins and rocked back and forth. 'At the third stroke, it will be twelve thirty-one and ten seconds.'

Laura took a step towards her. '*Do you understand!*'

There was distress in the girl's eyes, but not fear. There wouldn't be, of course – not after five years of love and security.

Nor would she scream. That would be to show an emotion. She never screamed or cried or laughed or smiled. But she would remember. She would remember this night for the rest of her life. Laura was grimly determined to make certain of that.

'Take off your nightie.'

André continued rocking, making a strange noise in the back of her throat.

'*Take off your nightie!*'

André pulled off her Laura Ashley nightie and folded it the way she had been shown. She stood naked before her mother, still making strange little whimpering noises in her throat. It was impossible to believe that in that pale, skinny body lay such a terrible, unimaginable power. Perhaps it was a power that couldn't be exorcised like a demon; but it could be made to remain dormant for the rest of André's life.

Laura hooked the Elizabeth Ann dressing-table stool into the middle of the room with her foot and tightened her grip on the hairbrush. She pointed to the stool.

'Bend over.'

André stood rooted, her dark eyes staring at her mother with what might have been a hint of disbelief.

'*I said, bend over!*'

André knelt in front of the stool and did as she was told.

Five minutes later Laura staggered into the bathroom and was violently sick into the basin. Her hands were trembling so much that she had difficulty in turning on the cold water tap. She used her tooth-glass to rinse her mouth, and splashed water onto her face before reeling blindly into her own bedroom, hardly knowing where she was or what she was doing. She flopped fully-dressed onto her bed without drying her hands. Tears streamed unchecked down her cheeks and soaked into the bedcovers.

Please, God, forgive me, but I had to do it.

After a few minutes she felt sufficiently in control of herself to rise and listen at André's door. There was not a sound from within – not that she expected to hear anything. She returned to her bedroom, undressed and slipped into bed. The first twitterings of the dawn chorus were beginning when she finally drifted off into a fitful sleep.

There was a brief furore in the local press over the missing man, which was soon forgotten.

In the years that followed that fateful night in 1985, Laura saw to it that André led as near normal a life as was possible. In the tiny circle of friends she cultivated, the only new additions were Khalid and his parents. Sajii and Hamet and their son became frequent visitors to Durston Wood, and on several occasions Khalid stayed with Laura when his parents had to return to Baghdad at short notice. Iraq was locked in a bitter conflict with Iran; and although they never spoke out, being Kurds, the boy's parents loathed Saddam Hussein and had no wish for their son to be sucked into the tyrant's war-machine. They never told anyone about the large bribes they paid out to ensure that Khalid's name stayed off the reservist draft list.

The Iraqi boy was five years older than André, and mentally more advanced. Yet despite these differences they seemed to share a strange rapport – at least, as far as Laura could judge; it was impossible to tell with André, how much she really liked anyone, but one important indication was that she never showed any signs of distress when Khalid was around. They went for long walks together, watched the same Tom and Jerry cartoons, and André showed Khalid how to perform seemingly impossible stunts on her bicycle. The real difference between them was that André never laughed, whereas Khalid smiled all the time.

In early 1991, the impending war between Iraq and the coalition forces of the United Nations meant that the London branch of the Kurdish National Investment Bank had to close. The British Government had been tolerant. The bank and its customers were opposed to Saddam Hussein and therefore they had been allowed to remain open and not have their assets frozen. Now all Iraqi nationals would have to return home or face deportation or internment. Khalid's mother tearfully told Laura that her husband had visited the British Home Office with a deputation of employees. Their plea that they weren't Iraqis but Kurds was rejected; Kurdistan was not a sovereign state – most of it was part of Iraq. They would have to go home.

'We never wanted to be part of Iraq,' said Sajii on her last visit to Durston Wood. 'The British forced Kurdistan to become a province of Iraq after the First World War. And when people like my grandfather fought against Baghdad rule, the British sent troops and planes into Kurdistan and helped the Iraqis to massacre us. The British have fought more wars against us Kurds in this century than any other nation.'

Laura comforted the distraught woman as best she could. They had become very close friends in the five years since they had first met in the rehearsal room on Waterloo Station. They had so much in common.

'So will you look after Khalid for us until all this terrible Kuwait business is over? Please, Laura – we beg you. Saddam Hussein cannot last much longer.' She added with sudden vehemence, 'We will rise up and destroy him.'

'But the Home Office have said that you must all leave.'

'They cannot make Khalid leave! He's a child. He's happy staying here with you!'

'Sajii,' said Laura softly. 'Khalid is twenty-one. Under British law he's been an adult for three years. He cannot expect special treatment.'

'He's a reservist. They will send him to Kuwait!'

'Oh surely not, Sajii. What use would Khalid be? I know his IQ is higher than André's but – '

'Laura – you do not understand. We have been paying money to the army draft officer in Baghdad not to have Khalid called up. He's completed his basic training, but that is all. Now the officer has been replaced. Hamet has received a fax saying that Khalid is to serve.'

'But couldn't you ask to be interned here?'

'Don't you think we've asked!' the woman flared up. 'They said there would be legal problems. I tell you, the British hate the Kurds. They always have. They said nothing when five thousand of us were gassed at Halabji. They carried on trading with Saddam Hussein . . .'

Laura moved to the woman's side to comfort her when she started crying.

'But we could leave him here with you, Laura,' Sajii pleaded through her tears. 'It is quiet. No one would know. We will pay you well.'

Laura thought of the consequences of having the police nosing around, looking for an alien. An enemy alien at that. They might link Khalid's savant talents with André's abilities. They might delve back into the past to the time when a drunk disappeared one night on his way home from the pub. It was a risk she dared not take, no matter how much she hated herself for what she had to say to Khalid's mother. 'No, Sajii . . . I'm sorry, but I cannot do it.'

Sajii had been staring at the floor, but now raised her red-rimmed eyes to Laura. She was a striking woman, always tastefully dressed in expensive Western clothes; although approaching fifty she had clear skin and soft dark eyes. Those eyes held more sorrow now than reproach. 'There is only Khalid,' she said. 'He is all we have. We wanted brothers and sisters for him but it was not to be. There were problems when I was carrying . . . But I've told you all this.'

'Sajii – you know I would do it if I could; but I can't. Anyway, there won't be a war. Saddam Hussein is bound to see that he can't possibly win.'

Sajii rose and turned away from Laura so that the English-woman would not see her fresh tears. 'You do not understand how the Arab mind works, Laura. No one in the West does. It is not your fault, but it is our tragedy.' She went to the door and called in Kurdish to Khalid, who was showing André how he could balance on her bicycle while it was stationary.

Later, André's hand slipped into Laura's as they watched Sajii reverse her BMW out of the drive.

'Khalid go home?' André asked.

'Yes – he's going home.'

Two nights later a television news report included a brief shot showing a group of Iraqis in a check-in queue at Heathrow Airport. There as a fleeting glimpse of Hamet and Sajii, both looking pale and drawn as they piled their luggage onto the weigh-in conveyor. Khalid was with them.

Smiling, as he always did . . .

213

50

Saturday, 9th March 1991

During Harry Mathison's thirty years as a private detective he had discussed work with prospective clients in some odd places, but never in the Travellers' Fare cafeteria on Waterloo Station. He had also been given some strange commissions – but this one out-stranged them all. He looked up from his notebook and met Mr Simmonds' sad, yet somehow rather steely, grey eyes.

'This is going to be an expensive task, Mr Simmonds, so let's make sure I've got everything straight. You want me to take one photograph of the front entrance of every apartment block in the London area whose name ends with "– ingham Court", and you want the postal address of every such block? Correct?'

'Correct, Mr Mathison. The photograph I caught a glimpse of in my wife's handbag shows her outside the block where her lover lives. I know I'll recognise it again. I'm determined to find her and get her back. I love her very much.'

'It could be a lengthy job.'

'I'm sure you have electoral rolls for the entire Greater London area?'

Harry said nothing. He never divulged his operating methods to anyone, and certainly not to strangers who gave him false names and refused to disclose their addresses. He wondered about Mr Simmonds. Expensive charcoal-grey suit, regimental tie to go with his military bearing; not a hair out of place. Perhaps a man whose pride had been injured? Perhaps not.

'You'd be able to look up places such as Fellingham Court, Nottingham Court, and make a list to cut down on the leg-work,' Mr Simmonds continued. 'But I'm sure I don't need to tell you how to do your job.'

'No,' said Harry evenly. 'You don't.'

'There's no need to investigate council developments,' Mr Simmonds added. 'Concentrate on middle-class and upwards blocks. What little I saw of it looked smart. I shall call your portable number each day for a progress report, starting tomorrow. We must keep our conversations circumspect. I'm sure I don't have to tell you that cellular phone calls are not secure.'

'No,' said Harry. 'You don't.'

'The number of cheap scanners on the market that cover the nine hundred meg. to one gig band is amazing.'

Harry made no comment. He made regular use of scanners to monitor calls on cordless and cellular phones.

'If,' Mr Simmonds continued, 'from your description of the properties, you come up with something that sounds promising, I shall come up to London to collect the photographs.'

'I could always post them to you,' Harry suggested. He preferred to know his clients' addresses.

'That won't be necessary. I enjoy my visits to London – even this early. I want some fast results on this, Mr Mathison. I've checked with your association. They tell me you have six operatives. I want you to put all of them on this project.' His usual lazy smile returned. 'Once I've shown Edith just how determined I can be, I know she'll come back to me.'

Harry decided that he didn't want the job. It smelt. And he didn't like this know-all military type with his close-cropped hair and mocking smile. There was a simple way to get rid of him.

'It's going to cost you fifteen hundred per day inclusive of VAT and expenses, Mr Simmonds. It's an open-ended commitment, I don't know your address, and I suspect you've given me a false name – so I shall need two days' fees in advance.'

Mr Simmonds was undeterred. He produced a genuine Gucci wallet and counted out thirty £100 banknotes. 'It's your lucky day, Mr Mathison. Three thousand up front in cash and no receipt required. And here's another three hundred because I want you to start work immediately.' He finished his coffee and stood. Suddenly his easy smile was gone, to be replaced by an icy stare that made even a hardened private investigator like Harry feel decidedly uncomfortable. 'Good luck, Mr Mathison. And because I've handed over a large sum of money, please don't think I'm a soft touch. That would be a very foolish assumption indeed.'

'I don't like threats, Mr Simmonds.'

'And I don't like uttering them. Less still, having to carry them out. But I'm sure that won't be necessary. I've been assured that you are the best. Good day to you.'

Mr Simmonds left the cafeteria and crossed the station concourse to the row of payphones. He called Leo Buller at Kimmeridge House.

'Well, Leo?'

'Max – I'm going through every damned file going back ten years. I told you it would be a waste of time. I had a big clear-out before I left England – there was no point in shipping a load of dross across the Atlantic. And I know I wouldn't keep letters from what I assumed to be a neurotic mother.'

Max checked an impulse to express his displeasure. It would achieve nothing. 'Very well, Leo. We'll just have to hope that my approach produces something.'

'How's everything your end?'

'Mission somewhat expensively accomplished,' Max replied. 'My train leaves in twenty minutes, so we should have time left today to finish those tests. Be seeing you.'

51

CENTRAL IRAQ

Nuri's and Khalid's exceptionally long run of good luck faltered when they were only three kilometres from the fly-blown, oil-lamp-lit motel at Sammara where they had spent an uncomfortable night. They had decided to break their journey quite early the previous day, in order to get a good night's rest and be fresh and alert for this morning's start. Now there was a small side-road at Daur they had to look out for just south of Tikrit, if they were to avoid the town.

They were still heading north, but they were now travelling on the east bank of the Tigris, with ancient mud-brick villages built on high, even older earthworks to their right, and the palm-fringed embankment of the Baghdad to Mosul railway line on their left. The scenery was undergoing a subtle change as they climbed. Already they could see the yellow foothills of

Jabal Hamrin far to the east, and Tikrit itself marked the end of the rich, fertile flood-plain between the Tigris and the Euphrates. From Saddam Hussein's home town, the land rose steadily until it became the mountains and valleys of the two travellers' beloved homeland.

Khalid drove fast, as he normally did, overtaking a stream of military vehicles also heading for Tikrit. Nuri remained silent. He supposed that, in a perverse way, Khalid's bravura acted as a sort of protection: no Kurd who was involved in the uprising, and no army deserter in his right mind, would travel this road.

They found the turning at Daur, but it was signposted as being closed to all but military traffic.

'Keep going!' Nuri snapped when Khalid slowed down to take the turning.

'But we can't go to Tikrit, Nuri.'

'We don't have any choice. This map's useless. We'll take the next turning off to the left, no matter where it goes.'

Khalid gave his companion an unhappy look and accelerated. Nuri studied the map intently, not knowing if the pecked lines that wandered all over the Western Desert were proper roads or goat tracks. His blinding wish now was to get as far north as possible and join one of the pershmarga guerilla groups. Once they were in the mountains, they would be safe. If only they had an off-road vehicle like a Land Rover. Maybe they could steal one?

A blaring horn startled Nuri out of his reverie. He saw to his horror that Khalid had overtaken a smart transporter bearing the insignia and pennants of the Presidential Guard, 1st Tank Battalion. On the back of the vehicle was a T–72 that had been smartened up with new camouflage paint. Khalid hooked the wheel to the right to swerve back in lane in time to avoid an oncoming truck, which also flashed its lights and sounded its horn.

'Don't you ever learn!' Nuri snarled at Khalid. 'Ease up! Don't draw attention to us!'

'But there are many of them, Nuri. We never get anywhere.'

And to prove his point another transporter appeared ahead.

Khalid accelerated, and they passed the slow-moving vehicle without trouble.

Nuri's first thought when he heard the explosion was that they had been shot at. Then he saw the smoke and fumes blowing around the bonnet and thought they had hit a land-mine – before realising that it couldn't be either, otherwise Khalid wouldn't have been able to retain control of the car.

'Engine dead,' Khalid announced as he steered the slowing car off the road and onto the dusty verge. He released the bonnet catch as soon as the car stopped, and Nuri jumped out to inspect the engine. A mixture of steam and exhaust gases billowed into the air when he pulled the hood up. Steam and boiling water was jetting across the engine compartment and soaking the electrics.

Khalid joined him, and both men stared disconsolately at the engine. Nuri swore bitterly.

'What is it, Nuri?' Khalid was a brilliant driver but his mechanical knowledge was sadly lacking.

'Blown head-gasket. What does it look like?' The older man banged his fist impotently on the wing and roundly cursed their misfortune. 'Now what do we do?'

'Buy another car?' Khalid suggested.

Nuri resisted the temptation to punch Khalid in the face. 'Good idea. Wave down a passing car and offer to buy it off the driver.' Nuri had to grab Khalid's arm to prevent him doing just that; he should have known better than to waste irony on the young man. 'Idiot! I was joking. We have to be careful with our money. I'll leave you here and hitch a lift back to Sammara – see if I can find a garage that'll come out.'

'No! Please, Nuri,' Khalid implored. 'We must stay together!'

'We can't leave the car unattended. It's got decent tyres. It'll be stripped. Do you understand?'

Khalid didn't understand and clung forlornly to his companion's sleeve. 'Must stay together, Nuri! Otherwise good luck won't work.'

'Well, it's not working now, is it?' Nuri pointed out angrily. He spotted the tank-transporter that Khalid had carved up

218

approaching. 'Look busy in the engine!' he hissed, and bent over the engine compartment.

Both men peered industriously into the stricken Escort's innards, pointedly ignoring the big army transporter that ground past them in low gear. There was an explosive hiss of compressed-air brakes as the laden vehicle pulled onto the verge in front of them and stopped. The door of the driver's cab opened, then slammed shut.

'What about your good luck now?' Nuri whispered.

A single pair of footsteps drew near. There was a deep, rich chuckle. 'The curse I put on you,' said a voice, 'I did not expect it to work so quickly.'

Nuri pretended to notice the transporter driver for the first time. He looked up, and was about to offer a sheepish smile and an apology to the soldier, when he saw that it wasn't a soldier but a stocky, unshaven, unwashed civilian in oil-stained dungarees. The man was eyeing the smart business suits of the two travellers with ill-concealed dislike.

'I must apologise for what happened back there,' said Nuri, much relieved that he wasn't dealing with a Presidential Guard.

'Nearly ran me off the road,' the driver accused.

'We were late for an appointment.' Nuri shrugged and gestured to the Escort's engine. 'Now, it doesn't matter.'

The driver moved forward and looked down at the engine. 'What's the trouble?'

'A blown head-gasket,' Nuri explained. 'Is there a garage back at Sammara that could do repairs? We are strangers here.'

The driver laughed. 'You won't find anywhere there. But there's a good garage in Tikrit that might be able to get help. Spares are a big problem now unless you've got money.'

Nuri was a good actor. Mention of the dreaded town failed to shake his bland smile. 'Thank you. We will try to get a lift there.'

'I'll give you a tow,' the driver offered, hauling a hank of oily rope from under the tank. He brushed Nuri's protests aside. 'It's no problem. That's where I'm going anyway. Got a victory parade on soon, that's why they want the tanks.' He grinned at Khalid. 'You used to being towed?'

Khalid nodded vigorously. 'Yes. I've been trained.'

The driver grunted and hitched the Escort to one of the shackles that was holding the tank secure. 'Nothing to it. Uphill all the way so it won't be a problem for you. But no overtaking. Okay?'

'Okay,' Khalid agreed, not seeing the driver's joke.

Once they were moving, Nuri let out a long sigh of relief. 'You know, for a terrible moment I thought you were going to tell him that you had been trained in the army.'

Khalid's forehead was creased as he concentrated on keeping the tow-rope taut. 'I didn't think that would be a good idea, Nuri.'

Despite their plight, Nuri managed to raise a smile. The two men fell silent. Nuri looked out of the window. His heart sank slowly in step with the roadsigns counting down the kilometres to Tikrit. They had just passed the two-kilometre marker when the transporter stopped outside a lonely, tumbledown mud-brick garage that had once been a wheelwright's workshop. Outside was a faded board bearing the owner's name above an American Express Welcome Here sign. A huge poster of Saddam Hussein had been cut to fit under the ramshackle building's gable end. A ten-year-old Nissan Bluebird in good condition, with a 1,000-dinar price tag, stood on the packed mud forecourt. The ancient workshop doors hung open on broken hinges. In the dark interior could be seen several old cars on axle-stands.

'We're in luck,' Nuri breathed. 'We're well outside the town.'

The transporter driver unhitched the Escort, waved aside Nuri's thanks and offer of money, and continued on his way.

The two men entered the garage's gloomy interior and found the owner asleep in a van. He was a swarthy Turkoman wearing a filthy, oil-stained galabiya, and had a temper that matched his short stature.

'Come back in an hour,' he snapped when Nuri shook him gently by the shoulder.

'We need help. Our car is broken down.'

'So's my recovery waggon.'

'We're parked outside.'

220

Muttering to himself, the Turkoman climbed out of the van and regarded the two strangers suspiciously.

'A Ford Escort with a blown head-gasket,' Nuri explained.

'I don't have no head-gaskets.'

Which was not strictly true because the grimy walls of the workshop were festooned with a huge assortment of head-gaskets hanging from rusty nails.

The garage owner glanced through the doors at the Escort parked on the opposite side of the road. 'I don't have a gasket for that model.'

'Couldn't you send for one?'

'Take a week to get one from Ankara. Plenty of hotels in the town if you want to wait.'

Nuri preferred not to think about spending a week in a Tikriti hotel.

'You're Kurds?' the garage owner asked.

'Businessmen,' said Nuri. He mentally calculated how much money he had left. 'We have some urgent business in the north. Perhaps you are interested in an offer for the Bluebird?'

The Turkoman shrugged. 'A thousand dinar. No more, no less.'

'Four hundred US dollars,' said Nuri. 'And you keep the Escort.'

Now the garage owner was very suspicious. Nuri wondered if he had been over-generous. The Turkoman's crafty eyes had narrowed. 'Dollars? You have American dollars?'

'We've had business dealings with Kuwait since before the troubles,' said Nuri evenly, watching the Turkoman carefully and wishing he knew the latest exchange rate the moneychangers were giving for US dollars against the Iraqi dinar. A businessman would be expected to know such things.

'Cash?'

'Cash,' Nuri agreed.

'Six hundred and fifty dollars.'

'Four fifty,' Nuri countered.

The garage owner spat onto the oil-stained floor. 'That is what I paid for the car.'

Nuri shrugged indifferently and turned to leave. 'Very well. There will be garages in Tikrit.'

'Five hundred.'

Nuri pretended to weigh the offer. Eventually he nodded. 'Agreed.'

The two men smacked palms.

'Is the car ready?' Nuri asked.

'Yes, but first I see your money.' The Turkoman held out his hand, his eyes alight with greed.

Nuri unzipped the inside pocket of his jacket and felt for five $100 bills with his fingertips. The garage owner was suspicious enough as it was without producing a thick wad of dollars. The Turkoman snatched the notes from Nuri's hand and held them up to the light.

'They're good bills,' said Nuri, smiling.

The garage owner grunted and stuffed the money in a pocket in his smock. He ushered Nuri and Khalid onto the forecourt. 'You wait in your car while I fix the Bluebird's papers. Ten minutes.'

'One point eight litres,' said Khalid excitedly, sliding behind the Escort's wheel. 'More powerful than this car, Nuri.'

Nuri was about to sit in the passenger seat when he noticed the overhead telephone wire serving the garage. It was such a tumbledown wreck of a business that he hadn't expected it to be on the phone. Also, the garage owner had disappeared smartly once the two men had crossed the road. Nuri started to recross the road.

'Nuri – we must stay – ' Khalid's protest was silenced by an angry gesture from Nuri, but the young man's eyes went round with worry as his comrade disappeared into the dark shadows of the workshop.

Through a doorway at the back of the workshop, Nuri heard what sounded like a telephone cradle being rattled impatiently. He moved forward on his toes. The door opened onto a small, dark room that served the Turkoman as office, kitchen and bedroom; he was sitting at a cluttered desk with his back to the door.

222

'Hallo?' said the Turkoman. 'Put me through to police head-quarters. It's urgent . . .'

Nuri looked around quickly for a weapon while the garage owner made impatient noises down the telephone.

'Listen carefully. I'm calling from – '

The Turkoman got no further. He made a gagging sound and dropped the telephone. His hands flew up to the speedometer cable that Nuri had looped around his neck. He fought with extraordinary strength, his feet lashed out and kicked the desk over, but Nuri forced him to the floor and used his entire weight to pin the man down. A socket-wrench tommy-bar caught Nuri's eye. He snatched it up. The chromium-plated bar slid smoothly into the centre of the knot of Bowden cable at the nape of his victim's neck. Four hard twists of the deadly tourni-quet were enough. The cable sank into the Turkoman's neck like a wire cheese-cutter and closed his windpipe. His silent struggles weakened rapidly. A few convulsive spasms, and it was all over.

Nuri wasted no time checking that the man was dead. He grabbed the telephone handset, apologised for the mistake, and replaced it on the cradle. He searched quickly through the things that had fallen to the floor when the desk overturned, and found the Bluebird's papers and keys in a marked envelope. He recovered the $100 bills from the dead man's smock, and searched the rickety shelves until he found a proper road map of Northern Iraq, which he stuffed in his pocket. His last task was to dump the Turkoman's body in the back of the van and cover it with sacking. The chances were that they had an hour or two before the body was discovered; three at the most.

He walked casually onto the forecourt, surprised at how calm he felt. But after a month of being bombed by B52s and strafed by A10s, this was nothing.

'Bring our things,' he called out to Khalid.

While the young man transferred their few possessions to the Bluebird's boot, Nuri checked its fuel and was relieved to find that it had a full tank. A sortie into the garage proved even more successful – he returned with four full ten-litre army issue

223

gasoline cans, and several one-litre bottles of engine oil. All were dumped in the boot.

Khalid sat in the Nissan's driver's seat and waggled the steering-wheel. 'Good steering, Nuri – no play.'

Nuri unfolded the map and spread it out on the car's bonnet. 'We're going to have to head west and work our way north.'

Khalid stopped playing with the car's controls. 'Into the Western Desert, Nuri?'

'We can't risk any more roadblocks. The permit your policeman friend stamped for us doesn't cover this car. Shit . . . We *have* to go through Tikrit.' His finger had stopped on the sixty-kilometre length of the great stretch of water that lay to the west between the Tigris and the Euphrates, the Tharthar Basin. The turning off the main road that skirted the lake was to the north of the hated town.

Khalid fretted about the danger of venturing into Saddam Hussein's home town. 'Do we have to, Nuri?'

'It's either that or we head back to Baghdad. And we'd never get through all those roadblocks.' He folded the map and sat beside Khalid. 'Okay – let's get going.'

52

SOUTHERN ENGLAND

The cliffs hurtled towards Leo at a thousand knots. At that unnerving velocity, nearly twice the speed of sound, the scrubland beneath the fighter was a buff-coloured blur with no discernible detail apart from the brief flash of roofs in the occasional village.

'Target landmarks found, daddy,' said a soft, sweet voice in his headset. It was the computer-sampled voice of his daughter, whom he rarely saw since his marriage and career had folded in California. The day would come when all military pilots would be guided by the stress-alleviating voices of their loved ones.

The visual identification system and its radar backing had probed the cliff, found the target, and signalled the flight controls. The aircraft banked sharply towards the cleft.

'Fifteen kilometres. Target acquisition, daddy.'

The incredible approach speed made the tiny opening swell like the automatic iris of a high-speed camera that is suddenly exposed to intense light. It was a tunnel, and the steel doors were open.

The white box around the target changed to a red hexagon.

'Ten kilometres. Missile lock, daddy.'

The mission profile was on full automatic, including stores release. The missiles leapt away from the fighter and streaked towards the yawning tunnel, but Leo didn't see them complete their flight. The control column jerked towards his groin, causing the mighty concrete edifice to drop below his line of vision. The stress gauges howled, but the experience of many such flights told Leo that the sudden appearance of blue sky hadn't been fast enough. There was a tremendous crash that shook the entire cockpit. At that instant all the instruments died, the head-up display went blank and the scream of the engines ceased. They didn't die away – they simply stopped. The sudden silence and cessation of all visual information brought its own sense of disorientation.

Leo slid back the plastic canopy. The flight-simulator pod was frozen in a ninety-degree climb so that he was tipped on his back. He touched the reset button that caused the actuators to settle the gimbal-mounted pod in the level position. He released his seat harness, removed the bulky Virtual World helmet and looked questioningly across the test laboratory at Max, who was sitting at the control console. The laboratory had once been the banqueting hall of Kimmeridge House; the Burroughs mini-computer was up in the minstrels' gallery, and the ungainly flight-simulator – looking like an advanced arcade machine – was in the centre of the hall where the long dining-table had once stood. The gleaming modern machines contrasted oddly with the hall's mellowed oak panelling.

'Well?' Leo demanded, gingerly easing his lanky frame out of the cockpit. His height did not lend itself to gung-ho gymnastics.

Max looked up from the control console. 'One point six milliseconds too late.'

'Damn. All that work and we've only shaved point-two milli-secs?'

'You also shaved a rock,' said Max humorously, making a note in the flight-simulator log in his meticulous handwriting. Inwardly, he was seething. The two men and their small team of technicians had achieved much with their neural network brain-emulators, but real success was eluding them. At times it seemed that the targets set by the Ministry of Defence in the research and development contract were impossible to achieve unless they made a major breakthrough in their neural-mapping and understanding of the brain.

'Methinks, Leo,' murmured Max, 'that we are coming to the end of the road with visual-recognition neural networks based on porpoise brains. A law of diminishing returns is setting in. It's needing more and more work to edge up the approach speed. And it's becoming routine work that can be handled by Stevens and Harding, leaving you free to concentrate on our other problem.'

'Max – we can't afford to let this work go. It's our bread and butter.'

'And a defence system like that T–55 had would be our jam. Quite a lot of jam.'

'Would it, Max? The world's changing fast. The Soviet Union's on the verge of collapse. Third World countries are now having to toe the US line because they can no longer turn to Russia – '

'The world is becoming more unsafe,' Max interrupted. 'There'll be a massive nuclear proliferation if the Soviet republics get their independence. And it's only a matter of time before Southern African blacks get their hands on white South Africa's nuclear arsenal. Imagine the effect of long-range nuclear-tipped Bull artillery shells being used in tribal wars.'

'I hadn't thought of that,' Leo admitted.

'Nor has anyone else. And Pakistan will be carrying out underground tests within the next three years. A Moslem bomb will be used to settle a few old scores, don't you think? The point is, Leo, that the world is going to become an extremely dangerous and unstable place. Anyone offering the sort of defen-

226

sive umbrella that that T–55 had out in the Gulf is going to be on course to make a lot of money.'

Leo looked hard at his colleague. Although Max had been speaking softly as he always did, there was a hard light shining in his steel-grey eyes. 'You never give up, do you, Max? I thought we argued this out on the flight. We don't have a manipulative savant. And for all we know, that bloody tennis ball could be a fake.'

Max reached into a pocket and unfolded the letter they had found in the T–55 tank. He read it aloud. ' "Dear Andy, Your letter came with Red Crescent and took three weeks because of bombing. I can't say where I am but I was very happy for me to hear from you. I can now make thunder like you showed me and I can still do tricks with tennis balls. More bombing started so will finish this letter tomorrow." ' Max folded the letter carefully and returned it to his pocket. ' "I can now make thunder like you showed me," ' he repeated. 'We most certainly do have a manipulative savant, Leo. Maybe this Andy is not in our grasp. Not yet. But he will be.'

Leo clenched his fists in tight-lipped anger. 'And when he is, do you really think I will agree to neural-mapping him to find out what makes him tick, and possibly killing him in the process?'

Max's easy smile never wavered. 'I know you well enough by now, Leo, to know that you will.'

53

NORTHERN IRAQ

The outskirts of Tikrit where just like those of any other Iraqi town, endless tenement houses and shops built of dun-coloured bricks from the mud of the Tigris – but they had ten times the number of Saddam Hussein portraits strung up across their narrow streets. The other big difference was that here the central plaza was dominated by a huge, diamond-shaped monument bearing pictures of a benign Saddam Hussein on each facet. The remarkable talent of Iraq's architects, working in a tradition that went back two thousand years, had given the monument a

227

grace of proportion and delicacy of design that it was somehow impossible to reconcile with the brutalities it represented. It could not have been more different from the unyielding Gothic edifices that commemorated the triumphs of Hitler's Third Reich.

Nuri watched the monument out of the corner of his eye as Khalid followed the flow of traffic around the edge of the plaza. The town was the seat of Saddam Hussein's power, and the monument its very centre. If the Allies had had an understanding of the Arab mind, the plaza would have been number one on their list of priority targets. That the town was unscathed by bombing was a vindication of the claim by Saddam Hussein's followers that their leader was invincible.

'We could destroy that thing, Nuri,' said Khalid expressionlessly, dropping into second gear when the traffic came to a standstill.

Nuri glanced at his companion. 'Sure, it would be easy,' he answered morosely. 'All we need is a few kilos of explosive and a death wish.'

'I mean *I* could destroy it,' Khalid corrected. 'Like I destroyed that man.'

'You concentrate on your driving,' Nuri answered.

The traffic started moving again.

'I could, Nuri.'

'How?'

'The same way I killed that man who followed us.'

Nuri grunted. Conversations with Khalid sometimes went around in circles. 'But he had a booby-trapped rifle.'

'Not his rifle,' said Khalid flatly. 'I killed him.'

Nuri recalled their extraordinary run of good luck in the Gulf War and the strange death of the Mukharabat agent. He was about to argue with his companion – but what was the point? In truth, Nuri didn't know what to think.

Once clear of the town, both men felt they could relax a little. The increasing frequency of the signposts to Mosul were reassuring, even though, as Iraq's fourth largest city, Mosul had always been heavily garrisoned. But more important to the two travellers, it marked the southernmost border of Kurdistan, where their countrymen were in the majority and where they would find friends.

They stopped at a scruffy truck drivers' roadhouse for a cheap but filling meal of lamb stew.

'If you're going north, don't go to Mosul,' a Kurdish tanker driver warned them when he heard Nuri's accent. 'Mosul's bad. Republican Guards everywhere, taking it out on anyone they suspect of being pershmarga. Take the oil pipeline road to the west at Baji for fifty kilometres, then turn north just before the big dam at Qaddissiya. It's a desert road, but it's in good condition.'

Nuri had no wish to discuss their plans with strangers, but he thanked the friendly truck driver for his advice. They pressed on northwards. At Baji Khalid turned off the main highway and drove west along the neglected, dusty service road that ran alongside the disused Amman-Kirkuk pipeline.

The terrain changed rapidly from the fertile meadows of the Tigris to the broad, irrigated, cotton-growing plains of the Jazirah. Occasional ranges of barren yellow foothills rose out of the plains – harsh reminders that the entire area would be desert where it not for the enterprise and industry of the generations of peasant farmers who worked this land. Their crop was used to make muslin – the fine, gauze-like cloth that derived its name from Mosul.

By late afternoon the road had degenerated to a rough track that forced Khalid, at Nuri's insistence, to reduce speed. The villages they passed through were noticeably fewer and poorer as the land become more arid and hilly. Gradually the cotton gave way to wheat and other cereals; they were now close to the unmarked border with Syria. It was here that Iraq's great Western Desert of the Hamad to the south was trying to reassert itself.

The track straightened to cut a broad swathe through fields of tall but immature stands of bright-green maize.

Khalid pointed ahead. 'Look, Nuri.' There was excitement in his voice.

There had to be something special about the two teenage girls for Khalid to slow down to pass their gaily-painted donkey cart,

229

which was loaded with an early crop of potatoes. The answer was in their clothes; they were wearing long, richly embroidered black cotton dresses which, unlike Arab dress, had been carefully tailored to fit the girls' youthful figures. The garments were of a similar cut to Western-style dressing-gowns.

The girls were special. Very special.

They were Kurds.

They were tall, proud and haughty, although the younger girl gave the travellers a shy smile as they drove by. The breeze flattened the thin, jet-black cotton provocatively against their breasts. The older girl was holding the reins. She looked straight ahead, pretending to ignore the admiring glances of the travellers.

'We're home, Nuri!' Khalid cried elatedly, banging the steering-wheel with his fist.

'Just keep driving,' Nuri answered caustically, not caring to admit that the sight of the girls had been a welcome tonic.

They drove on into gathering dusk.

Just as they approached the crest of a hill, Nuri yelled at Khalid to stop. 'Switch off the engine!' he snapped, winding down his window.

Khalid did as he was told. The two men listened. Both heard the dull *wap wap wap* beat of helicopter rotors and the crackle of distant gunfire.

'Get the car under those trees!' Nuri hissed.

Khalid pulled off the road and parked beneath the straggling, half-dead branches of an abandoned almond grove. Nuri jumped from the car and stared upwards at the darkening grey sky. The cover afforded by the almond trees was useless; any helicopter visually scouring the area in the present light would be certain to spot the Bluebird. Nuri yanked the driver's door open and half-dragged Khalid from his seat.

'Come on! We've got to get away from the car!'

They raced deeper into the neglected grove, stumbled down a steep slope and plunged into the thick reeds growing in the boggy soil of a nearly dried-up irrigation canal.

Nuri breathed more easily once he looked up and saw that they were well-hidden.

'Now what do we do, Nuri?' Khalid whispered.

'We wait until that chopper's gone.' He pulled the road map from his pocket. As near as he could make out, they were two kilometres from the village of Afan, where he had planned to find accommodation for the night.

The sound of the unseen machine's turbines deepened and became louder. It was coming towards them and flying very low – although Nuri dared not look up. For a panic-stricken moment he thought it was going to pass immediately overhead and flatten the reeds that hid them. And even if the reeds weren't disturbed, if the crew were using passive infra-red scopes they would be certain to spot the fugitives. But the helicopter climbed and hovered for a few moments as though scouring the landscape, then it spotted something and veered away, apparently following the road the two men had just driven along.

'Those girls!' Khalid cried. 'It's seen those girls!' He tried to stand and break cover, but Nuri grabbed his legs and pulled him down.

'We stay here!'

'But those girls! We have to help them!'

'We stay here and we stay hidden!' Nuri snarled, pinning Khalid down. 'They won't be interested in them.'

But the helicopter was interested in something, and Nuri guessed it had to be the girls. The sound of the thrashing rotors died to idle, as though the machine had settled on the ground. A few minutes later Nuri thought he heard a scream, though he could have been mistaken. Khalid heard it too, and moaned softly in his throat, but he made no attempt to break away. After fifteen minutes there was a sudden burst of automatic fire.

'No!' Khalid wept. 'No! No! No!'

Another burst of fire.

The turbines opened up again and the unseen helicopter headed back in the direction of Afan. The roar of the turbines became muted as it lost height and dropped below the ridge. As before, the beat of the machine's rotors dropped to an idle as if it had touched down.

It was now twilight. Nuri signalled to Khalid to follow him. The two men broke cover and raced up the far bank of the

231

canal. They kept to the shadows of the scrubland and worked their way cautiously on their stomachs to the crest of the hill just as the shooting started.

Two kilometres below them was the tiny village of Afan, little more than a group of farmhouses. No doubt it was the home of the two girls. The buildings were bathed in a cold halogen light from powerful searchlights on a helicopter that was resting on the ground near by. Clouds of fine, swirling dust thrown up from the idling rotors drifted across the scene like bonfire smoke.

The shooting had stopped. The helicopter's turbine rose to a roar. The machine lifted, playing its powerful lights in the dust storm created by its downwash. A ghost-like shadow moved on the ground, seeming to seek the protection of the billowing dust-clouds. Spears of light flicked from the machine's multi-barrelled cannons, and the shadow stopped moving. The helicopter reached one thousand feet and exposed its silhouette to the smear of crimson light across the western sky.

Nuri swore. 'A Super Frelon gunship!'

Actually it was a troop-transporter, but the difference was academic; it was one of Saddam Hussein's killing-machines – the machine made in France, optics made in Switzerland, rockets and launchers made in England, and the whole allowed to pursue its murderous pleasure by courtesy of the United States. Now it tilted its nose down and headed east. Khalid tried to scramble to his feet when it had dwindled into the distance, but Nuri grabbed him around the ankles and forced his comrade to the ground.

'We must help them, Nuri.'

'We are not going falling about in the dark. We'll stay here until morning.'

'Couldn't we go back to the car?'

'If they've left troops behind with infra-red sights, the heat from the engine will show up like a bonfire. We'll stay here and sleep. At first light we'll take a look around.'

With darkness came freezing temperatures, forcing the two men to return to the Bluebird. Once out of the biting wind, Nuri thought he would be able to sleep – it had been a long, eventful day – but he passed most of the night staring up at the Bluebird's headlining. Even though he had served many years in the army and taken part in many operations which, like his killing of the Turkoman garage owner that day, could hardly be described as military, he was dreading what they would find at Afan in the morning.

54

SOUTHERN ENGLAND
Sunday, 10th March 1991

Several pounds of multi-sectioned *Sunday Times* crashing through the letterbox and landing on the doormat like a newborn foal woke Laura early, as it did every Sunday. There had been a time when Sunday mornings, or any morning of the week for that matter, was a time for lazing in bed. Mornings were when she and David made love; the more hectic the party of the night before, the more passionate their love-making. The bitter-sweet memories began to invade her . . .

No!

She kicked back the duvet and jumped from the bed. Denial was part of her punishment, and after eleven years it had become nearly automatic. But there were times when her needs threatened to gain ascendancy, and she had an uncomfortable feeling that it wouldn't take much for her supposed iron control to slip . . . She pulled a dressing-gown over her baggy, sexless pyjamas, retrieved the newspaper and went into the kitchen to make herself a cup of tea.

She gaped in astonishment at the huge spray of carnations standing in a vase on the kitchen table with an envelope propped against it. Her hands shook as she opened the envelope and took out the home-made card.

HAPPY MOTHERS DAY TO THE NICIST MOTHER IN THE WORD FROM ANDRÉ NORMANVILLE.

Laura sat down and read through the message spelt out in awkwardly formed capitals with a red felt-tip pen. The base of each letter was unnaturally straight, as though André had used a ruler as a guide – something Laura had shown her many times how to do, but the principle had never sunk in. She read the simple message over and over again, and the emotion that welled up in her threatened to choke her. It wasn't so much the spelling errors or André's incongruous use of her full name that moved her; it was that this was the first time André had written a message without help. Her letters to Khalid when he was out of the country had been joint efforts that usually took an evening to write. Perhaps they had helped her at school? Laura thought suddenly. But no – that would suggest planning on André's part, and André did not have the ability to plan ahead. And yet the evidence that she could make plans was filling the kitchen with its rich perfume. Where had she got the money for the flowers? Perhaps she had saved it out of the weekly £10 she was given every Wednesday? But again, saving meant planning – and the André she knew wouldn't even understand that Mothering Sunday was coming up, or what it signified.

Laura cradled her head in her hands and wept, not knowing if she cried from simple joy at her daughter's gift, or because of the profound changes taking place in André that the magnificent carnations represented. André must have looked up the telephone number of a local florist, and used the telephone to order the flowers *and* arrange for them to be delivered when she was alone. On top of that, she had arranged them beautifully, made a card, written the message, and left the flowers where Laura would see them as soon as she got up. In other words, André had employed a huge range of social skills that did not equate with her last Vineland assessment. The psychologist at the Candice Webb Special School had said that André was improving, but this wasn't improvement – this was a giant intellectual leap.

And then a thought crossed Laura's mind that turned her bewilderment to stark inner terror.

Supposing André's other powers were also undergoing a change?

How much longer before another 'event' took place? How much longer before the authorities discovered André's powers and took her away? They would have to protect society from her. They would build a special secure unit for her, and lock her away in a drugged stupor for the rest of her life.

234

55

The bar of the Rose and Crown in Salisbury was crowded. Harry Mathison spotted Mr Simmonds sitting alone at a table and armed himself with a pint of bitter before pushing his way carefully through the lunchtime throng, briefcase in one hand, beer in the other.

'Good evening, Mr Simmonds.'

Max looked up from his *Sunday Telegraph* and beamed. 'Mr Mathison – punctual to the minute. This gives me confidence in your efficiency.'

'That's what you're paying for, Mr Simmonds,' Harry replied, sitting down. Christ – no wonder this oily prat's wife had buggered off. 'Tell me, does your technique for rubbing people up the wrong way come naturally or do you practice in front of a mirror?'

Max chuckled, and finished his gin and tonic. 'Let's hope that my abilities are outshone by your talent as a private investigator. From what you told me on the phone, I gather you've done rather well.'

'We've found fifteen apartment blocks so far whose names end with " – ingham Court".'

'Excellent.'

Harry opened his briefcase and handed Max a large manilla envelope. 'My lads had to take flashlight photographs of most of the front entrances. Sorry about that, but you wanted fast results so they had to work through the night.'

'They may be fast results, but I'm afraid they're disappointing so far,' said Max, having skimmed quickly through the eight-by-ten glossies. 'But don't be disheartened – you're doing excellent work. Keep it up.'

'The addresses are written on the back of each print.'

'So they are,' said Max easily. 'I'm impressed by your thoroughness.'

'Those are all blocks close to central London,' Harry replied, wondering whether this oddball client was taking the piss or trying to be pleasant. He suspected the former. 'We've located another ten or so that are further out. We should have the job sewn up by this time tomorrow.'

Max stood and tucked the envelope under his arm. 'Thank you for your sterling work, Mr Mathison. You're doing an excellent job. I'll call you tomorrow and arrange another meeting – somewhere near your office. I'm going north, so it might be late when I'm on my way back.'

Harry shrugged.

'Sorry I can't stay and chat with you, but I'm a busy man,' said Max. He walked out of the bar, leaving Harry Mathison seething.

Max had avoided parking in the car park, he had left the BMW several streets away. He didn't want the private detective peering through a window and noting his number – he was certain to have access to the Police National Computer. As always, Max thought out everything in advance.

Once settled in his BMW, and having made certain that he hadn't been followed, he went through the photographs again. He had been delighted with one particular print but, in his usual calculating manner, had seen no point in letting the private investigator know that. Now he compared Harry's third print with the photograph of the al Karni family group on the fore-court of their London apartment block. There was no doubt about it: the main entrance doors were the same, as were the flowerbeds, and the lettering on the front of the building. Every-thing matched. In the picture taken by Harry Mathison's operat-ive, the entire name of the block was shown:

Tushingham Court.

He turned the glossy print over. Tushingham Court had a Swiss Cottage address.

Max felt he was getting somewhere at last. He was confident that the mysterious Andy, the manipulative savant who held the key to a fortune, would be in his clutches by the end of the week.

56

NORTHERN IRAQ

The donkey was still harnessed to its brightly painted cart. It chomped unconcernedly on the waist-high young maize at the side of the track and ignored the two men walking cautiously towards it.

There was no sign of the girls, but the huge circle of down-wash-flattened crop, and the two swathes of down-trodden maize radiating out from the circle in the form of a V, spelt out in graphic terms what had happened. The Super Frelon had landed, disgorging at least twenty men who had chased across the field after the girls, who had split up. The story written on the field was so stark that even Khalid could read it.

'There's nothing we can do here. Let's go to the village,' said Nuri quietly.

'No – we must find them.' Despite Khalid's resolution, there was an echo of fear in his voice.

'They've probably been kidnapped. They were pretty.'

'They don't always do that, do they, Nuri?'

Nuri had heard tales of Kurdish girls taken by helicopters, gang-raped in flight and thrown out at a thousand feet. Once he had seen the smashed remains of such a victim – but he didn't want to get into an argument with his companion.

'You check that way, I'll go this way,' said Khalid, taking the initiative for once. 'We have to do this.' Before Nuri could object, the younger man was striding off along one of the trails of wrecked maize, the early morning sun burning on his fair hair.

Nuri followed his appointed trail for about two hundred metres. It ended quite suddenly. The other girl must have run faster and further, because Khalid was still moving through the green corn.

When confronted with horror – real horror – the human mind behaves in a manner that makes those who have experienced it reluctant to talk about it afterwards, for fear of being thought heartless. The eyes seize on anything that hints at normality. In

Nuri's case it was a blackbird at the edge of the circle of damaged maize, scratching for worms. It was darting in and out of the stalks, listening with its head cocked before plunging its busy beak into the soil. Next, there was the pattern of light and shade across the corn, made by the breeze, the morning sun and the scudding clouds . . .

Please, God – make everything normal!

As a teenager Nuri had had an accident with a friend's moped in which he was catapulted over the handlebars. Despite a broken ankle, he had struggled to his feet and righted the machine – such was his anxiety to re-establish normality in the face of disaster. During the protracted war against Iran, he had seen a fellow soldier trying to stuff back the spilled intestines of a dead comrade.

Nuri forced his gaze back to the naked girl. She lay on her back, grossly exposed because her legs had been forced apart so that her lifeless body formed an unnatural T. It was impossible to tell whether she had been the younger or older of the two girls because her face had been completely obliterated by 9-mm rounds. Her breasts had been clumsily hacked off, probably with a bayonet. Nuri knew why. During the Fao campaign there had been an officer who was inordinately proud of his tobacco pouch – a curious skin bag, brown and wizened, and tied with pull cord.

'Kurdish tit,' he had boasted, twirling the pouch around his finger when someone asked him what it was. 'Keeps tobacco fresh for weeks. Yanks used to make them in the Indian wars.'

A week later, during a particularly fierce battle, Nuri had seized the opportunity to shoot the officer in the back.

For seconds, now, he was unable to move. The sun was shining on the pathetic body, and he could see that her pubic hair was matted with congealed semen. Below that was a mass of dried blood where a soldier had hacked at her in an attempt to remove her clitoris as a souvenir.

He turned at the sound of a cry. Khalid was running towards him, tears streaming down his face. He clung to Nuri sobbing piteously and pointing back the way he had come.

'She looks like Andy!' he cried in abject despair. 'So much like Andy!'

Before Nuri could ask him what he meant, Khalid saw the second girl. He gave a little moan and fell to his knees beside her. Oblivious of her terrible head-wounds, he cradled her lifeless form to his breast and rocked her back and forth while great sobs were wrenched from the very core of his being.

Nuri stared down at them and reflected that at least the poor girl had someone to weep over her; he doubted if anyone would be left alive in her village.

57

SOUTHERN ENGLAND

Among the vehicles parked along the metalled Forestry Commission track was Detective-Sergeant Barr's Escort. Laura's first instinct was to turn around and walk back to the main road. She tightened her grip on André's hand. But her cunning in protecting André had been sharpened by recent events, and instead of turning back, she decided it would be sensible to carry on. Most of Durston's villagers had already paid a visit to the meteorite site; it would look suspicious if she didn't share their curiosity.

The two walked along the track. There was a chill easterly wind rippling the profitable stands of larch, spruce and fir. Both women were dressed for a walk in the country, Laura in a shabby, full-length quilted anorak, André in a sheepskin driving-coat. They came to a new gate across the narrow road. It was open, and there was a small green caravan beside it. Rob Jones appeared in its open doorway.

'Afternoon, Laura . . . Andy.'

'Hallo, Rob. We've come to see where the meteorite fell, if that's okay.'

'No problem. It's the grockles I have to keep out. Place is crawling with university types. Be glad when they get bored and go home so we can start on clearing up.' He waved them through the gate. 'About another two hundred yards. Stay within the markers when you get there.' He winked at André, but her answer was a blank stare. Funny kid. Those green eyes always gave him the creeps.

The two women reached the scene where André had evaded Dabber and Greaser the previous Wednesday evening.

'Is this it, Andy?' Laura asked unnecessarily, surveying the wrecked woodland and at the same time struggling to keep the shock from her voice.

'Yes.' There was no fear in André's voice, but the tightening of her grip on Laura's hand conveyed her tension. Perhaps she was sensing her mother's emotion.

'It's all right, Andy, darling – there's nothing to worry about.'

But there was everything to worry about. The pictures Laura had seen on television and in the newspapers were no preparation for the scene that confronted her. It was as if a giant chain-plough had crashed through the pines, dragging them down, ripping off their bark to expose raw white cambium, and creating a huge, ugly gash in the forest. Woodland in the area had suffered considerable damage in the wake of the 1987 hurricane, but nothing as concentrated as this. The scene was strangely illuminated by the late afternoon sun, breaking through the leaden sky and imparting an eerie, cheerless glow to the plantation.

A party of young men and women were working at the head of the damage, and there were several policemen in old clothes searching among the fallen trees on the far side of the devastated area. The broad avenue of stripped soil down the centre of the swathe was criss-crossed with white ribbons to form a grid pattern of squares.

There was a well trodden path through the undamaged trees along the edge of the destruction, marked by two rows of road-works bunting and traffic cones. The coloured plastic tags fluttered cheerfully in the early spring breeze, as if mocking Laura's mounting terror. They followed the path and came to a clearing near the working party. The students were excavating one of the ribbon-defined squares with the aid of fine-mesh sieves and a hose driven by a puttering motorised pump. As soon as all the mud and grit had been hosed through the sieve, the hose was moved to the next group, leaving the first lot to pick over the contents of their sieve. Small, gleaming rock fragments were dropped into brightly coloured plastic bins marked with numbers. Despite the quagmire and the appalling conditions, the students were obviously working to a well ordered procedure.

'What are you doing?' Laura called out to the nearest student.

'Rounding up all the tektites,' he replied. They had been briefed to be polite to the locals.

'Tektites?'

He fished a golf-ball-sized piece of gleaming rock from one of the plastic bins and gave it to Laura. She looked at it curiously. It had the colour and waxy, semi-matt sheen of freshly broken flint.

'Vitrified clay,' the student explained. 'Caused by the heat released by the meteorite when it evaporated – burnt up.'

'You mean, the meteor turned clay to glass?'

'It certainly did. Once we've rounded up all the tektites we can calculate the amount of energy that was released, and from that we can work out the meteorite's approximate size when it burst.'

Laura started to count the filled plastic bins, but gave up; there were dozens of them. 'You seem to have found rather a lot,' she remarked, hoping she sounded like an interested bystander.

'About four tonnes so far. Most of it's been taken away. Those bins are just today's work. Latest estimate is that the burst released energy equivalent to ten tonnes of TNT.'

Laura held out the rock, hoping that the student would attribute the trembling of her hand to the cold.

'That's all right – you can keep it,' the student said. 'One bit like that won't upset the calculations.'

Laura thanked him, and slipped the piece of vitrified rock into her coat pocket. As they returned along the path, she glanced across at the group of policemen searching among the fallen trees, and saw that Detective-Sergeant Barr was among them. The policeman had seen her too, and was staring across the clearing at her and André. Laura shifted her grip on her daughter's hand and forced herself into her routine of chatter.

'As soon as we get home, Andy, I must ring the school bus company and tell them to pick you up at the normal time tomorrow morning. Let's hope their answering-machine is working. Remember all those problems we had during the power cuts? Would you like to wear that blue dress I got for you in Singapore, or would you rather keep it for best? On second thoughts, I don't think it's warm enough for it yet, so perhaps you'd better stick with the skirt and jumper for another couple of weeks. I thought I'd take the rest of the week off anyway, and finish getting the garden into shape. That means I'll have time to do all your favourite meals. That'll be nice, won't it, darling?'

They neared the main track. Laura was uncomfortably aware of the policeman's eyes boring into her back. Also there was the hard lump in her coat pocket, pressing against her hip – a chilling reminder of the awesome powers André possessed. The sky darkened as the leaden cloud base closed the gap the sun had found in its defences. The biting east wind strengthened, heightening Laura's sense of grim foreboding, and André's hand felt unnaturally cold. Laura knew she was being irrational, but the bleak message of the sky, the wind, and her daughter's icy grip seemed to be that there was worse to come.

Far worse, the wind seemed to whisper.

58

NORTHERN IRAQ

Nuri was wrong; there were villagers left alive in Afan. The six survivors were all women, wrinkled with age, huddled together at the far end of the barn. It was the muffled, keening wails of one of the women over the body of her husband that gave away their hiding-place. They whimpered in terror when Khalid hauled the sliding door open, and Nuri spoke to them at once in Kurdish to allay their fears. They watched the strangers with wide, frightened eyes, but none of them made any attempt to speak, or to leave the barn.

Chickens and goats scattered before the two men as they searched for the rest of the villagers. They found them in the well-tended kitchen garden of a modern stone-built bungalow – probably the home of a land-owning family. The villagers had been lined up against the wall and shot; about thirty men, women and children, although the blood-stained pile of rags and protruding limbs made an accurate count impossible. Nuri carefully turned the body of a woman over; flies rose in protesting swarms. He knew what to expect even before the lifeless eyes stared up at him; the severed genitals of one of her menfolk had been stuffed into her mouth.

The two men stared down at the unspeakable. High above, a lark perfumed the still, clear air with its song. A goat cropped the grass nearby with a soft tearing sound.

'Why, Nuri?'

Nuri could think of nothing to say. Khalid repeated his question.

'I don't know the answers to your stupid questions!' Nuri suddenly shouted. 'How should I know how their minds work! Ask them!'

Nuri needed a drink badly. He strode to the water-pump in the centre of the village and yanked on the pull switch. Nothing happened. Of course, the bastards would have destroyed the generator – that was what they always did. There was a hand-crank for emergencies. He worked the lever several times and felt the pump prime. Water splashed into his cupped palm.

'No! Don't drink!' The command was shouted in Kurdish.

Nuri looked up. One of the old women had ventured from the barn. She shuffled towards Nuri with the aid of a stick, her back crooked and bowed with osteoporosis. She pointed to the borehole inspection cover set in concrete that Nuri was standing on. 'They opened that and poured in some powder.'

Nuri sniffed his hand where the water had trickled through his fingers. The faint smell had echoes of childhood – the almond cakes his mother used to make.

The borehole had been poisoned with potassium cyanide.

Khalid appeared, and stared at his companion and the old woman in turn.

'Don't drink the water,' Nuri warned, and added, 'I'm sorry about just now.'

But his outburst was forgotten. The young man stared first at the old woman and then at the pump. 'What is wrong with the water, Nuri?' His face was even paler than usual. There was a tension about him that threatened to snap at any moment.

'Poisoned.'

The old woman turned and shuffled back to the barn where all the women were now wailing. Khalid gazed after her and turned to the older man.

'We have to stay here awhile, Nuri. We have to help them. We have to bury the dead and see that they have food. We must do this.'

Nuri remained silent, staring down at the inspection cover. He looked up at his friend and saw his tears of anguish. At least someone was crying for these people. As for himself, the events he had witnessed that day had robbed him of the will to argue or think straight. Eventually he nodded.

'We stay,' he agreed.

59

BARNSLEY, NORTHERN ENGLAND
Monday, 11th March 1991

Dunlop Slazenger's chief production engineer, a good-humoured, rotund Yorkshireman, was proud of his production line and was keen to take his guest through every stage. Unlike most visitors, this snappily-dressed character who had telephoned out of the blue had actually offered to pay for his brief conducted tour. He wondered if Mr Simmonds' bland smile had been permanently fixed in place at birth.

It did not require a very advanced technology to make tennis balls. Once the putty-like rubberised compound had been mixed, a forming machine shaped it into hemispheres which were bonded together in a press and at the same time pressurised with compressed air.

'Interesting,' Max observed at this juncture, hoping that the tour would soon be over. The real reason for his visit was in his briefcase.

After that, the balls went through an automated inspection machine which tested them for weight, compression and rebound, and then a steaming process cleaned and teaselled the melton nap, giving the now yellow balls their characteristic hairy appearance. Finally they were stamped with the Dunlop Fort trademark and packaged in pressurised containers.

'And that's about all, Mr Simmonds,' said the engineer. 'Any questions?'

'Several,' said Max. 'Is there somewhere we can talk?'

The two men entered a small office. Max opened his briefcase and passed across the desk to the engineer the inside-out tennis ball he had obtained from the Iraqi POW.

'What do you make of that?' Max inquired.

The engineer turned the ball over in his hands. 'It's one of our ball cores before it's been – ' He broke off in mid-sentence and frowned. He was studying the fine rings and dimples moulded around the ball. 'By heck,' he muttered. 'This is weird.' He hunted in a drawer for a magnifying glass and studied the ball more closely.

Max waited patiently.

'You see these rings and dimples, Mr Simmonds? They're our batch mark codes which are set up on the mould. They tell us when the ball was made, and from that we can tell who it was supplied to.'

'I guessed that was what they were,' Max replied.

'But they should be on the *inside* of the core. To check a returned ball, we have to cut it in half.'

'I think it's a tennis ball that has been turned inside out,' said Max drily. 'That's the real reason why I'm here. I want you to tell me whether or not it's genuine.'

The engineer smiled suddenly. 'Doubt it. We try not to make them inside out.' His smile faded as something occurred to him. 'If you're serious, I'll have to cut into it.'

'Be my guest.'

The engineer rooted in his drawer again and produced a scalpel. Max pulled his chair nearer and watched intently as the engineer held the ball firmly down on his desk and worked the blade through the rubber. There was a soft hiss of escaping air. 'It's a core all right,' the engineer grunted. 'It's been pressurised.'

He pushed the blade right through the rubberised wall and used a sawing motion to cut a small circle, which fell out onto the desk. Released from the tension of the ball, the dish-shaped disc popped into its original shape so that the yellow nap was on the outside curve.

'Bloody hell,' the engineer muttered, picking up the disc and looking closely at it.

'I take it that the ball is genuine?' Outwardly Max was maintaining his usual icy calm; inwardly he was seething with excitement.

The engineer didn't answer at first. He repositioned his table lamp, peered into the ball's interior, and felt inside the hole with his little finger. The brief inspection seemed to be enough. 'Where did this come from, Mr Simmonds?'

'From this factory, I fancy.'

'Mmm . . .' The engineer used his magnifying glass to take a close look at the disc. He teaselled the nap by scratching it with his thumbnail. 'We use a special melton for covering our tennis balls, which gives them their unique quality. The weft yarns are made from a wool and nylon mix, and the warp yarns are cotton. Take a look.' He passed the magnifying glass and the disc to his visitor.

Max leaned forward on his elbows and studied the disc under the table lamp. He could see immediately the differences in texture and quality between the warp and weft. 'So it's definitely genuine?'

'No doubt about it, Mr Simmonds.'

'Would it be possible to fake a ball, but use genuine Dunlop materials?'

'It would be impossible.' The engineer looked speculatively

at the visitor. 'This isn't the first time we've had one of these balls returned to this factory.'

Max's bland smile never flickered. 'How interesting. I'd like to know more.'

'You tell me how you came by this ball, Mr Simmonds, and I'll tell you what little I know. Fair?'

'Perfectly fair,' said Max, seeing no reason why he shouldn't tell the truth. 'I've just returned from the Middle East. I swapped it off an Arab in exchange for some cigarettes.'

There was a silence while the engineer picked up the ball and examined it again. 'I've never actually seen one of these before,' he admitted. 'And I don't mind saying that I still don't believe the evidence of my own eyes. But my predecessor told me about an identical ball that was brought to him for verification at this factory. Must have been five or six years ago. I've been here three years.'

'Where is your predecessor now?'

'He died last year.'

'So what do those code marks tell you?' Max pressed.

The engineer looked closely at the fine rings and dimples on the outside of the ball and scribbled down some numbers. He made an internal telephone call, read out the numbers and asked for a batch identification. He waited, drumming his fingers while staring down at the strange ball on his desk. The person he was calling came back with some information.

'Okay – fine. Do we know who placed the order . . . ? Okay – fine. Cheers.' He replaced the handset and looked levelly at his visitor. 'I don't know if this is any help, Mr Simmonds, but the batch number is definitely one of ours. The ball was part of an export order three years ago.'

'Exported to where?'

'A wholesaler in Baghdad.'

'Oh, come on, Linda,' Lloyd protested down the telephone. 'You're the last person I expected to have a silly job's-worth attitude.'

'I can't do it, Lloyd. The society's rules are very strict. I'm not allowed to give out names and addresses.'

'You gave me plenty of information on autistic children for my article,' Lloyd pointed out.

'That's because your visit was cleared by the committee,' the secretary replied tartly. 'Anyway, this girl . . .'

'André Normanville.'

'André Normanville. It's possible that her parents aren't members of the society. Only sixty per cent of all autistic children are registered with us.'

'Her mother's middle-class, and you yourself told me that most middle-class parents are members. Right?'

'Right,' Linda agreed. 'But I still can't go giving out addresses.'

'I don't want addresses, Linda – just one address. André Normanville.'

'No.'

'I know – you're cross with me because I didn't have my wicked way with you after that dinner?'

Linda laughed. 'I would have been cross if you *had* tried anything.'

Lloyd tried a different tack. 'So how am I going to get this colouring-book back to the kid?'

'What colouring-book?'

'The colouring-book she left on the aircraft,' said Lloyd glibly. 'Expensive. Only half-completed. I'd like to return it to her. I know. Give me the name of the special school she goes to and I'll post it to the school secretary and ask her to pass it on. How about that? Now don't go telling me that the rules don't allow you to give the names and addresses of special schools, because I won't believe you.'

'They don't,' said Linda doubtfully.

'*Please*, Linda. It's a lovely book. I'm sure the kid will be only too delighted to get it back.'

There was a brief hesitation before Linda capitulated. 'All right,' she said resignedly. 'What's the girl's name again?'

Lloyd told her, and spelt it. He could hear the clatter of a computer keyboard. There was a pause. 'Found her?' he asked hopefully.

'I'm not saying, but if you send the book care of the secretary of the Candice Webb Special School, Billingshurst, West Sussex, it stands a good chance of being returned to its rightful owner. It's a private school. One of the best in the country. 'Nuff said?'

Lloyd scribbled down the information. 'Linda?'

'Yes – I know – you love me.'

'Passionately,' Lloyd declared jubilantly. He blew her a kiss down the line and hung up.

His next call was to Ted Prentice, to explain about his visit to Rikki Steadman's recording studio and the digital analysis techniques used to extract the sound of thunder from the video-tape. 'She certainly did make thunder, Ted,' Lloyd concluded. 'It was very faint and distant but it's been on your tape all the time.'

'I'm intrigued,' the psychiatrist admitted.

'I've dropped a copy of Rik's recording in the post to you,' Lloyd continued. 'You should get it tomorrow. The other thing is that I've found André, or at least, I've found the special school she goes to. I'm now on my way there, to see if her mother picks her up and to follow them home.'

Prentice grunted. 'You're a tenacious fellow. Can't understand why you're not in gutter journalism.'

'Because I'd keep running into miserable old buggers like you,' Lloyd retorted. 'I'll keep you posted.' He hung up, and studied a large-scale map of Southern England. With a high-lighter pen he drew a rough twenty-miles radius around Billingshurst. The circle covered several telephone areas. The next step would be to check each area with Directory Inquiries to pinpoint all the Normanvilles. But that would take time; he preferred direct action.

It was 2 p.m. Traffic willing, he could just make it to Billingshurst in an hour.

61

NORTHERN IRAQ

By noon Nuri and Khalid had finished the grisly task they had begun the previous day. After a sleepless night in one of the now uninhabited cottages, they had been in no state for hard work, yet they had toiled ceaselessly through the morning, digging out a deep pit at the edge of the clearing that served the village as a graveyard. They used a tractor and trailer to collect the bodies from the kitchen garden.

Nuri went in search of the old woman who had warned him about the poisoned water. He found her in the barn, where she and the other survivors were sitting on the concrete-hard earth floor, drinking tea. A circle of listless, wrinkled faces framed by headscarfs watched him as he approached the woman.

'We're ready to bury them,' he said.

She nodded and bowed her head.

'We want to place husbands with wives, children with mothers. We need your help.'

Nuri helped the old woman to her feet and found her stick. They walked into the sun. He learned that her name was Shenna and that the village had been attacked because the Iraqis were convinced that a prominent member of the PKK was a villager.

The old woman identified the bodies one by one. Only when they came to the last body, a man aged about fifty, did she show signs of emotion. Even then her tears were silent – not the distraught, keening wails of her neighbours in the barn.

'My son,' she said simply. She tried to bear her grief with dignity, but her legs gave way. Nuri helped lower her onto a log. It was some moments before she could speak again. 'It was his house where they took them all. Then we heard the shooting.'

'The modern bungalow?' Nuri asked. He indicated to Khalid to begin filling in the pit.

The old woman nodded, watching the dry soil cascade onto the still forms. 'He had a good job in Baghdad and only came home sometimes. We never knew when to expect him. He was the man they were looking for. They knew that – I heard the officers talking – but no one betrayed him.' There was a catch of pride in her voice. 'No one. So they killed them all.'

'But someone betrayed him,' said Nuri. 'Otherwise how did they know to come here?'

She shook her head. 'I don't know. I was with my son and his wife all day yesterday. He has the only telephone in the village and no one else used it.'

'Did he use it?'

She thought for a moment, then nodded. 'He made a telephone call to his friends in Ankara. Thirty minutes later the helicopter comes.'

A telephone tap, thought Nuri. A signals sergeant had told him that they had automatic equipment for monitoring long-distance calls on lines serving Kurdish villages. As a member of the PKK the old woman's son would have known that. Either he was a fool – or it was a very urgent message.

Nuri covered the woman's weathered hands with his own. 'We will avenge your son, Sheena. We will avenge all of them – I promise you that.' It was a hollow-sounding promise, but he couldn't think of anything more constructive to say. He smiled into her aged eyes. 'I'd better help my friend, otherwise he will get angry with me.'

'If you stay tonight, you must stay in my son's house. It is comfortable.'

Nuri smiled his thanks and helped her to her feet.

The two men finished filling in the pit by mid-afternoon. They quenched their thirst with water they had found in a rain butt, boiling it first to kill the wriggling shoals of mosquito larvae. Both men then flopped on their backs, exhausted by their efforts, every muscle in their bodies screaming.

'Shall we be moving on now?' Khalid asked.

251

'After this you should want to join the PKK – not your parents.'

'Yes – but we must help these people first, Nuri. We must stay and make them a well.'

Nuri closed his eyes at the prospect of more digging – but he realised that to set off on their journey again would be foolish in their present exhausted state. A good meal – there were plenty of vegetables in store in the village – and a night's rest in proper beds would do much to restore their spirits. Also a wash and a change of clothes, especially after the tasks they had performed that day. He decided to check the house that Sheena said they could use, and climbed wearily to his feet. He prodded Khalid with his foot but the young man was sound asleep.

Nuri entered the bungalow and was surprised to discover that it hadn't been ransacked. Even the television and VCR, normal targets for looting, were in place. The officers must have had a good reason for not permitting the place to be trashed.

The answer was on a small table in the living-room. An intact telephone.

The Mukharabat automatic tape-recorders would be listening, of course. Listening for any other members of the PKK who returned to the village and made long-distance calls to cells in Turkey.

Nuri ripped the telephone from the wall and smashed it on the stone hearth. He gathered up the tangle of wires and shattered pieces of plastic, and dumped them in a chest.

62

SOUTHERN ENGLAND

The Candice Webb Special School turned out to be a large, sandstone-faced house about a mile west of Billingshurst on the winding A272. Uncertain whether the school day finished at 3 or 3.30, Lloyd had thrashed his Lotus down the A29 and managed to get himself in position by 2.50.

He parked at the entrance to a field; not the best vantage point, but it was probably best for a young man keeping schoolgirls and schoolboys under surveillance with binoculars to exercise discretion.

At 2.55 cars driven by women started arriving. They disappeared around the back of the school and reappeared with offspring on board. None of them was driven by André's mother. An elderly thirty-seater bus emblazoned with the name of a Guildford coach company passed Lloyd's observation-point and turned into the school entrance. A school bus? Stupid of him not to have thought of that. He debated whether to follow it or wait and see if the girl's mother turned up. Of course, there was always the chance that André hadn't started back at school yet.

The coach reappeared and waited at the school gates for a break in the sparse traffic. It was crowded with boisterous youngsters. Lloyd carefully refocused the binoculars as the vehicle edged out, and caught a fleeting glimpse of a familiar face just before the bus turned towards him. He tossed the binoculars onto the passenger seat, pulled out, and began to follow the coach at a safe distance.

As one would expect of a school bus, the vehicle led him a merry dance through the byways of West Sussex and Surrey: Wisborough Green, Northchapel, Plaistow. Every time it stopped to drop off children, Lloyd reduced speed and hung well back. None of the kids shed by the bus was André. After twenty miles there didn't appear to be any children left on board. The bus crossed over the county border into Surrey – for the tenth time, as far as he could judge – and grated its gears through a tiny village called Durston – a one-horse hamlet where they had shot the horse.

Durston?

Now why was that name familiar? The road straightened and seemed to cut right through a sombre Forestry Commission plantation whose profitable but land-sterilising stands of spruce and fir crowded down to the verge on both sides. The coach increased speed and so did Lloyd. He was so intent on keeping his quarry in sight that he almost didn't see the two uniformed police officers manning what he supposed was a vehicle check roadblock. Lloyd swore and jammed on his brakes as the coach, apparently not of interest to the two policemen, was waved on and disappeared round a bend. Lloyd was not in luck. He wound down his window and had a suitably sheepish smile ready by the time one of the police officers approached him.

'I trust we weren't dozing at the wheel, sir?'

'In this car, officer, no one sleeps.'

The policeman eyed the classic sports car and wondered what it was worth. 'That I can believe, sir.'

Another car was waved down by the second officer. It drew up behind Lloyd.

'Do you travel this route often, sir?'

'No. I can't remember ever coming along here before.'

'Were you in this area last Wednesday evening, sir? That would be the sixth of March – five days ago.'

'No, definitely not.'

The police officer handed Lloyd a HAVE YOU SEEN THESE MEN? pamphlet, bearing photographs and descriptions of 'Dabber' Young and 'Greaser' Evans. A third photograph was of a Kawasaki Z–1000, captioned with two registration numbers.

'Those two bikers disappeared last Wednesday evening, sir,' the police officer explained. 'If you see them, or their bikes, we'd be grateful if you would call that phone number. Sorry to have detained you.'

Lloyd drove on, fuming inwardly. Once clear of the police, he accelerated, but there was no sign of the school bus. The roundabout he came to shafted his slender chances of finding it, so he decided to head for home.

Then a thought occurred to him. He had no idea why, but something in his subconscious was telling him it had to do with a piece of the jigsaw that was tantalisingly out of reach. He pulled over, called the office on his mobile telephone, and asked Della to put him through to Gary Pepper.

'Gary. It's Lloyd. Have you done anything about that meteorite that came down in Surrey last week?'

'You said not to.'

'I know what I said, Gary. But I've no doubt that you've been nosing.'

254

'London University are supposed to be publishing an interim report next week.'

'Where did it come down?'

'Surrey.'

'Yes, I know that, you clown. Where in Surrey?'

'Near a one-eyed place called Durston. Please don't ask me if I've been there. I shall deny all knowledge and say that we're just good friends.'

Lloyd laughed. 'I thought Durston rang a bell. I'm not two miles away. There's about an hour's light left so I'd like to take a shuftie.'

Gary gave him directions and added: 'Tell the Forestry Commission warden that you're from the university. They don't check.'

Lloyd thanked him and hung up. He followed Gary's directions and found the metalled track that led into the forest without difficulty. There was no one in the caravan at the gate, so he drove straight through and parked behind a pick-up truck at the head of the great swathe of demolished pines.

The failing light did little to detract from the awesome scale of the disaster that had struck the remote plantation. A man wearing muddy jeans and a Garfield 'I HATE MONDAYS' T-shirt was leaning against the truck. He ended his conversation into a PMR radio as Lloyd approached. Lloyd showed him his press card and introduced himself.

'Gordon Walters,' said the T-shirt owner cheerfully, returning Lloyd's handshake. 'Always pleased to talk to *Science UK*. I'm in charge of all this, and beginning to wish I wasn't.'

'Why's that?' Lloyd asked, glancing at the working-party at the far end of the fallen and uprooted trees. 'I should have thought anyone would give their right arm to investigate a major meteorite impact.'

'Well, I certainly would if I thought it definitely was an impact site or a comet break-up,' Professor Walters admitted ruefully. 'But we're beginning to have serious doubts. The meteorite impact theory is out because there's no crater and there were no unusual seismic shocks recorded for last Wednesday. Now the comet nucleus break-up theory is falling flat on its face because the damage is too localised and none of the Earthwatch telescopes have logged a comet anywhere near the Earth. But what's got us really stumped is the amount of heat that was released at the time of the impact, or whatever it was. Want to see today's collection of tektites?' Without waiting for an answer he dropped the pick-up's tailboard and gestured to the load of plastic bins.

Lloyd picked out one of the largest pieces of vitrified clay and examined it. The nodule had been exposed to so much heat that it was almost ceramic. 'Any unusual levels of background radiation?' he asked.

'Thank God there aren't,' said the professor with feeling. 'Otherwise we'd be bandying a theory about that someone let off a home-made H-bomb here. It's no more loony than some of the other ideas we've been looking at.'

'So what's the looniest theory?'

'One of mine.'

'Which is?'

The professor hesitated. 'Unattributable?'

'Unattributable,' Lloyd agreed.

'What fits nearly all the evidence is that this isn't the site where something arrived, but where something left. And something that left the bloody planet in a fucking hurry, too.'

'Any idea what?'

'None at all. We haven't a clue.'

Lloyd stayed another ten minutes at the site, and left when the working-party of students started trudging back to the pick-up truck. A few minutes after pulling onto the main road, he spotted the inviting lights of a greasy-spoon transport café and decided that he was in need of a cup of coffee. It was too early for the pubs to be open, so it was just the place to pick up some local gossip.

Jacko was slopping down his chipped, formica-topped tables with an evil-looking rag that smelled of drains when Lloyd entered the steamy, empty café.

'Coffee and a cheese sandwich, please,' Lloyd called out, and sat at a dry table. He was disappointed that the place was empty.

Jacko grunted and contrived to wipe congealed sauce from

256

the tops of ketchup-filled plastic tomatoes. The unwritten rule of his establishment was that customers approached the high altar of the hissing, chromium-plated tea-machine to place their orders. He went behind the counter, busied himself for a minute, then reappeared with a mug of bog-black coffee and a doorstep sandwich. These culinary delights were banged down in front of Lloyd.

'I've just been to the meteor site,' said Lloyd, taking a tentative bite out of the sandwich. The filling was a fine example of the cheese-maker's craft – ready-sliced processed stuff that had the colour, texture and taste of soap. He opened the sandwich and decided that the butter, if it was butter, had been applied with a spray gun. 'Must have been a tremendous bang . . . Last Wednesday, wasn't it?'

'A real big bang,' Jacko agreed sourly, opening a copy of the *Sun*. 'Broke a few of my windows. When they finds out who done it, they gets the bill.'

Lloyd tasted the coffee and was impressed; for a catering establishment to serve war-time, ersatz, chicory-based coffee and still be in business in 1991 was a remarkable achievement. He glanced around the timber shack. The 1950s grease-encrusted Coca Cola, Tizer and 7-Up posters were probably worth money if they could be cleaned up and steamed off the walls. A more recent poster, apparently stuck to the wall with tomato ketchup, was an enlarged version of the police handbill about the missing bikers.

'So what was the bang like?'

'Like a bang,' Jacko grunted, eyeing the Page Seven girl. Not a real woman, she weren't. Far too skinny.

'Was it a sort of sharp crack, or more a rolling noise like thunder?' Lloyd pressed.

Jacko sighed. Clearly this was another Londoner berk who wasn't going to leave him in peace. There had been a lot of them around recently making a nuisance of themselves by ordering food and drink, and whingeing about the coffee and the crisped edges of his fried eggs. 'It was a sort of rolling noise like thunder, only it died away more slowly than thunder. Could still hear it when we all rushed outside.'

Suddenly, out of the blue, Lloyd remembered the lightning-strike that had nearly hit the Boeing 747 at Heathrow. It was as if a logic-defying piece of the jigsaw had suddenly fitted neatly and terrifyingly into place.

'You one of them smart-arses from the university?' Jacko demanded.

Lloyd assured him that he wasn't. When he set his mug down he realised that his hand was shaking.

'Bleedin' toffee-nosed gits,' Jacko growled. 'Don't know nothing, the lot of 'em. I went down there yesterday. Saw 'em buggering about with their stupid sieves and plastic bins. Bleedin' obvious what happened. Oughta bite 'em on the nose.'

'So what do you think happened?'

Jacko pointed across the road. 'Dunsfold aerodrome not four mile away. Harrier jump-jets buzzing around all day. Right?'

'Right,' Lloyd agreed.

'One comes down in the plantation. Forced landing, only they keeps quiet about it because they're flogging them to the wogs. Bad publicity, see? So they nips out there smartish, fixes it up and it takes off and gets away smartish. The bang was when it goes through the sound barrier. Simple.'

'Simple,' Lloyd echoed, full of admiration for the café owner's reasoning.

Jacko rested his brawny arms on the counter. 'That mess out there weren't caused by nothing arriving. No way. It's bleedin' obvious – it were caused by summat leaving.'

63

NORTHERN IRAQ

The sun was hanging blood-red and bloated over the western hills when the mass burial was finished. The great mound had been smoothed over by tying a baulk of timber to the tractor and dragging it back and forth over the long grave. The mound would settle in time, and headstones could be set up. For the time being, each of the thirty-five souls consigned to the earth was identified by a fragment of paving with his or her name painted on it by the old woman.

The kites caught Khalid's eye. They had been circling most of the day, attracted by the scent of blood; the two men had ignored them. But now the birds had found something to the south. They dropped towards the ground, their spoiler wing-tip feathers spread wide to stabilise their eager descent.

'The girls,' Khalid whispered. 'We forgot them!'

'We'll get them tomorrow,' Nuri replied. All he was interested in was cooking a meal of potatoes and crawling into the big double bed in the bungalow.

'We must do it now, Nuri. We will use their cart. And tomorrow we start on a well.'

Nuri groaned. 'You fetch them if you're so keen.'

'*Please*, Nuri. We must stay together.'

Nuri nodded. 'Okay. Let's get moving.'

They returned to the village an hour later, just as it was getting dark, leading the donkey by the reins. The pretty little cart belonged to the girls; somehow it seemed respectful that they should not have to share it with anyone else for their last journey. Khalid pointed to the smoke rising from one of the cottages as they drew near the little huddle of buildings. Sheena hobbled across, glanced in the cart and called out in a shrill voice. A woman appeared in the barn doorway. She saw the cart, gave a great wail and rushed across. When she saw the bodies, her wail became a long cry of anguish. Despite her age, she threw herself on the corpses, clutching them to her, screaming piteous grief at the darkening sky and beating her chest. The other women emerged from the barn and cottage. When they saw the cart they fell to their knees and with pleading hands held aloft, added their tortured lament to the evening stars.

'Her grand-daughters,' Sheena said listlessly. 'We thought they had escaped.'

As before, the tears that formed rivulets down her wizened cheeks were silent but unrestrained, and did not detract from her inner strength that symbolised the courage and fortitude of her people.

64

SOUTHERN ENGLAND

Max was tired after his long drive from the Dunlop factory, but not too tired to forget his customary caution. He parked his BMW in a Swiss Cottage back-street, well away from the street lights, and walked the quarter of a mile to his objective.

Tushingham Court was one of those small suburban apartment blocks that sprang up in the 1960s, when property developers hit on the idea of buying three or four substantial Edwardian properties that looked good on the landscape and replacing them with one property that looked even better on the balance-sheet. The smart neighbourhood, the block's well-kept gardens, floodlit car park and closed-circuit security camera suggested that one had to be reasonably well-heeled to afford to lease a flat here. There was a small lobby, with a panel of speaking-porter buttons which indicated that the block consisted of sixteen flats on four floors. Max rang the porter's doorbell in the lobby. A small, grey man with wispy hair appeared.

Max beamed at him, and explained that he was looking for Mr al Karni.

'You've got a long wait,' said the porter, neatly palming the £10 note that Max offered. 'Iraqis. Kurds they called themselves – they were kicked out of the country around the beginning of the year.'

'By they, that would be Mr and Mrs?'

'Hamet al Karni and their son, Khalid. Nice kid. Nice parents. Never any trouble.'

'Good tenants are so hard to find these days,' Max sighed.

The porter shrugged. 'No skin off my nose. They've paid their rent and service charges for a year in advance.'

Max thought fast. 'So their flat is still in their name, Mr . . . ?'

'Straw. Benny Straw. It's just as they left it.'

'Ah. Now that explains everything, Benny. My wife took a phone message from Mr al Karni, asking me to value his pictures. She must have assumed he was calling from his flat. He said that he might want to sell them. Would it be possible for me to take a quick look at the flat?'

Benny was about to say that it was impossible, but Max's production of two more £10 notes made it possible. He disappeared into his flat and reappeared with a set of keys. Max followed him up the stairs to the first floor. The porter fiddled with the unfamiliar locks on number 11. There were two: a conventional mortise, and a Spanish triple-turn dowel mortise. When the porter finally got the door open, Max noticed that the single hinge was a piano-type hinge running the full height of the door. It was an apartment that would be next to impossible to break into. On the other hand, Benny's ground floor flat could be a walk-in job, and no doubt he kept keys to unoccupied apartments on a rack.

Max entered the apartment. It was expensively but simply furnished. He guessed that the tapestries and the glowing Laristan Persian carpets were probably worth more than the apartment, and were a good deal older. The room's centrepiece was a low, circular tea-table made of hammer-beaten copper which was starting to lose its golden patina from lack of polishing. The only modern piece was a long wall-unit that housed a television and hi-fi stack, and provided shelves for framed family photographs. The rest of the flat consisted of an elaborate Smallbone kitchen, a simple bathroom, and two sparsely furnished bedrooms. There were no paintings anywhere.

'Looks like they took the pictures with them,' Benny commented when they returned to the living-room. He had not taken his eyes off Max for an instant since they entered the flat.

'So it would seem, Benny,' Max replied. A silver-framed postcard-sized colour picture taken at a children's party caught his interest, although he was careful not to show it. The picture was propped up on the wall-unit. He gestured to the far wall. 'They'd have to be Old Masters to equal the value of that tapestry. Before those tapestries are sold, you know, they're aged by letting camels and goats walk on them. Smell that, and you'll see what I mean.'

The porter sniffed the tapestry. 'Sort of dank smell.'

'That's a sign of a genuine tapestry,' Max replied, slipping the photograph into his jacket pocket.

He thanked Benny Straw profusely and returned to his car. He drove half a mile, and pulled over to examine his trophy. The photograph had been taken at a children's party held in a Happy Eater. He recognised Khalid from the photographs found in the T–55. He was older in this picture; Max guessed about seventeen. His mother, fair-haired like her son, was smiling benignly in the background, but it was the other children in the photograph who held Max's interest. With one exception, they were all laughing, and all were wearing bright-yellow Happy Eater smile badges on which their names had been written with a felt-tip pen:

Alan, Stacy, Khalid, Peter, Andy.

Andy was the only one not laughing. She was closest to the camera, and staring fixedly at the lens.

Max slipped the picture into the glove compartment of his BMW alongside the inside-out tennis ball.

So the mysterious Andy was a girl, and a young girl at that. Interesting.

Of course, he would have to make another visit to Tushingham Court to search the flat, but without Benny Straw's watchful presence. No doubt those drawers would be worth checking.

Max's next port of call was a pub in the Edgware Road where Harry Mathison handed over a set of photographs. Of course, a small red herring was called for.

'Excellent, Mr Mathison,' said Max, enthusing over a picture of a nondescript apartment block in Roehampton. 'That's definitely the block where my wife is shacked up. You've been of excellent service.'

'There's a small refund due on the fee you paid me,' said Harry Mathison. 'So if you let me have your address . . .'

'Buy your operatives a drink, or put it in the private eyes' old age benevolent fund or whatever it is you have,' said Max generously. 'Thank you, Mr Mathison – you've provided a first class service.'

An hour later Max was heading south-west on the M30, tired

but elated. The success of his exhausting day's investigations gave him new confidence. It was now only a matter of days before he and Leo tracked down Andy and determined the extent of her strange powers.

And exploited them.

65

Tuesday, 12th March 1991

Ten minutes in Cybernet Consultancy's flight-simulator did nothing for Stephen Ramsay's unhealthy pallor. If anything, the experience added five years to the senior civil servant's appearance.

'Remarkable,' he muttered shakily to the laboratory assistant who slid back the canopy and helped him out. Max, sitting behind the control console, avoided chuckling at his visitor's discomfort and made room for him in the spare chair at the side of his broad desk.

'Nine hundred knots, the target destroyed, and the attack aircraft safe,' Max observed. He dismissed the laboratory assistant and added when they were alone: 'As the advert says, we're getting there.'

'Yes, well, there's still a lot of getting there to be got,' said Ramsay acidly. 'It's very good, Max. I don't deny that I'm impressed.'

'So you don't envisage problems clearing the warrants for this quarter's work?'

'None at all, Max.'

'And for the next two quarters?'

'The new financial year? Yes – the cover's there. I'm sure I can swing it.'

'Excellent,' Max beamed. 'That means we can put our top researchers onto this project, which will leave Leo and myself free to work on an entirely new project.'

Ramsay looked worried. 'Any new R and D project expenditure will need a vote, Max.'

'I was thinking of carrying the costs from our own resources.'

'*Your* resources, Max.'

Max chuckled. 'Forgive me, Steve. I keep forgetting your sensitivity about your wife's holding in the Cybernet Consultancy . . . Tell me, have you thought about taking early retirement?'

Ramsay thought about little else these days. He nodded. 'I'd like to go at fifty-five – in five years. But it would knock a hole in my pension.'

'The Ministry of Defence will be losing an excellent Director of Advanced Weapons Research and Development,' Max observed, watching Ramsay carefully but not appearing to do so.

'What the devil's going on in that twisted little mind of yours, Max?'

'What would you say if I told you it was more than likely that your holding – correction, your wife's holding – in our company could be worth several million in five years' time?'

'I'd say you were mad.'

'Of course. Now – some hard thinking, Steve. What would be the old science fiction dream-come-true for everyone in the defence business?'

'I'm sure I don't know what you're talking about.'

Max's grey eyes were unblinking. 'Think, Steve. There's an extremely useful invention in the realms of science fiction that's been around for years. I can even remember it as a kid. So what is it?'

'The death-ray?'

Max nodded. 'And that's not so far off now, with the latest developments in laser technology. Anything else spring to mind?'

Ramsay thought the conversation was bordering on the absurd and said so, but Max was persistent. 'Very well,' said Ramsay with a bad grace. 'If you insist on childish games – the force wall.'

Max smiled. 'Bingo. A protective but invisible wall that can repel incoming missiles, shells, bullets – anything. A useful invention, wouldn't you say?'

'Let's talk about it around AD 2050, Max.'

'Let's talk about it now,' said Max mildly.

The civil servant looked hard at Max. Usually he could sense when the grey eyes were mocking him, but not this time. Surely he wasn't serious? 'Has this anything to do with the fiasco of that T–55 with the charmed life?'

'It has everything to do with it. Listen carefully, Steve.'

Max talked for five minutes. He outlined Leo's theory about manipulative savants and how it might be possible to develop neural-network artificial intelligence systems to duplicate their talents, using the latest techniques in neural mapping. He showed his visitor the tennis ball and filled in its background, but made no mention of his tracking down Andy.

'Amazing,' said Ramsay, returning the inside-out tennis ball to Max. 'But you're going to have to find a manipulative savant.'

'Let's say we've traced one, and leave it at that.'

'In this country?'

'Accessible,' Max replied enigmatically.

The senior civil servant looked sharply at his host. 'You're serious about this, aren't you?'

'We're talking about patents that could make your share in the firm worth not millions of pounds, Steve, but billions.' Max paused and smiled blandly at his guest's shocked expression. 'I think your estimate of 2050 is a little out. We'll have a patentable system working by 1997 if we keep our mouths shut, act fast, and act now.'

66

Ted Prentice was unimpressed by Lloyd's flat.

'Typical yuppie dwelling,' he announced, glaring belligerently around at the expanse of varnished floorboards. 'Damned if I could live with my conscience if I'd thrown thousands of dockers out of their jobs by living in a converted warehouse.'

'They perform a valuable social function by providing small businesses with cheap premises,' Lloyd answered from the kitchen area, where he was cooking a lasagne in his microwave oven.

'Like this woman who's coming round?'

'Yes. It was good of you to come here at such short notice.'

Prentice grunted noncommittally and examined a rented videotape. It was the classic science fiction movie *2001: A Space Odyssey*. 'Well, if it's the only evening she could manage . . . Is this the sort of rubbish you watch?'

Normally Lloyd would have staunchly defended his taste in movies, but he was intent on serving up the evening meal. 'Okay, Ted. Prepare yourself for the big culinary event of the year in your narrow little life. It's ready.'

They sat at Lloyd's dining-room table by a window where they could watch the passing lights of the river traffic.

'Frozen food,' said Prentice, poking suspiciously at his serving.

'It's not frozen now.'

'The only food that keeps well in a freezer is ice-cream.'

'This is an expensive lasagne from the gourmet supermarket,' Lloyd explained, filling their wine-glasses.

The psychiatrist tried a mouthful and reluctantly agreed that it was good.

'Your trouble, Ted, is that you're getting too narrow-minded in your old age. Dangerous, in your line of work, I would've thought, where new ideas and theories are constantly being advanced.'

Prentice grunted, tried the wine, and was disappointed to discover that he liked it. 'The latest being your theory that your manipulative savant was responsible for that meteor impact in Surrey?'

'The University of London doesn't think it was a meteorite impact. Or a comet nucleus break-up,' Lloyd replied. 'In fact, they don't know what to think.'

'Well, I saw the damage on television. No savant could do that. You've been watching too many junk science fiction movies.'

'But they can turn tennis balls inside out,' Lloyd observed.

'Yes, but where's the logic in zapping a plantation?'

'Where's the logic in turning tennis balls inside out?' Lloyd countered.

'Because it's a tangible demonstration of the impossible made possible.' Prentice was getting agitated. 'With fallen-over forests you can argue natural causes, hurricanes, meteors or comets. But there's no arguing with my tennis ball that Khalid turned inside out. It exists – a challenge to logic and reason. Fallen trees aren't.'

'You're arguing on the grounds of scale rather than basic principle,' said Lloyd, enjoying the discussion because it was acting as a catalyst for his own thoughts. 'You can accept the inside-out tennis ball but not a wiped-out plantation. I've seen both. Your reasoning reminds me of the story about the girl who justified her illegitimate baby on the grounds that it was a very small baby. Once you bend or break our perceived laws of the universe, scale is not a factor. They've been broken, and that's that.'

Prentice suddenly laughed. The wine was loosening him up. 'I see your point. But I think scale is important. You can hold a tennis ball in your hands, but you can't hold a forest.'

'You're assuming that a manipulative savant has to be able to hold something in order to manipulate it?'

'I should have thought that was obvious . . .' Prentice broke off as something occurred to him. 'Damn . . .' he muttered.

Lloyd looked at the older man with interest. The psychiatrist seemed to be struggling with a concept he was having difficulty in rationalising. 'A little problem with your theory?' Lloyd inquired.

'A big problem,' Prentice admitted ruefully. He finished his meal and declined Lloyd's offer of more. 'Mind if I smoke? This is a draughty hole, so it won't linger.'

'Go ahead.'

Prentice stuffed his pipe and lit up. The actions gave him time to marshal his thoughts. 'Contrary to what you may think, I'm not narrow-minded. I'm always willing to admit when I might be wrong. There's a manipulative genius who now lives in this country: Uri Geller – an Israeli millionaire. Made his fortune as a rare minerals consultant. He tells a mining company where to dig for, say, cadmium. They dig, and bingo – they find cadmium.'

Lloyd had an idea that he had heard the name before. 'Is he a savant?'

Prentice sucked hard on his pipe and shook his head. 'Not him. A man of great wit and charm. Before he became a clairvoyant prospector he made a name for himself back in the seventies, bending spoons. An old friend of mine, a BBC TV producer, was determined to expose Geller as a fraud – he really had it in for him – so he got a glass-blower to seal a Mappin and Webb silver spoon in a glass tube. He even filmed the glass-blower doing his stuff. Just for the publicity, he had a twenty-four-hour Securicor guard placed on the tube until the programme went out.

'Uri Geller was wheeled into the studio and told in a polite, round-about sort of way that they had a spoon he couldn't possibly bend, and that the game was up. The presenter produced the tube. Geller examined the tube – tipped it up and down and asked for a camera to go in close. Shock, horror, general consternation and much studio audience mirth when the close-ups showed that the bloody spoon inside the glass tube was bent in half. More studio audience falling about when Uri offered to straighten it out again. The presenter had to smash the damned tube in front of ten million viewers to get at the spoon. The Mappin and Webb bod they had in the studio confirmed that it was definitely the original spoon. After that, my friend retired to the country to grow roses and talk to them.'

Lloyd smiled. 'And Uri Geller didn't touch the spoon once?'

'That's right. After that programme I heard that airlines were wary about flying him because they imagined he could flatten fuel pipes in his sleep. He probably could, too. The point is that people with manipulative talents are not unknown, just extremely rare. Perhaps it's some quirk in their brain-structure – no one knows.'

'Quirk,' Lloyd commented. 'Now there's a sound medical definition I never expected to hear from a professional.'

Prentice bridled and then chuckled. 'We like to pretend we know it all. But the truth is that we're really rather good at identifying and classifying psychogenic phenomena without actually understanding what *does* go on in the human mind.'

268

'In other words, we know nothing?'

'But we've turned knowing nothing into a remarkably exact science,' Prentice replied. 'But it'll change. There's new neural-mapping techniques being developed – PET scans and SPECT – '

'SPECT? What's that?'

Prentice relit his pipe. 'Single Photon Emission Computed Tomography. It's a method of introducing low-level radioactive gases into the brain that enables precision dynamic mapping of individual neurons and axions as they're working. Physical structure, chemical changes, electrical changes – everything gets recorded.'

'It sounds dangerous.'

'All intrusive mapping methods are dangerous, but SPECT is particularly so. It's only being used on mammals. But I wouldn't mind betting that there's more SPECT work being carried out on higher mammals, such as dolphins and porpoises who have a similar brain to us, than anyone cares to admit. The world is slowly filling up with loonies who think animals are more important than people.'

Lloyd cleared away the meal and made coffee.

'So why didn't you stake out André Normanville's special school today?' Prentice asked.

'I was going to, but a lot of things cropped up at the office,' Lloyd answered. 'I do have a magazine to run. I've juggled some appointments tomorrow so I should be able to get away early. Much as I'm fascinated by the whole thing, my job must come first.' He looked at his watch. 'Miss Dyson will be here in ten minutes. Try to be polite to her. She can be every bit as cantankerous as you.'

'What gave you the idea of using a lip-reader?'

Lloyd gestured to the rented videotape. 'That movie that you rubbished . . . I was thoroughly pissed off when I got in last night: my girlfriend's buggered off – we always played squash on Monday evenings – there was crap on television, so I went to the local 7–11 and rented out *2001*, one of my all-time favourites. There's a scene in it where two astronauts hatch a plan to disable

269

their spacecraft's computer but don't realise that the computer can lip-read . . .'

The interphone buzzed. 'That'll be our redoubtable Miss Dyson,' said Lloyd. 'It's no good me answering it, of course.'

He raced nimbly down the spiral staircase to greet the new arrival. Prentice stood up when the small, iron-grey lady entered the flat, and shook hands with her.

'So what's all this nonsense about you wanting me to watch a videotape?' she demanded when Lloyd had completed the introductions. She perched herself on the settee and frowned her disapproval at the flat's open-plan layout. 'God knows how you can stand this place. It must be like living in a department store.'

'My sentiments exactly, Miss Dyson,' Prentice agreed, warming to the visitor. He was interested in anyone who had developed special skills to overcome a handicap. Her voice, although clear, had an unusual quality because of her inability to hear herself. She placed very slight but incorrect stresses on particular syllables, which tended to make her sound ruder than she actually was. She had even trained herself not to appear to be overtly lip-reading when engaged in conversation, so that when she turned her head to see anyone talking, it seemed like the normal movement of someone giving a speaker polite attention. It was hard to believe that she lived in a world of total silence.

'It's just a few minutes of tape, Miss Dyson,' Lloyd explained, pouring his guest a coffee and adding a tot of rum. 'There's some youngsters talking in it, but without sound. We'd like to know what they're saying. What shall I do? Play a few seconds or so at a time and see what you make of it?'

Miss Dyson sipped her coffee and nodded at the television. 'Okay. Fire away.'

Lloyd had already loaded his VCR and primed the memory with the sequences he was interested in. He switched on the television, picked up the VCR's remote-control, and checked that Prentice was ready with a notebook. He played the scene in which Khalid was talking to André. It was a medium shot, with the two children unaware that the camera was on them.

'Stop!' said Miss Dyson imperiously after a few seconds. 'The girl has her back to the camera. Had you been more specific when you called, I would have brought my crystal ball.'

'Just do the best you can, Miss Dyson,' said Lloyd patiently. He caught Prentice's eye and had trouble keeping a straight face.

'The boy said: "My name is Car Lid". Absurd names parents give their children these days.'

'Khalid,' Lloyd explained. 'Spelt with a K. It's foreign.'

'I didn't think it was English,' Miss Dyson retorted. 'Anyway, the girl must have answered then, because there was a pause. Then the boy said: "I am fifteen years old. How old are you?" Never mind his looks, it's obvious from the way he speaks that English is not his first language.'

Prentice looked at the woman in some surprise. He leaned forward to give her a visual clue that he was about to speak. 'You can tell that from lip-reading, Miss Dyson?'

She turned her head quickly to catch what he was saying. 'Of course. If English was his first language he would have said: "I'm fifteen." When one is deaf, Mr Prentice, one looks for clues that may not seem obvious to someone with hearing. Play some more, please.'

Lloyd ran a few more seconds of tape, as far as Khalid's sudden laugh at something André said. Both men looked questioningly at Millicent Dyson.

'The boy said: "Why are you here?" And as you saw, the girl's reply caused him some amusement. Then he said: "Whoever heard of making thunder? Only God makes thunder." More, please.'

During the next shot the cameraman had changed his position slightly, to bring André's face into profile. 'Rewind that bit and play it again,' Miss Dyson said, but it was no good. 'The girl's hair is in the way and the youth's in profile,' she said. 'Extremely difficult, lip-reading in profile. Next.'

Lloyd skipped over several shots with sound, including the one that showed André catching the tennis ball Khalid had thrown at the wall. 'Ah – this is the one we're really interested in, Miss Dyson.'

The picture had changed to a wide-angle shot of André and Khalid sitting side by side on chairs against the wall. Khalid was holding a normal tennis ball, apparently showing it to André. It was the out-take in which Prentice and Lloyd guessed that Khalid had been trying to teach André his amazing new-found ability to turn tennis balls inside out.

'Camera's too far away,' Miss Dyson complained. 'I can't read that.'

'If you could try, we'd be most grateful, Miss Dyson. It's very important. The boy is trying to teach the girl something, and we need to know what.'

'They're too far away, the lighting's awful, and they won't keep still.'

'*Please*, Miss Dyson.'

The woman muttered to herself. She rose and sat in an armchair so that she was nearer the television. 'Play it again, Sam,' she commanded.

Lloyd rewound and reran the silent scene. Prentice puffed impatiently on his pipe as the seconds ticked by.

'And again.'

The woman sighed after Lloyd had run the scene for a third time. 'I think the girl's saying something about it being easy . . . But it's not easy for me. I don't think she's forming her words properly. Ah! Stop!'

André's face froze on the screen.

'Just then I think she may have said something about holding the ball in both hands and squeezing it tight. Run it again.'

Lloyd ran the sequence yet again.

Miss Dyson leaned closer to the television and nodded emphatically. 'Yes. As near as I can make out, she said: "That's right . . ." Something . . . Something . . . "It's easy, Khalid. You hold it like . . . Yes – like that . . . Now squash it and think the time back." And the rest of the scene she just kept repeating that . . . Saying: "Think the time back. Think the time back." '

'Think the time back?' Lloyd echoed. 'Are you sure?'

'Of course I'm not sure!' Miss Dyson snapped. 'Didn't you hear what I said just now? That's what it looks like, but I

272

couldn't swear to it.' She broke off and looked contemptuously at the two men. 'You can't even read body language properly. If you ask me, that boy isn't teaching the girl anything – she's teaching *him*.'

The same thought had occurred simultaneously to Lloyd and Prentice. They stared at the woman. She glared at them in return, and looked at her watch. 'If you've finished your silly games, it's time I went to bed.'

Lloyd was profuse in his thanks as he showed Miss Dyson down to the front door. He returned to his chair and sat staring at Prentice. 'Looks like we got it wrong about Khalid,' he observed.

Prentice took his gaze off the television and nodded. His voice had a curious strangled note when he replied. 'I think, Lloyd, that you had better find that Normanville girl as a matter of some urgency.'

67

Wednesday, 13th March 1991

At twenty-eight, Father Denis Foxley was not the youngest curate in West Sussex, but he was the most determined to succeed. He threw selfless enthusiasm and energy into every task he was given, one of which was to take the weekly religious study group for Catholic children at the Candice Webb Special School. Mercifully, it was a relatively small group of six hyperactive youngsters; he had been running the group since Christmas and was just beginning to feel at home with them. The kids had learned to like him, so that fourteen-year-old Michael Thomas had stopped banging on his table, Carol Rogers no longer had a screaming fit whenever he looked at her, and Jenny Carson – fourteen, and grossly over-developed and over-sexed despite hormone treatment to reduce the excessive testosterone her body was producing – no longer insisted on yanking up her blouse at him. And these kids were among the less disruptive in the school!

Of course, it was his acting talents that had won the group

over. Rather than read from the Bible, he preferred to act out the scenes, playing every character with tremendous aplomb. He was particularly proud of his ranting Herod, which was holding the kids entranced now as he strutted up and down berating John the Baptist; rapid role-switches were accomplished by changes of voice and stance. He was an accomplished actor in the John Sessions school, but he had no illusions about what he was achieving; the youngsters gave him the same attention they would accord a party conjurer, and for much the same reason. They were absorbed by the messenger, not the message.

'So where is this God?' Herod demanded of his captive.

A quick change of posture. 'He is all around,' John the Baptist proclaimed.

'Ha!' Herod exclaimed, looking about him and fixing a beady eye on Peter Cardew, who squirmed and gurgled in anticipation. 'So where is he? Is he hiding under Peter's table?' Much to the autistic boy's delight and the laughter of the others, Father Denis made a great show of peering under Peter's table.

When he straightened, he was uncomfortably aware that one child was not joining in the hilarity. As always, André Normanville was sitting quiet and unmoved at her table, neat as a pin in her knife-pleated skirt and spotless silk blouse, watching the good priest with those large, luminous eyes that always made him feel so foolish and self-conscious. It was as if the compelling eyes were windows into a dungeon where a frantically signalling adult was trapped in the prison of the young girl's retarded mind. She wasn't a Catholic, but her mother was keen for her daughter to receive additional Christian instruction.

'Is he in Carol's pencil box?' Herod roared.

'No!' Carol shrieked back in delight, nearly dropping her pencil box in excitement as she snatched it up to safeguard it from the attentions of the crazed Herod.

'Then where is your God?' Herod thundered.

'Andy's hiding him!' someone piped up.

The thought of involving André in his play-acting unnerved Father Denis. He quickly switched characters.

'God is all around. All-seeing. All-loving,' declared John the Baptist defiantly.

A sneering Herod reappeared. 'So show him to me. Point out where he is.'

'He is everywhere! He is with us now! Watching over us!'

'And where is this heaven?'

'All around!' John the Baptist proclaimed.

'No,' said André abruptly. 'Wrong. All wrong.'

Father Denis was so surprised that he momentarily forgot what character he was. He abandoned both of them, and smiled benignly at André. 'Sorry, André. What did you say?'

The green eyes stared fixedly at him. Father Denis repeated his question.

André shook her head. 'All wrong.'

'What's wrong, André?' the priest asked gently.

'Not all round.'

Dear God, Father Denis thought. I'm getting through to one of them at last. Maybe she's getting a distorted message, but at least something is registering.

The other five children were forgotten for the moment. They had fallen strangely silent, as though sensing that something even more entertaining than Father Denis's performance was about to happen.

'Do you mean that God is not all around, André?'

The girl looked uneasy at the sudden attention, and nodded, not taking her unblinking gaze off the priest for an instant.

'Then where *do* you think God is, André?'

'Not here. Not all the time.'

Father Denis knelt, so that they were conversing as equals. He was experiencing a little tingle of excitement at the realisation that here was a girl with an IQ below 60 who could handle an abstract. 'Where, then?'

'At the place where time begins.'

You couldn't get much more abstract than that. The priest remained outwardly calm. There had been a spate of theological articles in *The Tablet* recently, debating whether God had been present at the exact point in the Universe that marked the location of the Big Bang and the Creation – the so-called singularity. One writer had referred to such a theoretical point as the place where time began, and had postulated that it marked the physical location of heaven. There had even been a piece by the noted rabbi scientist who suggested that the spiritual concept of God was a mistake of man's own making. There was precious little of the spiritual in the Big Bang, he argued, so why should the follow-up be spiritual? It was now time to search for God with instruments and probes rather than prayers. The physical fundamentalists were having a field-day.

'And where is the place where time begins, André?' Father Denis asked, and cursed himself the moment the question was out. It made him sound patronising, which he hadn't intended.

But there was no theology or philosophy in André's reply. She screwed up her eyes as if in deep thought and pointed towards the ceiling above the door. 'There,' she said simply. 'That way.'

A bell rang in the corridor, signifying the end of the school day and triggering a chorus of cheering and table-banging. The school bus pulled into the quadrangle and waited outside the window, its diesel ticking over with an uneven beat. Father Denis stood and smiled down at the girl. 'A pity there's not more time to continue this, André.'

The girl stared hard at the priest and said, 'At the third stroke, the time sponsored by Accurist will be two fifty-seven and ten seconds. Beep . . . Beep . . . Beep . . .'

Such a pity, thought Father Denis regretfully. For a few magical moments the priest had believed that he was reaching beyond the blank stare and into the dull mind that lay beyond, jealously guarding the girl's soul and denying it to him and to God. But it had been just a phantom flash of intelligence – the brief, tantalising opening of a shutter that was now firmly closed.

68

Laura gave up struggling with the stump of the pine tree. It rocked in the ground, but refused to break free no matter how much she heaved it back and forth. It was one of those jobs Jeff

Harcourt would tackle in ten minutes and charge her a fiver for. But she had learned that it was better to pay Jeff to do such jobs, rogue though he was, than accept favours from the husbands on the estate, who would willingly do any job for nothing – and then hang about for a couple of hours drinking tea and paying compliments in the hope that such kindnesses were a route to her bedroom. That was the annoying thing about being a widow in a small community – and of course the wives regarded you with suspicion because they saw you as a predator. No, hiring Jeff Harcourt for jobs she couldn't do herself had proved to be sound, if expensive, politics. Also, the big, amiable odd-jobber had never shown the slightest interest in her, or any woman for that matter. The obsessive loves in his life had two wheels rather than two legs.

She went into the house, called Jeff's number and explained the situation to him.

'Could do it right away, Mrs Normanville. Still got plenty of daylight.'

Laura chuckled. 'What you mean, Jeff, is that you could do with some drinking-money for tonight.'

'Given up boozing, Mrs Normanville,' said Jeff cheerily. 'Got a new bike to pay for.'

'Not another, Jeff. How many's that this year?'

'Ah, but this one's a real beaut. A Kracker.'

'Kracker?'

'A Kawasaki. Be round on it in ten minutes with me pickaxe and axe. Okay?'

'Okay, Jeff. And thanks.' Laura went into the kitchen to start preparing the evening meal. She glanced at the clock radio. 3 p.m. Andy would be home in thirty minutes. Damn – it was a Wednesday. Andy's one evening out by herself at Jacko's cafe.

Laura sat at the kitchen table, rested her chin on her hands and debated with herself what to do. Thinking about the dreadful events of the previous Wednesday made her skin crawl with terror. Andy was certain to want to go out. Her Wednesdays had become part of her routine. Laura knew that if she really put her foot down she could stop André's weekly jaunt, but there would be a bitter scene. On the other hand, Laura had

277

sensed the suspicion of Detective-Sergeant Barr when he called around to make inquiries about the missing bikers. He was certain to have questioned Jacko and everyone in the café about last Wednesday, and would have discovered that André visited the place at the same time each week. Maybe he would be keeping watch. If André didn't visit Jacko's this evening, the change in her routine would arouse his suspicions even more. The sensible thing would be to let her go.

Laura rose and crossed to the vegetable rack. Some tired leeks sprawled in the wire drawer, reminding her suddenly of the broad avenue of smashed pines in Tanner's Plantation.

This time the terror that stirred in her was of an intensity that forced her to flee to the bathroom, where she was violently sick.

69

NORTHERN IRAQ

'Look out!'

But Nuri's shouted warning was too late. The sides of the well collapsed, burying Khalid's legs to his groin. Nuri threw himself flat and stretched a hand down to his companion, and Khalid grabbed the offered hand and hauled himself free. Luckily the soil was dry and sandy. It was the fourth collapse that afternoon. When they started digging the well the previous day, they had made it a little over a metre square so that there was enough room for one man to dig and fill the spoil basket. With this latest collapse, the pit was twice that size, and still only three metres deep.

'This is useless,' said Nuri savagely. 'We've been digging for two days. As fast as we dig, the walls fall in. At this rate, we won't reach the water-table for a month.'

Khalid scrambled out of the pit and regarded his friend with large, solemn eyes. 'Couldn't we use bits of wood to hold the sides up?'

'Shore it up?'

'Yes.'

Nuri sighed and looked around. Two of the old women were toiling along the track towards the village. A yoke rested on their bent shoulders from which hung two five-litre plastic water-containers which they had filled two kilometres away, at the gully where he and Khalid had hidden from the helicopter. They would pour the muddy water into a trough for the chickens and goats to quench their thirst, then two other women would settle the yoke on their shoulders and set off back to the gully again.

By now Nuri was resenting the time spent in the village. This wretched well they were digging at the edge of a field, a safe distance from the poisoned borehole, was going to take longer than he had thought. All he wanted now was to press on north, to join the PPK.

Khalid broke in on his thoughts. 'So what do we do to shore up the well, Nuri?'

The older man gestured angrily at the buildings. All were built in the traditional Kurdish style: mud-brick walls supporting roof rafters cut from fast-growing young conifers. 'You tell me what to use for materials! We need boards, you stupid cretin!'

Khalid was too intent on wrestling with the problem for the insult to register. His face suddenly brightened. 'There's the workshop at the house we're using, Nuri. It's made of wooden boards. And there are plenty of tools to saw them up with.'

The older man was about to voice automatic objections when he realised that Khalid was right. The house possessed an expensive prefabricated workshop made of larch-lap boarding. 'Okay,' he said with bad grace. 'Let's take a look at it.'

70

SOUTHERN ENGLAND

The school bus took exactly the same route as it had on Monday, dropping children off in ones and twos at villages and hamlets in West Sussex and Surrey.

Lloyd followed it at a respectful distance in his Lotus Super

Seven, slowing to check the children who had disembarked, then accelerating to close the gap in case the bus took a turning he missed. The lanes were too narrow to overtake, so there was no reason why Lloyd's continuous presence behind the bus should arouse the driver's suspicions. It took twenty-five minutes to reach Durston, where the police had stopped him on Monday afternoon. Half a mile further down the road, the coach signalled and pulled into a bus lay-by. Lloyd drew up a few yards before a turning marked Durston Wood, and waited.

One girl got off the bus and walked towards him. There was no mistaking that tall, angular build. The last time he had seen André was in the baggage hall at Heathrow Airport. In the short time since then, her awkwardness seemed to have gone; she was moving with a sinuous grace. It was her clothes, of course: a high-buttoned long coat, well tailored, with a nipped-in waist that imparted a sophisticated elegance and accentuated her height.

A motorbike approached her from behind. The rider spotted André in front of him. He revved the engine hard, producing the familiar harsh crackle of a Kawasaki, dropped into low gear and veered onto the grass verge. Rather than turn to see what the noise was, André seemed to give a little cry. She clapped her hands to her ears and sank to her knees in obvious distress.

Suddenly it seemed as if the atmosphere was becoming massively charged with positive ions. Blue sparks cracked from Lloyd's fingertips as he grabbed the door handle. He jumped from the car and sprinted towards the girl. The motorcyclist was now less than twenty yards away from André and reducing speed.

'No, André!' Lloyd screamed. 'No! It's all right!'

The girl looked up at Lloyd. The anguish of her expression changed to fleeting recognition. At that precise moment there was a deafening crack, followed by a tremendous whoosh of air that hammered into Lloyd's back like the kick of an elephant and sent him sprawling on the grass in front of André. The blast nearly jerked the Kawasaki's handlebars from the rider's grasp. The machine snaked as he wrestled to regain control, but he was forced to lay the machine over and jump clear. The fibreglass fairing ploughed a deep groove in the soft verge; the footrest hit a hummock and whipped the machine around. It came to rest on its side within a few feet of where the girl had collapsed, its engine still running at a fast tick-over and its rear wheel spinning.

Lloyd struggled onto one knee. His first thought was for the girl, but he was badly winded by the fall and unable to move for some seconds. He looked up and saw that the rider was well-protected, and had fallen well despite wearing what looked like a pickaxe and an axe lashed to a haversack. He was beside André and helping her to her feet.

'Bloody hell,' he was saying. 'Sorry, Andy. Didn't mean to frighten you. I knew the timing was out but I didn't think it could cause a backfire like that.' He glanced up at Lloyd. 'You all right, mate?'

Lloyd stood. 'I think so,' he replied, badly shaken. 'How about you?'

'Yeah – I'm all right,' said Jeff Harcourt calmly. 'Not the first time I've had to lay a bike over. Won't be the last, neither.' He was about thirty-five, an experienced rider because he had virtually walked off his machine when he lost control, rather than stay with it. He had the look of an ageing hippy. Lloyd guessed that his riding days had started back in the '70s.

Both men helped André to her feet and brushed grass and soil from her coat. She stared straight ahead, either unaware of or not interested in the anxious attentions of the two men. Once Jeff was sure that she was okay, he slipped the haversack from his shoulders, stood his machine upright and switched off the ignition. He gave the motor-bicycle a quick inspection. 'Seems all right,' he observed. 'Blowback like that sometimes buggers a silencer, but the Japs build 'em well, I reckon.' He frowned at the deep gouges in the grass. 'Must've hit something, but I can't see nothing.'

'Compact,' said André suddenly when she realised who Lloyd was.

'Hallo, Andy,' Lloyd replied, smiling at the girl. 'Are you okay?'

'Bugger. Lights aren't working,' said Jeff, flicking a switch in annoyance. 'You know Andy then, do you?'

Lloyd managed a crooked smile. 'Oh, yes – we know each other, don't we, Andy?'

'Do me a favour then, mate. I'm Jeff Harcourt. Run Andy home and tell Laura what happened. I was on my way to do a job for her, but I can't now because I don't have no lights.' Jeff settled his haversack over his shoulder. 'I'll have to get back home now and fix 'em. Tell Laura I'll be along same time tomorrow. All right?'

'Understood,' Lloyd replied. He took André gently by the arm and steered her to his car. Jeff swung his leg over the Kawasaki's saddle and turned the ignition key. The sound of the engine caused André to give a little shudder.

'It's all right, Andy,' said Lloyd soothingly. 'It was silly of him to ride up behind you like that. Anyone would be scared. Especially a big bike like that.'

He opened the passenger door and made room on the seat.

'Do you live near here, Andy?'

'That road.' The girl sat demurely in the cleared seat and pointed to the turning into Durston Wood. Lloyd secured the girl's seat-belt, started the engine and turned into the estate. The Lotus's firm suspension did not take too kindly to being humped by sleeping policemen. Normally the strange un-English mixture of houses would have intrigued him, but his mind was wrestling with the awesome implications of the missing bikers and the nearby devastation supposedly caused by a meteorite.

'Which number, Andy?'

'Sixteen.' She pointed out the road that led to her bungalow. Number sixteen was at the far end of the short cul-de-sac. The timber-framed bungalow was hemmed in by pines, larch and spruce, with a sprinkling of the ubiquitous silver birch and ash that grew well in the impoverished soil of this part of Surrey. Lloyd turned into the drive, wondering how he was going to deal with Laura Normanville's undoubted hostility. The fury that had blazed in her eyes when she discovered André telling the time for him on the flight from Singapore was still fresh in his mind.

'Compact?' André inquired. She was looking at him intently.

Lloyd chuckled. 'It goes with me everywhere.'

The bungalow's side-door opened and Laura appeared. She was wearing scruffy, baggy jeans and a grubby but tight T-shirt that looked better on her than the dowdy clothes Lloyd had last seen her in. A pity about the ridiculous bun her hair was tied in. She approached the Lotus, frowning. André released her seat-belt and jumped out.

'Mother! It's Compact!'

I do believe she's actually excited, thought Lloyd. He opened his door and stood up. 'Hallo. Nice to see you again.'

The woman's eyes opened wide in alarm. 'You!' she almost spat. 'What are you doing with my daughter?'

'There was a slight accident just after André got off the school bus – '

'*Get out of my drive this minute. How dare you come here!*'

'But – '

Laura took a threatening step towards him. 'If you don't leave this instant, I shall call the police!'

Lloyd hadn't wanted to be brutal, but the woman's attitude left him little choice. He reached into his car and produced the handbill about the two missing bikers. He had expected a sudden look of fear in Laura's eyes even before he unfolded it, but there was no response. 'I thought perhaps you'd know what this is.'

'It's a police poster. So what?'

'Compact,' André repeated.

'Go inside, Andy,' said Laura brusquely.

'Compact!'

'*Do as I say!*'

André walked down the path and stood by the kitchen door, regarding the two adults.

Laura turned to face Lloyd. Her initial fury was gone, replaced by the steely reserve, the cunning, that had protected André all these years. 'What do you want, Mr Wheeler?'

'You remembered my name.'

'I never forget anyone who interferes. Say what's on your mind, and go.'

'Quite a lot's on my mind. A huge area of destroyed plantation not a mile from here. Two missing bikers, and a man called Jeff Harcourt nearly suffering the same fate just now . . .' Lloyd watched the woman carefully, looking for the slightest sign of discomfort, but there was none. That she stared straight back at him made him wonder if perhaps he had made a serious mistake. Either that, or she was a skilled actress.

'Jeff?' she queried, deigning to show some concern. 'What happened? Is he all right?'

'Thanks to my coming along at the right moment, he's fine. The sound of his motorbike frightened Andy. A Kawasaki.' He fingered the handbill pointedly. 'I think I can guess why.'

'Why?'

'Can I come in? Just for a minute?'

Laura was briefly undecided. Then she gave a sigh and held the door open. 'Come in if you must, but I'm very busy.'

Lloyd followed her into the kitchen. It was a snug, homely room, dominated by an Aga so big that the bungalow must have been built around it. Against one wall was a cluttered Welsh dresser with residues of paint still showing in the cracks in its ancient panels. The pine table looked as if it had been rescued from a jumble sale, as did the fan-back Windsor chairs, made comfortable with the addition of lace-on cushions. Lloyd's nose was assailed by the rich smells of home cooking, reminding him that it was a long time since he had visited his parents.

'Compact,' said André.

Lloyd smiled at the girl. 'Would you like to play with it, Andy?'

She nodded.

'Go and fetch it, then. It's on the floor in the back of my car.'

Laura opened her mouth to remonstrate with Lloyd for his familiarity in using André's nickname, but before she could speak her daughter did something even more extraordinary than her purchase of flowers the previous Sunday: she threw her arms round the intruder's neck and kissed him on the cheek, quickly and unselfconsciously, before rushing out to the car.

Lloyd was also taken aback, but not to the same extent as Laura because he was unaware of just how out-of-character the gesture was. André returned, clutching the portable computer and the rented video cassette of *2001* that Lloyd had dumped in the car with the intention of returning it to the library. She started to unzip the Compaq from its slipcase.

'It might be a good idea if you took it into the living-room or your bedroom,' Lloyd suggested. 'And you're welcome to watch the tape. It's a very good movie. I've got to return it, so be careful with it.' He smiled wryly at Laura as André vanished with the machine and the tape. 'You should have bought her a computer in Singapore.'

'I was too busy,' Laura replied coolly, confident that the effect André's extraordinary action had had on her did not show.

She threw her arms around him and kissed him! She kissed a stranger, and never once in all these years has she ever kissed me!

'And I'm still busy,' she added pointedly. 'I've a meal to get ready.'

'May I sit down?'

She checked the words that sprang to her lips and shrugged instead. 'Please yourself.'

Lloyd sat at the kitchen table. As he did so, he glanced at the telephone on the dresser. There was no number on the label; she was definitely ex-directory. British Telecom warned their ex-directory subscribers not to label their telephones, but there were ways of finding out what the number was. 'I think a cup of tea might be a good idea for both of us.'

Laura bit back the invective that sprang to her tongue. Ye Gods – this bastard had a nerve! But fear of what he seemed to know moderated her simmering fury to a constrained anger. The sooner she heard what he had to say, the sooner she could get rid of him. He was the outside world intruding on the quiet, insulated little world she had painstakingly built over the years – threatening to tear it apart. Already in her mind she was planning her move from the village, but the problems were almost too great to contemplate: selling the bungalow during a recession; the disruption of André's schooling and routine; having to find a new job . . . And trying to cover her traces effectively would be hopeless. The outside world would always find her, forcing its uncaring way through the most inconsequential chink in her armour. She clenched her hands tightly on the electric kettle as she filled it to prevent them trembling. *No! Why should we run?*

'So what's your interest in André?' she asked quietly, without turning around.

'As I said – I know about the two bikers who disappeared. And I also know that Andy's powers had something to do with it.'

Suddenly she knew what she had to do. She had to kill this man – this interloper. In those few seconds while her back was turned to Lloyd, she worked everything out. She would kill him, and take his body out to the car when it was dark, and drive off with it. She would hide the car and the body in some nearby woods and come back for André. André would be able to make the car and the body disappear.

Laura gave a hollow laugh. 'Really? And you think anyone will believe you?' There was a large Kitchen Devil knife close to her right hand. Twelve inches of razor-sharp stainless steel. Her right-hand side when she turned would be to his left-hand side. She would drive the blade straight into his heart.

'No. But I don't intend to tell anyone,' Lloyd replied.

'But you're a journalist.' Her fingers edged towards the knife.

Her strange calm worried Lloyd. 'Well – yes. But please believe me, Laura . . .'

Laura! The bastard has even found out my first name!

'. . . I give you my word that I won't – '

Lloyd's gruelling squash sessions with his girlfriend paid off. His reflexes were fast enough to grab Laura's right wrist – but not even his superior weight and strength were sufficient to counter the momentum of her demented rush. He twisted his body sideways, and at the same time shoved her hard away from him. The blade of the heavy Kitchen Devil drove deep into the pine wall-boarding just above his shoulder. She tried to snatch it out, but she was off-balance and Lloyd was too quick. He held grimly onto her wrist and twisted savagely, forcing her fingers open so that he could yank her hand away. She gave a little whimper of pain and tried to beat his face with her left fist. Lloyd spun her around so that her back was to him, pinioned both arms to her side and held her in a breast-crushing double arm-lock. Had she started kicking, he would have had no compunction about kicking her back, much harder.

'Listen, you stupid bitch!' Lloyd snarled in her ear. 'There's only two of us who know about Andy and we're not going to tell anyone! Do you understand? *We are not going to tell anyone!* Now for Christ's sake act sensibly, woman.'

'You're hurting me!' she spat.

'Good. Nothing like a bit of agony to concentrate the mind. I'm going to shove you into a chair and let go of you. If you try another stunt, by God I'll hit you hard enough to put you in hospital for a week. I've no scruples whatsoever about thumping women who come at me with knives. Savvy?'

The fight seemed to go out of her, but he wasn't taking chances. He thrust her into a chair, yanked the knife out of the wall and menaced her with it.

But the threat wasn't necessary. She stared at him, breasts heaving and tears streaming silently down her cheeks. Strangely, there had been very little noise during the fracas. Through the open door he could hear the faint explosions and laser-cannon blasts of André making life difficult for the wicked Egrons.

Lloyd suddenly felt sorry for this woman. He had come barging into the cosy, well-protected little world she had built of stripped-pine dressers and hanks of dried garlic cloves, and his knowledge and presence were threatening to destroy her life and take her daughter away from her. Small wonder that she had attacked him. He put the Kitchen Devil on the drainer and poured her a plastic beaker of water. He expected her to knock it from his hand, but she accepted it.

He sat down to make her feel less intimidated, but pulled his chair close, ready to grab her if he had to. 'Listen, Laura,' he began gently. 'Please don't be afraid of me. I promise you I'm a friend. I really do want to help. I beg you to believe me.'

'I don't need anyone's help.' The sobs she was struggling to suppress made the sentence come out as a shuddering gasp.

'I think you do, Laura. I don't know for how long you've struggled, trying to give André a normal life, but – '

'No – you don't,' Laura snapped back with something of her old spirit. 'No one does. But I don't care. I'll go on looking after Andy for the rest of my life if I have to – '

'Laura, you can't. Sooner or later there's going to be another accident like last Wednesday – '

She sat upright and stared at him. There was a wild look in her eyes. 'What do you know about last Wednesday? What can you prove? Nothing! So leave us alone.'

'Laura – please, I don't want to prove anything. But I can guess what happened from what nearly happened to Jeff Harcourt just now.'

She raised her head and looked at him. She was more in control now. 'What *did* happen to him?'

Lloyd told her.

'Is he all right?' Laura interrupted anxiously, this time genuinely concerned. 'I could never forgive myself if – '

'Yes, he's fine, but I don't think he would've been if I hadn't shouted at Andy. He thinks his motorbike backfired. It really was extraordinary. An instant before the crack, it was as if the entire atmosphere was charged with static electricity. A massive positive charge; sparks jumped between my fingers and the car as I got out. It was all very strange. Have you ever known that happen with Andy before?'

Laura's eyes focused on him. 'Do you swear to say nothing of this?'

'Yes. There's someone who knows – Ted Prentice. He produced that television programme that Andy auditioned for. I know he won't say anything.'

After so many years as a loner, Laura found it difficult to trust anyone, but she realised that she had little choice but to trust this deceptively mild-looking, big-boned man.

'About the static,' Lloyd reminded her. 'Have you ever known that before?'

Laura shook her head and took another sip of water. 'No – nothing like that – not static.' She hesitated. Talking about André like this was a struggle – the breaking of a long habit.

'She's . . . She's changing. Last Sunday she bought me flowers for Mother's Day. And just now . . . Just now . . . She kissed you. She hasn't done that since . . .' But the memories which were painful to recall were even more painful to relate.

Lloyd thought that perhaps he was crowding her, so he moved his chair away – and to her horror Laura realised she was sorry.

No! Don't be fooled by his soft voice and understanding manner, or his promises! He's the enemy. You've got to fight him, otherwise they'll take André away!

Lloyd sensed her sudden chilling. 'Perhaps I could make some tea?' he suggested.

Normally the thought of anyone using her kitchen would have horrified Laura, but now she was in a state of acute inner turmoil, part of her determined to fight this interloper tooth and nail, part of her feeling immense relief that here was someone with whom at last she could share her problems. Finally she nodded. 'Everything's in the cupboard over the sink. The kettle's full.'

Lloyd switched on the electric kettle, found two mugs and set them down on the table. While waiting for the kettle to boil he told Laura the entire story, starting with his interest in André's time-telling abilities on the flight from Singapore and his visit to Ted Prentice in Epsom. He broke off to make the tea, and related the rest of the story.

'So André *did* make thunder at the audition?' Laura interrupted when he told her about Rikki Steadman's analysis of the audition recording.

Lloyd grinned. 'Ted Prentice owes you an apology over that. He feels guilty about it. Does Andy still turn tennis balls inside out?'

'No. She couldn't do that. That was Khalid. Sajii's son. We met at the audition and became friends. They're Iraqis – Kurds. The Home Office expelled them at the beginning of the year.'

'You remember at the audition a cameraman going around making random recordings of the kids?'

Laura nodded. 'I think so. It was to get them used to the camera.'

'Well, the lip-reader who looked at the tapes of Andy and

289

Khalid when they were talking together thinks that it was Andy who was showing Khalid what to do with the tennis balls.'

'André *can't* turn tennis balls inside out. It's something she's never done.'

'Maybe not,' said Lloyd thoughtfully. 'The lip-reader did say that she couldn't be a hundred per cent certain of what they were saying to each other. Maybe Andy motivated a latent talent in Khalid?'

Laura grimaced. 'If turning tennis balls inside out was all she could do, we wouldn't be in the mess we're in now.'

'You're thinking that she killed those two bikers?' He saw the shock flicker in her eyes and wished that he hadn't been so blunt.

'Well, what do you think?' she asked after a pause.

'I don't know what to think, Laura,' Lloyd admitted. 'What puzzles me is that all the savants I've read about have only one talent. They can tell the time or do calendar calculations or mental calculations, play any piece of music, or draw any scene from memory with amazing accuracy. But André has two distinct talents; she can tell the time, and she can make thunder that can blow up half a forest. Two talents, unless there's a link between them – and I can't see that there is. Also she's a female savant, and that's extremely rare.'

'That's because she suffers from acquired savantism,' said Laura quietly.

'Sorry?'

There was a long pause before Laura replied. When she spoke, her voice was low and strained. 'She wasn't born autistic. She had it thrust upon her by my stupidity.'

'I'm a good listener,' Lloyd prompted after another long pause.

The oven timer suddenly shrilled.

'I have to see about dinner,' said Laura, rising. 'Thank you for bringing André home, Mr Wheeler.'

'You can thank me by calling me Lloyd.'

He rose, his mind going into overdrive to think up a reason for seeing her again. 'I suppose we'd better wrest my computer from Andy. She's certainly hooked on it.'

'I'll have to buy her one.'

Lloyd suddenly had an idea. 'Well, don't buy a new one, Laura. What with all the firms going bust these days, you can pick up a first-class machine at an auction for a fraction of its original cost. Look, there are auctions held every Thursday in Putney. Thursday is always a quiet day in the office and I'm owed a lot of leave, so why don't I pick you up tomorrow and we could take a look? Make a day out of it.'

Laura looked doubtful. 'I'll have to think about it. I'll get your computer.'

She found André sprawled across her bed, banging away at the Compaq's keys with grim determination. The almost continuous tinny explosions from the machine's speaker suggested that the alien ships belonging to the evil Egrons in 'Star-Glider' were suffering a massive defeat.

Lloyd heard the sounds of an argument. He snatched up the telephone and punched 175 – British Telecom's engineering test number. A woman's computer-sampled voice responded by telling him what number he was connected to. He committed it to memory and replaced the handset. Laura returned to the kitchen a minute later, looking apologetic. 'She's playing "Star-Glider". Is it possible to save the game she's playing like we can save games on our BBCs at school?'

'Er . . . No. If you switch the machine off, you have to start the game at the beginning.'

Laura frowned. 'Damn.'

'So what's the problem?'

'She says she's reached Level Five and doesn't want to stop.'

Lloyd looked incredulous. 'Level Five? That's impossible.'

'My daughter isn't a liar, Mr Wheeler.'

'No, of course not,' said Lloyd hastily. 'It's just that I've never been able to get beyond Level Three.' He broke off and grinned. 'Look – there's no problem. There's a greasy-spoon caff near here. Jacko's. I tried it on Monday. I'll get myself a bite and come back in, say, an hour, and pick up the machine. I don't suppose she'll be able to hold out for much longer. It's bloody near impossible to play for long at Level Three.'

Laura gave a wan smile. 'I couldn't let you eat at Jacko's.

I've enough on my conscience as it is.' She hesitated. 'Would you like to have dinner with us?' Even before the invitation was out, she couldn't believe that she had uttered it.

'Oh, I couldn't . . .'

Okay, then – enjoy the food at Jacko's. But she didn't say that. What she heard herself saying was, 'It's steak-and-kidney pie, so there's plenty for three.'

'Home-made?'

Get rid of him, you stupid bitch!

'Oh yes. I've got some time off. I've been enjoying the chance to do some cooking. But there's a snag . . .' She nodded at the little black-and-white kitchen television on the dresser. 'You'll have to sit through "Neighbours" at five thirty.'

Lloyd grinned. 'That's very kind of you, Laura. For home-made steak-and-kidney pie I reckon I could sit through an hour of Des O'Connor.'

Laura joined in with Lloyd's laughter. She looked quite lovely when she laughed.

71

NORTHERN IRAQ

Nuri shaved away the sandy soil behind the timber frame with a spade and drove the shoring-board into place with a club hammer. He straightened, and retied his sweat-band before wedging the board securely with shingles taken from the roof of the bungalow's workshop. It was hot, exhausting work in the well-shaft. He looked up at the square of light six metres above his head. The boards and cross-bracing struts that lined the rectangular hole looked ramshackle but were structurally sound. Khalid's idea of using the timber workshop as a source of materials had been a good one; the boards were two centimetres thick and would last many years.

He went back to loosening the hard semi-sandstone with a pick. Another thirty minutes' work and it would be Khalid's turn at the bottom of the hole. The soil was now soft and yielding as a result of seepage; the water splashed the baggy trousers and boots he and Khalid had found in the bungalow. Far from being welcome, the water increased the weight of the basket-loads of spoil that had to be hauled up the shaft.

He felt a dull vibration through his feet, and stopped work to listen. The borehole seemed to resonate and amplify the strange sound.

It was the menacing rumble of heavy trucks.

Khalid was perched on the ridge, yanking nails out of the roof timbers of the half-demolished workshop, when he heard one of the old women cry out. He looked up. From his high vantage-point he could see the cloud of dust and what was causing it. He leapt down from the roof in near panic and ran the hundred metres towards the pile of spoil that marked the new well.

'Nuri!' he screamed. 'Army transporters!'

The older man's head appeared at the top of the makeshift ladder at that exact moment. They had already worked out what to do, and Khalid did not need reminding despite his terror. When he saw Nuri emerging from the well, he veered towards the nearest barn, scattering startled chickens. The Bluebird was partly concealed behind a pile of hay in the dark recesses of the mud-brick building, with its bonnet facing the open doorway. He dived behind the wheel a moment before Nuri jumped into the passenger seat and seized the loaded shotgun that lay on the floor. Khalid's fingers gripped the key that was already in the ignition. Their plan was simple: if soldiers started searching the barn, Khalid would drive straight out and take off out of the village, while Nuri blasted tyres with the shotgun.

They waited in the cool gloom, hearts pounding, nerves stretched, eyes fixed on the splash of bright daylight at the barn entrance, listening to the sound of diesels grinding nearer and nearer. Khalid turned the key to release the Nissan's steering-lock. The hard-packed earth shook. Nuri guessed, with relief, that they were heavy transporters; they were too heavy to be armoured personnel-carriers.

A Soviet-built truck in camouflage paint laboured past the barn entrance, its engine roaring in low gear to negotiate the village. At first Nuri thought the tracked vehicle on the back of the first transporter was a tank.

'A bulldozer!' Khalid hissed, his eyes wide.

The second vehicle rumbled by. Its cargo, too, was a bright-yellow International bulldozer. The sound of the vehicles faded into the distance, but dull shocks continued to be felt through the ground as the giant tyres struck potholes.

When he judged the transporters to be a kilometre away, Nuri put the shotgun back on the floor of the car and cautiously walked out into the sun. He shaded his eyes and stared at the distant vehicles as they laboured up the hill to the north.

'What do they want with bulldozers, Nuri?' Khalid asked at the older man's side.

Nuri shook his head. 'I don't know.' Then he remembered the JCB excavators and bulldozers they had seen being moved north on the main road.

Something big was happening, or was about to happen, in his homeland. Fear closed icy fingers around the Kurd's heart.

72
SOUTHERN ENGLAND

The dinner in Laura's cosy kitchen was a great success, largely because Lloyd seemed to have forgotten how close his hostess had come to murdering him less than an hour before.

His easy-going manner seemed to bring André to life; she hardly took her eyes off him. At one point she even managed what looked like a smile at one of his jokes. It was a reaction that surprised Laura, and was a sharp reminder of what her daughter had missed in not having a father to respond to. Lloyd didn't know it, but he was the first man to share a meal in Laura's kitchen. As soon as they had finished eating, André dived straight back into her room and resumed battle with the villainous Egrons in 'StarGlider'.

'Not too long, young lady,' Lloyd called after her. 'Your mother will be wanting to throw me out soon.'

'Not long, Lloyd,' André promised.

'I prefer that name to Compact,' Lloyd remarked. 'It doesn't suit me.'

André's positive response to Lloyd's friendly admonishment was yet another disturbing surprise for Laura in a day of surprises. André had always shared her mother's suspicion of strangers, but her attitude to Lloyd showed that she was now forming her own judgments. André the little girl was inexorably slipping away from her, Laura knew, and she wasn't sure if she was pleased or sorry.

'This has been very kind of you, Laura. I've not had such a good meal in months,' said Lloyd anxiously. 'But I don't want to outstay my welcome.'

She looked carefully at him and decided that his concern was genuine. 'Don't worry,' she said, setting out two coffee cups. 'Wednesday evenings are when André slips the parental leash and goes out.'

'Where does she go?'

She poured coffee for them both from a jug. 'Jacko's dump.'

Lloyd chuckled. 'She's not very fussy.'

'There's nowhere else for youngsters around here.'

He became serious, knowing that he was about to tread on dangerous ground. 'Is that where she went last Wednesday?'

'Yes.'

'Maybe she won't want to go out tonight?'

'She will,' said Laura emphatically.

'Tell me about the accident. How old was she when it happened?' Lloyd asked gently.

Laura looked sharply at him. 'How much did your journalistic digging really unearth?'

'I've told you everything I know, Laura. Tell me, please.'

She idly stirred her coffee. It gave her time to think. *He's perceptive. If I don't tell him he'll find out anyway by other means, so what the hell?*

'It happened in 1980. David and I had been to a party – '

'David?'

'My husband. He had drunk a lot more than me so I drove . . .'

Lloyd saw the pain in her eyes and was tempted to tell her

295

to stop, but he sensed that she actually wanted to talk so he remained silent.

'Andy was in the back of the car. She was five. Those proper child seats weren't very common in those days . . .'

Over the next thirty minutes the entire story came out. Laura omitted very little. She related the misery of having to live with the double guilt of being responsible for her husband's death and André's terrible head injuries. She told of her efforts to give her daughter as normal a life as possible, and of the endless visits to specialists – the dozens of letters written to individuals and institutions all over the world. She recounted the first time André had demonstrated her strange powers, when she made a stick she had thrown for a dog vanish. She hesitated only when she came to the time when she and Andy had driven home from Witley Station after their visit to London for the television audition. There was no point in adding to the danger they were in by telling Lloyd about the man who had vanished. Anyway, even after six years she could not bring herself to face again the one occasion on which she had deliberately inflicted pain on André.

There was an embarrassed silence when she finished talking; Lloyd's coffee had gone cold. He was trying hard to think of something to say when André marched into the kitchen, carrying his Compaq zipped into its slipcase. She was ready to go out, looking surprisingly elegant in a long, fur-trimmed leather coat that Lloyd guessed must have cost in the region of £300. He took the machine from André and decided that it was time to go. He thanked Laura profusely yet again for the meal – and to his delight she agreed to accompany him to look for a computer for André. He arranged to collect her at eleven the following morning.

As he drove home, he reflected that he had achieved far more that day than he had dreamed possible. But he could not break his promise and write his planned article on savants now: it would be a betrayal. For a moment he regretted getting too closely involved; accepting Laura's offer of a meal had undermined his professionalism. Then he recalled his pleasure at seeing her laugh at his pathetic joke about Des O'Connor, and decided that was the sort of undermining his professionalism needed.

73

Detective-Sergeant Barr had parked his car in Jacko's car park, near the lights of the café, so that he could see clearly the comings and goings of Jacko's customers. George Michael, mixed with laughter and arguments, throbbed from the other side of the condensation-drenched windows. Near his car was an assortment of 'L' plate-festooned Hondas and Suzukis – hardly more than mopeds – and there were also a few push-bikes. When you saw just how popular the grubby little shack in the woods was with youngsters, Yorkie thought, it made you wonder if local councils, with their ambitious plans to build expensive youth centres, had got it wrong.

A light to his left caught the sergeant's attention. A cyclist was coming towards him, expertly weaving to avoid the car park's potholes. It was André Normanville – the reason why he was here. She took a line across one area that was a mass of puddles without getting her tyres wet. Sergeant Barr was impressed, but then one of the girl's neighbours had remarked that she had brilliant control on two wheels. He lowered his window and watched the girl's progress on what had to be several hundred quids-worth of Dawes sports bike.

She drew up in front of the café, and braked. Then she did something that the policeman hadn't seen anyone do outside a circus. She stopped, but instead of putting one foot to the ground, she remained perfectly balanced on the stationary machine with both feet on the pedals. She was less than two yards away, yet she seemed to be ignoring him – although Sergeant Barr was certain she knew he was sitting in the car, watching her. His suspicions were confirmed when she pad-locked her bicycle and straightened up. He held her gaze for a few seconds. The all-knowing green eyes that bored into him were devoid of expression, and yet the policeman had an uncomfortable feeling that she was mocking him. She looked away, not because she was dragging her stare away through guilt, but because it suited her to do so. George Michael spilled into the car park as she pulled the café door open and entered the steamy interior of Jacko's without a backward glance.

Sergeant Barr sat deep in thought for some moments. He had half-believed the girl wouldn't turn up – not that it would have proved anything either way if she hadn't. The unpalatable truth was that Yorkie didn't know what to think. First Crabbie Howard disappears, pissed as a newt, and now two bikers.

When he had won his transfer to plain-clothes, he had believed that somehow he would be endowed with a capacity for infallible hunches. Well, there was no shortage of hunches; the trouble was that four years' plain-clothes experience had demonstrated that ninety-nine per cent of them were all too fallible, and the other one per cent weren't much use without proof. He sighed, and pulled his clipboard onto his lap. He had over fifty cases on his plate. The disappearance of Dabber and Greaser would have to go to the bottom of the pile and stay there. Two living, breathing human beings turned into statistics by a retarded girl with haunting green eyes and an amazing sense of balance – and there was bugger-all he could do about it.

74

Thursday, 14th March 1991

For an hour after packing André off to school, Laura sat around, unable to concentrate on any task – although there were several clamouring for her attention. The meeting with Lloyd Wheeler the previous day had unsettled her. How could he have had the nerve to do what he did – tracking her down like that? And yet, she had ended up giving him dinner! It was absurd – and so was her agreeing to go out with him today. It wasn't going to be just a shopping trip, either, but a day out, with lunch and conversation, and all the other trimmings and commitments she could well do without. She had managed perfectly well for over ten years by herself, so surely she was more than capable of buying a computer without male help . . . She was tempted to call him and tell him the whole thing was off, but it was 10.15 – he'd be on his way. She remembered that he had a mobile phone, but God knew where his business card was.

10.15! Heavens! Was that the time?

She flew into the bathroom and showered. What to wear was a problem. On impulse she opened the left-hand door of her wardrobe, the side she never looked at, and examined the few polythene-shrouded dresses she had saved from those far-off, happy days with David. They were pushed to the far end of the rail, but among them was a navy-blue, all-wool, button-front dress, with a white collar, simple enough to be ageless, short enough for the fashion to have come full circle. It had been one of David's favourites – and it was still a perfect fit.

Strange how her weight had hardly changed in ten years. It was something she had never thought about until now, because it had never mattered . . . Tights, which she rarely bought for herself, were no problem because André had dozens of unworn pairs. A twinge of guilt as she pulled them on – but she would transfer the money for them from her black purse to the red purse she used for André. Shoes – a pair of once-worn white high-heels that had been part of her going-away outfit. The heels were a problem; she hadn't worn high-heels since the accident. A few experimental totters up and down the bedroom, and she decided that she could manage.

God – I'm behaving like a teenage kid on her first date.

She looked at herself critically in her dressing-table mirror. The bun would have to go . . .

Five minutes later, having brushed her hair straight and applied some make-up raided from the Mary Quant box in André's room, she caught sight of herself in André's full-length mirror and nearly fainted from shock. Confronting her was someone she thought was dead: the despicable creature who had killed the man she loved, destroyed her daughter and deprived her of a father. Her first instinct was to tear the clothes off – but the sound of a high-performance engine turning into her drive stayed her hand.

75

Lloyd wasn't the only one to be astonished by Laura's transformation. The tall, elegant woman who walked down the drive to the waiting bright-yellow Lotus caused much net-curtain-twitching among neighbours who had known Laura ever since she first moved to Durston Wood.

Lloyd recovered his senses and jumped out of the car to open the passenger door. 'You look fantastic, Laura,' he exclaimed, feeling self-conscious in his casual slacks and pullover. He hadn't expected this, but he was delighted and flattered all the same. He nearly told her how good she looked without the bun, but decided that might be overstepping the mark.

Laura flashed him a warm smile; his obvious admiration went a long way to stilling her guilt. It was years since a man had paid her a compliment – and now she even found herself experiencing a little thrill of pleasure when she saw Lloyd looking appreciatively at her legs as she swung her feet into the footwell. The old, suppressed Laura, which had been fighting all these years for rehabilitation and recognition, began to feel that it was gaining ground.

76

Max was too astute an operator to act suspiciously. There was no slouching lower in his seat, or any of that nonsense. Of course, he would have been happier parking some distance from Tushingham Court, but it was necessary to be close to keep the place under observation. He wasn't unduly concerned; people rarely gave parked cars a second glance and Benny Straw, the Tushingham Court porter, was no exception.

The porter's elderly Ford Escort emerged from the car park belonging to the flats, and the wispy little man looked carefully left and right along the road while Max continued to sit unconcerned in his BMW, leafing through a London A to Z. The porter pulled out, drove past Max, reached the end of the road and disappeared – and immediately Max got out of the BMW, gathered up his briefcase, and locked the doors. The central locking motors closed with satisfying simultaneous clicks when he worked the key-ring remote-control. They were well engineered, these little devices, and Max liked that. He liked anything that did its job with maximum efficiency. Like his neat charcoal-grey suit and briefcase and brisk manner: the perfect disguise in this neighbourhood. Wear trainers, jeans and a bomber jacket in smart, residential Swiss Cottage and you'd jam the phone lines to New Scotland Yard's Information Room.

He crossed the road, pulling on a pair of kid gloves, and entered Tushingham Court's small lobby. The security camera outside the front entrance was a joke. As usual, it was mounted too high on its wall-bracket; the foreshortening effect meant that it would be difficult to judge the height of intruders – the single most important piece of information the police needed to identify suspects.

Max rang the bell to the porter's flat. He had been keeping the flats under discreet observation since the previous day and knew that Benny Straw lived alone, but there was no harm in double-checking. He examined the lock on the front door while he waited. From his previous visit, when the porter had allowed him access to Hamet al Karni's flat, he knew that over the years the smart apartments in the block had acquired a variety of complex locks. Not the porter's flat, though. Benny Straw's lock was a simple Yale and the door surround was painted deal and looked flimsy. Getting the crowbar out of his briefcase would be a waste of time. Max was small and dapper, but he was solidly built from his regular work-outs, and during his years in the army he had learned, and applied, many lethal skills.

The door popped inwards on his first charge. There was no splintering of timber – the Yale's striker-box merely stripped its two screws out of the door frame, so it would be possible to screw it back into place later, leaving no sign of a forced entry. But first things first.

He pushed a chair against the door to hold it shut, and looked quickly around. Five doors opened off the hall. The smallest of the two bedrooms served as an office – the nerve centre of Tushingham Court. An old-fashioned roll-top bureau was open, strewn with bills and receipts. The walls were lined with shelves cluttered with paint brushes, used pots of paint and varnish, and tools.

His gaze took in a black-and-white monitor that was taking a feed from the closed-circuit TV camera outside. To his relief, there was no video recorder. When he checked the living-room, there was a repeater monitor on top of the television – but the video recorder on the floor wasn't even connected to the mains, so there was no need to check it. If it had been connected, Max would have scanned the end of the tape; it wouldn't do to have his image recorded.

He returned to the office. His luck continued to hold: the bunches of keys to the flats weren't kept in a safe but, as he had hoped, hung on a home-made board, each hook labelled with the appropriate flat number. Max climbed over a partly dismantled electric lawn-mower and grabbed the keys to number 11. He left the flat, wedging the front door closed with a small wad of newspaper. He mounted the stairs two at a time, and let himself into Hamet al Karni's apartment.

Benny Straw was three miles from Tushingham Court when he realised that he'd left the measurements for Mrs Ridley's replacement window-pane in his office. He swore to himself. He was in half a mind to forget the glass and carry on with his shopping expedition, but he had promised Mrs Ridley in flat 32 that he'd fix her broken window at the weekend, and she'd be good for a twenty-quid tip if he kept his word.

Damn the stupid woman for leaving her window open in the wind. Did she really think that her bloody canary was going to come home now? It was probably inside a local tabby. He turned the Escort around and headed back to Tushingham Court.

77

Despite Laura's initial misgivings, she was agreeably surprised at how much she enjoyed herself in Lloyd's company. After so many years of independence, she realised that she had forgotten how pleasant it could be to let someone else take all the decisions. The admiring glances she and the yellow Lotus attracted were an echo of those distant days of David and his Porsche. Strange that there should be no pain at the recollection – perhaps it was because Lloyd was being so entertaining.

At the auction room she took his advice and bid for a virtually new PC Systems IBM compatible, with the latest colour monitor and a hard disk. It was knocked down to her at a tenth of its list price. It was the first time she had ever bought anything second-hand for André, but it seemed the sensible thing to do.

Lloyd noticed that she paid cash for the machine from a red purse that appeared to be crammed with £50 and £20 notes. Her purchase of a load of games from a Virgin software shop was also paid for from the red purse. But when Laura insisted on paying for their pub lunch on the way back to Durston Wood, Lloyd was intrigued to notice that the money came from a black purse with very little money in it.

78

Max worked quickly. He took a chance and decided to ignore the main bedroom: the dresser drawers were crammed with documents, but they were mostly in Arabic . . . He could always come back to them if he had the time.

The boy's room looked more promising. In a chest of drawers he found some English children's books: Khalid must have been given just about every Ladybird book ever published. In the bottom drawer were some rough sketches of tanks, motorcycles and cars – freehand pencil drawings – many of them surprisingly good. He went carefully through every document, missing nothing, sensing that he was getting close to discovering the whereabouts of the mysterious female savant called Andy. The carefully formed capital letters of the titles on the drawings reminded him of the letter that he and Leo had found in the Iraqi T–55 – words that he now knew by heart:

DEAR ANDY
   YOUR LETTER CAME WITH RED CRESCENT
AND TOOK THREE WEEKS BECAUSE OF
BOMBING. I CANT SAY WHERE I AM BUT I WAS
VERY HAPPY FOR ME TO HEAR FROM YOU. I CAN
NOW MAKE THUNDER LIKE YOU SHOWED ME
AND I CAN STILL DO TRICKS WITH TENNIS
BALLS. MORE BOMBING STARTED SO WILL
FINISH THIS LETTER TOMORROW . . .

He fumbled with the string on a legal folder. He hated the lack
of feel from having to wear gloves, but there was too much at
stake to risk taking them off. One thumbprint at Letherslade
Farm had led to the Great Mail Train Robbery gang being
nailed. But the £2.5 million of that heist was pin-money compared with the potential yield from this operation.

A letter written on a Peter Rabbit notelet slipped to the
floor. He snatched it up. It was written in a child's hand, with
immature little circles instead of dots on the i's.

ANDRÉ NORMANVILLE
16 DURSTON WOOD
NEAR ALFOLD
SURREY RH14 0PN

DEAR KHALID
MUMMY SAID YOU ARE GOING HOME. HERE IS
MY DIARY FOR THIS WEEK.

Max didn't read any further. He thrust the letter in a pocket,
put everything back exactly as he found it, and locked the flat.
He returned to the porter's flat and, after a short, desperate
hunt, found some matches in Benny Straw's messy kitchenette
to pack into the screw-holes in the front door, and a screwdriver
in the office. He searched the floor for the striker-box and screws
– which like all fallen screws, had obeyed Murphy's Law by
bouncing into inaccessible corners.

Three paces away, in the office, the TV monitor was showing
Benny Straw parking his car outside the main entrance.

Max thrust the matchsticks into the screw-holes and snapped

them off flush. He held the striker-box in position with one hand while trying to start the screw with the other. Eventually the threads bit. He tightened the screw, and was about to put the second one in position when he heard footsteps in the hall. He darted into the office and saw Benny Straw's Escort on the monitor.

A key turned in the latch, and the door opened. Max heard Benny give an exclamation of surprise as the partly fixed striker fell to the floor.

Benny entered his office and blinked in surprise at Max.

'Hallo,' said Max pleasantly, tightening his grip on the long Posidrive screwdriver. 'I'm awfully sorry about this, old chap, but I'm afraid you weren't gone long enough.'

79

The feminine opulence of André's bedroom astonished Lloyd as he carried in the computer. While Laura cleared a space on the Maple's black-lacquered work-desk, a quick glance around took in the divan and its luxurious duvet, the deep-pile carpet, the white Bang and Olufsen television with matching video recorder, and the vanitory unit. The mirrored floor-to-ceiling sliding doors on the built-in wardrobe were open, revealing a profusion of fine clothes and lingerie, expensive shoes, boots and slippers. And yet it was not an over-elaborate room; the smooth blend of pastel-shaded wallpaper and curtains, the concealed lighting, suggested that an interior designer had been employed. Sarah would have approved. Lloyd had passed Laura's open bedroom door as he carried the computer from the car. The plain pine bed and cord carpet he had noticed contrasted sharply with this extravagance.

'Do you think you'll get it working by the time Andy gets home?' Laura asked.

Lloyd plugged the keyboard into the system box and looked around for a power-socket. 'Do my best,' he smiled. 'Sometimes setting up a PC can be a pig.' He found a socket behind a photograph of a fair-haired young man that he recognised as Khalid from the audition tape.

'I'll get a meal under way,' said Laura, moving off. 'Hope you like lamb chops.'

'I can't impose on you two evenings running.'

She returned and laid her hand on his arm. 'You can and you will, Lloyd. I expect you live on beans on toast in your flat, now that your girlfriend's gone.'

Lloyd chuckled. Laura had plied him with relentless questions about himself over lunch. 'Beans on toast?' he said in a mock broad Yorkshire. 'Nay, lass – sheer bloody luxury. Dinner's a lump of black pudding made with sawdust, garnished with a slice o' month-old gravy, and a crust and dripping for afters.' It was a good impersonation of the classic Monty Python 'When I Was A Lad' sketch, and it sent Laura into peals of laughter as she left the room.

He eventually got the machine connected and fired up, but the previous owners had wiped the hard disk, including the operating system. By the time he had reinstalled the DOS and set the system configuration, Jeff Harcourt was in the garden, attacking the pine stump with an axe. Laura put her head around the door. 'Coffee, if you're ready for a break.'

'Good idea,' said Lloyd, following her into the kitchen. 'I'm nearly through.'

She had changed out of her smart clothes, which was understandable, but he was sorry to see that the bun was back in place.

He stood by the sink, sipping his mug of coffee and chatting to Laura while she prepared the vegetables. The kitchen window looked out on the back garden, where Jeff Harcourt was working in the fading light to remove the pine stump. He seemed none the worse for his misadventure of the previous day. André was pedalling her bicycle up and down the lawn, still wearing her school clothes. Her tyres were making ruts on the soft ground, prompting Laura to open the window and tell her to stay on the paths.

'She can be a real pest with that bike,' she complained to

306

Lloyd when she closed the window. 'And I told her to stay out of your way until you'd finished.'

'Good God!' Lloyd gasped.

Laura followed his astonished gaze, and laughed. André was now cycling very slowly along the top of a narrow ornamental garden wall, and expertly hopping the tyres over the straggling tresses of the previous year's trailing plants.

'I told you she was a pest. She used to unnerve the neighbours and me by riding along the tops of their walls. Now we're all used to it.'

The girl reached a point where the wall had suffered frost damage, so that there was only a narrow ledge for her tyres; yet she steered the machine along the crumbling section of brickwork with unerring accuracy.

'I've never seen anything like it,' Lloyd declared.

''Course you have,' Laura replied. 'Haven't you seen the stunts kids perform on mountain bikes on television?'

'Doesn't she ever fall off?'

'Not her. Serve her right if she did, though.'

Lloyd drained his mug. 'Better get back,' he said, moving off. 'Give me another ten minutes.'

He sat at the computer and wrote some small batch files that would make it simple to load the games – the standard PC disk operating system being about as user-friendly as a cornered rat. He was nearly finished when he heard Jeff Harcourt and André enter the kitchen. After Laura had paid him and said goodbye, mother and daughter remained chatting in the kitchen for some minutes, Laura, as usual, doing most of the talking. She sounded happy and animated. He tested each game in turn to ensure that they loaded correctly. Then movement in the wardrobe mirrors caught his eye. It was André, with Laura just behind her to see her daughter's reaction to the new acquisition.

'Hallo, Lloyd,' said André. As near as he could judge from her flat, expressionless voice, she was pleased to see him.

'Hi, Andy. What do you think of the computer mummy bought you? Smart, eh?'

André moved beside him and regarded the colour monitor. 'Big,' she commented unemotionally.

307

'Big, and much easier to use than my laptop. Aren't you pleased?'

There was no reaction from the girl.

Disappointment clouded Laura's face. 'I'll leave you to get on,' she said quietly, and returned to the kitchen.

Lloyd wondered how many such disappointments she had endured over the years. André stood beside him and watched him finish writing the batch files.

' "StarGlider"?' she asked.

'It's among all these games that mummy bought you today. You're a very lucky young lady. No one bought me stuff like this when I was a lad.'

She didn't answer but, apparently unconcerned by his presence, removed her skirt, blouse and underslip. Lloyd's initial reaction was to leave the room, and he certainly would have done if she had removed her underwear, but he decided to chat on, unperturbed. 'I'll install "StarGlider" next, Andy,' he remarked casually, relieved when she wriggled her long and surprisingly shapely legs into a tracksuit. She wasn't so gawky after all – just very tall and slender. 'There's a joystick and a mouse, which will make it much easier to play.'

He showed her how to use them. Translating the horizontal movements of the mouse on her desk to matching vertical movements of the mouse-pointer on the computer's screen was no problem for her, nor were the more simple movements of the joystick.

'Very good, Andy,' he said, much impressed when she shot up a tank in a war-game program using the mouse. 'You know, there are several people where I work who've given up learning how to use the mouse properly.' He was no longer surprised by her intuitive skill. At the back of his mind a theory was developing that André had an extraordinary understanding of spacial relationships. She was immediately at home with anything to do with space and movement. He wasn't sure how this linked with her other talents, but he had an uncomfortable feeling that there was a common denominator – something so utterly fundamental about the girl's talents that he would roundly curse himself for his blindness and stupidity when he stumbled on it.

She stood at his side, watching intently as he copied the 'StarGlider' files from the distribution diskette to the machine's hard disk. He loaded it, and up came the 'StarGlider' intro screen in bright, vivid colours on the monitor. André gave a squeal of delight and threw her arms around Lloyd's neck. It wasn't so much the deliberately provocative pressure of her breasts against his chest that alarmed him, as the passionate, albeit clumsy and inexperienced way she kissed him on the lips. She even tried to thrust her tongue into his mouth.

Bloody hell. How do I handle this?

He pushed her firmly away, and she saw from his expression that he was annoyed. 'You shouldn't do that, Andy,' he said sternly, wagging a finger at her. 'Who taught you to kiss like that?'

The green eyes were expressionless. 'Friend.'

A local boy, probably, he thought – then changed his mind when he saw her looking at the framed photograph of Khalid. Over lunch Laura had told him about her friendship with the al Karnis, and how Khalid had often stayed at Durston Wood – the last time being just before all Iraqis were expelled from the country in January.

'Wanted to say thank you,' said André.

He gave her a little hug to show that he wasn't angry. 'A kiss on the cheek is sufficient. Or just say thank you. And another thing, Andy; you shouldn't undress like you did just now when there's a stranger in your room.'

'Not a stranger.' Was there just a hint of reproach in her otherwise flat voice?

'Yes I am. If there's anyone in the room other than mummy, you *do not* undress in front of them. Not any more. Do you understand?'

She nodded.

He looked at her quizzically, pleased and a little surprised at the level of communication he was achieving. Then he recalled Laura's surprise the previous evening when André had kissed him because he allowed her to use his Compaq. 'It was mummy who bought all this for you. Don't you think it would be nice to thank her? To put your arms around her and give her a kiss?'

The girl continued to stare at him. Lloyd would have given anything to know what was passing through her mind. 'Go on, Andy,' he said firmly, turning her around and giving her a little push towards the door. 'Go and say thank you to mummy.'

She left the bedroom and returned to the kitchen. Lloyd finished installing all the games and went into the kitchen a few minutes later, with the intention of calling Andy back into the bedroom to show her how to use the computer. Laura was alone, standing by the Aga. When she didn't turn round, he crossed to her, and saw silent tears coursing down her cheeks. He knew at once what was wrong. Or, perhaps, right. He put his arm around her waist and gripped her firmly – it wasn't the time for tentative, testing-the-water measures. He was pleased that she made no attempt to resist him. 'She said thank you . . .' Laura whispered. 'For the first time . . .'

Lloyd tightened his grip. 'You mustn't blame her. She's never understood. And you said that she bought you flowers for Mother's Day. All she needed was a little prodding.'

She nodded. 'I guessed it was you. She came in and hugged me and kissed me. After all these years . . . Not that I've ever looked for gratitude. God knows, that's the last thing I deserve. But when she kissed you yesterday . . .' She faltered, unable to find the right words. 'You're good for her, Lloyd. Maybe I've deprived her of the right kind of guidance . . . Maybe I should have remarried . . .'

Lloyd was tempted to kiss the back of her neck: the stupid bun would have made it easy. But fear of rejection made him hold back. 'You are talking rubbish. She's got a lovely, devoted mother – the best guidance in the world.' His words renewed her tears. He tore a tissue off a kitchen roll and dabbed her cheeks tenderly. 'Ee, lass. 'Tis only hanky I've got. I've nowt better on my pension.'

Laura smiled suddenly. 'You're a nutcase, Lloyd Wheeler. How can I ever thank you?'

'By letting me introduce you and Andy to Ted Prentice. He wants to meet Andy again, and to apologise to you over the audition.'

'He doesn't have to. Anyway, I was glad Andy wasn't used.

At the time I was keen for publicity for her in case there was someone out there who could cure her. But I'm now learning to accept that a cure is impossible for at least another ten years.'

'You should never give up hope.'

'After ten years – it's getting easy. Okay – I'll leave you to fix it up.'

'Forgive me if I'm being nosey, Laura, but does Andy have a boyfriend?'

He sensed her stiffen. 'Good heavens, no. Why do you ask?'

'How about Khalid?'

There was a slight hesitation before she answered. 'They were like children together. They played kids' games together, went for bike rides together. Did all the things that children do together.'

And probably a few things they shouldn't have done together, Lloyd thought.

'She doesn't form relationships easily,' Laura continued defensively. 'It's been enough of a struggle to form a relationship between her and me over the years. And from what I've been told, she hardly talks to the other kids at Jacko's Café. She just goes in, listens to the juke-box and spends half her pocket money on Cokes. Why do you ask?'

Lloyd gave a dismissive shrug. 'Oh, nothing. She's such a smashing kid, I couldn't help being interested.'

Question: How do you tell a mother that you think her sixteen-year-old daughter, who's led an incredibly sheltered life, might not be a virgin? Answer: You don't. Firstly, you could be wrong; secondly, it doesn't matter unless the girl's pregnant; thirdly, it's none of your business. So you keep your big mouth shut and say nothing.

80

Benny Straw opened his mouth to protest, but Max was too quick. The ex-officer knew exactly what he had to do. He stepped forward, seized a handful of grey, wispy hair and jerked the man's head back. He followed through with a swinging, upward drive of his right hand. The long screwdriver penetrated

Harry's jaw, went through the roof of his mouth, punched into the sinus cavities where the bone is at its thinnest, and continued into his brain. The upward blow was delivered with such force that when the point of the Posidrive jammed against the inside of Benny Straw's skull, it almost lifted him off his feet.

Leo Buller had once told Max about the astonishing amount of damage the human brain can sustain without its owner dying. Max had never killed anyone with a screwdriver before – he had always favoured a blade, quick and silent – so he took no chances. He grabbed the lapels of Benny's jacket to keep him on his feet and worked the screwdriver back and forth, using the porter's jawbone as a fulcrum. But there was no need; Benny Straw didn't gag or choke or kick or struggle: he just died. His assailant's single thrust had killed him outright.

Max clasped both hands around the screwdriver's handle, braced himself and supported Benny's weight, hanging like a carcass on an abattoir meat-hook. He walked the corpse backwards into the living-room and dropped him into a worn armchair in front of the television. He yanked the Posidrive out, causing the porter's head to slump forward as though he had nodded off. He was surprised at how little blood there was – just a trickle onto the man's grubby shirt. Maybe a screwdriver was more efficient than a knife; certainly it went home easily. He checked his suit: whistle-clean. He guessed his victim's heart must have stopped immediately. A perfect killing.

He liked that.

Max returned to the office and pulled open the drawers of the roll-top bureau. The police would think the break-in and killing were the work of a professional – which in a way, of course, they were. He found a cheap petty-cash tin, forced it open with the murder weapon, and scattered the handful of coins around the room. He froze when he heard footsteps outside, but they went on up the stairs. The telephone rang, but an answering-machine kicked in and took care of the call. He finished fixing the lock, and gave a last careful look around to ensure that he hadn't overlooked anything. The monitor was showing a deserted car park. It amused Max to think that the closed-circuit television system was aiding crime. He left the flat, pulling the door closed behind him.

He walked to the road, wondering if anyone had seen him from the flats – but not unduly concerned one way or the other, and certainly not glancing around to check. That would be asking for trouble. A few years before, ITV had networked a movie called *Elephant*. It wasn't much of a movie; in fact, all it consisted of was a series of re-enactments of sectarian murders in Northern Ireland. Most of the camera's time was spent following gunmen on their way to their various killings. In all cases they were ordinary-looking men, walking in an ordinary manner along ordinary streets, entering ordinary shops and offices, opening ordinary doors, and then pulling guns from their pockets and emptying them into their victims. Then they turned on their heels and repeated the whole ordinary process – walking along ordinary streets to their ordinary homes. There was no darting from shadow to shadow, no get-away cars, no screeching tyres; no music. Just ordinary, efficient killing. And no passers-by took any notice of them; just as no one would take any notice of Max.

He reached his car, sat in the driver's seat and removed his gloves. Later they would be burnt, but for the time being they went into the glove compartment. He consulted a road map of southern England and worked out a route to Durston Wood. Then he carefully refolded the map and started the engine.

It had been a most profitable day, and it wasn't over yet.

81

Lloyd was helping Laura clear away the meal when André appeared in the kitchen doorway. She stood on the threshold, watching Lloyd intently, not speaking.

'Something the matter, Andy?' Laura asked.

'Game stopped working,' she answered, not taking her vivid green eyes off Lloyd.

'Which one?' Lloyd wanted to know.

'Flying game.'

'Sounds like the system's hanged,' said Lloyd, drying his hands. 'Some of those flight-simulator games are badly behaved.'

'You see to it,' said Laura. 'I'll finish up in here.'

Lloyd had no intention of being alone with André in her bedroom again. 'It might be a good idea if I showed you how to reset the computer as well,' he remarked casually to Laura. 'I won't be around all the time.'

Laura looked as if she was about to say something, but she changed her mind and nodded. 'Okay.'

The three trooped into André's bedroom. Lloyd sat at the machine and talked the two women through the routine of rebooting the machine and reloading the software. The school Laura taught at had several BBC computers, so the procedures were familiar to her. But André got bored. She slotted a cassette into her video recorder and sat on her bed to watch television. The strains of Richard Strauss's *Thus Spake Zarathustra* filled the room.

'*2001*,' Lloyd commented, while showing Laura how to create a sub-directory on the computer's hard disk, and copy files into it. 'I wonder what she'll make of it? The ending baffled me when I first saw it.'

'Wrong!'

Startled, Laura and Lloyd looked around at André. The girl was staring at the television and appeared to be in some distress.

'What's the matter, Andy?' Laura inquired.

'Wrong!' André suddenly jumped to her feet and stood confronting the television. 'All wrong!' she screamed.

'*Wrong! Wrong! Wrong!*'

Her tormented expression was just as Lloyd remembered it when the Singapore Boeing landed at Heathrow. Laura moved fast. Long experience had taught her that prompt action could arrest the onset of a fit. She quickly folded the distraught girl in her arms and whispered comforting words to her, but her voice didn't stop the sudden, uncontrolled rush of tears. André's transformation from a young woman to a little girl in need of love and protection was almost instantaneous, and very frightening. Laura gestured to Lloyd to turn the television off. It was showing the glorious opening shot of the movie in which the

314

sun, the earth, and the moon were in magical alignment, with the sun rising, spreading its warmth and light as an expanding crescent illuminating the faces of its children – the planets of the solar system.

Lloyd stopped the tape and switched the television off. He turned to the two women. André was sobbing, her face buried against her mother's shoulder. Laura rocked her gently back and forth while stroking her long black hair. The sobs were gradually subsiding.

'It's all she needs when this happens,' said Laura quietly. 'Remove the cause of whatever's upsetting her and give her love and comfort, reassurance. It always works.'

Lloyd removed the tape from the VCR and frowned at it. 'But why should a movie upset her?'

'I don't know. It's never happened before.'

A thought crossed Lloyd's mind. 'Unless . . . No – it's too silly.'

Laura looked at him, still stroking her daughter's hair. 'Unless what?'

'Well, it's daft really. But you don't suppose a mistake in a movie could upset her?'

'What on earth are you talking about?'

'There's a mistake in the opening of *2001*. Well, not really a mistake – but use of artistic licence. That opening shot with the planets in line is not quite right according to the purists, because it shows the sun appearing to be outside the Zodiacal plane.'

Laura stared at him, her eyes wide. 'What on earth are you talking about?' she said again.

Lloyd gave a dismissive smile. 'Forget it, Laura – I'm rambling.' He knelt beside the two women. 'She's certainly quietening down now.'

'It's all she needs. Just to be held close and feel protected.'

'Why didn't it work on the flight from Singapore?'

The memory brought pain to Laura's eyes. 'I don't know,' she confessed. 'It's something that's always worried me.'

Lloyd touched André very gently on the shoulder. Her reaction astonished both of them. She suddenly released her grip on Laura and threw her arms around Lloyd and clung to him.

315

The expression in Laura's eyes spoke of her mixed feelings: André had never turned to anyone else but her when she was in this state. But the girl's trembling had stopped; she was now calm, at peace, and that was all that really mattered.

Lloyd's feelings were also confused as he held the now quiet girl close to him. But there was one thought that shone out like a beacon, its message clear and unequivocal: if there was anything worth doing with his life, it was to share with Laura the burden of protecting this strange girl from a harsh, hostile world that would never understand her.

82

It was nearly midnight when Max picked up the A281 at Godalming and followed the signposts in the direction of Plaistow. After fifteen minutes he found himself driving along winding rural lanes, where signposts consisted of easily-missed fingerboards set high on oak posts for the benefit of stage-coach drivers. After two stops to consult the map, he found Durston Wood.

He didn't drive onto the estate, but parked his BMW at the end of an anonymous line of cars outside a row of cottages. He locked the car, and set off at a brisk pace. To a casual observer, he was one of the local city-type commuters taking a late-night constitutional.

The walk took Max a little longer than he had calculated because number 16 was located at the end of a spur which he missed on his first circuit. There was no street lighting down the narrow turning – a great plus. Better still, the bungalow was shrouded in darkness at the end of a long drive. The disadvantage was that he couldn't get an idea of the lay-out unless he went in closer.

He slowed his pace and weighed up the options. To venture up the drive was risky – but good planning allowed for calculated risks. And all he needed was the briefest of reconnoitres.

He began to walk up the drive – and then he saw Lloyd's Lotus Super Seven. The electoral roll for the area listed only one voter living at 16 Durston Wood – Laura Normanville. Was it likely that a woman would run such a car? He considered it improbable. A light suddenly shone through a hall window at the side of the bungalow, and the front door opened. Max moved lightly on his toes and crouched behind a bush.

A woman's voice saying goodnight to a male guest.

Damn! That meant the car belonged to the visitor. Max backed quickly and silently away from the car, keeping it between him and the front door where the couple were talking. He dropped to one knee behind a privet hedge and waited. Luckily the ground wasn't muddy, but he could feel the damp seeping through his suit.

Damn!

He could hear their voices plainly.

'It's been a lovely day, Lloyd,' the woman was saying. 'Thank you for everything you've done for Andy.'

'It's nothing,' the man answered. 'I've thoroughly enjoyed it. I'm afraid my car may wake her, though.'

Laura laughed. 'She's whacked – she'll sleep through anything. Have you got everything? Your tape?'

'All safe and sound.' He paused. 'And Laura – I'll ring Ted Prentice first thing tomorrow. I know he'll be very keen to see Andy – he'll probably want to come down within the next few days. Is that all right?'

Max could hear the smile in her voice. 'All right.'

There was no kissing on the doorstep. A friendly wave and a couple of goodbyes, and the man climbed into the car and started the engine.

Max pressed himself into the depths of the privet hedge as the Lotus reversed down the long drive. He began to breathe a little easier when the car had gone. Now wait and see which room was the woman's bedroom.

A light going on at a front window a few minutes later answered that question. From there, determining which was André's bedroom was a simple process of elimination. The frosted-glass window was obviously the bathroom; the room with several waste pipes leading through the wall had to be the kitchen. The living-room was across the back of the bungalow

– French windows. That left one window at the side which could only be the child's bedroom. The bungalow had a concrete surround right up to the wall – no soft ground and footprints to worry about.

Treading softly, Max went right up to the bungalow and used his penknife to check the condition of the window frames. A firm push was all that was necessary for the blade to sink an inch into the wood. Better and better.

Max returned to his car and sat behind the wheel to ponder his findings. The remoteness of the place was a big plus, of course, but nevertheless, the kidnapping of André Normanville would require the most meticulous care. Every eventuality would have to be foreseen.

It was the sort of challenge he relished.

83

Friday, 15th March 1991

Peter Barber was a junior Health and Safety inspector, and right now rather wishing he had taken up something safer, such as the repair of faulty hand-grenades. He was at the top of a stepladder, with his body twisted sideways through a hatch that gave access to a dark, narrow space in the wainscoting of Kimmeridge House. Max and a secretary were below in the office, holding the step-ladder steady, but it wouldn't have made any difference had they taken it away, so firmly was he wedged in the hatch. As for using his hands, that was next to impossible because his elbows were pinioned by a roof truss and a wall. To make matters worse, he was being slowly suffocated by a Martindale mask that covered his nose and mouth, and blinded by close-fitting goggles that were steaming up. All things considered, it wasn't much fun being a junior Health and Safety inspector.

Somehow he managed to push his torch into position with his chin, so that it was trained on the suspect insulation board. He was examining in his tweezers some nasty fibrous stuff which he had just dug out of the insulation board, and which he had only ever seen before sealed in a Petrie dish when on a training course. The dish had been passed from student to student as though it were a bomb. Now he wiped the inside of his goggles and decided that the fibres had a decided bluish tint. That was bad news. He nudged the torch so that it shone deeper into the wainscoting. Stencilled on the side of the insulation board was: PRODUCT OF SOUTHERN RHODESIA.

And that was worse.

The normally simple task of thrusting the fibres into a polythene sample-bag and sealing it was a physical triumph of determination over environment.

'Coming down!' he yelled, for the benefit of those below. He wriggled backwards out of the hatch, releasing a cloud of dust, and climbed down the ladder looking appropriately solemn.

'Well?' Max demanded.

Peter removed his mask and goggles and produced the polythene bag. He held the sample under a desk lamp and examined it.

'Bad news, I'm afraid, Mr Shannon. This insulation material is definitely blue asbestos.'

'Damn,' Max breathed. 'It's not my field, so how dangerous is it?'

'Very dangerous. This is African crocidolite asbestos – the worst type. The fibres can cause not only asbestosis, but also lung cancer, and mesothelioma.'

'What's that?' asked Helen Frost anxiously.

'Mesothelioma? Lung tumours. Please don't worry – it's a close-fitting hatch so it's not likely that fibres have been escaping. I'll get back to my office, Mr Shannon, and fax you a list of specialist companies who deal with blue asbestos. There'll have to be a full survey.' He glanced up at the hatch. 'It could be, of course, that that's the only blue asbestos that's been used. But in the meantime, you'll have to move your business to temporary premises.'

Max looked suitably worried. 'How long could a clean bill of health take?'

'Hard to say. A week. Two weeks.'

Max swore. 'Moving our labs and equipment is out of the question at such short notice.' He thought for a moment, and

319

seemed to come to a decision. 'There's nothing for it – we'll have to close.' He turned to his secretary. 'See to it, please, Helen. Tell everyone to clear up and go home at lunchtime, and not to report back to work until Monday week. Tell them I'll be in touch, and that they're all on full pay, of course.'

'Right away, Mr Shannon.' Helen scuttled from the office to spread the glad tidings.

'It's very good of you to take such a responsible attitude, Mr Shannon,' said Peter. 'It saves having to issue an enforcement notice.'

'You might have to serve one on my wife, to persuade her to move into an hotel,' said Max grimly. 'Maybe you'd better put up some sort of official warning notice at the main gate?'

'We'll do that,' Peter promised.

Leo Buller entered the office after lunch. He stalked across to the window and stared down at the empty car park.

'Place is like a morgue,' he muttered.

'Good,' said Max, without looking up from the planning notes he was entering on his Psion Organiser. He knew from his partner's demeanour that something was preying on his mind. It didn't require a genius to guess what it was. 'My little ruse worked rather well, don't you think? The place to ourselves for the next week or so, and no one any the wiser. A big, empty, remote house. What could be better?'

'It's going to cost a fortune.'

'That's the trouble with this country,' Max observed. 'An unwillingness to invest.'

'I'm not going through with this.'

'Fair enough.'

Leo turned and glared down at his partner, who continued to work the Organiser's keypad, apparently unperturbed. God – Max Shannon could be infuriating. 'What the devil do you mean, "fair enough"?'

'Just that, Leo.'

'For God's sake, Max – we're talking about kidnapping *and* murder! We'll be using SPECT neural-mapping, using a particularly nasty isotope.'

320

'One that will give us fast and accurate results.'

'One that'll give us twenty years!'

Max opened his drawer and handed Leo a form. The scientist read it disbelievingly. 'What's this?'

'You can read, Leo. A dissolution of partnership. You asked for such a clause – now you can make use of it. As your input into the partnership has been brains and not finance, you can sign that form, I'll countersign it, and you can walk out with a severance cheque and be free of all commitments.'

'You need me, Max.'

Max smiled blandly. 'Well, I shall certainly need someone if you're no longer a partner, Leo. Someone like Nils Perelmann, perhaps?'

Leo paled with anger at the mention of his detested rival. The Swedish neuropathologist had once beaten him to publication of an important paper on melatonin receptors dysfunctions – a paper which had won the Swede international recognition and, more important as far as Leo was concerned, generous research funding from La Roche. It was time to call Max's bluff and show him that he couldn't manipulate everyone any way he wished.

'Perelmann wouldn't be interested in working for an outfit like this, Max, so think again.'

Max sighed, went through the papers on his desk, and passed a fax to his partner. It was from Perelmann. The Swede was very interested in Max's tentative offer and would be standing by, ready to fly to London if Max wished to discuss the matter further.

The fax slipped from Leo's fingers. Once again, he was beaten. The huge cut-backs in research as a result of the world-wide recession meant that the days when a scientist of his standing could walk into any university and grab a chair or department and the funds to go with it, were over. He met Max's smiling grey eyes.

'Tonight,' said Max, his friendly tone barely concealing the triumph in his voice.

'*Tonight!* As soon as that?'

'Tonight,' Max repeated.

Leo turned and left the office without a word.

Max picked up the fax and looked at it admiringly. Planning – that was the name of the game. Don't overlook any details. Simple details, like taking a genuine fax from Nils Perelmann and using the header and signature to produce a photocopy with a fake message. The photocopy was then fed through a fax machine using the self-copy facility, so that the result looked like a genuine fax reproduced on facsimile paper.

So simple.

Max was confident that the rest of the operation would be the same.

84

Lloyd had risen early, got to his office at 9, and telephoned Ted Prentice almost immediately. 'Well, what are we waiting for?' Prentice had barked. 'Come and get me!' And after a quick call to Laura to make sure she didn't mind her and André's domestic routine being disturbed two days in succession, Lloyd had set off in the Lotus for the round trip: Durston Wood via Epsom and the Horton Manor Children's Centre.

Ted Prentice arrived at Durston Wood complaining loudly about the lack of a heater in the Lotus and volunteering the opinion that anyone who bought such a car had more money than sense. Laura warmed to him immediately. He was the sort of man who radiated confidence; also, André seemed to like him. Lloyd was pleased to see that the tight little bun that Laura usually tied her hair into was gone. Hopefully for good.

Typical Asperger's Syndrome, was Prentice's first thought when he greeted André; the impassive expression, and the way she stared through him as though her gaze were focusing a few feet behind him. Truncated sentences, no first-person pronouns, adverbs contracted to verbs – but that was considered acceptable Plank Speak these days, as advocated by the sawmills of Comprehensive Education. On the whole, good communication skills. Mild autism. But he wanted to make a proper assessment, and ten minutes of coffee and small-talk was not enough.

'Take Lloyd on a thirty-minute country walk, Mrs Norman-ville,' Prentice suggested. 'It'll do him good. That pallid, unhealthy colour comes from living on junk food.'

'I'd thrash you at squash any day,' Lloyd retorted.

'Andy's always had me with her during assessments,' said Laura doubtfully.

'Time to break the mould, Mrs Normanville,' said Prentice, winking at André. 'Don't worry – being alone with teenage girls has few terrors for an old buffer like me.'

85

Max was pleased with his purchase as he drove it back to Kimmeridge House that afternoon. The Granada Estate handled well and had been carefully looked after. He would have pre-ferred a darker colour, but burgundy would do. Of course, he had examined it carefully first, and had even knocked £1,000 off the asking price after five minutes' brisk bargaining with the salesman. He had taken a ten-minute taxi ride to make the purchase – best not to buy locally – and had paid cash in used fifties, having provided the salesman with a false name. It would be difficult tracing the vehicle back to the partners. Leo had suggested a van – but Leo had no idea, of course. To drive an unmarked van any distance late at night was asking for trouble – the police in most counties considered them fair game for stop-checks. And the estate car was plenty big enough to hide a drugged child in.

He took advantage of a traffic hold-up to enter the purchase on his Psion. The pocket computer contained special infor-mation-erase software which he had written, and which could be activated instantly by pressing three keys. It didn't merely erase the directory pointers so that the information could be recovered, it over-wrote all the RAM. He scrolled through all the tasks that had to be performed that day. He would have preferred more time, but provided Leo continued to pull his weight as he was doing now, then they were an hour ahead of schedule.

86

They walked in silence. Lloyd didn't try to make small-talk, sensing Laura's concern for her daughter. They reached the main road and strolled for fifteen minutes in the direction of Jacko's café; then Laura decided it was time to head back.

'Let's give Ted a few more minutes,' Lloyd suggested when they drew level with the bus shelter near the turning into Durston Wood. The skid-marks across the grass where Jeff Harcourt had come off his Kawasaki were still visible.

They sat in the shelter, and Lloyd chuckled at the sexually explicit comments that had been carved into the wooden walls. 'Country graffiti are more enduring than town ones,' he remarked. 'A knife does more damage than an aerosol.'

Laura glanced around and mustered a smile. 'The locals call this the Durston Wood youth club.'

Lloyd laughed. 'I can believe it. Where all the local swains learn to be swines.'

'It's one of the reasons why I'm so possessive about André. She's so vulnerable.'

Lloyd was about to point out what had happened to the two bikers, but thought better of it. 'Understandable,' he replied. 'If these timbers could talk . . .'

'Judging by some of the drawings, they do.'

They both laughed at that.

'The truth is,' said Lloyd carefully, 'that I'm a bit worried about Andy too.'

She looked at him quizzically. 'In what way?'

'It's difficult to say.'

'You mean the crush she's got on you?'

Lloyd looked at her in surprise. 'You know?'

'Oh, don't be stupid, Lloyd – of course I know. I'm not blind. It's perfectly harmless. She's growing up.'

'I think she's already grown up.' He sensed her sudden chilling and wished he hadn't brought the subject up.

'How do you mean?' Laura demanded.

'When we brought the computer home, she undressed while

I was in the room. She didn't ask me to leave, or even give me a chance to leave.'

Laura seemed unconcerned. 'Yes – I guessed that had happened. So?'

'I told her that it was wrong. The point is that she didn't seem at all worried.' He hesitated. 'Also, she kissed me.'

'And me,' said Laura. 'You put her up to it. A thank-you kiss. So what?'

'This wasn't like a thank-you kiss,' said Lloyd seriously.

'Like what, then?'

Oh, hell. 'Well . . . An adult kiss.'

'How adult?'

'She tried to push her tongue into my mouth.'

Laura stood. 'Well,' she said abruptly. 'She's got further than I have.'

Lloyd fell into step behind her. She was walking quickly now.

'Don't bite my head off, Laura, but has it ever crossed your mind that maybe, just maybe, the relationship between Khalid and Andy grew into something that was more than brotherly–sisterly love?'

They were heading back to Durston Wood. She increased her pace as though the extra effort would help her ignore something that was refusing to go away. 'They were fond of each other,' she said defensively. 'Only natural – they'd known each other five years.'

'Now tell me what it is you're refusing to face.'

She slowed her pace. 'My instinct is to yell abuse at you and demand to know what you're insinuating. I'm angry because you're right. The last time Khalid stayed here was the month before last. January. Just before the al Karnis had to leave the country. When I returned from a shopping trip to Guildford, I found them laughing and joking, drying each other after taking a shower together. They didn't try to hide it, so I treated it as they seemed to – as an innocent experience. Now I'm not so sure. And there may have been other occasions. Certainly they had plenty of opportunities.'

'And André's not on the pill?' Lloyd ventured, knowing that the question was fraught with danger. He braced himself, but

325

the expected reaction never came. Laura merely shook her head and walked faster, not meeting his eye.

There was a dull rumble that could have been thunder, but it was low and barely perceptible, like the turntable rumble of a bad hi-fi system. The inexplicable sound snapped off Lloyd's sentence and froze his expression. For a moment he wondered if he had imagined the strange sound, but Laura had heard it too. He grabbed hold of her arm as she tried to break into a run.

'It was miles away, Laura.'

'No, it wasn't – it was from the bungalow!' She broke free of his grasp and started running.

87

NORTHERN IRAQ

One entire wall of the workshop and a large area of the roof had disappeared, the boards sawn up and used to shore up the sides of the well-shaft.

To get at a new section of wall, it was necessary for Khalid to shift a heavy work-bench. He removed all the drawers first: such fine tools – and such a fine workshop that they were pulling apart. It reminded Khalid of his father's workshop at their lakeside home near Duhok, where they garaged the speedboat every winter. In June, when the snows and the cold had gone, he always spent a weekend there, helping his parents prepare the house for the coming season. He loved the workshop in particular, with its smells of paint and oil, and the satisfaction of filling the boat's outboard with clean oil and carrying out the seat cushions. It was always an exciting time: it meant that the warm, lazy days of summer, away from the stifling heat of Baghdad, were just around the corner.

The bench was cluttered with old newspapers and tools, but Khalid didn't bother to move them; the bench would be light enough to shift now, without the drawers. He noticed the green wire as he pulled the bench away from the wall. He stared dumbly at it for a moment before he realised what it was. He traced the wire under the newspapers, pushed them aside, and there it was.

An extension telephone.

Of course, it wouldn't be working. Once the bombing started, telephoning his parents had been difficult . . .

He touched the handset. It was real – not a toy. He held his breath and picked it up. The hum in his ear told him that it was working. He would be able to phone his parents! Listen to their voices! Everything would be all right again.

'Khalid!'

It was Nuri's voice outside the workshop. He dropped the handset into its cradle with such a clatter that he was certain his friend must have heard it. He hid the instrument under the old newspapers just as Nuri appeared.

'Where are those boards?' Nuri demanded angrily. 'I've been waiting and listening, and I haven't heard anything that sounds like sawing.'

'Just doing them now, Nuri,' said Khalid hurriedly, and snatched up a claw hammer.

He set cheerfully to work, yanking nails and sawing up boards.

Tonight, when Nuri was asleep, he would use the telephone.

88

SOUTHERN ENGLAND

Laura burst into her living-room and took in the scene at once. Ted Prentice was trying to comfort André, who was sprawled on her stomach across the settee, sobbing and beating her fists in fury on the arm.

'Wrong!' André screamed. 'All wrong. Everything's wrong! At the third stroke, the time sponsored by Accurist will be – '

Laura pushed Prentice out of the way and folded the distraught girl in her arms. She rocked her daughter back and forth, clutching her head to her breast and stroking her temple. 'It's all right, darling. Mummy's here. Everything's all right. There's nothing to be scared of.'

Lloyd expected André's convulsive shudders to subside quickly, but they retained their frightening intensity. Her skinny arms went around her mother's neck. She clung desperately to her and they stayed like that for some moments, while Laura gently stroked her hair and kept up a constant stream of crooning, reassuring noises – which seemed to have no effect.

'What happened?' Laura demanded.

Prentice didn't answer her, but fired a question at Lloyd which, in his view, bordered on the ridiculous. 'Is there a globe in the house?'

'A what?'

'A globe! A map of the world printed on a sphere! Good God, do I have to draw one?'

'The neighbours have one,' Laura answered. 'But why – '

'Which neighbours?' Prentice demanded. 'Which side? Come on, woman!'

'That side!' Laura took an arm away from André and gestured quickly.

'Go and get it!' Prentice commanded Lloyd.

'What?'

'Go and get the globe! Don't stand there gawping, man! Fetch!'

Lloyd fetched. He shot out of the house and raced up Sally Fielding's drive. She had seen him coming, because she jerked the door open before he had a chance to use the knocker. Lloyd was back two minutes later, clutching a small plastic globe. Prentice snatched it from him, popped the sphere out of its plastic gimbal and base, and knelt in front of André.

'Andy!' he snapped. 'Listen to me! This is what I was telling you about!'

'There's no need to shout at her,' Laura protested.

'Let me be the judge of that. *Andy!* Look what I've got for you. Look!' Prentice sat back on his heels and waited, holding the globe out in front of him like a peace offering. Eventually André turned her head slightly away from her mother's breast. Laura brushed her daughter's hair away from her eyes, and they all saw that she was staring fixedly at the globe. Prentice's

328

voice became gentle. 'You see, Andy? Everything's just as I promised . . . Take a look.'

The girl appeared to calm down while her gaze remained focused on the globe.

'Hold it, Andy.' This time Prentice's voice was even more gentle. It was fatherly, the way Lloyd remembered him talking to the savant boy at the home.

Without taking her eyes off the globe, or even blinking, André disentangled herself from her mother's arms and reached out a tentative hand to the globe. It was as if she were a baby again, hypnotised by a shiny toy.

'Take it, Andy . . . It's yours.' Prentice was smiling encouragement. He took one of André's hands and placed it on the globe. She offered no resistance, while Lloyd and Laura looked on in wonder. The transformation was nothing short of miraculous: within a few seconds the girl had pulled herself out of the dark, lonely depths of hysteria and was now reaching for the globe with her other hand too, her face on the verge of a smile. Her eyes shone with joy and wonder as Prentice covered her hands with his and pressed her palms firmly against the globe's curved surface.

'This is it?' she asked in a small, frightened voice.

Prentice smiled warmly at her. 'That's it, Andy. It's beautiful, isn't it.'

'Beautiful,' André repeated, her green eyes burning with an emerald light. She wiped away her tears, then immediately slapped her fingers back on the globe as though frightened that the momentary loss of contact might cause it to disappear.

'What have you done to her?' Laura whispered.

'Shown her the truth,' Prentice replied, not taking his eyes off the girl for an instant. 'Something that no one has ever bothered to show her because they thought she was too stupid to understand. Damned special schools and well-meaning parents. My God, they've got a lot to answer for.'

'You're not making sense, Ted,' Lloyd observed.

Prentice looked at the young man in contempt. 'You've suffered a few moments of bewilderment, Lloyd. Whereas this lovely young lady has suffered years of not only bewilderment,

329

but terror. Terror you can't even begin to comprehend.' He turned his attention back to André. 'Let me show you where you are now, Andy.'

She looked anxious for a moment, and then allowed him to take her forefinger and guide it to southern England. 'Just there. You see how your finger covers nearly the whole country? If it were real, we'd all be in darkness . . . Where's the base for this thing?'

Lloyd retrieved the globe's base and gimbal. Prentice took it from him without taking his warm smile off André. 'Let me show you how it's mounted, Andy.'

With great reluctance, André allowed Prentice to take the globe from her. She watched intently as he sprung it back into its north-and-south-pole pivots and ensured that it spun easily. 'See how it turns, Andy? Do you remember what I said about the time it takes to go round once?'

'A day,' André replied. 'It can only be a day or else it's all wrong.' She snatched the globe back and clutched it protectively to her breast.

Prentice smiled wryly at Laura, who was looking at her daughter in rank disbelief. 'I think you're going to have to buy your neighbours a new globe, Mrs Normanville. Andy's not going to part with it now.' He touched the girl on the cheek. 'Do you think it would look good on your dressing-table, Andy?'

The girl nodded.

'Go and try it out, then.'

André scrambled willingly to her feet and moved to the door, clutching the globe like a rugby player going for a try. She paused, and looked back at Prentice. Her lips moved as if she were trying out a sentence before uttering it. 'Thank you,' she said shyly. 'Everything's all right now.' And then she was gone, leaving behind two stunned adults and an angry-looking Ted Prentice.

Laura shook her head slowly, still not believing or comprehending what she had witnessed. 'I don't understand.'

'You should have understood,' said Prentice evenly. 'You've had long enough, and all the clues were there. Ten years, isn't it, since the accident?'

'Understood what? What clues?' Laura demanded. 'I'm grateful for what you've done, Mr Prentice – at least, I would be if only I knew what it was.'

Prentice sat on the settee. He took a notebook from his pocket and glanced through some pages before looking critically at Laura. 'Let's take all the clues in order. Lloyd told me about the time when he first met Andy on a flight from Singapore last month.' He glanced at Lloyd. 'Correct?'

Lloyd nodded.

Prentice returned his gaze to Laura. 'But what happened on the flight *out* to Singapore, Mrs Normanville? Did Andy become agitated?'

Laura nodded. 'She was fine at first, but she got steadily worse during the flight. By the time we arrived at Singapore, she was hysterical. It took her a week to get over it – and then the same thing happened on the flight back to London.'

'Poor kid,' Prentice muttered. 'Poor little kid . . . She must have thought that the world was coming to an end.'

'Will you *please* tell me what all this is about?' Laura demanded.

'Your daughter, Mrs Normanville, has a total awareness of time and motion and space. Did you know that?'

'I'm a teacher, Mr Prentice. I've always known that Andy has excellent spacial understanding.'

Prentice looked contemptuous. 'That would be almost funny if it wasn't so bloody tragic. Heaven protect our children from teacher training colleges who have a one hundred per cent capacity for creating jargon, and a zero per cent capacity for creating understanding. I said that Andy has an *awareness*. What she didn't have until a few minutes ago was an *understanding*, because no one has bothered to explain to her until now. That globe was all she needed. Don't you realise that there's a link between all Andy's abilities? The way she can recite the time to within a hundredth of a second; her sense of balance; the way she can play computer games, and make thunder.' He paused, and looked in turn at Lloyd and Laura. 'André can stabilise the chaos of the universe. She understands space and time, and more than that, I believe she can send matter back to the

331

beginning of time, not by making it move but by *stopping it from moving!*'

There was a stunned silence in the living-room.

'The clues have been there all along,' Prentice continued. 'The biggest being what happened at Singapore. It's almost bang on the equator, where the earth's spin is at its greatest – a thousand miles an hour – which Andy could feel!'

Laura's mouth made a round O of surprise.

'At this latitude,' Prentice continued, 'the earth's spin is half that. We actually weigh a few pounds more here than we do on the equator. You took Andy from a high latitude, where the earth's spin is relatively slow and which she's had all her life to get used to, and flew her to Singapore. And when she'd got used to that, you came home again. Suddenly her whole perception of the universe was changed. The world was literally spinning about her! Can you imagine the hell she must have gone through on those two flights? She did her best to equate the change of the earth's spin with the aircraft's movements, but as soon as the aircraft stopped taxiing, her world was stood on its head.'

There was a long silence. Lloyd remembered telling Prentice how André had fainted at the precise moment the Boeing stopped moving. Prentice looked down at his notebook. 'As David Frost used to say on some daft TV panel-game, "the clues are there". Well, they certainly were. Let's take them in order . . .

'Lloyd – you said that Andy took naturally to computer games that involved space and three-dimensional movement, such as flight-simulators?'

'She didn't just take to them – she's brilliant at them.'

Prentice nodded. 'That's only to be expected. Her special appreciation is not merely good – it's honed to the point where she can actually live ahead of the game. There's probably a part of her brain that accelerates her awareness to a level that makes the outside world appear to slow down. She'd make a fantastic racing-driver.'

'Is that why she can perform such incredible stunts on her push-bike?' Lloyd asked.

'That's part of it,' said Prentice. 'She may not have what we would call a perfect sense of balance, but she does have an amazing gift of spacial understanding which gives her extraordinary anticipation. She's a very remarkable young lady, Mrs Normanville. I'd be proud to have her as my daughter.'

His words moved Laura. In all the years that she had been taking André to specialists, not one had ever complimented André or told Laura that she was lucky; none of them had ever referred to André's talents as gifts, and none had taken such a stupendous step in understanding her daughter. 'I don't know how to thank you, Mr Prentice . . .' she said quietly. 'You've done so much.'

Prentice shrugged dismissively. 'Maybe I've helped a little.'

'Are we any nearer understanding Andy's manipulative talent?' Lloyd asked.

The doctor shook his head. 'No, Lloyd. And I doubt if we ever shall understand it.' He looked at Lloyd and Laura in turn. 'I suppose it was the thunder just now that brought you storming back?'

Lloyd agreed that it was.

Prentice grunted. 'I told her that air was matter. That the breeze she could feel on her face was made up of solid particles that were too small to see.' He smiled ruefully. 'I didn't expect her to understand, but she did. I persuaded her to vanish a few molecules of our atmosphere. And yet it made that quiet but unnerving roll of thunder . . . Quite remarkable.' He smiled impishly at Laura. 'It was when I tried to explain about the world being round that she became upset. It was beyond her comprehension. So . . . I trust I'm forgiven, Mrs Normanville?'

Laura returned his smile. 'Yes, of course. But what I'd like to know is whether or not her condition is curable. Whenever I've asked, I've always got the same old answers: one day; maybe in the future. It's been going on for years. What I want to know is, when will the future be now?'

'But she'll be happier now that she understands everything around her,' Lloyd pointed out.

'Perhaps,' Prentice replied, staring at the floor. 'But understanding a roller coaster doesn't make you any more at ease when you're riding one. But there's another problem . . . A very big problem.' He raised his eyes to Laura. 'I've always condemned parents who've tried to suppress the talents of their savant children, and shall continue to do so. Most savants love demonstrating their abilities and it is the height of cruelty to prevent them showing off. They derive great satisfaction from seeing our amazement, and it goes a long way to offsetting their feelings of inadequacy.'

He hesitated. Until now he had spoken confidently, drawing on his experience to shape his sentences, so that what he said would come across as common sense and provoke a minimum of argument. But now he was venturing into the unknown; he had only instinct to go on. 'But in this case, Laura . . .' he said; '. . . may I call you Laura? In this case I believe you've done the right thing in actively discouraging Andy from using her manipulative skills. Telling the time, riding bicycles and playing computer games is fine . . . But nothing else. If what happened to those bikers ever got out . . .' He left the sentence unfinished.

'But can she ever be cured?' Laura persisted.

'You mean, by surgery?'

'Yes.'

The psychiatrist gave a contemptuous snort. 'You'll have neurologists falling over themselves to try and convince you that it's possible. But those buggers will be interested only in finding out what makes her tick and getting their names in print. Also there are some nasty, intrusive neural-mapping techniques that have been developed recently. No – my first thought is for the well-being of the child. Child? Hah – young woman. André's happy now. She's got a good home, a loving and understanding mother, financial security – or so I presume. She has excellent social skills too, which you've told me are improving. If she was autistic, she certainly isn't now. I can show you kids that live in a world of their own and don't acknowledge the existence of the outside world at all. Andy's certainly not like that. She's not violent; she's neat and tidy – doesn't dribble or wet herself. I'd say, leave well alone. You've done a first-class job over the years, Laura. No one could have been a better mother.'

Laura wanted to throw her arms around Prentice and hug him.

'How about her sexuality?' she asked doubtfully. She glanced at Lloyd. 'It's surfacing embarrassingly fast. How do I cope with that?'

Prentice thought for a moment. 'Yes – kids with limited egos can't always moderate their behaviour to what we in our world have decided is acceptable. Playing with themselves in public . . .'

'Well, André doesn't do that,' said Laura primly.

'Then that shows that she has some ego. Ten years ago the answer would have been simple – put her on the pill. But that's hardly adequate protection today . . . Don't worry about it, Laura. It's not a big problem. But if her behaviour changes, there's some hormone treatment I can prescribe.' He fixed his gaze on her. 'For Andy's sake, the really important thing now is to reinforce the conditioning you've instinctively used over the years. By all means let her tell the time, play computer games, and perform tricks on her bicycle . . . *But there must be no more making thunder or use of her manipulative skills.*'

'Mind if I poke my nose in where it's not wanted?' Prentice asked as Lloyd drove him back to Epsom.

'Yes.'

'Well, I'm going to anyway. What's the relationship between you and the mother?'

'None of your business.' Lloyd changed gear to overtake a truck.

'You're not lusting after a rich widow?'

'I'm *not* lusting after anyone. Why should you think that Laura is rich?'

The older man sighed. He tried to light his pipe in the speeding car and gave up. 'You disappoint me, Lloyd. I should have thought a sharp-nosed hack like you would notice that that young lady's wardrobe would have set her mother back several thousand pounds. Her trainers were top of the range, at least two hundred pounds; that Head tracksuit probably much the same. Crazy, but there you are. We live in a world that's investing heavily in designer insanity. Anyway, whether she's rich or poor is beside the point. She's an attractive, sensible woman. You need some moderating influence in your life to stop you wasting your money on stupid things like this car. But whether you get more heavily involved with her, or remain just good friends, you've got a problem with the kid. She's besotted with you.'

'Puppy love,' said Lloyd dismissively.

Prentice sighed. 'Give a problem a name and you think it's solved.'

'You told Laura that it wouldn't be a problem,' Lloyd observed coldly. The conversation was not to his liking.

'I've been thinking. Most adolescent girls can control their so-called puppy love – but it's much more than that in her case, Lloyd. She's been eroticized – had her emotions woken by a lover. My bet is that she's not a virgin.'

Prentice's perceptive powers were astonishing. 'How do you know?' Lloyd demanded.

'Seen it before. Sex can be difficult in an autistic kid who lacks cognitive control over her feelings. Her emotions are like a bomb – the full blast is likely to be directed at any nearby male who shows her kindness and consideration. If you develop any sort of relationship with Laura, you're going to have to tread very carefully for a time. Any advances the girl makes will have to be rebuffed very gently, without alienating her or making her feel rejected. She's coming out of her shell and I'd hate to see any reversion. After two years you might achieve some guilt-conditioning which will make her lay off, but I wouldn't bank on it.'

'Which is a long-winded way of saying that that I've got to be diplomatic,' Lloyd retorted.

Prentice sighed and looked at the scenery, which was passing a little too quickly for his liking. 'If only it were that easy,' he said sadly.

89

Max tested the stout boards that Leo had fixed across the windows of his flat in Kimmeridge House and beamed at his partner.

'Excellent, Leo. Of course, we'll keep her heavily sedated most of the time, so there's little danger of her attempting to escape.'

Leo said nothing. Until now he had been having trouble accepting that Max was serious about going ahead with the crazy and dangerous scheme, but as he watched him now, carefully entering information on that wretched Psion, he began to realise just how deadly serious his partner was. What little doubts Leo had left were swept away by Max's next question.

'Have you checked the furnace?'

'Oh, for God's sake, Max! Are you really -?'

'Have you checked it?' Max's tone was dangerously mild.

'No.'

'Then do so, please, Leo.'

'Max – we can't do this! A kid!'

'One kid measured against the future security of mankind, Leo.' Max smiled. 'Of course, if you can destroy her memory of us when we've finished . . . But you've said that you can't guarantee that, so it's necessary to ensure that the furnace and filters are in good working order.' He moved to the door. 'We'll do it together.'

The Cybernet Consultancy's induction-boosted argon gas industrial furnace had been installed in the ground floor laboratory two years before to produce prototype high-tension insulators made of molybdenum. Since then the bulky ceramic housing had been more useful as an incinerator, working at its maximum operating core temperature of nearly 3,000 degrees centigrade to dispose of electrolytic capacitors and the occasional porpoise corpse.

Now Max pulled the heavy circular door of the furnace open and placed one of his wife's ivory ornaments on the platen, while Leo set the controls to maximum. Max slammed the door shut and nodded. Leo pressed the ignition button.

There was a muted roar from within the chamber as the oxygen-fuelled gases burst into life. An incandescent white light flared through the mica inspection window. A one-minute burn was sufficient to vaporise the ornament to its component molecules.

Leo cut the power, and Max swung the door open when the safety interlock deemed that the core temperature had dropped to a safe level. There was no sign of the ornament. Max chuckled, and patted the furnace affectionately.

'I always thought it would come in useful again. A remarkable beastie. It can even destroy teeth.'

90

André's dolls had been banished from her bed. Mr Chips, the giant panda, was too large to be dumped in the bottom of her fitted wardrobe so he was stuffed ignominiously under her bed; the others, Kermit, two Garfields and a dachshund called Fritz, were now languishing in darkness. The sole survivor was Minnie Mouse, who gave Caesarean birth to André's nightie or pyjamas every night through a zipper. The usurper was the plastic globe donated by Sally Fielding. André was sitting up in bed, clutching the globe to her chest and watching television when Laura entered the bedroom to say goodnight.

She reached her arms out to her mother for a goodnight hug. Although she never smiled, Laura could feel the contentment in her daughter as she held her close.

'Lloyd staying?' At Laura's request, after delivering Ted Prentice back to Horton Manor Lloyd had returned to the bungalow, and the three of them had spent a happy, relaxed evening together.

Laura shook her head. 'No. I'm about to throw him out.' She held André at arms' length and looked carefully at her. 'You like Lloyd, don't you?'

André nodded vehemently. 'Can I say goodnight to him?'

'Of course, darling.'

Lloyd entered a moment later. 'Just off,' he said cheerfully.

'Mummy's chucking me out. Early nights all round. Hey – you look good enough to eat.'

André hopped onto her knees for another hug, pressing her breasts against Lloyd with perhaps a little too much enthusiasm. But such advances no longer alarmed him, and instead of over-reacting, which Ted Prentice had warned him against, he carefully disengaged himself and gave her a kiss on the nose. She seemed so happy that she was virtually on the brink of a smile.

'Coming tomorrow, Lloyd?'

'Can't, angel. I've got loads of work to get through. But mummy's asked me down for dinner on Sunday, so I'll see you then.' He paused at the door. André was clutching her globe again, watching him with large, soulful eyes. ''Bye, angel.'

''Bye, Lloyd.'

André turned down the television sound and listened to the muted conversation in the hall. A minute later she heard Lloyd slamming his car door.

Sunday. Two days' wait.

She turned up the sound as Laura returned and sat on her bed.

'Don't watch for too long, darling. You've had a lot of excitement today. Would you like a sleeping pill?'

'No.'

'Well, I'm going to take a couple. It's been quite a day. But a happy day.'

'Happy day,' André agreed. 'Everything right now.'

Laura took hold of her daughter's hands. 'I want you to listen to me, Andy. Today, that nice Mr Prentice asked you to make thunder.'

The girl stared blankly back at Laura. 'Thought it would be all right.'

'It was all right, darling. I'm not cross. But you must never do it again. Not ever, ever again. Do you understand?'

'Not even if Lloyd asks me?'

'He won't ask you. But even if he does, you must promise me you'll never do it again. If you do, nasty men will come and take you away from mummy and lock you up in a big cold room and you'll never see me again.'

'Never see Lloyd?'

'You'll never see *anyone* again. So do you promise me you'll never make thunder again?'

André nodded.

'Say, "I promise never to make thunder again". Say it, please, darling.'

'I promise never to make thunder again,' André repeated solemnly.

Laura pulled André close to her and kissed her. 'You're a good girl, darling.'

André suddenly pointed at the television. 'Dresses like the one Sajii showed us.'

A late-night news report was running a story about Kurdish families preparing for civil war. The picture cut to enthusiastic, chanting pershmargas training at a camp in northern Iran. The commentator was confident that the vanquished and demoralised forces of Saddam Hussein would be no match for the fervour of a massive Kurdish rebellion. The scene changed to some library footage of Iraqi helicopter gunships attacking rebel positions in the mountains during the 1988 rebellion. It would be another two weeks before the tragedy of the abortive 1991 uprising, and the Kurds' flight into the mountains unfolded on the world's televisions.

'It's awful what they've been through,' said Laura, wondering how much André was understanding. 'All those refugee camps in Turkey – and the Turks hate them. Sajii told me that it was illegal for Kurds to speak their own language in Turkey.'

'But they speak English and go to church.'

'That's because Hamet and Sajii are Christian Kurds.'

'And Khalid?'

'Yes, and Khalid.' Laura looked carefully at her daughter, but there was little sign of emotion.

André turned the globe in her long, delicate fingers. 'I can't find their place on my world.'

'Kurdistan?' Laura queried. 'No – you won't. It's part of Iraq and some other countries. Let me show you.' She took hold of André's forefinger and guided it to Northern Iraq. 'There –

that's Kurdistan. Where Hamet and Sajii have a summer house in the north – near Turkey. You see Turkey?'

'Always say a prayer for them before I go to sleep.'

Laura kissed her. 'So do I, darling.' She touched the globe. 'Do you want me to put it on the dressing-table for you?'

André tightened her grip on her new talisman. 'No. Want to hold it.'

Laura was about to insist, but changed her mind. What did it matter if André now preferred a globe to her dolls? The change brought about by Ted Prentice was wonderful; now the future held few fears. But the lost years infuriated her. She railed inwardly against the army of doctors and so-called experts who had pontificated about her daughter's distress and done nothing: Ted Prentice, in a few minutes, had not only discovered what had been tormenting André all these years, but had come up with a solution. It was all so bloody unfair.

She kissed André's cheek again, and stood up. Damn all duvets – they denied mothers their inalienable right to tuck their children in. 'Anyway, I'm bushed. It's been a long day so I'm having an early night. Don't have the television turned up too loud. 'Night, darling.'

'Good night, Mother.'

André aimed the control box at the television and turned the sound up. There are some things that will never change, Laura thought. I'll need those Mogadons.

91

'Spare wheel?' asked Max, forefinger poised on his trusty Psion Organiser.

'Fine.'

'Check the pressure.'

'It feels fine,' Leo protested, nearly banging his head on the Granada's open tailgate when he straightened up.

'Check the pressure, please, Leo,' Max insisted.

Leo grumbled but complied. 'Two bar,' he reported.

'Good. Blankets, travel. Large. Two of.'

'Blankets, travel. Large. Two of. All present and correct.'

'Gloves. Black. Cotton. Two pairs.'

'Gloves. Black. Cotton. Two pairs. This isn't a military operation, Max.'

'Its success depends on its being run like one,' Max countered. 'Good. That's the transport taken care of. Now for the supplies.'

The two men broke open a large carton that was lying on the floor of the goods inwards bay beside the Granada. It had been delivered by the pharmaceutical company courier service. The Cybernet Consultancy was a valued account, therefore orders were always delivered.

Max lifted out a small gas cylinder. He opened the valve and took a cautious sniff at the brief burst of gas. 'One of their better halothanes, I fancy.' He screwed an adaptor to the outlet valve which was fitted with a metre length of small-bore plastic tubing. 'Let's hope the girl sleeps with her bedroom door closed. And these are a sample – for assessment purposes only, you understand.' He produced a bubble pack with transparent blisters on each card, each blister containing a flat, red disc. They looked like hermetically-sealed roulette chips.

'If you look closely you'll see the barbs,' said Max in answer to Leo's query. 'Slow-release sedatives, but powerful. One of those taped to the nape of your neck will keep you docile for six hours.'

'How about keeping the girl nourished while I carry out the mapping? It could take up to two days.'

Max pointed to another carton. 'IV feed and body-waste gear. But it can wait – this stuff and a few more tools is what will be needed *en voyage*.'

'Which begins when?'

Max checked his Psion Organiser. 'We leave at midnight. Our ETA at Durston Wood is zero-two-thirty hours. The girl should be sound asleep by then.'

92

NORTHERN IRAQ
Saturday, 16th March 1991

Khalid lay awake, listening to the sounds of the night. He had left the door open so that he would be able to hear Nuri's breathing. His body cried out for sleep and every muscle in his body ached from the full day's toil on the well, but he forced himself to remain awake.

The well was finished at last. That evening the grateful women survivors of the Afan massacre had drawn their first bucket of clear water and had cooked their benefactors a goat stew to celebrate. At first light, he and Nuri would be on their way again.

Khalid waited until midnight to be on the safe side, and then slipped from his bed. Apart from his boots, which he now pulled on, he was fully dressed in working-clothes. Nuri insisted that they always sleep fully dressed in case they had to flee at a moment's notice. He listened at Nuri's door. Nuri was snoring softly.

Khalid lit a candle and crept out into the freezing night air. The Bluebird was parked outside, with food, water and clothing on board. He made his way to the skeletal remains of the workshop. During the last stages of the building's demolition, he had taken great care to ensure that the telephone remained hidden and undamaged. Now he moved aside the newspapers that concealed it and lifted the handset. The line clicked and hummed. It was still working! His finger trembled and his heartbeat quickened in anticipation as he punched the number of his parents' home near Duhok. Any second now he would hear his father's voice!

But the ringing tone went on and on.

Perhaps he had misdialled? He doubted it. There were three phone numbers that were engraved on his heart: the number of his home in Baghdad was one; Duhok was another. Nevertheless, he replaced the handset and dialled again. The result was the same. Perhaps his parents were visiting friends? They had many. He would try again in half an hour.

343

Khalid settled down to wait, too excited to notice the bitter cold of the cloudless night.

93

SOUTHERN ENGLAND

Max's ETA was five minutes out.

He turned the Granada into Durston Wood at 2.35 a.m. The car purred softly in the dark estate. He turned into the spur road that led to number 16, and parked. He set the handbrake by holding the button in, so that the pawl and rachet would not make a loud rasp. The bungalow, like all the other homes, was in darkness. The hard-working folk of Durston Wood kept sensible hours.

'A pity lover-boy didn't turn up tonight,' Max commented, noting that there was no Lotus in the drive.

Leo rubbed his eyes. 'Why's that?'

Max sighed. 'You never think, do you, Leo? What do lovers normally do on their nights together?'

'Make love?'

'Exactly. An exhausting business. Uncoupling couples usually fall into a profound sleep.'

The two men slipped from the car, leaving their doors ajar. They were wearing dark clothes and black gloves. Max clicked the tailgate open. He had taken the precaution of spraying moving parts with oil so there was little noise. One by one they shifted the necessary pieces of equipment to beneath the window that Max had identified as André's bedroom. But he had to be certain.

He flashed his pen-light beam on a TV cable that passed through a hole in the window frame. There was a forgotten doll on the sill between the glass and the curtains, but Max craved perfection in his planning. He switched on the audio amplifier and fitted the earpieces in his ears. Next he wetted the microphone sucker, and pressed it firmly against the glass. He listened intently, gradually turning up the amplifier's gain. The white-noise hiss he heard in his earpieces was the bedroom's background noise, the result of convection air currents caused by a radiator under the sill. The amplifier had a two-inch-square illuminated gas plasma screen that showed spikes dancing in harmony with the background noise. Max backed off the gain until the spikes dropped below the trigger line – and as he did so, the screen registered a fresh burst of spikes that his ears failed to detect. He watched and listened, then passed the ear-pieces to Leo and tilted the screen towards him. Leo checked the regular intervals between each burst of sound, and nodded.

'Regular breathing. Someone asleep. Definitely a bedroom.'

'Probability that it's a bedroom – high,' Max murmured. 'Not definite.'

He wriggled the TV co-axial cable where it passed through the window frame. Whoever had installed it was top of the Roy Rogers bodge-it-and-bill-it league; the hole was twice as large as necessary, and it was simplicity itself for Max to push the plastic tubing attached to the gas cylinder through the hole alongside the cable. He had planned to use an awl, but he wouldn't need it. He gave Leo a lazy smile of triumph.

'Watch out for the increase in respiratory rate when the gas takes effect,' Max whispered. 'Okay?'

Leo nodded.

Despite his outward calmness, Max was unable to conceal the slight tremble in his fingers as he opened the valve on the cylinder.

Anaesthetising gas hissed softly into André's bedroom.

94

NORTHERN IRAQ

Khalid didn't understand about recall buttons on modern tele-phones. He repunched his parents' number with great care, recalling the digits from memory one by one. As before, the ringing tone went on and on.

He let it ring for five minutes, and gave up. He was about to return to his bed when he recalled the third number that he knew by heart. He felt in his pocket for the photograph of

André. She always looked beautiful, but was even more beautiful by the light of the candle. He touched her hair and remembered the last time he had seen her.

'Andy . . .' he whispered to the picture.

He picked up the telephone again. The earpiece hummed reassuringly. It was a much longer number, of course, but he could see the line of digits clearly in his mind. First you punched 00 to tell the system that you wanted to make a call out of Iraq. Wait for the tone, then press 44 to tell it that you wanted to call England. Then press . . .

95

SOUTHERN ENGLAND

The sound of the telephone ringing in the bungalow nearly deafened Leo. He cursed, and tugged the audio amplifier's earpieces out of his ears. 'Hell,' he muttered. 'Who would phone anyone at this time?'

Max spun the gas valve closed the instant the telephone started ringing. He quickly pulled the tubing out of the hole in the window frame and shifted the gas cylinder under a privet hedge. Bending down enabled him to hide his face from Leo. The sudden ringing had been a bad shock.

'I don't know,' he said calmly. 'But we'll have to wait. You'd better keep listening.'

'Not until that damned phone stops.'

But the telephone didn't stop.

Ten feet from where the two men were crouched beneath her window, wondering what to do next, André stirred. The ringing telephone in the kitchen eventually filtered through her sleep. She reached instinctively for her globe beside her on the bed and clutched it snugly against her breast. Its cold roundness was a strange but reassuring comfort in the darkness.

The telephone kept up its insistent clamour. She wondered why her mother didn't answer it. In her mind she worked out that it had been ringing long enough for the caller to have passed the point of no return in the hope that someone would answer.

For her to slip out of bed now was a certain invitation to it to stop ringing.

But it didn't stop; the bell went on and on, muffled by two doors, yet shrill and demanding like a crying baby. André swung her feet to the floor and pushed them into a pair of furry slippers that looked like hairy snowballs. She shuffled into the kitchen, hitching up her pyjama trousers, knowing that the phone would stop ringing the moment she touched it. She lifted the handset.

Apart from an occasional speaking-clock check to verify her remarkable body clock, André rarely used the telephone; the last time was when she ordered flowers for Mother's Day. And she hardly ever answered it simply because calls were not usually for her. Mother always gave only the last four digits of their number when answering the phone, so André did just that, adding importantly: 'I am André Normanville.'

Understandably, there was much that she didn't know about telephones. She didn't know that international calls are digitally amplified, which makes the voices of overseas callers sound almost unbelievably loud and clear.

'Andy!' The voice burst upon her. 'Hallo. It is Khalid!'

André's head spun. 'Khalid? *Khalid!*' Her voice shrieked across Europe and Asia. Her legs lost their strength. His three words were enough to trigger a sudden wetness, just as his questing fingers and lips had done when she had last seen him.

'*Khalid! Khalid! Khalid!*'

She was unable to frame a coherent sentence and didn't realise that she was screaming.

'Andy, darling. Do not shout. Please not shout! I can hear you.'

André's head felt as if it was about to burst. Her tear-ducts and vagina wept. Her body became a battleground between despair and sexual ecstasy, and despair emerged triumphant. She beat her fist on the kitchen dresser in utter fury as she struggled to force her brain to translate into words the feelings that were churning in her stomach like a pair of brawling sumo wrestlers. Her shocked brain managed the impossible feat – clarity exploded for a blinding second, giving her enough control over her left hemisphere to blurt out:

347

'Khalid! Love you!'

'Andy . . . I have missed you so much.'

'Where are you?'

'I am calling in Iraq. Do you understand?'

Her mind reeled. Yesterday she would not have understood, but today she did. 'Iraq! Yes! Yes! It's on my world!'

'I am going to my parents' place by the lake. Do you have the pictures I gave you?'

'Yes – the lake,' André cried. 'Iraq.'

'I have to go now, Andy. Someone might hear me and your voice is loud. It is dangerous. People have tried to kill me in a war.'

The fear in his voice tore a blizzard of torment through André's already shredded reason. Khalid was always laughing. He was never afraid. And now there were hateful people trying to kill him! He wouldn't lie, not to her.

'Khalid!' she cried.

'I love you, Andy. Always I have loved you. Goodbye, Andy.'

She thought of the newsreel library footage on television, of the helicopter gunship killing Kurds. She didn't understand that the film was made three years before. To her it was happening now – the helicopters were after Khalid and they were trying to kill him!

'Khalid! Khalid!'

But the line was dead.

She sank to the floor, her heart torn out through her throat along with Khalid's name, which she screamed and sobbed over and over again into the dead handset. Her thrashing legs kicked a chair over, but no physical pain was capable of penetrating the whirling frenzy of her mental anguish.

And that was how Laura found her.

96

NORTHERN IRAQ

Someone else heard Khalid's telephone call.

In the big, air-conditioned communications truck parked on

the outskirts of Mosul, Signaller Ali Hassan was waiting for Radio Free Kurdistan to come on the air. The VHF scanners in the mass of rack-mounted equipment before him were scouring pre-set segments of the FM broadcast band and would hang if any new frequency came to life. A direction-finding fix could then be obtained in a matter of seconds. It was late now, so it seemed unlikely that the rebel station would come on air. Nevertheless, the blurred display digits on the Icom receiver continued their endless cycling through the band. There were several other similar receivers on the racks, all scanning their allotted bands.

Even the telephones were quiet, but that was normal at this hour. The General Motors truck was connected by a thick umbilical to the telephone junction-box that gathered together all the lines from this region on their routing to the digital exchanges at Mosul.

Ali Hassan yawned and cracked his knuckles one by one. It was something to do. He considered making himself another cup of coffee. Allah knew what the stuff was doing to his insides. He yawned again.

Bored. Bored. Bored.

It had all been so different the previous week, when he and his entire signals group had been operating in the south to help crush the Shiite rebellion. Now it was the turn of the despised Kurds. So far there had been only a few skirmishes, but the big showdown would come soon. In Ali's HQ there were rumours of movements of armour going northwards. Not in columns – that would alert the American spy satellites – but in ones and twos. Even Ali's truck was now painted to look like a furniture removal wagon. It had been joined by several more during the past two days, as the flags on the map showed. All communications throughout the Kurdish enclaves were now staked out. When called upon to support the glorious cause against those who sought to stab Iraq in the back during her hour of need, Ali knew that he would not be found wanting.

The alarm on the Teac logging-recorder bleeped. Ali gave a shove with his foot to bring his swivel chair opposite the tape-recorder. The recording light was on and the giant reels were

349

turning. You had to look carefully to see that they were moving; the tapes recorded very slowly. Along one of the 500 lines that passed through the comms. truck, someone had sent the tones of a double zero to access international trunking. The sending telephone number and the receiving number were displayed on the Packard-Bell monitor. The receiving number had a 44 prefix. Someone was calling the enemy United Kingdom.

Ali entered the number of the sending line on his keyboard, and had to wait three seconds while the system searched its hard disk for the name and address of the subscriber.

Afan flashed up. A village.

There was only one telephone subscriber in Afan. Ali had seen his name and address a few days previously: a PKK suspect. Someone hadn't been as thorough in following orders as they should have been. He saw no need to listen in to the conversation. It was an overseas call to an enemy country, and that was enough.

He picked up his red telephone.

97

SOUTHERN ENGLAND

With an earpiece each, and the gain turned down on the audio amplifier, Max and Leo could hear every word of the drama being played out in the bungalow at Durston Wood.

'Got to go to Iraq!' André was screaming. '*Got to! Got to!*'

'Andy,' Laura pleaded. 'We can't go to Iraq. There's been a war on. You've seen it on television, for God's sake – there's been hardly anything else on!'

'Got to help Khalid!' Andy raged. 'Got to go to Kurdystand!'

'Please, Andy – we can't help him. There's nothing we can do but pray! *Nothing!*'

'You don't care!'

The row got louder as mother and daughter entered the bedroom. There was a sound that could have been the girl hurling herself on her bed. Muffled sobs, then the mother's voice, much nearer:

'I do care, Andy. I care very much what happens to all of them – to Hamet and Sajii and Kha – '

'*You don't! Hate you! Hate you! Hate you!*'

'We'll talk about it in the morning, Andy.' The woman sounded utterly drained.

The sound of the woman leaving the room. Max increased the gain. The girl remained behind – crying into her pillow, judging by the muffled sobs. A cupboard opening and closing in the background, a tap running briefly. Then the woman was back.

'Take these, Andy – they'll help you sleep.'

'Shan't!'

The acrimonious row was renewed, with the girl screaming that they had to go to 'Kurdystand'. It ended quite suddenly with the sound of a loud, hard slap. The girl's hysteria subsided rapidly to frightened whimpers.

'You will take these and we'll both get some sleep! Swallow!'

The sound of swallowing.

'All of them!'

More swallowing.

'Now lie down!'

The rustle of bedclothes.

The woman's voice moved off. 'That's better. And if I hear another peep out of you tonight, young lady, I'll use the hairbrush on you, as big as you are.'

A terrified little: 'No, Mummy . . . *Please no.*'

'Then go to sleep!'

A click. The light around the curtains went out.

The two men crouching under the window glanced at each other and continued listening intently. The girl's sobs went on for another ten minutes. Occasionally she muttered Khalid's name, and repeated the phrase about going to 'Kurdystand'. Another ten minutes slipped by, and she fell silent; there was only the regular pattern of spikes on the amplifier's tiny screen.

Max straightened and stretched. The bungalow was dark and silent again. While Leo continued to listen on his earpiece, he pushed the plastic tubing through the window frame and opened the valve on the anaesthetic gas cylinder.

98

NORTHERN IRAQ

Nuri heard the menacing beat of the approaching helicopters first. More than two – a lot more than two. He raced into Khalid's room and shook him awake.

'Choppers! We're getting out! Come on! Move!'

A minute later the two men stumbled out of the house and scrambled into the car. The sky around the village was lit up with strobes and searchlights. One of the old women was wailing. Khalid was a second slow in starting the engine, and Nuri screamed at him and beat the dashboard in frustration. The engine caught. The Bluebird's rear wheels spun clouds of blue smoke before they bit on the dust and the car shot forward, its rear end fish-tailing from the second-gear torque Khalid was pumping through the transmission.

'North!' Nuri yelled, pointing through the windscreen. Dark shapes of deserted cottages leapt at them. Khalid spun the wheel left and right. He clipped a barn, but the car continued its mad charge, the rev counter climbing into the red as the speedometer hit 100 kph.

'You'll blow up the engine, you cretin!'

But Khalid had already snicked into third gear and was hurling the car at the rise. The track straightened where it left the village, enabling him to pile on even more speed. All four wheels left the ground momentarily at the top of the rise, then the engine screamed briefly and dropped back as the tyres crashed down on the ruts and potholes. Nuri was about to yell something about the suspension when he saw the strobe lights and humped outline of the helicopter ahead. It had come down in a harrowed field near the edge of the road. Its powerful searchlights came on and bathed the Bluebird. Soldiers in full combat gear jumped from the machine, casting long, grotesque shadows across the bare earth as they fanned out. Their automatic rifles went to their shoulders. One dropped to his knee and swung a rocket-launcher tube onto his shoulder.

Nuri braced himself for the 180-degree handbrake turn that

he was sure Khalid would perform. But instead the young man hauled the wheel towards the soldiers, dropped into second, and jammed the throttle to the floor.

'What the hell are you doing!' Nuri screamed as the Bluebird hit the soft soil. He couldn't believe it; Khalid was grinning! The stupid imbecile was actually grinning from ear to ear!

'Need good luck!' Khalid yelled back. He snapped on the headlights and flipped the main-beam stalk switch. The halogen lamps would dazzle the troops, but there was no chance of them missing the car as it bucked crazily towards them. The helicopter that had dropped the troops lifted into the air, spraying the charging Bluebird with several kilowatts of blinding white light. As the soldiers' rifles went to their shoulders, Nuri experienced again the strange fear he had known when they tried to flee from Kuwait in their tank. The air seemed to become electrified, causing the hairs on his arms, his head and his beard suddenly to go rigid. The troops opened fire at twenty metres.

The thunder crashed against Nuri's eardrums like a 155 mm. Howitzer bursting its barrel. The terrible concussion broke something – it was his side-window shattering – and the uproar wrenched his jaw open. It seemed to roll on and on. His body was hurled from side to side as the car slewed around, yet it seemed to him that he was detached from his body, and floating. Then the roar of the engine and the howling helicopter turbines reached through his numbed senses. The blinding flash that had overloaded his optic nerves left explosions of coloured light dancing dementedly on his retinas. He closed his eyes to spare them, but the visual assault continued unabated, tearing at his reason.

When his vision cleared he expected to see Khalid's lifeless body slumped over the wheel, his dead foot jammed on the throttle pedal. But he was sitting upright. Nuri wondered if death had given him another life but had taken his sanity. Mercifully darkness had closed in. The note of tyres changed as the car left the field. Then he thought he heard singing. He forced his eyes open again, and stared in disbelief at the rutted track that was being swallowed under the speeding car's bonnet.

Singing!

It was Khalid. He poked Nuri in the ribs and grinned broadly. 'Lot of good luck just then, eh, Nuri?'

Nuri's reply was drowned by the sudden scream of the helicopter's turbine. The cluster of searchlights wheeled in the black sky fifty metres ahead of the Bluebird, and charged straight at it.

99

SOUTHERN ENGLAND

The two men knew exactly what each had to do. They worked without speaking and without unnecessary movements.

The window was a poor fit in its frame. Max teased the thin strip of flexible plastic under the catch and levered upwards, while Leo pressed the opening light sideways. The latching tongue slipped out of its groove, enabling Max to pull the window open. He pushed the curtain aside and flashed his penlight on the bed.

She was older now, and much prettier, but it was the same girl as in the photograph he had taken from the flat in Swiss Cottage. The halothane gas cleared quickly once the bedroom was ventilated. The girl stirred. Max knew he would have to work quickly. Leo folded one of the travel blankets over the windowsill and helped him climb soundlessly into the room.

He crossed to the bed and turned André over. Odd that she should be clutching a small globe instead of a doll. Her luxuriant hair dragged across the pillow, exposing her neck. The backing was already peeled off the tranquilliser patch; it was only necessary to push it firmly against the nape of her neck. The original plan had been simply to snatch the girl and leave, but Max was flexible enough to modify his plans to make use of unexpected opportunities. That opportunity had arisen with the row between mother and daughter.

He slid the wardrobe doors open and was surprised by the large selection of good-quality clothes. He found a large tartan travel bag at the bottom of the closet and quickly crammed it with underwear, jeans, socks, a tracksuit, sweaters, T-shirts, and two pairs of trainers. He passed the bag out to Leo, together with a full-length fur-lined leather coat. Satisfied that he had taken all the clothing that a girl running away from home would choose, he turned his attention to André.

Pulling off her pyjama trousers was no problem, but the jacket proved awkward because of her tight grip on the globe. Max forced her fingers open. Despite the depths of her unconsciousness, she moaned softly and actually tried to renew her grip. Once she was naked he realised that she was much more mature than he had anticipated. Fully grown, in fact. He wrapped a travel blanket firmly around her and picked her up. Her dead weight caused him to stagger a little, but Max was strong. He passed her through the window to Leo, and began to breathe a little easier once his partner had her lying flat in the back of the Granada.

'You'd better let me have the globe, as she seems so attached to it,' Leo whispered.

Max shrugged and gave him the globe.

He looked around the bedroom. It was neat. Very well, if André was a tidy girl . . . He plumped the pillows, retucked the bottom sheet and straightened the duvet. Next he folded her pyjamas and fitted them carefully into the zip-up Minnie Mouse. What else would a girl running away take?

Money.

There was no sign of a piggy-bank or money-box in the bedroom. He conferred in low tones with Leo at the open window. What Max was going to do now was a departure from the plan. It was a risk, but one that Max considered worth taking. He was going to leave the bedroom.

'Well, don't be long,' Leo whispered anxiously.

Luck stayed with Max. His pen-light picked out the woman's handbag on the settee the moment he entered the living-room. There were a few £1 coins in the black purse, but the contents of the red purse astonished him: it was stuffed full of banknotes, mostly £50s and £20s. He grabbed a handful, crammed them into his pocket, and left everything as he had found it.

One quick, final look around the girl's room.

The pen-light beam paused on a mother-of-pearl dressing-table set. Max wondered if the hairbrush was the same one that had instilled such fear in the girl when the mother threatened her with it. If it was, it might be useful for persuading the girl to co-operate.

He picked up the entire set, hand-mirror, brush and comb, and crossed to the window.

100

NORTHERN IRAQ

Had the helicopter that chased after the speeding Bluebird been a gunship equipped with cannons, it might have been a different story, but it was a Chilean-converted Bell 205 troop assault machine, and carried minimal armament. The two soldiers hanging out of the open doors stood little chance of maintaining their precarious perch *and* bringing accurate rifle fire to bear on the weaving Nissan. The soldier on the right side had an opportunity when the Bell dropped back and turned sideways to its quarry, but it was lost when he was dazzled by the glare of the searchlights off the car's rear windscreen.

The pilot tried a different tactic. He altered cyclic pitch and hurled his machine after the Bluebird. He had good downward visibility through the side-windows at his feet. He lined up the up-turned ski-shaped prong of his right-hand landing-skid on the car's rear windscreen and lurched the Bell forward. The skid smashed into glass.

'Do something!' Nuri screamed as the rear windscreen shattered like a miniature bomb and the Bell's savage downwash blasted shards of heat-toughened glass into the car.

'Trying to think!' Khalid yelled back, wrestling with the wheel.

The scream of the Bell's Avco turbine drowned the sounds of the landing-skid grating and tearing at the Bluebird's roof. The machine could lift fifteen troops and full equipment; yanking the Nissan's rear wheels clear of the road so that the car lost drive was theoretically possible, provided the pilot had the skill, the training and, more importantly, a co-pilot to maintain a forward watch. At the precise moment that Khalid accelerated, the Bell's rotors sliced into the galvanised-steel lattice-work of a mains voltage distribution tower. It was not a large tower or even very sturdy, but it didn't have to be. Shorn of its rotors, the helicopter's unbalanced pylon was torn from its mountings. The tail rotor broke, so that the energy stored in the turbine's spinning compressor was transferred to the airframe. The tumbling Bell crashed into the road in the wake of the Nissan, and the somersaulting wreckage was absorbed into an incandescent fireball of burning fuel.

'Didn't need good luck that time,' Khalid shouted in triumph. 'What do I do now, Nuri?'

It was some seconds before Nuri could take his eyes off the receding glow. He twisted around to face the front.

'Just keep going,' he ordered. His heart was heavy. Their luck could not hold much longer. It had lasted so far because they had papers and no one had been looking for them. But it would be different from now on: all the formidable counter-insurgent forces of Northern Command would be hunting for them.

101

SOUTHERN ENGLAND

Lloyd stood on the threshold of André's bedroom and took everything in. The neatly made bed; the hairy slippers side by side; the early morning sun playing on the fitted carpet; Minnie Mouse grinning pregnantly at him; the open window; Laura clinging to his arm, her nails digging into him.

'And there's clothes gone?' he asked.

Laura nodded. Her nails sank deeper. 'A travel bag, clean underwear. Clothes . . .'

'What sort of clothes?'

'A couple of tracksuits. An overcoat. Sensible clothes. Also some not so sensible.'

Lloyd looked sharply at her. 'How unsensible?'

357

'A skirt and a sweater that fitted her last year. I should have given them to the WI jumble sale.'

'So where are the police? If I can get here in an hour, how come the police can't?'

'Because I haven't called them.'

'But on the phone you said – '

'That was to stop you calling them before you got here,' Laura interrupted.

Lloyd stared into her eyes and saw that she had been crying. 'Why?'

'Because she's run away.'

'Well, that's obvious, but why would she do such a thing, Laura? She seemed so happy when I left you.' He remembered how André had pushed herself provocatively against him and wondered if he had overdone the rejection. He had been gentle enough, but the emotions of young girls were as volatile as sodium in water.

He followed Laura into the kitchen and sat down while she made tea. 'Has she ever done this before?'

'Never.'

'Perhaps it was something I did or said?' he wondered aloud.

Laura set cups and saucers on the table and poured tea for them both. She sat opposite Lloyd, her face taut with worry but her emotions now under strict control. 'No – it's not you, Lloyd. Something happened after you'd left.' She told him about the telephone call in the night and the row that had followed.

'Bloody hell,' he muttered. 'Has she taken that globe?'

'Oh yes. And just after you went I used it to show her where Kurdistan was.'

The thought that crossed Lloyd's mind would have been comical if the situation hadn't been so serious. 'You think she'll try to head for Northern Iraq?'

Laura sipped her tea. Her trembling fingers caused her to spill some in her saucer; Lloyd steadied her hand. 'André sees things in very simplistic terms, Lloyd. There's point A, and there's point B. To get from one to the other, you move in as straight a line as possible between the two.'

'So maybe everything isn't as bad as it looks?' Lloyd suggested. 'We tell the police and they put out an alert that concentrates on the Channel ports.'

He sensed her stiffen suddenly. She was looking at him with an expression of steely resolve. 'I *don't* want to tell the police. Do you understand?'

'But – '

'*No!*'

'Because of those two bikers? They'd never be able to prove – '

Anger surfaced through Laura's anxiety. 'They wouldn't have to – she'd tell them. She's a truthful girl.'

'But they wouldn't ask her, Laura.'

Her anger mounted. 'Listen. The police pick up Andy at Newhaven or Folkestone or somewhere like that. They know who she is, so they get in touch with the police here. That's how they work. There's a detective on the local force who I *know* suspects something. He'd question Andy and she'd tell him everything . . .'

'What if she does? She's autistic. Do you think he'd risk his career by – '

'It's not just those two bikers – there was someone else about five years ago.'

Lloyd lowered his cup and stared at her. Without further prompting Laura told him about the late-night drive from the railway station and the drunk who vanished. 'And he was never found,' she concluded. She looked down. Her shoulders sagged, and all her fighting spirit seemed to abandon her. When Lloyd moved his chair beside her and put his arm around her, her resolve collapsed. She held on to him and wept silent tears. 'I'm so scared, Lloyd . . . So scared . . . They'll take her away from me and put her in a home and keep her drugged for the rest of her life – like a vegetable. Or they'll do worse to her . . .'

'No one's going to do anything of the sort.'

'Promise you won't go to the police . . . Promise me – *please!*'

'But you have – '

'*Please promise me!*'

'All right,' Lloyd agreed reluctantly. 'I promise. But what do we do? A kid wandering around . . . I don't want to frighten you, Laura, but you must face up to it – someone could find her and . . .'

'No one would take advantage of her.'

Her naivety angered him. 'Of course they would, you stupid woman! For Christ's sake, face reality – don't keep waiting for it to catch up with you. What do you think those bikers wanted her for? An innocent game of hide-and-seek? They wanted to rip off her clothes, hold her down with her legs apart, *and take it in turns to fuck her!*'

The deliberate shock-tactic worked, but not in the way Lloyd intended. Laura fled into her bedroom and slammed the door. If she expected Lloyd to tap nervously and ask if she was all right, she was mistaken; he burst in after her and grabbed her before she had a chance to throw herself on the bed. He spun her around and shook her.

'Bastard!' she spat. 'Filthy, sadistic bastard!'

'I said it to shock you! But it happens to be true! Pretty girls without money are vulner – '

'She's got money!'

Lloyd looked surprised, and released her. 'How much?'

'Enough to stay out of trouble.'

'*How much!*'

'Nine hundred and fifty pounds.'

'*What!*'

'She took the money from my bag. I always keep a record of how much there is. That's what's missing.'

'She stole that much? Oh hell – this changes everything.'

Laura flushed angrily. 'She didn't steal it! It's her money. She knows that.'

'Why the hell do you carry so much cash about?'

'Look, it's my life and none of your business!'

'All right, I'm sorry,' said Lloyd in a reasoning tone. 'We're not going to solve anything by going for each other. But if she's got such a large sum on her, that changes everything.'

'She can't get out of the country. She hasn't got a passport – she travelled on mine to Singapore. And that's still in my drawer. I checked.'

'Can't get out of the country?' Lloyd echoed. 'With that sort of money, of course she can get out of the country. She can buy new clothes, put five years on her age. Okay – so maybe she'd have problems at an airport, but she'd have no trouble at a seaport. She could get a trucker to smuggle her out in return for favours. Jesus, Laura, have you travelled on a cross-Channel ferry recently? Controls are virtually non-existent between EC countries these days! She could be on a boat at this very minute, so what the hell do you want to do?'

102

NORTHERN IRAQ

The first light of dawn was seeping into the eastern sky as Khalid drove into the wide, wooded valley. Nuri experienced a surge of relief. At least they were no longer in the open, where marauding helicopters with infra-red scopes could spot the car at a distance of several kilometres. The valley widened, and soon they were driving through a vast, ghostly orchard where the neat rows of fruit trees were shrouded in muslin to protect them from frost. Peaches, damsons and plums grew on the southern slopes, and orderly lines of the more hardy pears and apples to the north. In the half-light small groups of workers, a few in Kurdish dress, were already removing and carefully folding the expanses of white cotton.

Nuri ordered Khalid to stop so he could get directions from a party of chattering girls. They sent him to an inn that was open all day to serve the needs of the workers on the huge co-operative.

The innkeeper at Al Fathan was a Kurd, a huge, pot-bellied, laughing man. He served Nuri and Khalid with a jug of delicious-smelling coffee and freshly baked bread, which he set down on the table in front of them with an exaggerated flourish. The smoke-filled bar was crowded with farm workers – Kurds from the poorer northern villages who lived in the co-operative hostels. They were a noisy, good-natured crowd and the two travellers felt at home in their company.

'The latest is that Mosul, Kirkuk and Arbil are all sealed off by the military,' said the innkeeper, resting his brawny arms on the bar. 'Nothing goes in or out without their say-so.'

The news alarmed Nuri. 'Why? Is there fighting?'

'No more than usual. But everyone thinks something is going to happen soon. I went into Mosul yesterday for supplies. You could taste the tension.'

'Has there been anything on the radio?' Nuri asked.

The innkeeper shook his head. 'The Kurds in Baghdad who were rounded up last week have been released.'

'Anything recently?'

'Nothing,' said the innkeeper. 'Also, we can get Turkish TRT by satellite. Nothing.' At his mention of the despised Turks he turned his head and spat accurately into a spittoon. 'We don't know what's going on. There's a pershmarga PKK FM station on 104 that comes on air at odd times. They're calling for volunteers to join the militia. But they're probably up on the border and know as much as we do. All we know is that something big is brewing.'

'Big American air bases in Turkey,' said Khalid. 'Sometimes they fly over my parents' house. They won't let anything happen.'

The innkeeper was unimpressed. 'And they have to get permission from the Turks before they can do anything. You think the Turks will give the Americans the okay to defend us? They hate us even more than Saddam Hussein.'

'We need to get near to Duhok,' said Khalid abruptly.

Nuri's kick under the table was too late. How many times has he impressed on Khalid that they mustn't give away their ultimate destination?

'Forget it,' said the innkeeper.

'My parents are there,' Khalid protested. 'They have a fine summer house on the lake.'

The innkeeper shrugged his massive shoulders. 'And to get there by car, you'll have to use the main roads. Maybe nothing will happen to you. But maybe not. There are rumours about

362

big army movements – not just helicopters. You'd best stay here – get a job on the fruit farms. Right now there's a big shortage of workers. They'll train you. Pay's lousy but you'd be safe in the hostels. Stay until the emergency is over, then go north.'

Nuri glanced around the bar, but no one was paying them any attention. The innkeeper's plump wife was trying to tune an ancient valve-driven radio. 'We can't stay.'

'You must do what you think necessary.'

'Is there another route around Mosul?'

'There's a road of sorts that will take you to Tall 'Afar. It goes through several groves – a link road. But it's dangerous in the hills: it was an old silk road, only used during floods, and now it's nothing more than a goat track in places. Maybe okay with four-wheel drive.'

'We're prepared to chance it.'

The innkeeper turned to bawl out an impatient customer. He turned back to Nuri. 'You can stay here for a few nights. Three dinar a night. Tomorrow I'll draw you a map.'

Nuri smelt a trap, even though it seemed inconceivable that a fellow Kurd would betray them. But after their days on the run, he was learning to trust no one but himself and Khalid. 'We'd like to be on the move today.'

The innkeeper's laugh rumbled in his belly. 'You both look as if you need several hours' sleep. You'd go over the edge in your present state. You need to be fresh and alert, believe me, my friends – it's a dangerous drive, but it'll get you north. You stay here today and tomorrow. Rest, and have two good nights' sleep, and I send you on your way on Monday morning with a map.'

'Why do you want to keep us here two days?' Nuri asked casually.

The innkeeper looked surprised. 'Obviously you are both Christians? Yes?'

'Yes.'

'I'm thinking of your safety, my friend. Tomorrow is the first day of Ramadan. There will be very few people about during daylight. Most of us take the first day seriously – so if you travel

363

you will be conspicuous. But on the second day – perhaps not so conspicuous.'

Nuri relaxed and smiled. 'I had forgotten,' he admitted.

The innkeeper's wife suddenly yelled for quiet. The bar fell silent and all eyes turned to the radio. An announcer was speaking. By presidential decree, a dusk to dawn curfew would come into force north of the 35th parallel at midnight. Anyone found abroad beween midnight and sunrise that night, and between dusk and dawn on all following nights was liable to be shot.

'Right at the beginning of Ramadan,' the innkeeper growled. 'The swine want to ruin us first, then destroy us . . . So a room, my friends? It's comfortable. Only three dinar. Yes?'

'Okay,' Nuri agreed.

'Each.'

'Okay.'

'And two dinar for food.'

'Okay.'

'Each.'

'Fine.'

'And a dinar for the map.'

'Agreed.'

'In advance.'

The innkeeper was undoubtedly a true Kurd with a deep regard for Kurdish traditions; Nuri knew that he could be trusted.

103

SOUTHERN ENGLAND

André opened her eyes, focused them on the cadaverous face looking down at her, and screamed.

Leo set the orange juice down on the bedside table and hurriedly withdrew. 'She's awake,' he said unnecessarily to Max, who was emerging from his living-room.

'I think I would scream if you were the first face I saw after a long sleep,' Max observed. 'Wish me luck.' A warm smile spread across his face, and he strode purposefully into what had been the spare bedroom of his flat at Kimmeridge House.

He crossed the room and beamed down at André. 'Andy, my darling. I do hope you're feeling better. You were sick a couple of times in the night, and when I told mummy on the phone just now, she said that maybe she'd given you too many sleeping pills.' He pulled up a chair and sat, his friendly smile not slipping for an instant. 'We all did our best to wake you, and gave up. My word, you can sleep, young lady.'

André regarded him in bewilderment. Her gaze drifted around the strange room and snapped back to Max. 'Not my room,' she said hollowly.

'It's my spare room,' said Max cheerfully. 'Needs new wall-paper, don't you think?'

'Not home.'

'Well, you can hardly stay at home *and* go to Kurdistan, can you?'

André's eyes opened wide. 'Kurdystand?'

Max chucked her under the chin. 'After all that fuss you made last night? Of course you're going. Mummy rang me up and asked me to take you. She was worried about how upset you were. Trouble is, when I arrived, we couldn't wake you up properly. I'm an old friend of your mummy's. Leo – that's the ugly man who made you scream just now – is my business partner.'

André pushed herself onto her elbows. The bedcovers fell away and she looked down at the blue tracksuit she was wearing.

Max held out a hand. 'I'm Max. I hope we can be friends, Andy.'

She stared first at the offered hand and then at the grey, smiling eyes. Although cautious with strangers as a result of her mother's constant admonishments, she decided that she liked this friendly man. After a hesitation, she returned his hand-shake.

'Drink,' she muttered.

Max gave her the orange juice and watched her gulp it down without pausing for breath. Her disturbing gaze never left Max for an instant. Strange how those impossibly green eyes seemed to be focusing behind him. 'I expect your throat feels awful. Mine always does after a drive. Is the bed comfortable?'

'Friend of mummy's?'

'That's right, Andy,' Max replied, beaming. 'Gosh – how you've grown. The last time I saw you was at that party in the Happy Eater. Do you remember? With Alan and Stacy and Peter, and Khalid – of course.' He felt in his pocket and showed her the birthday photograph he had stolen from Tushingham Court. 'Of course, I don't suppose you remember me.'

Her blank stare answered his question. 'Kurdystand?' she queried at length.

'Mummy's too busy to go, so she asked us to take you. She was very upset after your quarrel last night and wants to make it up to you.'

'See Khalid?'

'Of course.'

'Hamet and Sajii?'

'Yes.'

The news seemed to be a long time sinking in. The girl continued to stare through him with those remarkable luminous green eyes. Then something snapped, and what happened next took even the imperturbable Max by surprise. André launched herself at him and threw her arms around his neck. 'Going to Kurdystand!' she exclaimed. 'Going to see Khalid!'

'That's right,' Max laughed, returning the girl's embrace. 'We're going to Kurdistan.'

'When! When! When!' Her excitement was totally uninhibited.

'In two days.' He became serious and held her away from him. 'Now you must listen carefully to me, Andy.' He made certain he had her attention before continuing. 'Because I'll be looking after you, mummy told me to tell you that you're to do exactly as I tell you. Do you understand?'

'Yes! Yes! Yes! Going to see Khalid!' She threw her arms around Max again, and clung to him as though frightened that he might disappear.

Leo appeared in the bedroom doorway and looked down at them, his face haggard. Max grinned at him over André's shoulder and patted her affectionately on the shoulder. 'Going to be a piece of cake, old man,' he murmured.

There was a gleam of triumph in his eyes. Everything was going even better than he had planned.

104

NORTHERN IRAQ

That night Nuri lay on the innkeeper's hard, horsehair-and-straw palliasse, unable to sleep. He tried concentrating on the slow rhythm of Khalid's easy breathing in the hope that it would lull him, but it was useless. He was thinking of the last Kurdish uprising and the brutal manner in which it had been suppressed with mustard gas. He was thinking about his family who had perished.

Khalid, always the optimist, nursed the hope that the Allies would never allow such atrocities to be repeated, but Nuri knew better. The West had undertaken the operation to drive the Iraqis out of Kuwait purely and simply because it was worried about its oil supplies; no one cared about the Kurds. And yet this time, surely, things *would* be different. The PRK were broadcasting for volunteers, and there were rumours of big training camps set up in the Lebanon and Armenia. His countrymen were better organised than they had ever been. He would deliver Khalid to his parents, and then join up.

As he lay awake, he thought he heard the deep, distant rumble of heavy artillery.

105

SOUTHERN ENGLAND

Laura followed Lloyd into the hall. 'I'd like you to stay tonight, Lloyd.'

He had been expecting this, and had decided not to play along with her. But there was no need to be blunt about it. He kissed her on the cheek. 'I'd better get back, Laura. I don't have a toothbrush with me, and I don't like the idea of sleeping in Andy's bed.'

He could see that he had stung her. 'I wouldn't expect you to sleep in her bed,' she said quietly.

Lloyd remained silent.

Laura flushed with annoyance. 'It's been eleven years since I had a relationship with a man. You're not making it easy for me.'

'Why should I? You want me here to make sure I don't call the police. I gave you my word that I wouldn't. Obviously you don't trust me, and you're prepared to behave out of character – to use your body – to ensure I toe the line. Not a very good basis for starting a relationship, even after eleven years.' He tried to move past her to the door, but she stood in his way.

'Please, Lloyd. It's not like that.' She took hold of his hand and looked up at him, her eyes more angry than pleading. 'I don't want to use my body, as you put it. It's just that I don't want to be alone.'

'Well, you'll just have to get used to it, Laura.'

Maybe that was too harsh; he regretted his words almost as he uttered them, but he wasn't going to back down.

'You're not being very understanding, Lloyd.'

'That's right – I'm not. I don't understand why you won't go to the police, and I don't understand why I stupidly allowed myself to get involved in the first place. You've made me give my word that I won't go to the police, so that's an end of my responsibility. This is something you're going to have to sort out for yourself, Laura. I've done my best. Phone me if you change your mind.' He moved around her and opened the door.

He drove back to London with the hood down: the freezing air helped him think clearly. He agonised over whether or not he had been too hard on Laura and decided that he had done the right thing. It took him just over an hour to get back to his flat and in that time his mobile telephone had remained silent. That helped him convince himself that he was better off forgetting the whole sorry business. So what if it was a cop-out? He had his own life to run.

It was a tough decision, but a relief once he had made it. It was helped by a message from Sarah on his answering-machine, saying how much she had missed him and that she would be home the following Saturday. But as he tried to get to sleep in his cold, multi-layered bed, he was haunted by visions of what might be happening at that very moment to a frightened, lovely kid with haunting green eyes.

106

Sunday, 17th March 1991

'Nothing in any of the papers,' said Max, tossing the *News of the World* onto the pile of Sunday newspapers on his desk. 'Nothing on the radio, TV or teletext channels.' He tipped his swivel chair back and regarded Leo with a self-satisfied expression. 'So I think we can say my little ruse has worked rather well, Leo. The police are treating it as yet another of-age teenager who has run away from home after a row. As far as they're concerned, our precious little guinea pig is just another statistic.'

Leo glowered at his partner with undisguised loathing. 'That's all she is to you, is it?'

Max gave an unperturbed smile. 'Time we woke her up. Let's see how your misplaced moral scruples fare when we have the results of our assessments, shall we?'

André's skirt rode up as she sat beside Max, exposing her long, shapely thighs. She made no attempt to pull the hem down, but sat clutching her globe protectively to her breast and staring at Leo. Her expression was more wary than frightened, because the kind, smiling man with grey hair who had promised to take her to Kurdistan was also in the office.

Max's smile was friendly and welcoming. He laid his hand affectionately on her arm. 'Are you feeling better now, Andy?'

She nodded, glad that it was the small man she was sitting near and not the tall man with the frightening face like a skull.

'Would you like to change into a tracksuit, Andy? You'll be cold in that skirt when the heating goes off.'

369

'No. Like it. Don't tell mummy.'

Max laughed. 'It'll be our little secret, won't it, Leo?'

'Another little secret,' said Leo, with enough anger in his voice to cause the girl to give him a worried glance.

'Khalid tells me you can tell the time, Andy,' said Max casually, smiling warmly at the girl. 'Is that true?'

She nodded.

'Would you like to tell me the time?'

The girl looked confused. 'Mummy . . . Not with strangers.'

Max leaned forward and covered André's hands with his own. She shrank back, but relaxed when she realised he wasn't trying to take the globe from her.

'I'm not a stranger, am I, Andy? We're going to see Khalid together. We'll be travelling a long way together, won't we?'

She gave Leo another fearful glance, and nodded.

'So tell me the time, Andy.' Max's tone was soft and persuasive. 'Don't take any notice of Leo – he can't help being ugly.'

She bent her head and rocked in the chair as though trying to overcome an inner conflict.

'Come on, Andy . . . Surely you can tell me the time?'

She looked up at Max, and the warmth of his manner and smile gave her confidence. 'At the third stroke, the time sponsored by Accurist will be nine thirty precisely. Beep . . . Beep . . . Beep . . . At the third stroke, the time sponsored by Accurist will be nine thirty and ten seconds. At the third stroke . . .'

André continued reciting the time, not put off by Max picking up his telephone and punching the speaking clock. He listened for a moment, and passed the handset to Leo without a word. The scientist's expression changed to one of amazement as he listened to the girl and the speaking clock.

'Perfect sync,' he muttered, passing the telephone back to Max. 'Amazing. Absolutely bloody amazing.'

'At the third stroke – ' André stopped when the kindly man held up his hand.

'That's very clever, Andy. My word, you are a very clever girl.'

She looked pleased at the compliment.

Max was pleased with his progress. It was a start. An excellent start.

'You like that globe, Andy. Would you like to show it to me?'

André tightened her grip on the globe. 'No.'

'What do you like so much about it?'

She looked blank at the question, so Max rephrased it.

'Makes everything all right,' she answered.

'Makes what all right, Andy?'

She spun the globe on its polar axis. 'Goes faster in the middle,' she answered. 'Makes everything all right.'

The two men exchanged puzzled glances.

Max was at a loss. 'Goes faster in the middle?' he mused.

'I think she means that the earth's rotational velocity is at its greatest at the equator,' Leo volunteered.

Max beamed. 'Yes . . . of course. Is that right, Andy? The land moves faster in the middle of the earth?'

'Singapore fast,' said André.

'Have you been to Singapore?'

'Yes. Globe – Earth goes fast there.'

'Because it's right in the middle. Did you know that?'

She looked at the globe. 'Yes. Now.'

'It would seem that she can sense the earth's rotation,' said Leo, regarding André with great interest.

Max nodded without taking his eyes off the girl. 'It's what we expected . . . What else can you do, Andy?'

'Balance on my bike.'

'We can all do that.'

'Stopped. Not moving.'

Max ran his fingertips lightly over the back of André's wrist and stroked her gently. This time she didn't draw away. 'How about making thunder, Andy?'

She started rocking; clearly the suggestion distressed her. 'No. Can't.'

'Leave us, Leo.'

'What are you going to do?'

'Have a quiet little word with Andy. She doesn't seem to like you, so leave us.'

The scientist left the office. Max could sense the relief in the girl as she watched the door close behind Leo. He moved his chair so that he was facing the girl with their knees almost touching.

'Is that better, Andy?'

She nodded and looked up at Max, her eyes large and troubled. 'Mustn't make thunder.'

Max stroked her forearm. 'You're cold, Andy.'

'Bit.'

His hand dropped to her thigh. 'You're not wearing tights.'

The feeling of her smooth skin under his hand was of little interest to Max but he was interested in the girl's reaction. She gave a little start and avoided his eye, bending her head so that her long, straight hair hid her face.

'Would you like me to make you warm, Andy?'

There was no answer. Max ran his fingertips gently along her legs to the hem of her skirt and felt the tiny tremor that ran through her body. His emotions were detached, but the gentle, caressing movements of his hand on her thigh were deliberately sensual – a clinical toying with the confused emotions of a lonely girl which Max saw in the clear terms of a laboratory experiment. One introduced a stimulus and carefully observed the results of that stimulus. Interesting results, such as little gasping pants; her fingers opening and closing, allowing the globe to roll unheeded onto the floor; eyes tightly shut now; teeth clenched. A surprisingly fast reaction to the gentle movements of his hand. Excellent. Excellent.

'Khalid said you could make thunder, Andy. Was he right?'

A tiny, almost imperceptible nod. The fingertips moved insidiously to her knees and back to the hem of her skirt, leaving a rash of goose-pimples in their wake.

'But you don't like doing it for strangers?'

Max's neatly-pared nails were now digging a little harder, not too much, but enough to leave fine red marks, and cause André's breath to catch in her throat, and the tension in her thighs to relax so that her legs parted slightly. She was experiencing a strange and frightening up-welling, like pressure building up behind a fountain's closed valve.

372

'But I'm not a stranger, am I, Andy?' His voice was a beguiling whisper yet it rasped on her consciousness like file drawn across the edge of tin. 'Not a stranger . . . Not a stranger . . .'

'Not a stranger,' André agreed.

'Is that nice?'

She nodded; the touch of this gentle man on her sensitive skin was inexorably turning her mind into a spinning kaleidoscope of emotions beyond her understanding.

The fingers rode higher with agonising slowness, forcing her to wriggle forward involuntarily. Suddenly the fingers pressed home their advantage; the valve opened. Her lost soul forced a cry from her. She threw herself at him, arms around his neck, teeth sinking into his shoulder, and shuddering, demented gasps escaping from her throat as her body spasmed uncontrollably amid the torrent of explosive warmth that the questing, torturing fingers were unleashing.

The three figures walking across the stunted grass where the walled grounds of Kimmeridge House ended at the clifftop were well wrapped against the icy, blustery wind that blew off the white-flecked English Channel.

'Damn silly, coming out like this,' Leo grumbled, pulling up the hood of his duffel coat. The .22 target pistol felt cold and bulky in his pocket. A camcorder carrying-bag was slung from his shoulder.

'She said it wasn't safe indoors,' Max commented. Under his greatcoat was a lightweight three-quarter-length bullet-proof jacket. The discs of abalative plastic and the carbon-fibre mesh that formed the body-armour's core material were bonded together using a method patented by the Cybernet Consultancy.

'And she wouldn't say why?' Leo queried.

Max chuckled. 'I daresay she doesn't understand why, but we'll find out. Anyway, what if anyone does see us? We're three people out for a walk.'

They reached the safety fence and followed it in the direction of Lulworth Cove. The sea boomed against the foot of the cliff. There was no beach along this part of the headland; the sea surged against the cliffs at all states of the tide. André gave a squeal of delight and ran after a rabbit, which promptly dived down a burrow.

'She seems happy enough. Clever, how you got her to forsake that wretched globe.'

Max smiled, and said nothing.

André raced back towards the two men, her long leather coat flapping in the wind. At Max's suggestion she had changed into a tracksuit. She approached them at an angle, so that she came up on Max's side. She seized his hand and looked at him for approval, ignoring Leo.

'You make me feel old, young lady,' Max laughed. 'And short. I do believe you're taller than me.'

'Go to Kurdistan today?'

'Not today, Andy. Soon.'

'To the lakeside house?'

'To the lakeside,' Max agreed.

André spotted another rabbit and was off.

'You seem to have gained a place in her affections,' Leo muttered.

'I'm a loveable person, Leo. And you're an ugly old goat who frightens young girls.'

'What was all that about the lakeside house?'

'Khalid's parents' summer house in Northern Iraq. Unfortunately there has been no answer when I've phoned. I thought it might be useful if André heard Khalid's voice again.'

Leo was surprised. 'You traced the telephone number?'

'And the address.'

'But International Directory Inquiries don't give addresses.'

Max sighed. 'You never plan ahead, do you, Leo? You're forgetting that we have some high-level contacts in Iraq from our SAAD 16 contract . . . Andy!'

The girl ran back to Max, her long leather coat flapping wildly. The three stopped walking near a bench.

'How about here, Andy?' Max asked.

'Make thunder?'

'Yes . . . Like you promised.'

André's happy expression faded. She shook her head.

'Why not, Andy?' Max asked, his smile never wavering.

She thought hard and looked at the watery afternoon sun. 'Too early. Make thunder in twenty-one minutes.'

Max put an arm around the girl's shoulders; she welcomed the gesture and snuggled against him. 'Why not now, Andy?' As always, his voice was friendly and reassuring.

André pointed to the ground. 'Bang would go wrong way. Not into sky.'

'Where would the bang go, then?'

'Down. Into ground.'

The two men exchanged puzzled frowns and sat down on the bench. The view at this point was magnificent.

'Go and look at the view, Andy,' Max ordered, patting her hand.

She moved off and stood near the clifftop safety fence, staring out to sea.

'So what do you make of that?' Max queried. 'The bang would go into the ground? Odd.'

Leo thought for a moment. 'Maybe . . . No – it's too preposterous . . .'

At the beginning of their partnership, they had agreed they could voice their thoughts and ideas to each other without fear of ridicule, no matter how bizarre those thoughts and ideas were.

Max waited patiently.

'Crazy as it may seem, I think she must be talking about a fixed reference-point in space,' said Leo slowly. 'If she makes thunder now, whatever it is will hit the ground. But if we wait twenty minutes, the earth will have turned sufficiently on its axis for the reference-point to be above the horizon. Does that make sense?'

Max nodded. He looked his usual bland self, but there was a hint of uncharacteristic excitement in his voice. 'Yes . . . Very good, Leo – it makes a lot of sense. Andy . . .'

The girl turned and regarded him.

'Would you like to make that thunder now?'

'Not to wait?'

'No. We have a lot to do before we pack to go to Kurdistan.'

It was a calculated remark. Max had only to mention the magic word 'Kurdistan' to secure André's co-operation.

'Make thunder,' André agreed. She fanned her hand in front of her face. 'Move air.'

Max wasn't certain what she was talking about. He picked up a stone and showed it to André. 'How about making thunder with that?'

She looked at it doubtfully. 'Too big.'

Leo dug an even smaller pebble out of the turf and offered it to her. She weighed it in her hand. 'Still too big. Too noisy.'

Christ, thought Leo. He caught Max's eye and found a fragment of flint about the size of his fingernail. André considered it. 'No – still too big.' She spotted something in the short, wind-stunted grass. 'Cigarette-end!' she exclaimed. She broke the filter in half and rolled it into a small hard ball between her fingers, and gave it to Max. 'Throw it into the air, Max.'

'It's too small to throw, Andy. Shall I flick it like this?' He turned his back to the wind and rested the tiny ball of paper on his outstretched palm and poised his thumb and forefinger near the target.

André twisted his palm up slightly so that the ball would follow a higher trajectory. 'Like that,' she said. 'Goes further.'

'Okay. What shall I do? Count to three?'

'Count to three,' André agreed.

Leo unzipped his shoulder-bag and took out the camcorder. He moved a few paces back and framed André and Max. 'It's too small for me to follow.'

'Just do your best,' said Max irritably. He smiled reassuringly at the girl. 'Ready, Andy?'

'Ready.'

'I'll count to three . . . One . . .'

Leo rolled the camcorder and focused the image on the tiny viewfinder screen.

'Two . . .'

The picture on Leo's viewfinder suddenly distorted. He felt the hairs on the back of his neck prickling him like hot needles. He opened his mouth to stop Max, but he was too late.

'Three!'

Max's fingernails connected with the balled filter with an audible click. The ball arched upwards and was whipped sideways by the wind. The time and date digits on the camcorder's view screen went mad – all of them cycling crazily through zero to nine.

There was a tremendous crash, so loud that both men thought they had been permanently deafened. The shock wave that followed punched through the turf with sufficient force to send all three staggering backwards. Max lost his balance and sat down. He saw André mouth a concerned scream in his direction, but there was no sound other than the ringing in his ears. The camcorder spun from Leo's fingers and landed several feet away. There was an explosive whoosh of air that knocked all three of them flat.

But that was nothing compared to what happened next. Max tried to get up, but felt a dull rumbling through the ground. It was like sitting on a railway track and hearing an approaching express train but not being able to see it. The terrifying noise got louder and louder. Suddenly a thin tongue of hell geysered out of the ground at an angle not ten yards from where they were sprawled on the grass. The astonishing eruption – voiding fire, roaring gases and molten matter – lasted for less than three seconds, and yet to the three of them it seemed that the terrifying spectacle had endured for much longer. Suddenly the white-hot flame snapped out, as if a welder had closed a valve. There was an abrupt silence – apart from the residual screaming of their eardrums caused by the initial stupendous report. The fire and plasma-like tongue of burning gases vanished, leaving only the sensation of intense heat on their faces.

107

'Jesus Christ Almighty,' muttered Leo. He scrambled to his feet and stared at the point where the earth had briefly opened up, exposing the crucible of hell that raged deep below the planet's mantle. His expression was a mixture of fear and fascination.

Max was already standing. His eyes were gleaming in triumph. 'We're going to do it, Leo! We're going to do it!' His gaze went from the burnt patch of grass to André, who was rolled into a tight, protective ball. He knelt and touched her shoulder. She immediately flung her arms around him and clung to him in panic.

'Didn't mean to! Didn't mean to! Too early!'

Max carefully disengaged himself from her vice-like grip and helped her to her feet. She was trembling uncontrollably, trying desperately to hold back the tears that suddenly came in floods, soaking his overcoat. He rocked her back and forth, making soft, soothing noises while Leo looked on, inwardly hating himself for allowing this sweet, trusting kid to be abused by their greedy curiosity. And of course, there was worse to follow . . . At that moment he decided he could not go through with the rest of the project. He would have to find a way of getting André away from Max and back to her mother, regardless of the consequences.

'Sorry, Max,' André said in a small, quiet voice when her tears had subsided. 'Tried to make it small.'

'There's nothing to be sorry about, Andy. You did very well. We're very proud of you, isn't that right, Leo?'

Leo didn't answer. He recovered the camcorder, crossed to the burnt patch of grass and knelt down. There was a hole in the exact centre of the patch. He studied it cautiously, as though he expected it to blow again like a geyser. It was too small for a golf ball to be dropped down it, and his cheek could feel warm air rising from the opening. He touched the inside of the hole with his forefinger and quickly withdrew it. A shadow fell across him. It was Max.

'It's smooth,' Leo declared. 'And still hot.' He stood. It was ten years since he had smoked and now he found himself yearning for a cigarette.

'So what do we think happened, Leo?'

'Ask the kid.'

'Do you know what happened, Andy?'

'Little ball went to where time begins, but ground in way.'

Max stared first at André and then down at the innocent

beetle-sized burrow. Both men realised that the concepts implied by the girl's simple statement were almost too awesome to contemplate.

Max was the first to speak. 'You realise what happened, don't you?'

Leo nodded. 'I think so, Max.'

'She turned that filter tip into anti-matter. Think of the possibilities for harnessing energy!'

'I don't think so.'

'What do you mean, you don't think so? You saw what happened!'

Leo shook his head. 'That was my first thought. It makes sense – the conversion of matter and anti-matter into energy during their mutual annihilation. But I think what she does is something much more profound. Our universe is chaos. André establishes order.'

Max sent André to sit on the bench. Both men stood gazing out to sea. 'Let's hear it, Leo.'

'How fast do you think we're travelling at the moment?'

'How do you mean? The orbital speed of the earth around the sun?'

'That's part of it,' Leo agreed. 'The earth is moving around the sun at about a hundred thousand kilometres an hour. Roughly twenty miles per second. Think about that velocity, Max. *Twenty miles per second!* We don't feel it, of course, because we're all moving as one. But supposing something were to stop? Something as small as a rolled-up filter tip? What would happen?'

Max nodded. Leo was pursuing a sound line of thought. 'It would leave the planet at a great rate of knots, of course.'

'Precisely.'

'The ball of paper would possess a considerable mass,' Max pointed out. 'But without any calculations, my gut feeling is that even at twenty miles per second, it wouldn't be enough to generate the sort of wallop that we've just experienced.'

'Right,' Leo agreed. 'But what about at three hundred thousand kilometres per second? Nearly the speed of light?'

Max was silent as the implications of what his partner was

saying sank in. The concept was awesome, something that he could hardly comprehend, and yet he saw only too clearly what Leo was driving at. 'Hell,' he muttered. 'The recessional velocity of the most distant galaxies . . . Something like three-quarters of the speed of light!'

'You've got it,' Leo agreed. He thought for a moment, choosing his words as carefully as he would when writing a paper. 'The most distant galaxies we can see are receding from us at speeds approaching that of light. Therefore, to observers on those galaxies, we're receding from them at the same speed. Every particle of matter in the universe is hurtling away from the precise centre of the universe where the Big Bang took place some twenty thousand million years ago . . . Every particle, that is, except the ones that André has sent back to the beginning of time . . .

'Some physicists believe that eventually the expansion of the universe will slow down and stop, and that it will then start to collapse back on itself. That's when time will stop, and start to run backwards, and all matter will fall back to form a vast mega-black hole – which is the natural, orderly state of the universe. What we have at the moment is disorder – chaos. The Uncertainty Principle rules.'

Max's excitement mounted as Leo spoke. He strode to the safety fence and turned to face his partner, impatiently punching his palm. Leo had never known him to show such agitation. 'So what happened to that filter tip? Did it pass right through the earth?'

'Hell knows, Max. I'm not a physicist. At a guess, all its mass was converted to energy by the time it penetrated the earth's crust. Pressure sealed the hole it made as it was formed . . . On the other hand, what we saw just then may have been a glimpse of the earth's core.' A thought occurred to him. 'Max – just think of the possibilities! To tap the energy potential of the planet's magma!'

'Control!' Max snapped. 'We need to know what level of control she can exert. Nothing has possibilities without control! So – we carry out the control test.' He turned and shouted to the girl. 'Andy! Come here!'

André approached Max. She was nervous of the change in him. The constant, comforting smile was gone. In its place was a hard look that frightened her.

'Show her, Leo.'

'Max. I think we should – '

'Show her!'

Leo reluctantly produced the long-barrelled target pistol that had been weighing his pocket and conscience down. André's eyes widened when she saw it.

'Do you know what that is, Andy?' Max demanded.

The girl nodded unhappily.

'Show her a bullet.'

Leo dug into his duffel coat and showed a bullet to André.

'The gun fires those,' said Max brusquely. 'They kill people. Leo's going to fire that gun at me and you're going to stop the bullet with your thunder. Do you understand?'

The girl's green eyes went round with fright. 'No! Mustn't!'

Max was in no mood to argue. He took André firmly by the shoulders and turned her to face the sea. 'You stand there. Don't move.'

'Mustn't,' she said tearfully.

Max gestured to Leo to move back. The two men took up their positions so that the three formed a ten-metre equilateral triangle. They looked like a family about to toss a Frisbee to each other. Leo stood sideways on to Max, so that he was partly facing the girl. His right arm hung at his side, the pistol pointing at the ground.

'On the count of three,' Max instructed. He gave a grimace of exasperation at André's tears. 'You want to go to Kurdistan, don't you?'

André nodded. 'Don't want you to get shot.'

'I won't get shot if you stop the bullet. If I'm killed, then Leo will take you to Kurdistan. Won't you, Leo?'

'If you say so,' Leo muttered.

The girl turned her frightened stare on the older man. She wanted to close her eyes; she wanted to be with Khalid; she wanted to be with her mother and Lloyd; she wanted to feel safe and protected. Above all, she wanted to run away from these men. It would be easy, but fear of the consequences, her terror at the thought of ending up in the clutches of the man with the skull face, kept her rooted.

'Right,' said Max, facing Leo. 'On the count of three. One . . .'

Leo brought up his right arm to the horizontal and centred Max's chest in the open sights. He heard the girl give an anguished little sob. At that precise moment he asked himself whose death he wanted on his conscience. Perhaps a jury would deal leniently with him, once all the miserable facts were placed before them. His own future as a scientist was no longer of paramount importance. He could live with a jail sentence, but he couldn't live with his conscience . . . The decision was taken, and already he felt better.

'Wind,' Max cautioned.

But Leo had already made a tiny allowance for the blustery gusts.

'Two . . .'

Leo's finger tightened on the trigger without upsetting his aim. He had always been a good shot. Max's face was now haggard. Maybe he had read his partner's thoughts. Good – let the callous bastard suffer.

'*No! No! No!*' André screamed. '*All wrong! ALL WRONG!*'

The fine hairs on Leo's outstretched wrist suddenly went rigid, and the strange prickling sensation he had experienced before raced up his arm – but it didn't affect his aim. The pistol remained centred unerringly on Max's chest.

'Three!'

Leo's arm went up one degree. Enough to centre the open sights on Max's head. He squeezed the trigger.

It was the last thing he ever did.

108

Usually Lloyd enjoyed working in the office on a Sunday. With silent telephones and no constant stream of interruptions, he could get through a lot of work. Also, it took his mind off other things. By midday he had dealt with all the letters in his in-tray, paid several bills that should have been settled at the end of the previous month, and had scheduled what press freebies should be covered during the coming May.

With the intensive work out of the way, he switched on the office television for some background noise while he read the latest crop of press releases and patent application reports. The heavy political flavour of Sunday lunchtime television on the terrestrial channels irritated him; it was annoying, the way they abandoned their regular news slots at weekends so that one was never sure when to catch the headlines. He switched over to Sky News and settled down with a highlighter pen to read a lengthy judgement in an important patents case. The amiable mustachioed face of Scott Chisholm, looking like an educated pub bouncer, was on the screen, reading the top-of-the-hour news.

'. . . has just come in of an explosion near the army firing ranges on the Dorset coast in which a British scientist has died . . .'

Lloyd ringed a paragraph in the judgement with the high-lighter pen.

'. . . Another scientist escaped with cuts and bruises. Army experts investigating the explosion believe that it may have been caused by a war-time bomb, although they are puzzled by the absence of a crater in the vicinity of the blast.'

The highlighter pen froze in the middle of a half-completed ring.

'A Ministry of Defence spokesman has discounted the possi-bility that the scientist may have been killed by a stray round from the firing ranges. We'll bring you more on that story just as soon as we can . . .'

Lloyd snatched up his phone and called Laura.

109

'Really, miss,' Max assured the nurse who was tending his face. 'I'm perfectly all right. You've been most kind.' And to prove his point, he eased himself off the ambulance's boarding-steps and stood up.

'You ought to take that overcoat off and let us take a proper look at you,' said the doctor sternly.

Max smiled. 'I really am fine. I've been through much worse in my time, believe me.'

'Brigade of Guards, wasn't it, Mr Shannon?' the detective-inspector inquired. He had checked with the collator at Weymouth, who had information on all prominent local businessmen.

Max's hand went to his regimental tie. The knot was just visible above the collar of his overcoat. 'It was indeed, Mr Treloar. Cyprus, Aden, and a year in Borneo.'

Amazing, these army types, thought the policeman. His mate blown to kingdom come, and he's as cool as a cucumber.

An orange-striped Dorset Constabulary Range Rover bumped across the grass and parked near the huddle of vehicles. A group of newsmen with video cameras were at the safety fence, taping the efforts of the inflatable search boats coping with the dangerous waters at the foot of the cliff. Nearby was an area of grassland marked off with cordon ribbon. Treloar left Max assuring the nurse and doctor that he was okay, and joined the heated impromptu conference around the army bomb disposal unit truck. A Royal Artillery sergeant was holding his own against a captain from the bomb disposal unit.

'According to our records, sir, these grounds were cleared of all live rounds in 1950 when the War Office de-requisitioned Kimmeridge House. Since then, all firing has always been directed out to sea.'

'The sea is certainly a large target, sergeant,' the captain observed. 'But are you sure you've always hit it?'

The debate got quite acrimonious, and the Dorset policeman listened with great interest.

'So what's your verdict?' Treloar interrupted, directing his question at the captain.

'The ground around the site appears to have been exposed to intense heat,' the captain replied. 'It seems very likely that it could have been caused by a war-time cache of phosphorus or magnesium. Something like that. But don't ask me to explain the absence of a crater.'

Treloar nodded. This wasn't the first case of ordnance being found in the area, and it wouldn't be the last. In the wake of the Nugent Report over twenty years previously, the Ministry of Defence had been persuaded to open the range walks to the public. Even though the army had carefully scoured the coast before the walks were opened, members of the public were still coming across live rounds. But it was rare for such finds actually to explode. Rarer still for a find to turn up on private land, and to cause loss of life.

'So you don't think this has anything to do with our bomb-planting friends?'

'Definitely not, Mr Treloar.'

The policeman looked questioningly at the sergeant. 'I'd go along with that,' said the NCO. 'There would be a lump of the cliffs missing if it had been modern HE.'

'Right,' said the police officer. 'That's all I wanted to know. We'll treat this as another MOD incident.' He turned to the driver of the Range Rover. 'Anything?'

'I've just called the search off, Mr Treloar. It's too dangerous to get the Zodiacs in under the cliffs. We've already had a capsize. I suggest we keep a sharp eye open over the next few days. A fishing boat will probably find the body if it doesn't turn up at Weymouth.'

'That's good enough for me,' said Treloar. 'Thanks for turning out, gentlemen. I think we can all go back to our Sunday lunches.' He trudged up the rise to brief the press.

110

André didn't see what happened.

On Max's count of three, she screamed in terror and threw herself flat, bracing herself against the deafening implosion. Luckily she fell into a hollow. The mighty inrush of air sucked hungrily at her leather coat but left her unharmed. The thunder boomed and rolled around the bay as it faded into the distance.

When she lifted her head fearfully above the lip of the hollow, she saw Max staggering to his feet. There was no sign of the nasty man with the skull face who had wanted to kill him.

The enormity of what she had done slowly dawned on her. She had made the same terrible thunder that long ago had stopped the man who walked in front of mummy's car, and which had recently saved her from the two bikers. Max would be furious; mummy would be furious. The policeman who had come round asking questions and who had watched her in Jacko's car park, would arrive with a big black van to take her away.

'Andy!' Max's cry was whipped away by the wind. His face and forehead were cut and blood was streaming into his eyes. He was stumbling blindly towards her.

Panic seized André like a leopard pouncing on its prey. She jumped to her feet and ran down the rise. She had no idea where she was, but instinct steered her away from the big mansion when she reached the drive, and she ran past the gatehouse, stumbled over a cattle grid and kept going along a rutted, unmade road. Mud splattered her tracksuit, but she drove herself on. After ten minutes, exhaustion forced her to stop. She leaned against a rock, her breath hoovering and her heart pounding. She looked back the way she had come, but no one was coming after her.

After a few minutes she had recovered sufficiently to take stock of her surroundings. The road had been cut into the side of the downs. It ran parallel with the sea and followed the contour of a steeply sloping hill that was dotted with grazing sheep, its rounded slopes broken by the outcrops of granite thrusting through the thin topsoil. The sea to her right was now about half a mile distant.

She listened carefully, but the only sounds were the cries of herring-gulls and the plaintive bleating of sheep. The wind was bitterly cold, the sky sombre and threatening, heightening her fear. She zipped her coat closed and tucked her hair inside the fur-lined hood. With her frozen hands thrust into her pockets and beginning to warm up, she felt a little better.

She was about to start walking when terror struck again.

386

Something unseen was approaching. A shrill whine and a deep *wap-wap-wap*, as if something was beating the air. She looked frantically around: about a hundred yards up the slope to her left was an outcrop of granite that seemed to be buttressing the hillside. She raced up to the level patch of ground, and wriggled frantically into the narrow gap between an overhanging ledge of rock and the grass.

A few seconds later a Sea King helicopter appeared. It was flying low, following the valley towards the headland. It was like the machines that had hunted and killed Kurds in the report on television, but this one was searching for her. André shrank as far as she could into her hiding-place. She could hear the helicopter hovering over the headland but she was too terrified to look. The noise drew rapidly nearer. It swept overhead, so low that she was convinced she had been seen. But the whining turbines and thrashing rotors faded quickly into the distance.

Fifteen minutes passed before André mustered the courage to crawl out into the open – and then, as she started down the slope towards the road, the sound of approaching vehicles drove her back into her hiding-place. The ambulance and two police cars hurtled along the unmade road towards the headland and disappeared from sight. Tears filled André's eyes. First helicopters and now police cars. She felt so desperately alone and afraid.

'Mummy,' she wept. 'Didn't mean to do it. Didn't mean to . . .'

But there was no Laura to answer her plea; no comforting arms around her; no warm, soft words of reassurance. Beneath her was the cold, damp soil and above her the rough, moss-covered granite. Her cries of wretchedness were borne away on the icy wind and answered by the sheep and the seagulls.

111

'For God's sake, slow down!' Laura yelled, trying to hear the news bulletin on the car radio now that they were in range of 2CR's transmitters.

Lloyd dropped the Lotus's speed down to the legal limit. In

the past hour they had covered eighty miles. The New Forest was behind them.

'Kimmeridge House!' Laura cried, to make herself heard above the howling slipstream. 'They definitely said in the grounds of Kimmeridge House near Lulworth Cove! Where do you keep your maps?'

'Under your seat,' Lloyd answered, and wound the Lotus back to a steady 90 mph. 'There's a local guide-book in your door pocket. I grabbed it when I left the office.'

'You'll get busted,' Laura warned, hunting for a map of Dorset.

'Radar detector behind the dash.'

'These are all years out of date.' She found an Ordnance Survey tourist map of the Dorset coast and struggled to unfold it. 'What was that last town?'

'Wimborne.' Lloyd glanced at Laura. She had maintained a taciturn silence during most of the two hours since he picked her up; he guessed that she had had little or no sleep that night. When he telephoned her from the office, she had answered instantly.

'It's about fifteen miles to Lulworth Cove,' said Laura. 'Turn left at Bere Regis.'

Lloyd dropped speed on a winding section of the country road. 'See if there's any mention of Kimmeridge House in the guide-book,' he instructed.

Laura crammed the map into the foot-well without bothering to fold it, and searched through the book's index. Reading in a moving car usually brought on nausea, but now her nerves were too much on edge to give car-sickness a chance.

'Found it. There's a map. Three miles west along the coast from Lulworth. Near Durdle Door. God – it looks remote.'

'There must be a road to it.'

'There's a broken line that looks as if it leads into Lulworth Cove, but this is only a rough sketch-map. We shouldn't have any trouble finding it. West Lulworth is a village. David and I used to – '

'Used to what?' Lloyd prompted as his passenger's voice trailed into silence.

'Nothing . . . Bere Regis three miles, according to that last signpost.'

112

Max moved quickly once the police, army and ambulance had gone. That the experiment on the clifftop had gone disastrously wrong did not interfere with his ability to think clearly and revise his plans to fit the new emergency circumstances. Certainly there was no time to ponder the death of his partner – Leo was replaceable. In fact there was a brilliant neurologist at Baghdad University whom he had met on his last visit to Iraq. With Leo's detailed notes and the neural-mapping equipment, Max was confident that the threads of their research could be picked up. But first he had to find André and, more importantly, he had to dispose of her belongings in case the police found her first and she spilled the whole story.

Max raced back to Kimmeridge House, rounded up all the girl's clothes and stuffed them in the furnace. He left the machine running on a ten-minute burn on the time-switch, and quickly restored his flat to the state it had been in before it was prepared for André's occupancy. Next he grabbed a pair of powerful Zeiss binoculars and unlocked the garage that housed the company's Land Rover. It was an elderly vehicle but looked smart because Max had had it resprayed white. What was important now was that its four-wheel drive and Rolls-Royce Gypsy engine gave it a hill-climbing ability that was second to none.

It had not been used for some time. Its reluctance to start came perilously close to upsetting Max's customary imperturbability. Eventually the engine caught. He drove fast along the drive to the main gate, but not so fast as to arouse the suspicions of any watchers who might be about. Once over the cattle grid he left the track and headed up the steep downs. Occasionally the tyres spun on the soft ground, but the limited slip differentials kept all four wheels turning. Sheep bleated in protest and scattered at his approach. At one point the slope was too steep even for the Land Rover, forcing Max to make a detour, but all the time his direction was upwards. He was climbing determinedly to the triangulation pillar on the peak of Hambury Tor that lay halfway between Kimmeridge House and Lulworth Cove. At nearly 500 feet above sea-level, it was the highest point in the area, with stunning views in all directions. The sky was overcast but the air was clear. From the vantage-point of the great tor, Max was confident that nothing could move in the vicinity without him spotting it.

Lloyd drove as fast as he dared through the sleepy little village of Wool.

'There! There!' Laura pointed frantically to the signpost that marked the B3071. Lloyd took the left-hand turning and accelerated. 'How far now?' he asked.

'About four miles! Oh please, God, let it be her and let us find her. Please, God. *Please*.' She fell silent, as though self-conscious about her outburst. Then she reached out and touched Lloyd's hand, gently, so as not to interfere with his driving. 'I'm sorry, Lloyd . . . I've been a real bore and I haven't said thank you. It's so good of you to go to all this trouble.'

Lloyd glanced at her and gave her a reassuring grin. 'Let's find her first and then I'll claim my reward.'

Despite her concern for her missing daughter, Laura was able to muster a little smile.

After ten minutes slow, uphill grind in low gear, Max breasted the peak and stopped the Land Rover's engine. The wind was bitterly cold when he opened the door. He stood leaning against the radiator, grateful for its warmth, while he swept the area with the binoculars. The images in the beautifully-ground prisms and lenses were brilliantly sharp, with little colour aberration. The instrument came close to the perfection that Max always craved.

West Lulworth, just under a mile away, was virtually deserted. In the cove a few fishermen were working on their boats, which were pulled up on the narrow shingle beach. A couple of stalwart residents of the Lulworth Cove Hotel were drinking on the sheltered terrace. The lower fields in the valley were used by the landowners as a summer car park. They stretched westward from the village and were also deserted. On fine days the acres of grassland were thick with profitable ranks of parked cars and campers.

A movement caught his eye. He swung the binoculars and saw a yellow Lotus Super Seven following the winding road that led to the dead-end of West Lulworth. It was the same car he had seen reversing out of Laura Normanville's drive on Thursday night.

Another movement. He tilted the binoculars down slightly. A figure, half-hidden by rocks, had appeared briefly about half a mile in the direction of Lulworth, and had disappeared into a depression. He waited patiently, focusing the binoculars carefully on the point where the figure was likely to emerge. And then he saw her. There was no mistaking that flapping coat.

André!

She too appeared to have seen the Lotus, because she was running down the steep slope towards the valley car park and waving frantically.

Max leapt into the Land River and hurled the vehicle straight down the steep slope towards the running girl.

Lloyd braked to a standstill by the mini roundabout outside the entrance to the car park. A No Entry sign barred traffic from the final stretch of road down to the cove.

'Damn! We must've missed the turning to the house,' he fumed.

Laura pointed to the far end of the car park. 'There's a track leading off over there that looks as if it goes in the right direction.'

'Could be,' Lloyd agreed. He gunned the engine and drove into the car park.

'Mummy! Lloyd!' André screamed out. The slope was steep and the grass wet, making it difficult for her to control her headlong flight. Nevertheless, she was able to exercise that brilliant anticipation that prevented her from losing her balance. She skidded to a stop on a level patch of ground and clutched her sides. The car was driving fast along the grassy valley in her direction. She was certain she had been seen, but why weren't they returning her waves?

The sound of another engine was borne on the keening sou'westerly. She wheeled around. What she saw was enough to make her resume her headlong flight down the hill, even though she hadn't recovered her breath.

The vehicle looked like those jeep-like cars the police used. It was about a quarter of a mile away, bumping and swaying down the uneven slope, and heading straight towards her. She saw the Lotus stop in front of a five-barred farm gate. A familiar figure got out from behind the wheel.

'Lloyd!' André tried to scream. 'Lloyd!' But her anguished cries were little more than choking gasps.

Lloyd swore when he examined the steel gate and its padlock. Had he looked up he would have seen André some two hundred yards away, pounding down the slope, her arms windmilling frantically, with a Land Rover a quarter of a mile behind her and bearing down on her. But he ran back to the car without looking up.

'Can't you break it down?' Laura complained as he let in the clutch.

'In an aluminium-bodied car? Are you kidding? We'd both end up dead.' He spun the steering-wheel and headed back across the fields towards the entrance, the Lotus's rear wheels kicking up mud.

'Lloyd . . . ! Mummy . . . !'

'Lloyd! Stop!' Laura shouted above the roar of the engine.

There was enough urgency in her voice for Lloyd to heed her demand. He braked, and looked inquiringly at her.

'Now look,' said Laura in a reasoning tone. 'It's ridiculous charging about like this. We'll never find the place. Let's try that hotel and ask . . .'

André collapsed, sobbing over the gate. She was too late – they hadn't seen her! Suddenly the speeding Lotus's brake lights came on when it was about two hundred yards away. It had stopped! The police jeep was now less than three hundred yards away and closing fast.

André forced her aching legs to haul her exhausted body over the gate and half-fell into the mud on the far side. She picked herself up and stumbled blindly after the Lotus – just as its engine opened up and it gathered speed. She stood no chance of catching it unless she did something desperate. Something that only she could do . . . Something that required intense concentration and a degree of control that she had never attempted before. It could only come from a relaxed mental state, so she stopped running and tried her best to think hard.

The Lotus was nearing the car park entrance when the top six inches of the wooden gatepost at the side of the road in front of the Lotus suddenly seemed to explode with a deafening thunderclap. Windows were shattered in the hotel and nearby houses. The tremendous inrush of air shook the car with enough force for Lloyd's foot to slip off the throttle pedal and onto the brake.

'Jesus Christ!' he yelled, stalling the car.

'*Mummy! Mummy! Lloyd!*'

He and Laura heard the despairing cry at the same time. They turned around, and there was André racing towards them.

Max didn't hesitate. He aimed the Land Rover at the precise centre of the five-barred gate. The force of the impact was enough to snap the rusty padlock chain like a piece of rotten cord and to rip the gate clean off its pintles and fling it clear.

Laura had barely time to straighten up as she climbed out of the Lotus before André hurled herself into her arms. 'Mummy!' she cried hysterically. 'Policeman chasing me!'

Laura looked up and saw Max's white Land Rover roaring towards them. She bundled André into the Lotus's cramped rear seat and scrambled in after her. 'Get going!' she yelled at Lloyd, folding her distraught daughter in her arms. 'That Land Rover's after her!'

Lloyd saw the charging vehicle in his mirror and accelerated out of the car park, just as people came running out of their houses.

Max braked and slowed. He knew he didn't stand a chance of catching the Lotus on the open road, so he might as well let it go. After all, he knew where the girl lived. He stopped at the car park entrance. Men were rushing towards him and there were faces at all the cottage windows.

'What do you reckon? Rogue shell or supersonic bang?' an old man demanded.

'A Tornado, I fancy,' Max replied. 'Damned fighters. They're supposed to train much further out to sea. I shall be writing to the Ministry of Defence.'

'So will I,' another man declared. 'Buggers broke all me windows. Worse than that bang this morning, it were.'

The Lotus was two miles from Lulworth by the time André had recovered sufficiently to speak coherently, although she continued to cling to Laura with fierce strength, totally overwhelmed by everything that had happened to her since she had woken up in the strange bed and strange surroundings.

'*Go to Kurdystand! Go to Kurdystand! Help Khalid!*'

She repeated the demand over and over again, weeping and trying to burrow her trembling form deep into the warmth and security of Laura's arms and breast.

'Of course we'll go to Kurdistan. Of course. Of course.' Laura stroked and kissed André's mud-splattered hair as she talked.

'*Promise! Promise! Promise! PLEASE, MUMMY!*'

'Of course I promise, Andy. You're safe now, darling. It's all over.'

Lloyd waited until André was quiet. 'Kurdistan? Do you mean that?'

'Of course I mean it,' Laura retorted. She paused. Her voice had softened noticeably when she spoke again. 'I'm sorry, Lloyd. I've no right to snap at you, but I never make a promise to Andy unless I intend to keep it.'

Once the good citizens of West Lulworth had drifted back to their cottages, Max took a close look at the gatepost. The missing section had been burnt away, leaving a smooth, matt finish as though the timber had been sawn and then planed. But what particularly aroused his interest was the control the girl had demonstrated.

He had seen exactly what had happened as he sped towards

394

her. She had suddenly stopped running and put her hands up to her head as if she had been making a supreme effort of concentration. At that moment the top of the gatepost had exploded. At a distance of about one hundred metres the girl had managed to focus her extraordinary powers on a specific target.

Control – that was what it was all about.

He returned to the Land Rover and considered his next moves. As always, his thoughts were logical and analytical, and left nothing to chance. As he mapped out every possible contingency, this latest setback took on the status of a minor inconvenience. This time he would take no chances – somehow he would have to get the girl out of the country. Risky, but possible. And then he laughed to himself, and chided himself for not seeing the obvious right away.

He recalled the bitter row between mother and daughter he had overheard while listening outside the bungalow at Durston Wood, and how André's wish to go to Kurdistan had since developed into a blind obsession. It was obvious what would happen now. After this little debacle, the girl's mother was certain to be taking her daughter out of the country for him.

He permitted himself the luxury of a chuckle as he started the Land Rover's engine.

113

NORTHERN IRAQ
Tuesday, 19th March 1991

The innkeeper shook Nuri's shoulder.

'You must be on your way, my friend.'

The anxious note in the innkeeper's voice snapped Nuri fully awake. 'What's the matter?'

'Word from one of the canning hostels. Police are checking for two men involved in a garage robbery at Tikrit. The garage owner was killed. Also the army are looking for men who escaped from a raid on Afan.'

Nuri was out of bed and shaking Khalid before the innkeeper had finished.

'What's the time?' Nuri demanded, thrusting his feet into his boots.

'Four thirty-two and ten seconds,' said Khalid sleepily, groping for his trousers.

The innkeeper glanced at his watch by the light of the bedroom's low-wattage lamp. It wasn't the first time he had encountered Khalid's remarkable time-telling ability. 'One day, when the troubles are over, you will come back and tell me how you do that,' he commented.

'It is good of you to warn us,' said Nuri, pulling on his anorak.

The innkeeper shrugged. 'To have the police *and* the army looking for you is doubly unfortunate. You have the map?'

Nuri dug in his pocket and produced the sketch-map the innkeeper had drawn for them. It was a tracing from a large-scale map. The innkeeper had added in red a cross-country route to the north that avoided towns and main roads, where there were believed to be concentrations of troops and artillery.

'The curfew is still in force until daylight,' warned the innkeeper. 'So do not use your lights.' He pointed a grimy finger at the map. 'Also you must take great care along the Zab river gorge.' He pointed to a fork in the river. 'It starts there. But once you are past that, the going is easy. Good luck, my friends.'

Thirty minutes later, having eaten a hurried breakfast and settled their bill, Nuri and Khalid were heading north through the fruit-growing region of Mosul. The Bluebird's heater was on full blast, but it made little difference to the freezing night air being sucked into the car through the windows that had been smashed in the helicopter attack at Afan.

'Right at the next fork,' Nuri instructed.

Khalid flipped the main beam on for a second and committed the brief glimpse of the road ahead to memory. It was beginning to get light, so the trick would not be needed soon, but at the moment it was essential if they were to maintain a high average speed on the unmade road. Another flash of light and he spotted the fork.

The road he had turned onto was little used and in worse condition that the road they had just left. The Bluebird's tyres skipped and bounced from rut to rut.

'You rip a tyre and I'll skin you alive,' Nuri threatened, hanging onto the passenger's grab-handle.

Khalid grinned at his companion and reduced speed.

The road deteriorated even more. When they stopped for a break at 7 a.m., they had covered only forty kilometres since leaving the inn. But the terrain had changed dramatically and was more familiar to the two men. They were now in the hilly region of Mosul, where the many tributaries of the Tigris had cut deep valleys through the soft strata of limestone and sandstone. These were the oil-rich foothills that marked the southern extremity of the great mass of the Anatolian mountains on the frontier with Iran and Turkey. They had stopped where the road was cut into the side of a steep valley. Four kilometres away they could see a section of a main road – probably the Mosul to Mardin highway.

They were about to resume their journey when a deep throbbing note caused them to look at one another in concern and scramble up the slope to a dense clump of pines. The heavy beat of the helicopters' rotors echoed around the barren hills, making it difficult to tell where they were. Khalid spotted them and pointed them out to Nuri. They were three Super Frelon gunships, moving fast and low, following the lush, tree-lined valley. They were machines that many Kurds had learned to hate and fear during the years of oppression. They could bring the destructive firepower of a column of tanks to the most remote mountain village in a matter of minutes. The whine and beat of their rotors did not fade as they receded into the grey, overcast distance, and Nuri realised why when Khalid pointed again: three more gunships had appeared – also heading north.

'What is happening, Nuri?' Khalid asked fearfully.

As he spoke, a column of six slow-moving transporters appeared far below on the highway in the valley. Each one was hauling a G5 155-mm. Howitzer artillery piece – guns that could fire 50-kilo HE shells over a distance of forty kilometres. A true terror-weapon in mountainous terrain, where its range and effectiveness could be monitored from helicopters.

'They're not looking for us,' said Nuri savagely. 'Saddam Hussein is sending everything north. Troops, the army, heavy artillery, the airforce – everything. We don't stand a chance.'

'But the Americans will stop him, won't they, Nuri?'

Nuri gave a crooked smile and draped his arm across his comrade's shoulders. He guessed Khalid was thinking about his parents. 'Of course they will.'

He hoped he sounded convincing.

They filled the Bluebird's fuel tank with petrol stolen from the garage in Tikrit and pressed on, with Khalid driving and Nuri studying the map. The river they were following suddenly took a sharp fork and plunged into a ravine, and the road appeared to cut into the side of the rock-face. The track was blocked by what looked like a landslide of small boulders.

'We must have gone wrong somewhere,' said Nuri angrily. 'This can't be the road the innkeeper meant.'

Khalid pointed through the windscreen. 'Look, Nuri. Scratches in the rock. Sometimes trucks have come this way. It must be the road.'

The two men got out of the car and approached the track. Nuri saw that Khalid was right. This was the road. What he had thought was a landslide was in fact a place where the road had been roughly repaired by filling in the subsidence with small rocks. His gaze took in the road beyond the crude repair, where it was no more than a rough-hewn path a little over two metres wide. He looked at the map again. If the map was accurate, and so far it had been, the mountain track they were about to embark on snaked around the mountains for fifteen kilometres.

He groaned, and peered over the edge at the water cascading onto the rocks ten metres below. Ten metres was nothing. The map didn't give heights, but the way the road climbed, the drop could well be several hundred metres further up. As he looked down, something splattered on the back of his neck. He looked up. Damn! Wasn't it slippery enough underfoot as it was?

Rain!

He cursed softly.

That was all they needed.

114

VAN, EASTERN TURKEY

Laura pressed her nose against the window of the Turkish Airlines 737 and willed the circling aircraft to finish its turn over the glittering soda-bath expanse of Lake Van, and land. The captain had depressurised, so that the curious alkaline smell of the lake pervaded the aircraft. The rising sun came into view, its light burning white fire on the forbidding peaks of the Anatolian Mountains. Her fellow passengers numbered about a hundred and fifty, mostly men, and all packed into one aircraft run by an airline that didn't believe in no smoking areas on its domestic flights. Under these circumstances the term 'passive smoking' was meaningless; with Turkish cigarettes, everyone was an active smoker.

She looked at André to reassure herself that all was well. There had been no tantrums, although the girl had been sick after waking up just before they landed at Ankara – which Laura had attributed to travel pills. Now she was sitting quietly between Lloyd and herself, holding the miniature globe that Lloyd had bought for her, and looking at a picture-book of Eastern Turkey packed with photographs of the ruins of Troy, Pergamon and Ephesus. Turkey, and not Greece, as Laura had supposed, was the centre of classical Hellenic culture. The girl's bookmark was a favourite postcard that showed elegant villas grouped around a small artificial lake near Duhok – a luxurious enclave that was the result of co-operation between the hydro-electric company that built the dam and a Kurdish property developer. Occasionally André's long forefinger would reverently touch the villa that had been marked with a cross. Beneath the postcard was a photograph of Khalid that she gazed at whenever she thought no one was looking.

Laura thought how pretty André looked in her new, bright-red thermal tracksuit. All three of them were wearing the same brightly-coloured cold-weather clothing, the result of a hurried shopping expedition the previous day. Getting everything sorted out in time might have turned into near-panic but for Lloyd's level-headed good sense. The biggest battle had been persuading Lloyd that she should pay all his travelling expenses for the trip.

André sensed that her mother was looking at her. She lifted her head from her book and smiled. Laura took her hand, gave it an affectionate squeeze, and was pleased when the gesture was returned. There was no doubt about it – André's running-away-from-home escapade had brought about a marked change in her personality. Her hysteria when they snatched her from the car park at West Lulworth had ceased from the moment Laura promised her they would go to Kurdistan. After that, she had slept the rest of the way home. Since then, only when Laura or Lloyd tried to question her about what had happened in Dorset and how she got there did she become distressed and retreat into her shell. At all other times she was happy and smiling at the prospect of seeing Khalid again.

'We'll leave it,' Laura had told Lloyd. 'She'll tell me in her own good time.'

Lloyd had pointed out that the police Land Rover must have got his Lotus's number, and even if it hadn't, how many yellow Lotus Super Sevens were there in the country? It was only a matter of hours before the police came nosing around.

But they didn't come, and the questions surrounding André's running away remained unanswered.

The note of the 737's engines dropped. Lloyd yawned and looked at his watch.

'It's five thirty,' said André.

The two adults looked at the girl in surprise.

'What happened to the time sponsored by Accurist and all that?' Lloyd inquired.

André pouted. 'Silly. Taken it off.'

'We're ahead of London now,' said Lloyd, patting André's hand. 'But don't let it worry you. We'll make use of you whenever we want to know the time at home.'

The second officer made an announcement in Turkish which prompted some younger passengers on their side of the aircraft to shade their eyes and peer at the dazzling, snow-covered peaks. The co-pilot repeated his comments in English, and even Lloyd, who was a hardened traveller, tried to get a glimpse of Mount Ararat.

'I don't suppose we'd be able to see Noah's Ark from here,' he remarked drolly.

There was a rumble as the 737 lowered its main-gear. Laura suddenly realised how close the snow-covered roads and houses were. Snow looked wrong on minarets and the onion-shaped domes of mosques; she always imagined them rising mirage-like out of the shimmering haze of the desert.

There was the gentle bump of a remarkably good landing on Van airport's single runway.

'Welcome to Van, ladies and gentlemen,' said the chatty co-pilot after speaking a few sentences in Turkish. 'The outside temperature is minus ten degrees. Spring is in the air but there will be buses to take you to the terminal.'

Although they had cleared immigration formalities at Ankara, Turkish bureaucracy dictated that the few foreign nationals on the domestic flight had to pass through Van's passport control. Laura groaned. They had been travelling for thirteen hours. She wanted nothing more than to crawl into an hotel bed and sleep.

'No problem,' said Lloyd, taking André by the hand to spare Laura. 'Doesn't look like more than a dozen of us.'

There was no wait; the immigration officer opened and snapped shut each passenger's passport so quickly that she could not have registered details. But she did, because she was looking for only three names. And when Laura, Lloyd and André were allowed past her booth, she had found them. With the last foreigner cleared, she shut up shop and reported to her chief officer that the three had arrived. Her boss thanked her and picked up the fax he had received from Mosul. All he had to do was call a voice line number and report the arrival of the trio. Simple as that. As he picked up his telephone, he reflected that either someone had been chucking his money about or he had a great deal of influence.

*

Lloyd need not have worried about whether arriving in a pre-dominantly Muslim country in the middle of Ramadan would make it difficult to find a taxi. Outside the tiny terminal building was a lively throng of eager porters, turbaned peddlers selling kilims – the locally made Kurdish rugs – and taxi drivers. Turkey had separated state and religion, with the result that anyone who wished to make a fast lira during the religious holidays was free to do so.

They were virtually kidnapped by a smiling Turkoman who employed his two children to snatch travellers' luggage trucks: before Lloyd or Laura could object, their bags were lashed to the roof-rack of a battered Mercedes whose interior smelt of goats. A thirty-minute drive that took in the car ferry docks, the sports stadium, the famous Rock of Van, and some of the ruins of the old city – destroyed by the Ottomans – ended on the forecourt of the modern Bükyük Hotel where the smiling taxi driver relieved Laura of 100,000 lira. It was an extortionate amount even at the rate of exchange of nearly 4000 lira to the pound sterling, but Laura and Lloyd were both too tired and too intimidated by their strange surroundings to argue.

The helpful travel agents in Guildford had done their job well. Two comfortable, well-heated adjoining rooms with a com-municating door were awaiting them on the second floor.

'I'm too knackered to think of anything until I've had a shower and at least four hours' sleep,' Laura declared. She ordered André into the shower first and stepped out of her tracksuit trousers. She saw Lloyd watching her and propelled him gently through the door into the single room.

'I thought – ' he began.

'I don't want Andy sleeping alone after what's happened, Lloyd. You do understand?'

'Not really,' he answered mischievously. 'I was thinking of claiming my reward. Or had you forgotten?'

Laura took his hand and smiled. 'No – of course not. You've been so kind, but I don't want even to think of embarking on any form of new relationship until this crazy trip is behind me. I simply can't handle any more. And I'm too tired even to think straight. Do you understand?'

He smiled. 'Sure.' He drew her closer with the intention of kissing her lightly on the cheek, but Laura circled her arms around his neck and kissed him on the lips. Before he had a chance to respond, she pushed him gently through the door.

'You need some sleep as well, Lloyd.'

She gave him a warm smile before pulling the door closed.

115

NORTHERN IRAQ

It was Khalid's remarkable driving skill that saved them. He sensed that the Bluebird's rear wheels were about to lose their grip on the rain-slurried loess, and gunned the engine just the right amount to prevent the car slewing sideways into the gorge. It surged forward, bouncing off the boulders that were strewn across the track, banging Nuri's head on the roof in the process. He grabbed the handle above the door and hung on grimly as Khalid bucked the car half around and half over yet another rockfall. The wind-driven rain hammered incessantly against the cliff face, and giant drops came scudding in sideways through the car's broken windows – a solid wall of water exploding against metal and rock and turning into a blinding, heavy mist that prevented Nuri from seeing down into the ravine. He had no idea how deep it was, but they had been climbing for thirty minutes along this precipitous track which meant that it had to be very deep indeed. The windscreen-wiper on his side was useless – it aquaplaned back and forth over a solid stream of rain without clearing it.

'Go easy,' he muttered, and promptly clamped his foot on the dashboard to jam himself hard against the seat-back when the car oversteered suddenly. Khalid's door slammed and grated against the rock face. He grinned at Nuri, taking his eyes off the track for a second.

'Pretty frightening, eh?' He had to yell to make his voice heard above the fiercely revving engine and the nerve-shredding screech of metal on sandstone.

Nuri said nothing. When they had first started along the

track, he had marvelled at the tenacity of the ancient peoples who had carved out this track to ensure that the silk road was kept open when the Zab river was in flood. Now his only thoughts were fervent prayers, spliced into a loop, that this hellish journey would soon be over. The rough sketch-map provided by the innkeeper had slipped down the side of the seat, but he had no intention of even thinking of retrieving it.

The rain-squall stopped as quickly as it had started, giving Nuri a clear view of the magnificent gorge below them. He shuddered, closed his eyes and pleaded for the return of the rain into his prayer-loop.

'Better!' Khalid yelled, pointing gleefully.

Ahead, the track widened slightly where it had been cut deeper into the rock face. To Nuri's despair, Khalid used the improvement in the track to accelerate. He was about to shout his disapproval when a deluge of rocks and water cascaded onto the car with sufficient force to wrench the steering-wheel out of Khalid's hands. The toughened glass windscreen fractured with a loud report and turned into a sheet of opaque cracked ice.

Nuri had experienced shattered windscreens before. Without thinking, he smashed his fist through the glass so that hundreds of crystal-white shards burst across the bonnet and onto his lap. But he was too late: although a small area of windscreen in front of Khalid had remained clear, he had lost full visibility. For a few crucial milliseconds he failed to realise that the car was virtually facing the edge of the precipice. To complete the disaster, at that precise moment he made a fatal, if understandable, mistake when the car pitched around and crashed his door against a protruding rock, knocking his foot off the brake pedal. His foot went back to the brake pedal and stamped down hard.

Except that the pedal that connected with his foot wasn't the brake pedal.

The Bluebird's engine roared. The rear wheels spun wildly, splattering the rock face with slurry, and the car leapt blindly at the brink. The front wheels went over the edge, causing the car to crash down on its door sills. The Bluebird rocked forward like a child's seesaw, lifting the spinning rear wheels clear of the track just as they were about to catapult the car into the gorge.

Khalid twisted the ignition key to kill the engine and turned, white-faced, to his companion. Even the slight movement was enough to cause the finely-balanced car to rock alarmingly.

'What do we do now, Nuri?'

'Don't move!' Nuri snarled, staring in wide-eyed horror at the expanse of grey sky that lay beyond the end of the Bluebird's bonnet. 'Don't even breathe!'

Even the silence was terrifying. Khalid's hand went to his door release.

'*I SAID – DON'T MOVE!!*'

'We have to do something, Nuri.'

'We need some of your luck.'

'Too close, Nuri.' Khalid's voice was a contrite whimper. 'I'm sorry, Nuri.'

'We have to think!'

The two men sat in frozen silence. The icy wind keened into the car through the shattered front and rear windscreens, rocking the Nissan like a cradle. It started raining again with increased ferocity. Nuri quickly realised that their only hope was to shift the car's centre of gravity as far back as possible. Slowly, very slowly, he edged his right hand down to his side and groped for the handwheel that reclined the back of his seat.

His questing fingers failed to find the wheel. Perhaps if he sat up a little . . . but that would mean shifting his weight forward. The icy rain, driving straight into his face and soaking into his clothes, made it difficult to see, and to think straight.

'We have to get our weight back,' said Nuri hoarsely, terrified that even the energy expended when talking might upset the Bluebird's precarious equilibrium. 'See if you can recline your seat. Move very slowly. Don't argue – just do it!'

Khalid had more success in finding his handwheel. At first he turned it the wrong way.

'The other way!' Nuri hissed.

Khalid's body tipped backwards slowly in a series of jerks as he managed to crank the wheel. The Bluebird settled back-wards.

'Now push yourself backwards!'

By now the anoraks the two men were wearing were drenched through and clinging to them.

Khalid carefully straightened his legs and eased his torso into the back of the car.

'That's good, that's good,' said Nuri as he felt the rear of the car rock back a little more. He risked easing himself forward so that he could find his handwheel. This time he was successful. He reclined his seat as far as it would go and gingerly eased his weight back until the two men were lying side by side, staring up at the roof. The car seemed more stable now, and wasn't rocking so much in the wind.

'What now, Nuri?'

'I'm going to try to open my back door.'

Nuri's fingers found the door-catch. The door opened when he tugged the lever. He felt an overwhelming sense of relief, but they weren't out of trouble yet. As if to confirm his feelings, the rusty sills that were now supporting the entire weight of the car and its two passengers crumpled on his side.

Nuri suddenly realised that he wasn't thinking ahead properly. 'Can you release the boot-catch?'

'I think so, Nuri.'

The boot's cable-release lever was on the floor, between the driver's seat and the door. Khalid found it and gave it a gentle tug. Both men heard the boot lid click and swing open on its creaky, spring-loaded hinges.

'Good. Good,' Nuri muttered. 'Now for my door.' He carefully eased it open with his foot, only to realise that by doing so he was moving the car's centre of gravity in the wrong direction. He had managed to get it open a few centimetres when it encountered a rock, and jammed.

The driving rain continued soaking into the two men and into the Bluebird's front carpets.

'Try your door,' Nuri instructed.

Khalid's side of the car had taken the most punishment from the rock face, and yet the rear door required only a slight nudge to persuade it to swing fully open.

'Okay,' said Nuri, breathing a little easier now. 'This is what

406

you've got to do. You're to slide head first out of the car, but you must keep your weight over the rear wheel arch at all times. Are there plenty of small stones around the car?'

Khalid looked. 'Yes – plenty, Nuri,' he replied, and even managed a little grin.

Nuri bit his tongue. There was no point in shouting at the younger man. 'Pick them up one at a time – *without letting go of the car!* – and toss them into the boot. As many as you can to start with. Don't stop until I say. Do you understand?'

'Sure, Nuri – sure.'

The rain continued to tank down with unremitting ferocity. It was creating a problem that not even the normally quick-thinking Nuri had anticipated.

Khalid backed cautiously out of the rear door while at the same time doing his best to keep his weight bearing down on the wheel arch. He twisted around and half-sat on the arch in order to reach for a large rock. The Bluebird rocked, and the sills collapsed a little more. The driving rain, draining down from the cliff, was forming fast-flowing muddy rivulets that streamed over the edge of the precipice.

'Not too big!' Nuri warned when he saw the rock that Khalid was lifting. 'Small ones to start with!'

'Be quicker with big ones, Nuri.' With that, Khalid heaved the small boulder into the Bluebird's boot.

The shock wave that bounced through the car was nothing; no more than it would encounter when driven over a pothole. But combined with the extra weight of water that the car had taken in through the windscreen, it was enough to complete the collapse of the corrosion-weakened sills. The rotten metal crumbled like oven-foil. Soil and stones broke away from the edge of the precipice and rattled down the rock face. The car slewed forward on one side and tipped down, metal shrieking harsh and discordant on sandstone.

'Nuri!' Khalid cried out. As the car lifted, his body overbalanced onto the edge of the cliff. He tried desperately to grip the door-surround with his feet, but there was nothing for his heels to get a purchase on. Through the streaming rain he caught a glimpse of his friend's terrified face through the rear windscreen opening. Khalid rolled clear of the sliding car and frantically twisted his body around, with the intention of grabbing hold of the rear bumper. He managed to get a grip on the sharp underside of the pressing, but his weight was no match for two tonnes of saloon car with a centre of gravity that was now well over the edge. Metal screeched on metal and on rock as the sills were ripped through. Suddenly, the boot seemed to lift, but that was due to the entire mass of ironmongery pivoting downwards.

Khalid would have been dragged over the edge had he not let go of the bumper.

'Stay close to me, Nuri!' he screamed. 'Stay close!'

The rear axle rode over the edge and the car was gone.

'*Stay close! You must stay close!*'

Khalid threw himself prone and stared over the edge. The car seemed to glide downwards with an eerie grace until it hit the slope some twenty metres below. It shed wheels, doors, the boot lid and other components as it blazed a spectacular, cartwheeling trail of disintegration and destruction through some scrub. It came to rest some two hundred metres below the point where Khalid lay looking over the edge of the track in wide-eyed horror.

The expected sheet of flame never materialised. Only American cars in American films tend to become incandescent fireballs when they go over cliffs.

'Nuri,' Khalid moaned into the rain and wind. 'You should have stayed with me.'

116

VAN, EASTERN TURKEY

There was nothing about Bruno Keran's business-like demeanour as he smiled at Lloyd, Laura and André in turn, to suggest that his company, Keran Tours, was on the verge of bankruptcy. Indeed, at that moment, two of Van's commercial banks were squabbling over which bits of Keran's financial liver they were going to have on a plate. He was a small, dark-skinned man aged about forty. What was left of his black hair was slicked down like a coat of paint, giving his oval head the appearance of an olive.

'But you have two Land Rovers outside, doing nothing,' Laura pointed out.

Keran looked pensively at the Englishwoman, mentally undressing her as he did all foreign women. Very attractive, as was her daughter. The girl was watching him with large green eyes that seemed to be reading his thoughts. 'It is Ramadan, Mrs Normanville. My drivers will not work at this time.' He spoke English well enough to lie convincingly. No driver-guide would work for him because none of them had been paid.

It wasn't Keran's fault that his tour business was going broke. In 1987 a beautifully photographed Japanese television series 'The Silk Road' had gone on worldwide syndication, creating a boom in tourists visiting this magnificent but forgotten part of the world. But the Iraq border was within spitting distance just over the Cilo Dagi mountains, and the Gulf War had brought the boom to an abrupt end.

'So why can't you drive us?' Lloyd asked.

'I have pressing business matters here,' said Keran regretfully. This time he was telling the truth. He was involved in a deal to buy an old 5,000-litre petrol tanker to import oil from Kirkuk. With President Ozal paying lip-service to the UN embargoes on Iraq by closing the oil pipeline from Iraq, the new pipeline-on-wheels between Mosul and Mardin was growing rapidly into a major business. The Turks were buying oil at $2 per barrel in Mosul and selling it to the oil companies in Turkey at $10 per barrel. If the embargo continued, fortunes would be made.

'Very well, Mr Keran,' said Laura decisively. 'Perhaps you will hire us one of your Land Rovers for three days on a self-drive basis?'

'Where do you wish to go?'

'Duhok – just over the frontier, in Iraq. According to our maps, it's about a hundred miles . . .'

Iraq was bad news for Keran: the banks had slapped an injunction on him that prevented him from taking assets out of the country. That included his vehicles. He thought fast to come up with a plausible excuse.

'Is there a problem, crossing the mountains?' asked Lloyd, seeing the Turk's hesitation. 'We saw very little snow from the plane.'

'No. No,' said Keran hurriedly. 'The road to Duhok is via Cukurca. It is not a main traffic route, and the customs post on the Iraq side is not always manned.'

'Is it a difficult drive?' Lloyd demanded.

'No. Narrow in places, but not difficult.'

'So why can't you take us?' Laura pressed. She tapped her guide-book. 'According to this, Duhok has been in the Kurdish autonomous region for over ten years. It's almost self-governing. There's no Iraqi problem, so what's your problem?'

'I'm very sorry – but I always suspend my Iraqi insurance during Ramadan. There is so little demand, you understand.'

'This is ridiculous,' said Laura impatiently. 'All right, Mr Keran – we'll buy one of your Land Rovers.'

Keran was astute. He looked doubtful, even though he urgently needed ready cash for his tanker deal. 'That would depend on the currency and whether you can pay in cash,' he responded cautiously.

'How about English pounds?'

The canny Turk studied his fingernails. 'I'm sure we can do business, Mrs Normanville.'

Thirty minutes later the three emerged from Keran's office into the bustle of the Ipek Yolu, the Silk Road, and hailed a taxi. Two hundred metres away, the Mukharabat agent saw them leave and shook his Kurdish taxi driver awake.

The first thing Laura did when they arrived back at the hotel was call Hamet's number. As on all the previous occasions, there was no answer.

'Damn!' She banged the phone down.

'If it's a summer home, maybe they have it disconnected out of season?' Lloyd suggested.

'Then why do I always get the ringing sound?'

'It's called "ringing on the rack",' Lloyd answered. 'The

ringing tone is generated in the exchange. What you're hearing is not the phone ringing at the other end – it never is.' He glanced at André, who was lying on the bed reading a book, and lowered his voice. 'What do we do if they're not at home when we turn up tomorrow?'

'Simple. We leave a note and stay at a hotel in Duhok.'

'One night, Laura. I've got a magazine to run.'

'One night,' Laura agreed.

117

NORTHERN IRAQ

It took Khalid an hour to scramble down into the gorge and work his way back through the scrub to where the remains of the Bluebird had come to rest.

He approached the wreckage cautiously, slipping and sliding in the mud, fearful of what he knew he would find. It was more sheltered from the wind in the valley, but the icy rain sliced down with the touch of miniature circular saws.

What was left of the Bluebird's body-shell was on its roof. The door pillars had collapsed, so that the car appeared to be unnaturally low. One of the once fine Texan boots Nuri had been so proud of was thrust out of the wreckage – like a bizarre prank played by students with a tailor's dummy.

'Nuri?'

There was no answer.

He crept nearer.

'Nuri? It's me – Khalid.'

Silence, apart from the soft moaning of the wind.

Khalid reached out a fearful hand, touched the protruding ankle, and quickly withdrew it. The tears that streamed down his cheeks mingled with the rain that was now turning to sleet. He didn't know how long he stood there, alone with the turmoil of his confused thoughts; desperately afraid, now that his friend was gone. All his life he had been protected and cared for. Even in the army there were those who had befriended him and shielded him. Now there was no one.

'Mother! Father!' he cried out.

The wind answered by turning the sleet to snow.

Eventually it was the cold and wet that forced him to move. As he turned to leave, a little square of white caught his eye. It was lying in the mud under the wreckage. He stooped to recover it, turned it over, and saw that it was the colour photograph of a dark-haired, green-eyed girl that he had recovered from his vandalised room in Baghdad.

André! Dear, sweet, lovely André! She would help him. All the years they had known each other, they had both sensed that her powers were so much stronger than his.

Think the time back, Khalid. Think the time back to the beginning. To the very beginning of time.

It was thanks to her that he had come through the Gulf War alive. Now he needed her more than ever. He studied the picture for timeless minutes before slipping it carefully into his pocket.

It was now bitterly cold; the temperature was plunging as nightfall approached and the mud underfoot was already hardening. He turned away from the wrecked car and trudged along the valley.

118

Wednesday, 20th March 1991

It would be another week before the aftermath of the terror – the flight of thousands of Kurds into Turkey and Iran – was shown on the world's television networks.

It all began quietly enough, early on a cloudless morning, with a lone helicopter from the army base at Mosul cruising northward in the cold, crystal air.

From one thousand feet the blue-tiled swimming-pools of the villas and bungalows clustered along the southern shore of the artificial lake sparkled invitingly in the morning sun. The tadpole shadow of the Aérospatiale Alouette wheeled over the golf course that was set amid pines behind the villas, and lost height. A kilometre away, along the only approach-road to the estate, a JCB had moved into place and was digging a long, narrow trench in a pomegranate orchard at the side of the road; no doubt they were laying water-pipes, or a telephone cable. There were even two men on the fairway, playing golf. Everything looked perfectly normal – but the presence of the hovering Alouette brought people hurrying into their gardens, where they stared anxiously upwards, shading their eyes against the harsh glare from the sun. During the uprising of 1988 over two thousand Kurdish towns and villages had been destroyed by Iraqi forces. This area had been peaceful since the 1977 troubles, and had taken no part in the 1988 fighting, but the fear that the Iraqis would return was never far away.

Brigadier Anwar Tulfah's laughter rumbled in Max's headset as he pointed down at the running figures. 'Those cowards hear a helicopter now and they shit themselves,' he said contemptuously. He was a short, thickset man. Like Max and the helicopter pilot, he was wearing a heavy parka and over-trousers to protect him against the cold. The helicopter bore no unit markings.

'Which house is it?' Max asked. There was no need for him to raise his voice above the roar of the engine because they were communicating through their headsets.

The Iraqi officer looked at the map strapped to his thigh and pointed down through the Plexiglass side-window. 'House with the biggest boat and jetty.'

Max picked out the bungalow and its moored cabin-cruiser. He nodded.

'It is a good plan you have devised,' said the brigadier respectfully. He had been impressed with Max's simple but cunning plan for emptying the estate without signs of a struggle. It was well thought out, and gave him an insight into why this smiling Englishman who spoke good but slow Arabic had friends in high places. In good time, no doubt he would learn what this curious operation was all about.

'I have a reputation for careful planning,' Max replied. 'Don't forget that I want to be there.'

The Iraqi officer shrugged. 'You will need an NBC mask.'

'I've brought my own,' said Max, patting his trusty Adidas bag. 'It always travels with me on my visits to Iraq.'

The brigadier liked the joke and laughed. He pressed the PTT button on his Icom personal radio and spoke in rapid Arabic into his headset's microphone. When he had finished, he touched the pilot's shoulder and jabbed his thumb south.

The helicopter banked. The watchers on the ground saw its rotors become an iridescent ellipse of sunlight as it turned away. The sound of its turbine faded. It was replaced by a new and more sinister sound, and one which many of the residents knew: the heavy beat of Super Frelon gunships and the shrill whine of their Turboméca turbines.

The two machines appeared suddenly over the line of windbreak pines at the eastern end of the golf course. The lead helicopter approached the edge of the estate and dropped a flour bomb. The huge white cloud, billowing into the clear air, had the desired effect: the watchers rushed panic-stricken into their houses. Even the golfers abandoned their game and clubs, and dashed towards their homes. Within seconds, up-and-over garage doors were being thrown open and car engines feverishly started. Families piled into Mercedes, BMWs and Peugeots that were already crammed full of emergency supplies for just this eventuality. Two minutes later, the fine white dust drifting across the rooftops mingled with the dust thrown up from the access road in the wake of the fleeing convoy.

The lead car was a blue Mercedes driven by a dark-haired, middle-aged man wearing heavy sunglasses. Sitting terrified at his side was his pretty blonde wife. They were Hamet and Sajii – Khalid's parents. Hamet accelerated hard along the narrow road – and was forced to brake when the JCB swung across his path and stopped. Republican Guards in full combat kit, with AKS–74 assault rifles at the ready, vaulted over the tailboard of an unmarked truck that had been drawn up near the JCB.

'Leave the keys and get out of your cars!' yelled the captain in charge of the platoon. He was using a portable loud-hailer. He repeated the order several times.

The cars behind Hamet were stopping, but the Kurdish banker had had his fill of uniformed thugs. He was seized by a sudden, blind rage. After all he and his family had been through, there was no way he was going to surrender everything to this murdering scum without a fight. There was one slim, impossible chance of escape and he snatched it. He dropped into a low gear, wrenched the steering-wheel over and hurled the Mercedes onto the verge. The car's doors scraped along the JCB's bucket. Two guards were forced to leap clear.

The captain's movements were fast but precise. He yanked the firing-pin from a grenade and lobbed it accurately over the receding Mercedes so that it fell in the car's path. The explosion directly beneath the floor-pan split the fuel tank and threw the car onto its side. It dissolved into an incandescent ball of fire and came to a blazing stop nose down in an irrigation ditch. Within seconds even the car's acrylic paint was ablaze. The captain grinned at the occupants of the nearest car. He could have used his rifle, but the hand-grenade was a more effective demonstration.

White-faced with terror, the families got out of their cars. Altogether there were about forty men, women and children. One woman in a fur stole was clutching a baby protectively to her chest. Her husband tried to remonstrate with the soldiers as the pathetic group was herded to the edge of the trench. His answer was a savage blow on the temple with a rifle butt. Some pleaded with the captain; some kneeled and prayed; some clutched each other; some stood to shocked attention, gazing with unseeing eyes across the lake. The baby sensed its mother's distress and started crying; she shushed it gently. A woman wearing a long cape that reached the ground was trying to hide something. The captain spun her around, ripped the cape open, and looked down into the terrified eyes of a girl aged about thirteen, clutching her mother's dress. He stepped back and signalled to two of his men.

'No!' the woman screamed in Arabic when the soldiers dragged her daughter away. She tried to beat the Iraqis on the face and shoulders, but was doubled-up by a vicious punch in the stomach. The guards secured the screaming girl's wrists behind her back with a nylon cable-strap and threw her across the back seat of a Peugeot.

On a word from the captain, the soldiers formed a line along the road. The JCB driver settled his ear-defenders in place, leaned on his controls, and lit a Rothmans King Size with a Bic lighter while the shooting went on, temporarily drowning the girl's screams. The impact of the 5-mm. rounds sent all the bodies tumbling into the trench.

It was all over in a few seconds. The captain walked around the edge of the mass grave, firing his pistol at any movement. Satisfied with his handiwork, he holstered his firearm and turned his attention to the girl who was sobbing hysterically, face down in the back of the car. The guards who had dragged her away from her mother knew what to do. Watched by a grinning circle of their comrades, they hauled the girl roughly from the Peugeot and ripped off her clothes. Her wildly flailing legs seemed to add to the men's excitement. Once the girl was naked, they supported her between them, yanked her legs wide apart and carried her around the group like priests taking the host to their congregation. The ritual took fifteen minutes, during which the girl's screams of terror and pain continued unabated, rising to fever-pitch when one of the guards tried to cut off her left breast. But the girl was under-developed; the fold of bloody skin kept slipping through his fingers. He gave up in disgust.

The captain was last. He was always last for a very special reason. The girl had fainted, but he had learned from his experiences in 1988 that it didn't matter. The men supporting her adjusted her position to make it easy for him. He thrust forward, feeling her warmth closing around him like a soft mouth. He gripped her firmly around the neck and pressured his thumbs into her windpipe. Careful timing was important for maximum effect, but he had plenty of practice. She started to struggle. Her eyes flew open. She stared at the captain, eyes round with pain and terror. Her legs strained and kicked, causing the men holding her to stagger slightly to maintain their balance. The captain grunted and pushed deeper. The first spasms came one after another. More pressure on the girl's throat. Her windpipe squirmed under his thumbs like a snake; he could feel it closing. A croak escaped from her mouth. And then the waves of death-spasms came in a sudden, heavenly surge of powerful muscular convulsions, clasping and unclasping, milking him of his reason. He threw his head back and uttered a loud, spent cry at the

416

great vault of the blue sky, as though the spirit of the wretched dying girl had escaped through him to heaven. The divine contractions gradually lost their strength and finally ceased.

It was over.

He stepped back, buttoning his fly, and jerked his head at the pit. The girl's lifeless body was tossed on top of her mother. The captain fired a bullet into her head to be certain she was dead. Allah's law had been obeyed; there was no question of the girl having been a virgin when she was executed. He signalled to the JCB, and the driver flicked his cigarette-end away and set to work with his bucket to fill in the trench.

'The Audi's mine,' said the captain to his platoon. 'You can draw for the other cars.'

Apart from the incident with the Mercedes, he considered the operation a success. The flour-bomb ruse had worked well: there had been no need to drive the residents out of their homes or waste time ransacking every room, searching for car keys; the Kurds had done everything for their executioners, including driving themselves the kilometre to their grave. A good plan. Simple and effective. He wondered who had thought of it.

The guards were deliriously happy with their new possessions. Some ran their hands lovingly over the cars' shiny bodywork; some sat in the drivers' seats making childish engine noises, grinning from ear to ear at the acquisitions that were worth a lifetime's pay.

'Okay,' said the captain over his loud-hailer when the JCB had finished its gruesome task. 'Let's move out.' He slipped behind the wheel of his new Audi and turned the key. Listening to the sweet, almost inaudible purr of the finely-balanced engine gave him an orgasmic thrill. To think that this magnificent creation was now his. He admired the fine dashboard and ran his fingers over the padded curves as though savouring the texture of a girl's skin before raping her. An audio cassette was protruding from its slot. It latched home with a smooth click when he pushed it. The Dolby light on the Blaupunkt player winked on and the Beatles singing 'All You Need Is Love' boomed from the quad speakers. The captain turned up the volume so that everyone would know what a fine car he pos-

417

sessed. The column moved off, each car pulling wide and spurting past the now gutted and smoking Mercedes lest the fierce heat from the wreckage scorched pristine paintwork.

The JCB driver used his bucket to roll the remains of the Mercedes into the field. He reversed towards the road, obliterating the deep gouges in the ground as he went. When he had finished it looked as if the gutted car had been there many months.

The captain slowed where the road curved around the edge of the lake, and glanced regretfully back at the houses. His son would have appreciated one of the smart speedboats, but he had been given strict orders to leave the houses alone.

On a camouflaged hilltop observation-point six kilometres away, Max and the brigadier watched the departing convoy through British Army Barr and Stroud binoculars. Behind them, two technicians wearing NCB suits, but without the hoods, were fitting quick-release clips between the Alouette's landing-skids. The machine was draped with ICI netting to break up its outline. The senior technician reported to the brigadier that the clips were in place, and the two men ducked under the netting. Max examined the clips and checked the operation of the remote-control that had been strapped to the seat-frame beside his and the pilot's seat. The clips opened with loud clunks when Max pressed the button.

'Excellent. Excellent,' he approved. 'Now you can fit the canister.'

It took three men to manoeuvre the 500-litre gas canister into the clips beneath the helicopter. It resembled a bomb because it was provided with stabilising fins and a rounded nose to ensure that it fell straight. The brigadier recognised the type of canister – it was a ground-impact-fracture pattern that had been developed by his countrymen – but the markings stencilled on the side were unknown to him.

'What is this gas?' he asked Max.

'Cyclopropane. The fastest-acting anaesthetic in the world. Single whiff, instant knock-down. The Americans call it SWIK.'

'Dangerous?'

'It's hardly used because it's so damned volatile – although this stuff contains an explosion inhibitor. But I still don't trust it. That's why I've insisted that you cut the electricity and gas supplies to the estate.'

'That has been done,' the officer replied.

Max was not averse to helping the technicians hold the canister in place while the clips were closed around it. He was sweating slightly when he straightened.

'You've got to drop it from a height of at least four thousand feet,' Max insisted. 'The entire success of the plan is that they mustn't see the helicopter as a threat. Do you understand? It is vital.'

'I will instruct the pilot,' the officer replied. He looked curiously at the bomb-like device slung beneath the helicopter. 'An invisible gas?'

'Absolutely.'

'How many people could that one canister kill?'

'No one,' Max replied. 'That's the whole idea. Cyclopropane is an anaesthetic. The fastest in the world.'

The Iraqi officer grunted. Non-toxic gases were of little interest to him. Max lifted his binoculars to his eyes and trained them on the estate again. Clothes were hanging on a rotary airer in one garden; a wheelbarrow and gardening tools were spread out on the lawn of another. Apart from all the garage doors left open, the scene looked ordinary.

Max was pleased.

The trap was set.

119

It was the cold, rather than the grinding of heavy vehicles labouring up the hill, that aroused Khalid from his fitful sleep. He lay still, every joint apparently paralysed by the bitter cold so that he couldn't move, while he tried to sort out in his mind where he was. He remembered walking the previous afternoon after leaving the wreckage of the crashed Bluebird. He had no idea how long or how far he had walked, but it must have been a considerable distance. The road was close by because he could hear vehicles approaching.

He opened his eyes – and immediately shut them again, such was the harshness of the morning light. But his vision gradually adjusted and he tried to make sense of his surroundings. He turned his head and saw rust. There was rust everywhere: above him, beside him, even on his hands – as he saw when he held a hand up to shade his eyes against the sun.

The pieces dropped into place; he was in the gutted remains of a burnt-out truck that had been hauled off the road. The padding had been incinerated off the seats he was lying across, with the result that he was covered in rust. He massaged his neck and cautiously raised his head. Above what had been a dashboard and was now a mass of rust with holes where the instruments had been, he could see a long line of GM flat-bed transporters toiling up the incline. What should have been fresh, clear, morning air was thick with diesel fumes from the poorly adjusted, labouring engines.

He didn't count the transporters – there was no point. What puzzled him was that the drivers were in army fatigues, wearing Republican Guard shoulder-marks, but their cargoes were bright-yellow JCB excavators, one on each vehicle. All were fitted with bulldozer blades on their bucket-arms and also on their back-acters. He and Nuri had seen many of these road-making machines over the last few days. The only logical explanation was that a new military road was being built in the north.

He waited until the last vehicle had disappeared, then climbed stiffly down from the cab. He was on the edge of a smallholding that was strung out on each side of the winding road. In places plump winter cabbages grew right up to the edge of the tarmac. The sunlight was pleasantly warm but the air temperature was well below freezing, as he soon discovered when he had to hide behind the wrecked truck to avoid being seen when a military staff-car sped by.

What should he do now? What could he do? For the first time in his life he had to make a decision for himself. He wondered about thumbing a lift, but that would be dangerous.

The sun told him which way was north, but a deep, inner instinct would have told him had there been no sun.

The road was quiet now. As Khalid brushed the worst of the rust off his now shabby, mud-soaked anorak, he reasoned that this was not the main Mosul road but the secondary, more mountainous route that Nuri had wanted to reach the previous day.

Khalid crouched in misery, covered his face with his hands, and gave a keening wail of anguish when he thought of his dead friend.

'You should have stayed close to me, Nuri,' he wept. 'I told you to stay close to me.'

The sound of another approaching vehicle snapped him out of his misery. He wiped away his tears and remained crouching behind the wreckage until the army truck had passed. It was packed with lustily-singing troops.

He tried eating one of the cabbages but it tasted harsh and acid. He spat it out and started walking. It was then that he realised he had no money. Nuri had always looked after everything. It hadn't occurred to him to recover anything from the Bluebird, and even if it had, he would have been unable to search Nuri's body for the wallet containing their supply of dollars and dinar. He hunted through his pockets and found a $20 bill and a few fils. The discovery made him feel a little better; also the sun was getting stronger and the cold of the night was seeping from his bones.

A battered Cherokee pick-up loaded with parsnips, carrots and potatoes in net sacks clunked and rattled towards him. It clattered to a stop in response to his raised hand.

The driver was a weathered old farmer wearing a grubby, badly-knotted muslin turban and a work-stained smock. His rheumy dark eyes quickly took in every detail of the fair-haired hitch-hiker. Few Iraqis were blond.

'Taking this lot to Sammel,' he said sourly in Kurdish.

Khalid's heart leapt. 'Sammel!' he cried. 'It is only ten kilometres from my home. How far from here?'

'An hour. You help me unload at the market there and I'll take you. Deal?'

'Deal!' Khalid exclaimed, leaping in beside the old man and smacking his offered leathern palm.

The Cherokee moved off and Khalid settled happily in the seat. He was nearly home. That morning he would be reunited with his beloved parents. There would be water-skiing on the lake again using the cabin-cruiser he had begged his father to buy two years before; and fishing trips; and lazing in the sun beside the swimming-pool; trips to Sammel market to buy supplies for barbecues in the balmy evenings when they would invite friends around to drink, smoke hashish, and gossip into the early hours.

Everything was going to be all right again.

120

Although they had left Van at 6 a.m., it was noon when Lloyd stopped the Land Rover at the nondescript Iraqi frontier office. Six hours' arm-wrenching driving to reach a border marked by a muddy tributary of the Zab river that ran through a dismal valley. This was Turkey's desolate back door into the Middle East. At Hakkari, where they stopped for coffee, they had been seventeen hundred metres above sea-level. Since then the road had wound a tortuous, zig-zagging, climbing route into the mountains that took them to three thousand metres. Occasionally they had met laden petrol tankers using their crawler gears to grind them around the hairpins. All of them had been fitted with additional box tanks along the underside of the chassis, so hastily welded together and fitted that they were dripping black Iraqi crude onto the badly-maintained road. But for the tankers, Lloyd would have won the argument that they should turn back and take the longer main-road route from Mardin into Iraq. Laura reasoned that if tankers could make it, then a Land Rover should have no problems. Besides, according to the large-scale map that Keran had supplied, this road to Duhok actually passed the turning to the Zab River Paradise Estate where Khalid's parents had their summer home.

The Land Rover's external temperature-gauge was reading

minus 15 Celsius, yet it was surprisingly warm in the sun. Laura and André stretched their legs while a friendly Iraqi customs officer inspected their passports and stamped them with visitors' visas. Lloyd was glad of the chance to rest his arms – the Land Rover wasn't supplied with power-steering. The Iraqi seemed reluctant to provide change for a $20 bill and Lloyd didn't press the matter. The officer pointed to the big oil patches left by the tankers and advised the travellers in sign-language to take care.

'God – that air bites when you breathe it in, and yet it's hot in the sun,' Laura complained when she and André climbed back aboard the Land Rover.

'Kurdistan!' said André, bouncing excitedly on the back seat. 'We're in Kurdistan!'

Laura turned and smiled at her daughter. 'Happy, darling?'

André nodded vigorously. 'See Khalid soon.'

'Don't go building up your hopes too soon, young lady,' Lloyd warned as they moved off. 'We've not been able to get through on the phone.'

But nothing could dampen the girl's excitement. 'He's here. Very close. How long now, Mother?'

She's back to using 'Mother' again, Laura thought as she consulted the map. 'About thirty miles in a straight line. Say, fifty miles because the road winds all over the place.'

After twenty kilometres the winding road, threading its way between precipitous slopes of frost-loosened shale, began losing height. Occasionally the oil on the road caused the Land Rover tyres to skitter, but the downward gradient was gentle so the slicks were not a problem. The sun got hotter; the temperature-gauge crept past zero and climbed to ten. The scenery was unimaginably depressing: grey, boulder-strewn slopes on both sides of the vehicle, and not a trace of vegetation to relieve the impression that they were driving through an unending Welsh slate quarry.

They rounded a bend, and the vista that opened before them exploded on their senses like a bomb.

As a girl, Laura had been taken to see *The Secret Garden*. The film had been shot in black-and-white until the scene in which a drab door in a drab wall was opened. At the precise moment that the glory of the garden was revealed, the movie changed to colour. The tremendous impact of that moment was repeated now.

'Stop!' Laura cried. 'Oh do please stop, Lloyd.'

But Lloyd was stopping anyway. The three got out of the Land Rover and feasted their eyes on the glorious view.

'Beautiful . . . Beautiful,' André whispered.

Indeed it was. Spread before them in the brilliant sunlight was a view that seemed to go on for ever. Two thousand metres below were fruit orchards whose blossom seemed to lie along the wooded valleys like gentle clouds of coloured incense. Pomegranates; plums; damsons; peaches; apricots; cherries – all contributing to a riot of pastel shades that bewitched the eye with their variety. Immediately below was a cascade of terraced fields that had first been laid out seven thousand years ago when man first turned from being a hunter-gatherer. Dotted among the fields were the humped outlines of hundreds of tells – many unexcavated even to this day – which concealed the tranquil remains of man's first attempts to build civilised communities and to construct tombs that would deny his mortality. From this height it was possible to see the faint drainage lines of the ancient, long-vanished roads that had linked the great tells. It was a landscape older than written history. To their right was the silver ribbon of the Tigris, now parted from its sister, the Euphrates. The river was swollen with the melted water from the snow-covered mountains of Central Anatolia, bringing down with it nutrients and fertile loess in quantities that had ensured a superabundance of food for generations. Above them was the azure bowl of the sky, marred only by a few threads of cirrus.

'Dear God, this is magnificent,' Laura breathed. She pulled up the hood of her anorak so that Lloyd wouldn't see her tears. She felt André's fingers steal into her hand and grip her tightly.

Yes – in your way you're thinking the same as me, aren't you darling? You're thinking how tragic that such a lovely land, so rich in all the minerals of the earth, should be torn apart by hatred and war.

Laura's finger trembled as she pointed. 'Somewhere down there was the Garden of Eden.'

Lloyd was surprised. 'I didn't know that,' he admitted. 'My education was weak on mythology.'

Look at it, man! Where else could it have been?

A warning hoot from a tanker toiling past towards Turkey shook Laura from her reverie. She rescued the map from the Land Rover's door-pocket and aligned it with the Tigris. 'Look,' she pointed. 'You see where that river widens? That could be their lake . . . Yes – it must be – it's in the right direction. That big town is Duhok and the little town must be . . .' She checked the map. '. . . Sammel! That's where Sajii does her shopping.'

Thunder rolled up from the distant tree-clad foothills.

'Not me,' said André indignantly when they both looked at her.

'Must be a storm brewing somewhere,' said Lloyd unconvincingly. There wasn't a thunder-cloud to be seen.

The rolling echoes tumbled across the glorious landscape again. White smoke rose on the convection currents of the sun-warmed air from the direction of the little town.

'Come on,' said Laura hurriedly, herding them back to the Land Rover. 'We'll be there in an hour.' She caught Lloyd's eye when they were settled in their seats. 'It wasn't thunder, was it?'

He shook his head. 'No.'

' "To make famine when abundance lies on the land." '

'Pardon?'

'Your education didn't stretch to Shakespeare's sonnets either?'

'No,' said Lloyd, starting the engine. He had expected her to be frightened, instead she seemed angry.

The noise they had heard was guns. Big guns.

121

There was no warning.

The 155-millimetre Howitzer shell screamed down into Sammel's crowded market-place and exploded, scattering hundreds of steel splinters in all directions. The circle of bloody carnage raced outwards from the point of impact like a stone lobbed into the centre of a pond. Traders, women clutching bulging plastic carriers, excited children with new toys, mules – all were cut down. One second a peaceful little town going about its centuries-old business; the next a heaving, screaming, crimson pizza of death and mutilation in the centre of its outdoor market.

Khalid was saved by the last sack of potatoes he was unloading from the Cherokee for the old farmer. The impact of the splinter smashing into the sack on his back knocked him flat. Even before the first great wail went up, a second shell tore into one of the small, modern office blocks that lined the square. The building heaved and burst from the inside, bringing down tombstone slabs of reinforced concrete on neighbouring shops. A third mighty concussion hurled Khalid's head against the Cherokee's front wheel as he was staggering to his feet.

His senses reeled. More shells howled into the town centre. Buildings were collapsing all around. Between the mighty, death-dealing, ground-heaving crumps came the terrible, agonised screams of the maimed. The headless body of the old farmer fell across him. His second attempt to climb to his feet ended with his boots skating wildly on the ancient cobbles that were now slippery with blood and gore. He lashed out blindly and his fingers encountered the Cherokee's steering-wheel. It was something he understood in a world that was falling apart around him. In a blind panic he hauled himself into the driver's seat, and wiped the farmer's blood from his eyes. Despite still being disorientated by the blow on the head, he managed to start the pick-up's engine.

The holocaust he could see through the windscreen – the wails of the survivors, the bloody bundles of rags scattered among the spilled fruit and vegetables, the collapsing buildings and the ground-shaking eruptions – was a disembodied horror movie that was being played out on the other side of the Cherokee's tinted glass. He crashed the shift into bottom gear and threw the pick-up through the carnage. At times the wheels

426

spun impotently on the blood-slick, picking up a coating of red, and then bit on the cobbles and pitched forward again.

A filling-station took a direct hit. The shell exploded in the underground storage tank, and the resulting molten fireball added to the hideous carnage. The windows of a large florist's were blown out, bringing down a bizarre rain of flowers on the dead and dying. A corner of Khalid's reason retained sufficient grip in the turmoil of his senses to hammer the pick-up through the flames. He crashed into a Fiat Panda, but the Cherokee's bull-bars spun the vehicle to one side. He careered on, unconsciously applying remarkable driving skills but not caring where he was going as long as he was moving. A hill slowed his mad flight; there was a blur of yellow on his left. Several shots from behind smacked into the back of the cab and punched through the laminated windscreen. One even passed through the back of the passenger seat and shattered the speedometer. He was now partially blinded by tears.

Suddenly the explosions unaccountably stopped and there was no more firing. He pulled off the road, wrenching the wheel hard so that the unladen pick-up slewed round in the dusty lay-by. A tree loomed before him. He braked, and the force of the bull-bars colliding with the trunk pitched him over the steering-wheel. He stayed slumped like that for some seconds, sobbing uncontrollably, tears streaming down his cheeks and onto his trousers which were already wet with urine.

'Should have stayed close, Nuri!' he cried, beating the wheel with a clenched fist. 'Should have stayed close!'

His plaintive, despairing sobs were answered by the twittering of birds in the trees. Minutes passed before he was able to lift his tear-streaked face and take stock of his surroundings. The sun beat down on the cab roof. He fumbled for the window-winder and cranked it open. As his head cleared, he realised that he knew this road: perhaps some kind of automatic pilot had taken over during his mad dash. Either that, or incredibly good luck, had steered him out of the stricken town on the road that led to his parents' summer home.

From here he could look down on most of the little town. A pall of black smoke rose from its centre, and he heard the distant wailing of ambulances. The yellow blur he had seen was a column of giant International bulldozers and JCBs moving purposefully down the hill into the town like a giant caterpillar.

As he watched, the lead bulldozer suddenly swung to one side and tore its blade through the front walls of a row of houses. A JCB followed into the swirling dust-cloud, its giant, bulbous tyres crunching over the rubble, its raised bucket smashing through any walls the bulldozer had left standing; furniture, beds, televisions – all were crushed beneath its ponderous weight. Now the other machines formed a line like a formation dance team. Smoke plumed from their exhausts as the drivers revved hard. Then they plunged their collective bulk straight through the prefabricated buildings of a small industrial zone. The flimsy sheet-sections of pressed aluminium folded and jostled like houses of cards before crumpling beneath the relentless tracks of the massive Internationals. There were screams; people running into the street, pleading with the drivers, some standing defiantly in front of the advancing iron behemoths, waving their arms, clasped hands raised imploringly to heaven. All to no avail: those that didn't jump clear were crushed to smears under the steel tracks.

The line-abreast squadron of bright-yellow juggernauts disappeared into the dust, but the sounds of their handiwork continued to reach Khalid. The reason why he and Nuri had seen so many earth-moving and road-building machines being moved north was now hideously clear: bulldozers and JCBs could flatten towns and villages more effectively and much more cheaply than bombs and shells.

Khalid closed his eyes in remorse. If he hadn't panicked perhaps he could have used his luck to save the little town. But before, he had always been with friends and comrades; somehow, friendly company always made it easy to focus his mind. Now he was alone. But not for long. He cheered up when he remembered how close his parents were now. He started the Cherokee's engine and backed away from the tree. There was an angry hissing, and a thin jet of steam clouded from the radiator where something had punctured its core. But it didn't matter.

He was nearly home now.

122

Max parked his rented BMW in the bungalow's drive and got out. He avoided looking at the car; it was bright red, a colour he detested, but there had been little else available in Baghdad. The bungalow's front door was open. He entered, carrying his Adidas bag, and walked through a generously proportioned hall into the living-room. He admired the al Karnis' good taste. It was a fine house, marble-floored throughout, all in white, with windows sensibly arranged to take full advantage of the view across the lake. The furniture, in fine, silvery-cream damask, looked invitingly soft. He gazed pensively at a colour picture of Khalid hanging on the wall. The photographer had used top lighting to highlight the youngster's fair hair. Once André was captured, it would be a good idea to have the country scoured for him in case he had survived the debacle in Kuwait. To have two manipulative savants in his possession . . .

He checked that the power was definitely off by flipping a light-switch. He didn't trust Iraqi planning.

The smell of cooking drew him to the Miele fitted kitchen. A breakfast-bar table was laid for two. There was a combination gas-and-halogen hob set into the worktop. Having checked to ensure that the gas had also been cut off, Max pulled down the oven door and contemplated the roast shoulder of lamb surrounded by baked potatoes, swedes and parsnips. How very English. Still hot, too. Another twenty minutes and it would be ruined; a pity to let it go to waste.

He found a carving-knife, cut himself a generous portion of meat and added some vegetables to one of the Indian Tree dinner plates. There was a passable claret on the wine rack, but he opted for a ready-chilled bottle of Graves in the cold cabinet. He took his trophies onto the terrace, because it was now pleasantly warm in the sheltered valley, and settled down to eat with his usual fastidiousness. Silver cutlery and a crisp, white napkin. There was no hurry; the little Icom transceiver clipped in his breast pocket would warn him when the white Land Rover turned into the estate. He kept his Adidas bag close to hand. Inside was a miniature emergency breathing apparatus with an overcharged compressed-air bottle that would give him a ten-minute supply. Also in the bag was a Smith and Wesson revolver.

He wondered if it would be necessary to kill the mother and her companion and decided that, regrettably, it would be. A small worry was the method of delivering the gas. He wasn't happy with the helicopter idea but he had been unable to come up with an alternative in the available time. Also, the brigadier had every confidence in the pilot's ability to drop the canister accurately from a considerable height. Of course, accuracy was easy to achieve when dropping objects from a stationary point; there was no need for the complicated calculations involving ballistic trajectories that were necessary when releasing bombs from fast-moving aircraft. Wind was a factor, but it was a still day – the stabilising fins would ensure that the heavy canister plummeted straight down even if it were dropped from a height of six thousand feet. He made a mental note to re-impress Brigadier Tulfah with the need to fly high. He looked up at the cloudless sky and unfastened the top buttons on his smart pilot's shirt. A fine haze was forming across the tranquil lake. It was unseasonably hot, but then late March in England could produce unexpected spells of fine weather too.

The lamb was excellent.

123

Lloyd slid the Land Rover's side-window open a little more to increase the draught blowing through the car.

'Damned hot,' he muttered. 'Strange after half freezing to death a couple of hours ago.'

'We've come down well over two thousand metres,' said Laura, studying the map. 'Do you realise that those mountains we came over are around fifteen thousand feet high?'

'Half the height of Everest,' Lloyd commented. 'Two and a half miles. Christ – no wonder it was cold up there.'

They sped on, past ancient field-systems that were under intensive strip cultivation. Figures bent over their crops ignored the speeding Land Rover.

'How much more, Mother?'

Laura looked at the map. 'Six kilometres. We're nearly there.'

The Cherokee's waterless, over-heating engine finally seized when Khalid was a kilometre from the turning into the estate. He steered the pick-up off the dusty road and tried to restart the engine, but the starter solenoid emitted loud, protesting clicks when he turned the ignition key. After trying to push the vehicle in a futile attempt to free pistons welded into their cylinders, he realised how hot and uncomfortable he was from having wet himself at Sammel. He took off his outer clothes down to his trousers and shirt, and started walking. The soaked trousers chaffed, but they would soon dry in this heat. He quickened his pace when he realised how close to home he was. By the time he reached the turning, he was sweating profusely but he was too excited to notice. When he saw the distant cluster of bungalows across the bend in the lake, he gave a little cry of joy and broke into a jog.

Max wiped his lips on the spotless white napkin. An excellent repast; a pity there had been no mint sauce, but one couldn't have everything. A burst of selective calling tones opened the squelch on the Icom. He lifted the transceiver's miniature speaker-microphone to his lips and identified himself.

'A young man has turned onto the approach-road,' said Brigadier Tulfah, remembering to speak Arabic slowly.

Max took a sip of wine, thinking fast. 'A gardener, do you suppose?'

'Possible. He's on foot so it's likely he's from a local farm. They use a lot of casual labour to keep their gardens pretty.'

'I'll deal with him if it's necessary,' Max replied. 'Where's the Land Rover now?'

'Can't see the road from this point, but it can't be far. Don't worry, my friend – we're all ready here.'

Max could hear a turbine running to half power in the background, and was satisfied.

Khalid stopped walking and stared at the burnt-out Mercedes in the field. There was something horribly familiar about it that chilled his carefree mood. He walked slowly towards the wreckage and realised that the heat emanating from it couldn't be due to the effect of the sun. Also, he knew that all vehicles that had had their paint burnt off acquired a thin film of rust after exposure to even one night's dew.

His heart-beat quickened. He was now five metres from the car and the warmth on his face was very strong. Even the ground underfoot had absorbed the heat from the car and was re-radiating it. Everything was strangely still and silent, although the branches of the pomegranate trees above the line of the car's roof were twisting and dancing in the heat-distorted air like the waving arms of tormented spirits.

The car was sitting in a pool of heat and overpowering smells: burnt acrylic, PVC, leather, and oil. There was another smell that he knew from the horrors of that hellish flight from Kuwait: the sweet smell of burnt human flesh. At that moment he realised what it was that was familiar about the car. Not everything had been consumed in the fire. The Arabic and Roman characters on the front registration plate had partly melted but were still legible.

It was his father's car.

And when he crept nearer and saw the tangled mass of half-incinerated arms and legs inside the car, he knew the terrible truth.

'The Land Rover has just turned onto the estate road,' said Brigadier Tulfah's voice, sounding thin and reedy in the Icom's speaker-mic. 'The chopper pilot is standing by to take off.'

'Excellent,' said Max. 'Don't forget – it is imperative that he flies as high as possible.'

'I have instructed him to go straight up before he begins his approach,' the brigadier promised.

'Excellent,' Max replied. 'Tell him to step on the gas when I give the word.'

The Iraqi officer laughed. He liked the Englishman's jokes.

Max slipped the microphone back into his shirt pocket. He unzipped the Adidas bag, and the Smith and Wesson went into his jacket pocket. He draped the breathing-set around his neck. His movements were calm and methodical; his thinking, as always, clear and logical. The was no point in pulling the mask over his face and wasting compressed air until the last minute. He sipped another glass of wine and glanced across the lake. The layer of haze lying across the water was steadily thickening, and there wasn't even a hint of a breeze.

It was turning into an extraordinarily hot day.

'Lloyd! Stop! There's Khalid!'

Lloyd stamped on the brakes as André cried out, but she threw herself out of the Land Rover before it stopped. She should have gone tumbling head-over-heels in the dust, but she miraculously recovered her balance and dashed across the field to the fair-haired young man crouching by the wrecked Mercedes.

'Khalid! Khalid!'

The young man stood, his expression one of utter bewilderment. Before he had time to comprehend what was happening, André missiled into his arms, nearly knocking him over.

'Oh, Khalid,' André cried, tears streaming freely down her cheeks. 'It's me! It's me! Everything all right now.'

Laura started out across the field towards the joyously embracing couple, but Lloyd raced after her and grabbed her arm.

'Leave them,' he said quietly.

'But – '

'No – leave them.' He was very firm, his grip on her wrist determinedly tight as he steered her back to the Land Rover.

Kneeling facing each, Khalid and André smothered each other with frantic kisses, oblivious of the bubble of heat they were in, with the gutted Mercedes at its centre.

*

Max's customary cool was so close to shattering that he forgot to speak in Arabic. 'Where the hell are they?' he demanded into the Icom.

'We don't have a good sight-line from here,' said the Iraqi officer, guessing what Max had said. 'But they definitely turned into the estate road. The helicopter has just taken off.'

'Tell the pilot to hold back! Remember – get all the height he can. It's no good dropping the gas unless we can be sure of knocking the girl out quickly!'

'Perhaps they stopped to talk to the youth?'

'Did he look like a Kurd?' Max demanded.

'I think so – yes. He had fair hair. He could only be a Kurd.'

'Fair hair!' Max's brain raced. As always, he was quick to turn setbacks to his advantage. 'That could be the other one! We could get two!'

'I don't understand,' said Brigadier Tulfah.

But Max had stuffed the microphone back into his breast pocket and was racing out to the BMW.

Lloyd reversed the Land Rover fifty metres along the road in the direction they had come. He backed off the road so that André and Khalid were obscured by a thorn bush; the verge was soft, as though it had been recently dug and filled in. The couple by the wrecked car were too wrapped up in each other to notice that the car had moved.

'Why did you do that?' Laura demanded.

'A bit of shade here. It's getting bloody hot.'

Laura's hand moved to her door-catch but Lloyd leaned across and stopped her. 'Let them have a little privacy for a few minutes.'

'Oh, for goodness' sake,' she retorted. 'They've known each other since they were kids. They're very fond of each other – like brother and sister.'

Lloyd ran his fingers through his hair. It *was* getting hot. 'Sometimes, Laura, I think you're blind as well as stupid. Or is it that you can't face up to the truth? There's everything between them. Look at the way they kissed; and look at the state André was in until you promised to bring her here. She's never without his photograph. It's obvious that she's in love with the boy.'

Laura made no reply.

'When were Khalid and his parents thrown out of the UK? Around the first week in January?'

'About then.'

'And Khalid and André were alone together?'

That hurt. Her eyes opened wide. 'Just what the hell are you insinuat – '

'*Listen!*' Lloyd broke in, holding up his hand.

'It sounds like a car coming.'

'And there's something else!'

They both heard the helicopter approaching.

Max heard the helicopter as he accelerated along the approach road. He snatched up the speaker-mic. 'Tulfah! You idiot! Your pilot's too low!'

'He's at the maximum service ceiling of seven thousand feet,' the officer protested.

'Don't give me that! I can hear him! Tell him he needs another three thousand feet. Order him to climb!'

'You are forgetting the height of this land above sea-level,' Brigadier Tulfah retorted. He was getting tired of having to accept orders from this Englishman. 'We are already at over five thousand feet at ground level. He cannot go any higher!'

Max swore to himself. He had made a serious tactical error. No, worse. To have forgotten something as fundamental as their height above sea-level was more than an error – it was a monumental blunder. But, as always, his mind was racing ahead on a damage-limitation plan.

He stamped on the BMW's brakes the moment he saw Khalid and André by the gutted Mercedes.

'Change of plans!' he yelled into the Icom's speaker-mic. 'Tell the pilot to drop the canister near the wrecked car in the field on the approach-road!'

'He can hear you,' Brigadier Tulfah replied. 'He's patched through. Yes! He reports that he can see them!'

Max pulled on the miniature breathing-set and twisted the lever that supplied compressed air to the demand valve.

'It's too high to worry us,' said Lloyd. He was leaning out of the Land Rover door, craning his head back and shading his eyes to see the helicopter that was now nearly overhead. 'It's a French Alouette.'

Laura pointed at the bright-red BMW. 'Lloyd! That man's wearing a gas-mask!'

Max was over fifty metres away. He had stopped the car and jumped out.

'Canister released,' the brigadier announced.

Unlike André, Khalid was wise in the ways of helicopters. He pushed himself away from the girl's demanding embrace and looked up in time to glimpse the Alouette before André pulled him close again. At least it wasn't a big military machine. But although it was high, it was losing speed, and that frightened him.

'No, Andy!' he said hoarsely, returning her frantic kisses. 'That helicopter is stopping.' This time he thrust her firmly away and looked up. A cry escaped his lips when he saw the canister arrowing down out of the clear sky. In another millisecond he would have destroyed it, but he was too late. André hadn't seen the falling canister; she thought that Khalid's cry of horror was directed at the helicopter.

'Christ!' Lloyd yelled. 'It's dropped a bloody bomb!' He was out of the Land Rover and running towards André and Khalid before Laura could react.

The nine hundred kilos of aluminium, steel and plastic that made up the Alouette, and the blood and tissue of its pilot, ceased to exist in the earth's atmosphere. Its departure created a tunnel in the atmosphere in the same way a lightning-flash does, and as with a lightning-flash, air hurtled in to fill the vacuum. The colliding molecules smashed into each other with the force of a head-on collision between two express trains, and unleashed an expanding sphere of sound to equal that of an erupting volcano bursting through its cap.

André gave a scream of terror and sank to her knees, certain that the retribution following her act would be swift and dreadful.

The mighty, shattering crash of thunder, and André's scream, caused Khalid to lose concentration at the vital moment when the canister crashed down ten metres from his parents' wrecked car.

Max was nearly on top of the couple when the great pall of gas exploded into the air. As the mighty plume of cyclopropane erupted from the canister, its rapid expansion caused it to cool. In so doing, it condensed the water in the atmosphere to vapour, rendering the gas visible as a vast cloud of white fog.

Lloyd threw himself flat at the moment of the explosion. When he looked up, he saw that he was about twenty metres from the spreading gas cloud. It seemed to possess a malignant life-force that caused it to twist and swirl in the still air as it continued expanding upwards and outwards, blocking the sun.

It was the heat that saved them: the ball of rising warm air from the ground and the residual heat from the gutted car prevented the gas reaching the ground. There was a layer of clear air between the field and the heat-flattened underside of the dense cloud.

'Andy!' Lloyd yelled, picking himself up and running doubled-up towards the couple. '*Don't stand up! Don't stand up!*'

But his shouted warning was too late. André jumped to her feet and her head disappeared into the gas. Two breaths were all it took. She crumpled, unconscious. A shot rang out, sounding curiously deadened beneath the fog. The sudden pain in Lloyd's left calf caused him to cry out, and he went down just as Max, looking like a grotesque monster in his breathing-set, came rushing through the fog. Holding the Smith and Wesson, he stooped over André and tried to lift her, but he realised he needed both hands free, and jammed the gun into his pocket.

It was timing rather than good sense that prevented Khalid from staggering to his feet. He saw that the masked figure was lifting André over his shoulder and launched himself at Max from a kneeling position. He fought with the demented savagery of blind rage: this stranger equipped with a breathing-set had killed his beloved André . . . The girl's body flopped to the ground as the ferocity of Khalid's attack brought Max down and his breathing-set mask was torn off. The two men fought and grappled, rolling away from the sanctuary of the wrecked car where the gas was at its highest above the ground.

As they struggled, Max's hand encountered a large stone. He managed to lift it, and bring it down on the back of Khalid's head. But as he rolled clear, he saw that his assailant was only stunned, and tried to yank his Smith and Wesson from his pocket. To pull it free of his clothing meant having to stand. There was a certain satisfaction in firing a single round accurately into the young man's head; the exit wound caused his mop of hair to fly apart. It was then that Max realised he wasn't wearing his mask. The gas had a butane taste as he unwittingly sucked it into his lungs, and he came as close to panicking as he had ever come in his life – but unconsciousness closed in with a terrible suddenness.

Lloyd crawled to where André was lying on her back. There wasn't time to check if she was breathing. All that mattered was to get her away from this hellish place as quickly as possible. He grabbed her under the armpits and dragged her backwards. Then he heard the engine, and rolled over to see what was happening. The Land Rover was bumping across the uneven ground towards them.

'KEEP BACK!'

Laura heeded the shouted warning and Lloyd's frantic gestures, and stopped. She had seen everything from the moment the canister exploded. The horror had been played out in less than a minute. When she saw André fall, her instinct had been to rush forward, but she had retained enough grip on her senses to realise that getting herself killed would help no one. The gas was now dispersing rapidly – spiralling upwards in swirling, thinning tendrils of fog that were eventually vanishing into the warm air.

Lloyd didn't look up but continued dragging the dead weight of André towards the Land Rover. He changed his technique to holding her by one wrist as he wriggled forward on his hips and knees like a soldier crawling under a barbed-wire entanglement. Crawl, drag, crawl, drag. It was a desperately

438

slow business, slowed further by his frequent admonishments to Laura not to come near. Eventually she could bear it no longer. She rushed forward, keeping her head low and stumbling over the uneven ground.

'I told you to stay back!' Lloyd snarled.

'The gas is going. Look. Is she . . ?' The dread word caught in her throat. 'Is she dead?'

'I don't know.'

'She's breathing!' Laura gathered her unconscious daughter into her arms and held her protectively to her breast. 'Andy, darling . . . It's all right now.' She pressed her forefinger on the girl's neck. 'Her pulse is normal and so's her breathing!'

Lloyd looked up. All the gas had disappeared. 'I think it was an anaesthetic gas.' He stood unsteadily, and grimaced at the pain as he put his weight on his left leg. Laura saw the blood that had soaked through his trousers. 'You must let me look at that.'

'There's no time. We've got to get away from here.' He looked across to where Max and Khalid lay on the ground. There was no need to go nearer to know that the fair-haired young man was dead.

They lifted André between them and laid her across the seat in the back of the Land Rover.

'You look after her,' Lloyd instructed, sliding behind the wheel. 'I'll drive.'

'Can you manage?'

'I wouldn't be able to stand if he'd hit the bone. I don't think it's serious.'

Once the Land Rover was off the estate road and they were heading back the way they had come, Lloyd found he could think more clearly. André's condition seemed reasonably stable, so Laura went along with Lloyd's suggestion that they get out of the country as fast as possible, rather than try to find a hospital. Having lost a helicopter, it seemed likely that the Iraqis would launch a massive search, but it would probably take an hour to organise.

Once the decision was taken, Lloyd pressed the throttle pedal to the floor.

*

Of all the anaesthetics, cyclopropane has the most unpleasant recovery symptoms – as Max discovered when he tried to stand. He climbed groggily to his feet, and promptly fell to his knees, doubled-up in pain and throwing up the contents of his stomach. Three times he got to his feet and three times he was reduced to gagging and retching. It was some minutes before he was able to think clearly enough to take stock of his surroundings.

There was no sign of the girl or the Land Rover. He looked at his watch and saw with considerable disquiet that he had been unconscious for fifteen minutes. *Damn!* They could be fifteen miles away by now. His hand went to his shirt pocket. Luckily the Icom was still clipped in place. He pulled it out and tried to focus his eyes on the absurd rubber buttons. He managed to pick out the selective-calling-tones button and pressed it with a trembling finger. Brigadier Tulfah's voice answered immediately, demanding to know what had happened.

'They got away,' Max replied.

'What was that thunder, and what happened to the helicopter?'

Max felt a wave of nausea coming on again. The world spun madly and his now empty stomach heaved in frustration at having nothing to get rid of. He sat down and cradled his head in his hands. It took a massive effort of will to make his voice sound normal.

'The helicopter crashed. Listen . . . They'll be heading for the frontier into Turkey – the way they came in. You've got to stop them.'

'We've no units up on that road. We've been told to stay away from the border. We don't want a Turkish incursion on our hands.'

In his present state Max found it difficult, having to think for the Iraqi officer. 'Okay – get in touch with the customs post.'

Brigadier Tulfah's patience was wearing thin. This Englishman had been nothing but trouble. 'I don't have jurisdiction over customs. I shall need to get permission from Mosul. It will take an hour, perhaps two.'

Max closed his eyes. 'The Super Frelons – get them to go after them.'

'They're on an operation in the west. I can recall them, but it will be an hour or more before they can get here.'

Max's iron control was wearing dangerously thin. 'Then get onto them now, brigadier,' he said mildly. 'And get them here as soon as possible, with cyclopropane canisters on board. In the meantime, rather than do nothing I shall go after the girl myself.'

He jammed the speaker-mic into his shirt pocket and somehow found the strength to run towards his car.

124

The steep slope up the winding mountain road forced Lloyd to drop into bottom gear, but he kept up the revs so that they continued to make 25 mph.

'You'll blow up the engine!' Laura yelled, to make herself heard above the roar of the straining engine.

Lloyd backed the power off so that the rev-counter needle wasn't touching into the red. 'Got to keep the speed up!' he called over his shoulder. 'We don't stand a chance if he comes after us in that BMW!'

'She's coming to!' said Laura excitedly. 'Darling, it's all right. Mummy's got you. You're safe.'

A huge, unmarked tanker, belching thick black diesel fumes, appeared ahead of them when Lloyd rounded a bend. The rear of the massive oval tank, and the inspection ladder, were caked in black soot; only the row of handwheel valves on the bunkering manifold were reasonably clean – probably because they had to be used each time the tanker unloaded. Down both sides of the chassis were additional tanks. The driver was nursing his monstrous charge up the steep gradient using his crawler gear. There was no chance of overtaking on the narrow road, even though the giant vehicle was progressing at walking-pace. Lloyd closed up behind the tanker, leaning out of the window, looking vainly for an overtaking opportunity. He acceded to Laura's pleas to drop back as the stinking fumes invaded the Land Rover.

After ten minutes, all the hatred Lloyd was capable of mustering was directed at the tanker, although he realised that on this particular stretch the driver had little choice but to keep going. If he stalled or stopped, the chances that he would be able to get his grossly overloaded vehicle going again were nil.

The road widened slightly. Lloyd was about to grab the chance to squeeze by when he was distracted by the sound of André vomiting.

'Don't worry about us!' Laura snapped. 'Just concentrate on your driving!'

The cutting they were driving through suddenly opened out on Lloyd's side of the road to reveal an intimidating, unguarded drop. A thousand feet below he could see the snaking ribbon of the road they were on, where the many hairpin bends caused it to double back on itself. A red car was racing effortlessly up the steep slope, blue smoke spurting from its wheels as it took the bends at speed.

It was the BMW.

'Laura! He's behind us! About three or four miles back!'

He saw Laura's white face in the driving-mirror. 'Will he catch us?'

'There's no way that he won't catch us. *And* the bastard's got a gun.' He wanted to bang the steering-wheel in frustration. 'How about getting Andy to deal with him?'

'She's passed out again. We've got to get her to a hospital, Lloyd.'

'For Chrissake, woman, we'll all need a bloody hospital if that bastard catches up with us!'

The road levelled out and widened. The note of the tanker's tortured engine changed as the driver shifted up.

'I've got an idea!' Lloyd yelled. He pulled out and managed to force the tanker to give way by using his lights and horn. As he overtook the vehicle he realised how long it was and why the driver had been so reluctant to pull over when climbing. He drove two hundred metres beyond the tanker and stopped the Land Rover in a passing place that had been dynamited out of the rock face. He jumped out and limped into the road, cursing the pain in his calf and waving frantically at the tanker driver.

The giant vehicle ground to a standstill amid explosive hisses from its compressed-air brakes. The engine note dropped to a clattering tick-over from poorly adjusted tappets. A bemused, bearded face looked down at him, taking in his blood-stained trouser-leg, and spoke in rapid Turkish.

'I don't understand,' Lloyd answered. 'Do you speak English?'

The driver operated all over Eastern Europe and knew enough of several languages to negotiate fees and loads. 'A little just.'

'Our vehicle is giving trouble. Will you take my wife and daughter into Turkey in case I break down? We'll pay you.'

The driver was a hardened negotiator. The way the stranger kept glancing anxiously back along the road told him that these people were in trouble. What sort of trouble was of no interest to him, but they looked as if they had money, and that was very interesting. 'Extra people on board make me use more fuel,' he commented.

At any other time Lloyd would have viewed that as a statement bordering on the priceless, considering that half the fuel used by the tanker was being expelled, unburnt, from the exhaust. 'We can give you a hundred US dollars. American dollars – do you understand?'

'One hundred and fifty dollar I understand very well.'

'Done.' With that, Lloyd raced back to the Land Rover and quickly explained his plan to Laura. They supported the barely conscious André between them and carried her to the waiting tanker. The driver helped them lift the girl onto the bunk in the living area at the rear of his cab.

'My daughter is very travel-sick,' Lloyd explained, handing over three fifty-dollar bills to the driver.

The driver understood. He grinned amiably and pocketed the money. Laura returned to the Land Rover to collect her handbag and their valuables, then hurried back and accepted the driver's offered hand up into the cab. She slammed the door shut and looked worriedly down at Lloyd. 'I'll make him take it easy,' she promised.

Lloyd gestured ahead to the mountains they had yet to climb. 'I'll need ten minutes – if that. Okay – tell him to get going.'

Laura spoke to the driver and the tanker moved off, gears grinding and spewing black smoke in Lloyd's face. He crossed to the parapet and looked down. From here he had a splendid view of the road. He caught a flash of late afternoon sunlight heliographing on a windscreen. He shaded his eyes: it was the bright-red BMW about a mile back. He scrambled behind the wheel of the Land Rover, started the engine and set off at a moderate speed in the direction of the tanker. Two minutes later the BMW appeared in his mirror.

Despite the appalling headache he was suffering from as an after-effect of inhaling the gas, Max experienced a surge of elation when he saw the Land Rover. The blinding pain behind his eyes made rational thought difficult but not impossible; in his usual calculating manner he weighed up the chances of the girl being conscious. Even if she was awake, it was likely that she was still very sick and therefore unable to use her remarkable powers against him.

It was difficult to see the occupants of the Land Rover at this distance. He accelerated gently to close the gap. As his quarry rounded a bend, the low sun caught the Land Rover at the right angle. The only occupant appeared to be the man. That meant that the girl was probably lying down. He wondered where the mother was, and considered it likely that she was down beside her daughter.

He lowered the window. The hot air sucked the coolness from the BMW's interior. No – not here, he told himself, and raised the window again. The unguarded road was too dangerous. The last thing he wanted was to take out a tyre and send the Land Rover over the edge.

He jammed the Smith and Wesson barrel-first between the seat and the centre console, where he would be able to get at it in a hurry. When the opportunity arose, of course.

Lloyd drove on at a steady speed, not wishing to catch up with the tanker. It was about eight hundred metres ahead and kept coming into sight on the few straights. He was puzzled as to why the BMW didn't make a move.

He rounded a bend and came to a long, straight stretch of potholed, frost-damaged road that hugged the side of a valley

444

he remembered from the outward journey. The road-builders had made roughly-dressed rectangular blocks out of boulders dynamited from passing-points, and used them to provide a crude but intimidating crash-barrier along the edge of the road. He caught a glimpse of the tanker some way ahead, slogging up the long incline and virtually obscured by its cloud of exhaust smoke. He prayed that Laura and the girl would be safe if his plan failed.

Ideal, thought Max, and accelerated very gently to close the gap. The straight stretch of road extended for a long way – there was no hurry.

The deteriorating road surface caused the steering-wheel to buck and wrench in Lloyd's hands. The massive blocks lining the edge of the road seemed to be closing in. He remembered commenting to Laura that, although the passing-points were at frequent intervals, it was not the sort of road he fancied reversing along for any distance if they met an oncoming truck. He glanced in the mirror. The BMW was following about four hundred metres back. He looked carefully, and realised that it was gradually gaining on him. His mind dropped into a higher gear than the one the Land Rover was in. There was one particularly large block about two hundred metres ahead that had been struck at some time by a heavy vehicle, with the result that it was out of line and intruding slightly on the road space. Also it was on a slight bend where the BMW was likely to be unsighted for a few seconds.

It was now or never.

Once the decision was taken, Lloyd cleared his mind. Timing was of the essence for the plan to work. First, release the door-catch; second slip the shift into neutral; third steer the Land Rover towards the protruding block.

His timing wasn't perfect, but it was good enough. The moment the incline brought the Land Rover to a stop, he pitched himself onto the road, managed to kick the door shut with his good leg, and hauled himself behind the block. By the time he twisted his body around and peered out from his hiding-place, the Land Rover was rolling backwards and picking up momentum. It veered, grated on a boulder, and was deflected back into the centre of the narrow road.

Max's blinding headache slowed his reactions by a crucial second. His first thought when he saw the Land Rover hurtling towards him was that the driver was reversing. By the time he realised that the vehicle was driverless and careering out of control and therefore gathering a formidable speed, it was less than two hundred metres away and being thrown from side to side – first against the rock face and then against the blocks. The glancing blows smashed windows and caused loud screechings of metal on rock, but the minor impacts had no effect on the charging Land Rover's acceleration.

Max slammed the shift into reverse. The engine roared, the rear tyres smoked and the BMW shot backwards. Twisting around in his seat to look through the rear windscreen caused his headache to become a thousand neural lances driving into his brain. The passing-place was eighty metres back . . .

Sixty metres . . .

Fifty metres . . .

He dared not take his eyes off the road through the rear windscreen for an instant. His ears told him that the Land Rover was gaining on him as it was hurled from side to side like a giant metal shuttlecock.

Ten metres. He stood on the brake pedal and hooked the steering wheel. The BMW's remarkable ABS braking system worked extremely well in reverse; the wheels did not lock, with the result that, more by luck than judgement, Max was able to steer the rear of the car into the lay-by. Unfortunately for him, the manoeuvre resulted in the car's front end swinging out.

The Land Rover smashed into the BMW's wing, spinning the car through 180 degrees and cannoning the other wing into the rock face. The impact distorted the body-shell, causing the windscreen to flip away like a tiddlywink. The driver's door slammed sickeningly into a protruding rock with such force that it seemed a miracle to Max that it didn't punch right through the door's inner and outer skins and smash into his body.

The Land Rover reached the beginning of the straight stretch and sailed gracefully over the edge. It followed a ballistic curve, and vanished.

125

'Please!' Laura implored the tanker driver. 'You must stop!'

'I stop on this and I never go,' the driver protested. 'I stop now and I bugger clutch making her go again! Five kilometre road goes downhill. Plenty of valleys near frontier. I stop then. Ami promise. Ami always keep his word.' He pointed to a row of Polaroid photographs of children taped to the windscreen. 'I swear on the lives of my six children. Okay?'

'Okay,' Laura agreed worriedly, and turned her attention back to André, who was on the point of being sick again.

Lloyd hobbled out from behind the block and looked back along the road with some elation. The trick had worked: there was no sign of the Land Rover or the BMW. But the mounting pain in his left leg did not permit his pleasure to last. He looked down in dismay at the red wetness soaking into his trouser-leg and realised that the wound had started bleeding again.

He lifted his foot onto a rock and, after some effort, managed to rip his trouser-leg along the outer seam. At first sight the mass of blood made the wound look worse than it actually was. The fresh bleeding washed away the coagulated blood, which he wiped clear to reveal an ugly but superficial gash at the back of his calf. The leg could take his weight, albeit painfully, so he assumed that the muscle was not damaged. He fashioned a crude bandage from his pocket lining, which he bound around the wound to staunch the bleeding.

There was no sign of the tanker. Praying that Laura had persuaded the driver to stop, he started walking.

The silence that followed the crash came close to unnerving Max. His door was wedged against the lay-by's rock face. He scrambled out of the passenger door and ran a little way down

447

the road, to put solid rock between him and the BMW in case it caught fire. Two minutes passed, and nothing happened.

He moved cautiously forward and studied the car. It was in a sorry state. The nearside wing had been torn virtually off and had ripped into the tyre, and the side against the rock was stoved in. But most important of all, there was no sign of oil or petrol leaking on to the road, nor was there a smell of petrol. Max had always admired BMW engineering – it matched his craving for perfection – but on this occasion it had saved his life and had kept him in the race. There was a down side, though: even in a mangled state, the bodywork was astonishingly strong. It took him a sweated thirty minutes' methodical use of the jack as a crowbar, with the low sun beating directly into the lay-by, to prise the wing away from the wheel arch.

Disappointment came when he removed the wheel and its shredded tyre. The stub shaft that carried the front wheel and the front disk brake calipers was loose, and the front wheel-bearing was broken. By the time he had bolted the spare wheel in place, his shirt was soaked through and clinging uncomfortably to his back.

After a final inspection, he drove the car gingerly onto the road. The front wheel-bearing gave off loud clonks which were transmitted to the steering-wheel, but the brakes worked – although the car tended to shake alarmingly if he applied too much pressure. After what had happened, it was a miracle that the BMW was capable of moving. He wondered how many other cars could have survived a major impact with the tank-like Land Rover.

He increased speed to a cautious 20 kph. The noise from the front wheel smoothed out slightly at the higher speed. Sunglasses solved the problem of the non-existent windscreen. He accelerated very cautiously to 30 kph. Everything seemed to hold together. His guess was that the mother and daughter had hitched a lift on the tanker he had seen in front of them.

He passed a sign painted on a rock that said Turkey was forty kilometres. Only twenty-five miles. He would have to get a move on. The slipstream played on his face as he nursed a little more speed out of the crippled BMW. He chuckled to himself:

the lack of windscreen would make it easy to use the Smith and Wesson.

Laura shivered. The sun had dipped below the jagged peaks of the Cilo Mountains. Ami glanced at her and at André on his bunk berth. He tapped an altimeter that was held in place on the vibrating dashboard by a rubber sucker. 'Three thousand metre. Cold out of the sun. Blankets under the bed. You give one to little one.'

She thanked him, and wrapped the least smelly of the blankets around André. To her immense relief, and despite the sustained roar from the diesel beneath the cab, after her last bout of vomiting André was now asleep and breathing normally. Laura leaned out of the window and looked back, searching vainly for Lloyd. The scenery was changing. They were now high above the vegetation-line and the tanker was grinding at less than walking-pace through a sombre, slate-grey valley. There seemed no end to the continuous uphill slog.

Ami shouted, and gestured to a roof hatch overhead. 'You see more up there.'

Laura reached up, unclipped the hatch and pushed it open. Ami glanced at her as she swung herself up by the grab-handles and wondered why it was that so many young European women looked half-starved. No meat on them.

Laura pushed herself half out of the hatch and looked back along the road. From the high vantage-point above the long Swiss-roll shape of the tank she saw Lloyd about three hundred metres back, trying to maintain a shambling jog in the middle of the road. She could see that he had torn away his trousers and tied a blood-stained bandage around his calf. Beyond him was something that prompted her to climb onto the cab roof and crawl onto the railed catwalk that ran the length of the tank. Kneeling on the swaying, vibrating catwalk, she tugged off her jacket and waved it frantically. Lloyd saw her, and managed to put on a spurt, but it was obvious as he staggered and tripped on potholes that he was approaching the point of collapse.

What Laura had seen was a brief glimpse of the setting sun

flashing on a red car about two miles further back. She dropped into the cab, opened the door before Ami could protest, and climbed down the boarding-steps. The low speed of the grinding tanker meant that it was only a matter of stepping down onto the road and standing clear while the huge bulk crawled past her. She ran back to Lloyd. Despite the increasing chill due to their altitude and the disappearance of the sun, his golden hair was sweat-plastered to his pain-contorted face.

'Come on, Lloyd,' she urged, putting an arm around his waist and propelling him forward. 'You're gaining on it.'

'Can't . . . Can't . . . You get him . . . slow down . . . stop?'

'He's scared that if he stops he won't be able to get started again. He's overloaded.'

Lloyd stopped and doubled-up, his breath wheezing and rasping, his chest heaving. Fresh blood was streaming down his leg. Laura wondered how much he had lost.

'You've got to keep going!' she pleaded. 'That red car is behind.'

'What!' he choked. 'But I knocked it off the road!'

He straightened and looked back. The BMW was a long way back, struggling up the incline, its nearside front wheel wobbling as though it was about to come off. But the stricken car was making better progress than the tanker.

Max saw the couple break into a hobbling run, and smiled grimly. He had guessed right – the girl was in the tanker. The BMW's front end was bucking and clattering, but he risked exposing the wrecked front suspension and wheel-bearing to another couple of kilometres per hour.

The sel-call tones on his radio bleeped. He had forgotten all about the thing. He pulled the speaker-mic out of his pocket and acknowledged the call.

'The two Super Frelons are in the area now,' said Brigadier Tulfah.

'Armed with gas?'

'Two canisters each. Where are you?'

Max told him. 'There's a tanker ahead of me which has the

girl on board. Tell the pilots that's their target. I'll be close behind to mark it.'

There was a long pause before the Iraqi officer came back. 'They'll be with you in twenty minutes.'

'Twenty minutes!' Max snarled. 'Do you realise how near the frontier we are?'

'I am sorry,' the Iraqi replied. 'I cannot make helicopters fly faster than their maximum speed.'

Max thrust the speaker-mic angrily back in his pocket. As always, it was useless having to rely on others. All his current problems were because he was surrounded by bunglers who never thought anything through. Now, as a result of their incompetence, he was on the roof of the world, chasing a tanker in a crippled car, and not sure how he was going to get his hands on the girl without danger to himself if she was conscious.

He pushed his foot a little harder on the throttle pedal. The protesting noises from the wheel-bearing got louder and the steering-wheel juddered. To wait for the helicopters would be foolish. Besides, the pilots would probably get lost. It was best to get nearer the tanker. He was confident that he would think of a way around the current problem. He always did.

126

Laura cried out as Lloyd failed to grasp her outstretched hand. He stumbled and fell. She jumped down from the cab's boarding-steps and dragged him clear of the advancing tyres. Another second and the tanker's huge wheels would have crushed him.

'Sorry, Laura,' he croaked as the great vehicle ground past them. 'Legs like rubber.'

She dragged him to his feet. By now he was so weak that he could hardly stand. 'The ladder!' she gasped, pointing at the tanker's rear while supporting his weight. 'We'll get you on that. If you slip, it won't matter.'

They staggered after the tanker. The black, unburnt fuel belching from the exhaust made them cough and choke, adding to their misery. Laura lunged for the lowest rung but it was slippery with soot and she lost her grip. She tried again and this time held on tightly, wrenching Lloyd's arm towards the ladder. She banged his palm against the rung.

'Grab!' she yelled.

Lloyd's fingers refused to close on the rung.

'Hold on, Lloyd! Hold on!'

He was on the point of fainting, his feet were flopping drunkenly along on the potholed tarmac as though they weren't part of him, but Laura's urging and the touch of the cold steel on his hand caused his fingers to close tightly on the rung like the unexpected grip of a newborn baby.

'Now the other hand!' Laura shouted. The smoke was making her eyes smart so that she could hardly see what she was doing. She was about to grab Lloyd's arm, but he just managed to bring it up and grasp the rung unaided. His feet trailed on the road, but luckily there was more strength in his arms than in his legs. With Laura's help, he was able to lift his feet clear of the road and drape his lifeless legs over the row of discharge valves.

Laura looked back and saw that the BMW was now less than a kilometre away. Even with a front wheel whipping about, it was only a matter of minutes before it caught up with them.

'Got to get you on top of the tank!' she shouted in Lloyd's ear. 'There's a sort of catwalk up there that you can hang onto. You'll be safe.'

She supported his weight while he shifted his right hand up one rung and brought the other hand up to join it.

'That's it . . . That's it . . .' she encouraged.

A few more rungs. She was able to stand on the valves and thrust her shoulder into his groin.

'Rest! There's no hurry.'

He took the advice and relaxed a little. Now that he was no longer having to run, he was thinking more clearly. He opened his eyes. Mercifully his head was now above the worst of the poisonous black smoke. He felt Laura's hands guiding his feet onto the lower rungs. A couple of heaves and his head cleared the top of the tank. He closed his eyes and made a superhuman effort to pull himself up.

Once safe, he rolled onto his back and lay sprawled on the narrow walkway like a stringless marionette, oblivious of the icy steel on his back as he clawed fresh, cold air gratefully into his lungs. Laura's head bobbed up beside him.

'Don't try to move until you're ready to,' she warned.

'I wasn't planning to.' Already he was feeling better, although that served to remind him of the pain in his leg. 'Andy?'

'Sleeping.'

Ami bellowed at them. The driver's bearded face was sticking out of his hatch. He cupped his hands to his mouth. 'You both okay?' he yelled the length of the huge tank.

Laura nodded and gave an affirmative wave.

The tanker veered, and Ami promptly disappeared to bring it back on course.

'Think you can make it to the cab?'

Lloyd turned his head. The catwalk looked about a mile long. He nodded, and set off on an awkward soldier-fashion crawl, leaving a trail of blood from his injured leg.

When Max was two hundred metres from the tanker he decided that a risky but decisive experiment was called for. He tightened his grip on the steering-wheel with one hand while doing his best to spare the offside wheel the worst of the pot-holes. He aimed his Smith and Wesson low. The mother was hanging onto the back of the tanker. She would be certain to hear the ricochet, and it would be easy for her to jump off and run to the cab to warn her daughter.

Provided the girl was in a fit state to use her powers, that was . . .

A shot cracked out. The bullet whined over Lloyd's head. He twisted around and yelled to Laura to join him, but she waved and disappeared from sight. He assumed that she had jumped down and was running to the cab.

Max swore, and dropped the gun as the tyre clouted a deep rut. The pounding through the steering-column got worse; he needed both hands to bring the car under control. But the experiment had worked. The woman had not run to the cab; obviously the girl was still incapacitated, so there was no reason why he shouldn't pick the mother off first.

453

At that moment the tanker breasted the long incline and began gathering speed. Ami knew the road well. The valley narrowed here, but the road was straight enough for a couple of kilometres for it to be safe to slip into a higher gear and give his engine a chance to cool down.

Laura's reaction to the shot was more anger than fear. The big dump-valves beneath her feet gave her an idea. Hanging grimly onto a grab-handle, she tried to turn one of the hand-wheels. It refused to budge. She worked out in her mind which way it ought to turn and tried turning it in the opposite direction. It moved with unexpected ease and smoothness, but nothing happened, not even when she had rotated it as far as it would go. She peered underneath the handwheel and saw the lugged cap and its swaying retaining chain. Obviously the cap wasn't a good fit because oil had begun seeping around the threads and was streaming onto the road. The lugs were badly damaged, suggesting that the usual method of removing the cap was with a hammer or something similar.

It was then that she saw the copper-and-hide mallet secured to the chassis by a clamp. She reached down and discovered that the clamp's wing-nuts unscrewed easily.

Max realised what the woman was planning. He recovered the Smith and Wesson, took careful aim, and pulled the trigger. At the exact moment that the hammer struck home, the car bucked savagely, sending the shot wide. He swore, and tried again, but the distance between him and the tanker was too great. He would have to kill the woman at point-blank range.

It was hardly surprising that Laura's first swing with the mallet should miss, given the precariousness of her perch. She thought the heavy tool was going to pull her arm out of its socket, but she managed to swing it again. This time the blow landed square on the lug. The cap rotated half a turn, shifting the lugs into a more difficult position for her next attempt.

Max decided that it was time to discard caution. He stamped down on the throttle pedal and sent the BMW surging forward like a maddened bucking-bronco.

A hundred metres . . . Seventy-five . . . Fifty . . .

The mallet's copper head connected with a dull but satisfying

454

thud on the lugs. This time the cap spun a complete turn of its own accord. Oil sprayed out around the threads in all directions. It trickled down Laura's forehead and into her eyes, causing the mallet to miss.

The BMW was twenty metres from the tanker when the mangled remains of the stub shaft that was holding its front wheel in place gave up the unequal struggle and suddenly snapped. The wheel flew off at a tangent and the car crashed down on one side. Sparks flew up from the tarmac. There was nothing left to break, so Max piled on all the speed he could. There was just enough steering effect from the one front wheel for his purpose.

With one hand hanging onto a handle and the other holding the mallet, Laura tried desperately to use her forearm to wipe the stinging oil from her eyes. She partly succeeded, and aimed another swipe at the cap. The blow connected. The spraying oil increased suddenly, covering Laura's head and arms and causing her to drop the mallet. She gave a sob of despair and snatched at it, but it was gone. Now completely blinded by the oil, she reached down and felt with her fingers. The cap was still in place. Mustering all the strength she could in her wrist, she managed to coax another half-turn out of it.

Max saw his chance and rammed the BMW forward. The bonnet smashing into the tanker's chassis only inches below her fingers forced a terrified cry from Laura.

Ami heard the thump and took no notice. So many odd things were happening during this run. He wondered if he could get away with charging these strange foreigners an extra $50 for the honour of cavorting about on his tanker.

The impact ripped the BMW's bonnet away from its hinges and tore out the entire front section, exposing the radiator's header-tank. The bonnet fell away into the dust. Max allowed the car to drop back a few metres and charged again. The BMW's suspension repeatedly bounced off the road and crashed down again, like a power-boat pounding into a head sea. The oil spraying from around the cap looked like a grotesque black flower.

Laura felt the cap give another quarter-turn.

God dammit! It had to come free now! It had to!

The force of the BMW ramming into the tanker's chassis drove its wings deep under the tanker's massive steel sections and held the car firmly in place, with the front suspension screaming on the road.

Max half-rose from his seat and pushed himself through the windscreen opening. Laura was struggling less than two metres away, her face and hair were smothered in oil; she couldn't possibly see him. In a way that was rather a pity. He braced his body against the windscreen-surround and took careful aim at her head. He couldn't miss – not this close.

Another half-turn.

Dear God – let it come free!

Max thumbed back the hammer.

The steel cap was suddenly wrenched through Laura's fingers as though a giant had reached down and snatched it from her. The great gout of black oil hit Max square on the chest and hurled him backwards into the car. Through half-closed eyes, Laura saw a solid black jet, as thick as a man's leg, fill the BMW to window-level in less than ten seconds.

The sudden transfer of weight from the tanker to the car caused the big vehicle's rear springs to relax and lift. The BMW was torn free from the tanker's grip. The car's screaming suspension struts, now with a massive increase in load to cope with, ploughed into a deep rut amid a shower of white-hot sparks and spun the car around. Laura, wiping the worst of the oil from her eyes, closed the handwheel valve and stared goggle-eyed at her handiwork.

The BMW had stopped. As it dwindled, she saw a movement inside. It was Max, trying to escape, but he was too late. The fire seemed slow to start, but once the flames found the petrol they combined with the oil to create an expanding, fiery ball of furnace-intensity, with tongues of fire leaping up through the dense black column of smoke.

Ami saw the sudden glow in his mirror and brought the tanker to a halt. He jumped from his cab and surveyed the blazing BMW. An apparition whose head and shoulders were

456

covered in oil approached him. It spoke to him in the woman's voice.

'Where's Lloyd?'

The driver gaped at Laura. He uttered a cry and rushed past her. Another cry when he saw the oil vomiting from the valve. He spun the handwheel shut and shinned up the ladder to examine the sight-glasses that showed the contents of each of the tanker's four sections.

'A thousand litres!' he wailed, beating the side of the tanker. 'You have released half the middle section's oil. This is a crime!'

Ami's English was remarkably good when discussing matters relating to profit and loss. In this case, loss.

'I'll buy it from you,' said Laura tiredly. 'Where's Lloyd?'

'Fifty cents a litre?'

'Fifty cents a litre,' Laura agreed.

Ami looked mollified. 'Would you like to empty out some more? I give you a special price.'

They found Lloyd on the catwalk, sprawled near the cab hatch where he had fainted from exhaustion.

Thirty kilometres away, the lead pilot of the two Super Frelon gunships spotted the rising column of black smoke from Max's blazing funeral pyre and radioed a course-correction to the other helicopter.

127

Ami's cab was well equipped with solvents for removing oil. Once she had cleaned herself up at the tiny sink in the back of the tanker's cab, Laura felt better, and turned her attention to bathing Lloyd's wound using Ami's first-aid kit. Before setting off again, the friendly driver had insisted on making tea for them. It wasn't hot tea because water boiled at a low temperature at this altitude, but with two large mugs of the brew inside him, Lloyd was feeling much better. André was still asleep, wrapped in a blanket and curled up in a foetal position on the bunk.

Laura stared out of her side-window at the passing scenery. The sombreness of the bleak lunar terrain was enriched briefly when the tanker emerged from a valley into the setting sun. Lloyd felt a popping in his ears and noticed that the altimeter on the dashboard was reading nearly 5000 metres. He doubted its accuracy, but there was no doubt that they were very high. He tried to remember what the map had said. It would have been useful to have kept it, but it was now at the bottom of a ravine amid the wreckage of the Land Rover.

'Turkey five kilometres,' Ami announced as if he had been reading Lloyd's thoughts.

'Will there be problems at the customs post?' Laura asked.

The driver chuckled into his beard. 'At this time, no one on duty.'

The road dipped, and skirted the edge of a drop that fell away several hundred metres. Laura looked away. The disadvantage of the tanker's cab was that it was higher than the crash blocks that lined the edge of the road – not that there were many of them at this height, the road here was in an even worse condition than it was lower down, where Max had met his end.

Ami took advantage of the level road to shift into second gear. As the engine note dropped, Lloyd thought he heard something. He called out to Ami to stop. The driver was reluctant, but the urgency in Lloyd's voice caused him to comply. Lloyd lowered himself carefully down from the cab and hobbled towards the edge of the road where there was a wide gap in the crash blocks. He listened intently. The icy wind keened and moaned over the bare crags.

Laura joined him. 'What's the matter, Lloyd?'

'Listen!'

She listened, and heard the distant beat of rotors and the whine of turbines. There was a curious quality about the sound; it rose and fell and sometimes disappeared altogether. 'A helicopter,' she muttered.

'Helicopters,' Lloyd corrected, scanning the deepening shadows in the valley. 'Two identical choppers, from the way their sound keeps beating together and going out of phase.'

They both saw the machines at the same time. They were about two thousand feet below, and were hugging the steep, rock-strewn slopes of the valley as they climbed.

'Christ . . .' Lloyd breathed. 'Frelon gunships.' He grabbed Laura's hand and limped as quickly as he could back to the tanker.

Ami saw them returning and started his engine. 'Problems for you?' he called down, seeing Lloyd's troubled expression.

'See if you can make the border in five minutes.'

'Do you think they're after us?' Laura asked worriedly as she helped Lloyd back into the cab. They were both gasping for breath from their brief exertion in the rarefied air.

'Certain to be,' Lloyd panted, sinking onto the bunk but taking care not to disturb André. He glanced at the sleeping girl. 'It might be a good idea if you woke her.'

Laura shook her head. 'No.'

Lloyd stared at her disbelievingly. 'For God's sake, Laura. This is no time for scruples. Those choppers will be jumping us any minute. We've got to wake her.'

'It's not a question of scruples,' Laura flared. 'I've given her two of her sleeping pills! You want to wake her, you try, but it won't do you any good.'

Their disagreement ended abruptly when, not thirty metres away, one of the gunships suddenly reared above the edge of the road-lip like an avenging monster rising from the depths of Hades. The scream of its turbines and the harsh crackle of its rotors caused Ami to jump in his seat and swear roundly in Turkish. The tanker veered, and grazed its chassis along one of the rocks, adding a shrill scream to the uproar. Lloyd caught a glimpse of an ugly cluster of Gatling barrels mounted on the side of the helicopter, and canisters slung from its landing-frame, before it plunged out of sight. The sound was chopped off abruptly, as though someone had hit the mute button. The gunship rose again, spilling its hellish cacophony over the barren landscape before dropping back.

Almost instantly it reappeared two hundred metres away; at least, that was what it looked like until Lloyd realised that it was the second helicopter. That machine, too, promptly vanished almost as soon as it had appeared. The whole scene was taking on the character of an outlandish black comedy.

When the first machine bounced back again, Lloyd got a good

look at the flailing rotors. There was something odd about them that puzzled him. Then both machines put in a double-act appearance together, and vanished together like a pair of well-rehearsed comedians. It was then that he realised what was wrong with the rotors: they were at full cyclic pitch. That is, on their forward sweep, the spinning blades were advancing to full pitch, so that they were nearly square-on to the air in a frantic attempt to gain maximum bite. Also, the tips were reaching the speed of sound; the strange crackling noises were sonic booms.

He waited for the machines to reappear to confirm his suspicions, but nothing happened.

'Maybe they're resting,' said Laura with unwitting humour, although her face was white with fear.

'Maybe they try to frighten us,' Ami commented over his shoulder. Throughout the bizarre performance he had driven steadily, once the initial shock was over.

'Stop a minute!' Lloyd yelled.

'You're crazy!'

'No – it's okay. Stop!'

In his excitement Lloyd forgot his leg. He jumped down from the cab, winched, and hobbled to the edge. He leaned against a rock and stared down, a look of triumph lighting his face. He started laughing. Thinking that the thin air had affected him in some way, Laura jumped down and went to his side.

'Look!' He pointed excitedly.

Laura followed his finger and saw the two Frelons some two thousand feet below. They were heading south. 'What made them give up?' she asked. 'Have we crossed the frontier?'

Lloyd laughed and hugged her to him. 'It's our height! The service ceiling of most helicopters isn't much above eleven thousand feet! Their rotors lose lift above that. Those two did bloody well to get to this height. Lesson one, if you're ever hassled by helicopters – take to the mountains.'

Laura smiled and returned his embrace. 'I'll try to remember that,' she promised.

'Hey, you two!'

They turned. Ami was leaning out of his cab, looking indignant. 'I thought you wanted Turkey? Two kilometres now.'

Arm in arm, they retraced their steps to the tanker.

They walked slowly, arms linked, sensing each other's thoughts but not wanting to break the spell by talking.

EPILOGUE

FREE KURDISTAN
Tuesday, 20th March

The Kurdish immigration officer at Mosul International Airport looked at the young woman's date of birth again.

'Is anything wrong?' the woman asked.

The officer looked up from the passport and met again the arresting green eyes that had already made him feel decidedly uncomfortable. He transferred his attention to the studious-looking fair-haired boy at her side. He was an honest man, so he said what was on his mind.

'Forgive me, but you seem so young to have . . .' He groped for the right words. To say that she seemed too young to have a nine-year-old son might give offence; it was so easy to give offence with one's second language. Kurdish directness was not always appreciated, even though he had a right to ensure that the boy travelling on the woman's passport was definitely her son. 'A fine boy,' he ended up lamely, and grinned down at the lad.

'I was even younger when he was born,' said the woman sharply but without rancour.

The officer stamped her passport and wished the visitors a pleasant stay in Kurdistan. His next clients were an American couple; the queue at his desk stretched right across the terminal building. Tourism in Kurdistan was certainly booming.

The Hertz girl with the perfect English was quick at sizing up most customers, but this elegant, black-haired young woman in the expensively-cut black skirt and jacket defeated her. She had an Amex Platinum Card, too. No briefcase, so she was probably not a businesswoman. She wondered if the boy with her was a son or a younger brother. Certainly there was a strong family resemblance, although the boy's fair hair didn't seem right. She smiled when the woman signed the rental agreement.

'A Nexus soft-top,' she said brightly. 'It's still a little chilly

465

so we've left the top up. But the forecast for later is good. We're in for a hot spell.'

There were a few steps leading down to the rental car pick-up point. The boy took his mother's hand to steady her, knowing that her sense of balance had not fully recovered.

The sun was burning off the morning haze as the young woman threaded the car off the ring road and slotted it into the slow lane of the Mosul to Zakho motorway. She was in no hurry, and she found the hurtling juggernauts in the middle lane a little intimidating. This was her first trip abroad by herself. Mother had made a fuss of course, especially when she announced that she was taking the boy.

'It's his father's country, Mother. He wants to go; he has a right to go. Anyway, I'm taking him and that's that.'

'But you need another six months to recover fully.'

'I'm as well as I'm ever likely to be. So please stop fussing. My mind is made up.'

The boy sat silently at her side, taking everything in – wide-eyed and alert, missing nothing.

'They've all got nice cars, Mummy,' he observed, and pointed to the spidery lattices of the oil well heads near the road. 'They're lucky – they'll never run out of petrol.'

She laughed, and tousled his hair. 'Find my sunglasses for me, pet. It's getting very bright.'

The boy delved into her handbag. He unfolded the Leitz glasses and slipped them onto her nose, guiding the arms under her headband. His touch was gentle and caring, as his father's had been.

'Better?'

'Mmm . . . Much.' She relaxed a little. Driving was more comfortable wearing the sunglasses. Bright sunlight still worried her, as did the occasional migraines, but they were getting less frequent, as the neurosurgeon in charge of the team at the Atkinson Morley Hospital had predicted. The team were pleased with her progress.

Thirty minutes later she left the motorway at the Sammel intersection and drove into the prosperous little town. Everything was new; there was not one building in the town, apart from the mosque, that dated from before 1991. The market was crowded; two circuits of the bustling square were necessary before the boy spotted a parking place between a Cadillac and a Discovery.

The boy insisted on pressing the remote-control to lock the car. They entered a large florist's where they were greeted by the overpowering scent of thousands of flowers. The store's stagings were crowded with blooms of every conceivable variety, from pansies to magnificent displays of protea with brilliantly coloured bracts.

An assistant was found who spoke a little English. He listened carefully to the woman's request and promised that the order would be ready for collection in one hour. She paid with her Amex Platinum Card.

The two wandered around the square. They sat at an outdoor café and ordered soft drinks. There was a announcement in Arabic over loudspeakers – a signal for all activity in the market-place to come to a standstill. Traders ceased trading; customers were left waiting for change; shops closed. An unseen imam intoned a brief prayer. The eerie silence continued when the loudspeakers fell silent.

'What's going on, Mummy?' the boy whispered.

The woman raised her finger to her lips.

Two minutes later, normal activity suddenly resumed.

The boy looked bewildered. 'What happened?'

'I don't know, darling. But I think it must have been a commemoration from the times of the troubles.'

'That's why we're here, aren't we? A comm . . . A commem . . .' The long word defeated him.

She frowned suddenly.

'What's the matter, Mummy?'

The tension faded from her face. She glanced down at her watch and smiled at him. He thought his mother always looked beautiful, but particularly when she smiled.

'I was trying to think what the time was. I always used to know.' She stood abruptly and took the boy's hand. 'Come on. The flowers should be ready now.'

*

467

The weather changed. The bright promise of mid-morning had given way to a close oppressiveness by the time she turned the rental car into the approach-road to the lakeside estate.

She slowed down, content to let the car's tick-over automatically trickle it along the smooth black road surface.

There had been changes, of course. It was inevitable after so many years. The golf course had been extended to eighteen holes and had taken over the pomegranate orchard; several groups of players were on the fairways and greens. Strange, how prosperity had driven the Kurds golf-crazy. The lake was now surrounded by pleasant landscaped gardens, and there was a new, large clubhouse with a car park. There was even that ultimate symbol of affluence, a helicopter landing-pad.

The boy had fallen silent. He had never been here before, yet he felt that he knew this place. 'Here, Mummy?'

'Nearly.'

The road curved slightly. About a kilometre ahead, she could see the bungalows. There were more than she remembered. A few of the shallow-pitched roofs were bone-white rafters awaiting tiles.

'Can I put the top down now, Mummy?'

'Go on then. But it feels as if there's a storm brewing.'

The boy pressed the control and the car's rag-top concertinaed neatly into its well. The bubble of cool, conditioned air escaped, and the oppressive, thundery warmth of the afternoon settled on the two pilgrims.

'Look.' He pointed through the windscreen.

There was a vivid splash of colour at the roadside about a hundred metres ahead. A white Renault was parked by the verge, and its driver, a youngish man in a black suit, was standing with his head bowed. In front of him was a metre-high white memorial stone that was almost completely hidden by fresh flowers. The woman drew the Nexus quietly up to the verge and motioned to the boy to leave the car without slamming the door. She took his hand. They moved near the lone mourner and contemplated the columns of forty or so names that were lettered in Arabic and Roman script on the gleaming white stone.

468

The man said something in Kurdish and pointed to two names.

'I'm sorry,' said the woman slowly. 'But I do not understand.'

'My parents,' said the man simply in English. 'I come on this day every year.'

'I thought no one escaped?'

'I was with my . . .' He groped for the right word and gave up. 'I was with the sister of my mother.'

They stood for a few more seconds in silence. The stranger bid the travellers good day and returned to his car. The boy waited until the Renault had driven off, then moved some carnations aside and searched through the names with his fingers. He stopped.

'Daddy?' he asked, looking questioningly at his mother.

The woman nodded. Her face clouded with bitter-sweet memories. 'And the two names above are Daddy's mummy and daddy.'

The boy gently traced the names with his fingers. He read the date. 'Today's the twentieth of March. So that's exactly ten years ago.'

'Ten years ago to the day,' the boy's mother agreed. She looked at the watch. 'Almost ten years ago to the hour. Let's get the flowers.'

They opened the car's boot, releasing the delicate fragrance from the huge spray of spring blooms that completely filled the compartment.

'Aren't you going to write something on the card, Mummy?'

'You write something.' She gave him a pen.

He thought for a moment and wrote:

To Daddy. With all our love.

He looked worriedly at his handiwork. 'I haven't left you any room.'

She tousled his blond hair. 'It doesn't matter. You've said everything.'

They lifted the flowers out of the boot and carefully arranged them with all the other flowers in front of the memorial. To the boy's surprise, his mother did not want to spend time looking at the display. She took him by the hand and they returned to the car. She opened her handbag, took out an Iridium telephone, and pressed a memory button. The call was answered almost immediately once the satellite link to England was established. They had promised that they would be waiting anxiously to hear from her.

'Hallo, Lloyd. Mission accomplished . . .' She listened, and gave a little laugh. 'No. No – I'm fine. We're both fine. You're worse than Mother.'

'Hallo, Lloyd!' the boy yelled. The woman laughed and pinched his lips gently together.

'As you heard – as noisy as ever. Can I have a word with Mother?' She listened, and then spoke quickly. 'No. No. Don't wake her. Give her my love. Tell her we're fine. I'll call back in a couple of hours.' She blew a kiss into the mouthpiece and gave the handset to the boy for a boisterous sign-off. He was very fond of Lloyd.

She returned the telephone to her handbag and leaned back with her eyes closed. She was proud of what she had achieved.

Distant thunder rolled. It echoed ominously back and forth across the sullen sky and reverberated into a brooding silence.

She thought of the days when she could make thunder.

Now she was at peace with the world and herself, her family, and above all, her beloved son. Those deep recesses of her mind where there had once been turmoil and fear were now pools of sweet tranquillity.

The days of thunder were over.

THE END

Also available in Mandarin Paperbacks

James Follett
SWIFT

There is a satellite through which, daily, pass all the
interbank transactions between London and New
York, currencies to the value of billions of pounds –
moving not as bank notes, but as vulnerable streams
of electrons. This, the most vital computer system in
existence, is operated by SWIFT, guardians of the
system on which depends the delicate stability of the
world's currencies. And one man has a plan to
destroy it.

That man is Charlie Rose, disaffected mobster boss
with millions at his disposal. Assisted by a Soviet
Tass correspondent with his own motives to pursue,
and a brilliant but psychotic computer programmer,
Rose has the audacity, the power and the driving will
to dare the biggest, most sophisticated act of theft
ever conceived.

James Follett

DOMINATOR

High above the earth's surface orbits one of NASA's latest space shuttles, Dominator. But the crew and cargo on board are beyond the control of the US space agency. Dominator has been hijacked and a nightmare is about to be unleashed.

How could it happen -- and how will it end? James Follett's latest, heart-stopping novel spans three continents as it follows the fearfully possible outcome of a new deadlock between the Middle East factions and the United States. Standing innocently at the centre is Neil O'Hara, ex-astronaut, ex-drunk, whose rare skills and debatable loyalties may ultimately be the only barrier between us and the holocaust . . .

James Follett

CHURCHILL'S GOLD

1940 – Britain faces her darkest hour . . .

War has brought Britain to the verge of bankruptcy.
Her debts to America are crippling. Her precious
supplies of weapons and fuel are running desperately
low.

Her last hope is gold – £42 millions worth of it, held
in a bank vault in Pretoria, South Africa.

Only one man can bring that gold to Britain: Robert
Garrard, captain of the 'Tulsar'. But lying in wait to
intercept him is Germany's newest submarine U-330,
captained by Kurt Milland, a pre-war colleague of
Garrard's, handpicked to predict his every move.
The duel to the death will be fought in the lonely
wastes of the Atlantic . . .

A List of James Follett Titles Available from Mandarin

While every effort is made to keep prices low, it is sometimes necessary to increase prices at short notice. Mandarin Paperbacks reserves the right to show new retail prices on covers which may differ from those previously advertised in the text or elsewhere.

The prices shown below were correct at the time of going to press.

All these books are available at your bookshop or newsagent, or can be ordered direct from the address below. Just tick the titles you want and fill in the form below.

Cash Sales Department, PO Box 5, Rushden, Northants NN10 6YX.
Fax: 0933 410321 : Phone 0933 410511.

Please send cheque, payable to 'Reed Book Services Ltd.', or postal order for purchase price quoted and allow the following for postage and packing:

£1.00 for the first book, 50p for the second; **FREE POSTAGE AND PACKING FOR THREE BOOKS OR MORE PER ORDER.**

NAME (Block letters) ....

ADDRESS..

....

☐ I enclose my remittance for ....

☐ I wish to pay by Access/Visa Card Number

Expiry Date

Signature ....

Please quote our reference: MAND